# In the Land of Seas

## Nicolo's Renaissance Voyage

### Book Two of *The Lives of Nickolaus*

A Novel by

## Michael Roof

**Grass Roof Publishing**

San Francisco

First Printing: 2020

ISBN 978-1-943918-28-7

International Print Edition

Grass Roof Publishing

P.O. Box 14908

San Francisco, California, 94114

www.NicolosRenaissance.com

# Table of Contents

# Chapter 1 – Misgivings

**Mediterranean Sea off the Coast of Genoa – October 1555**

From the lofty forecastle deck of the Hanseatic carrack ship, *The Paradise of the North*, Nicolo and Michela Di Cottano gazed straight ahead into the open sea, afraid to look back for fear they might have to reckon with just how much they were leaving behind. The view was magnificent, with gleaming speckles of bright autumn sunlight prancing like fairies across the warm bubbling swells of the Mediterranean Sea, all overseen by a sky so clear and blue that it seemed to offer a direct view into the cosmos. In fact, its brilliance was so intense that it seemed to be causing Nicolo's eyes to water, or were those tears? That was the last thing he needed. Most of the crew already viewed him as a delicate little dandy, or so he erroneously believed.

Yet even in mid-afternoon, the sun was already hanging low in the sky – a vivid reminder that making the best possible time to their Baltic destination was absolutely essential. The captain had warned them there would be hell to pay if they failed to stay ahead of the late autumn storms in the North Sea. Indeed, the risks were truly overwhelming, probably even worse than they imagined; nevertheless, the Cottanos had chosen their path and were fully committed to seeing it through. All they could do now was to hope for the best.

Getting this far had not been easy. By means of careful timing and brilliant strategy by Captain Zannaro and Genoa's Harbormaster, the young couple had managed to evade a final and possibly fatal confrontation at the wharf. Having just barely escaped the wicked clutches of local crime boss, Il Rossone, and his comrades at the Genoan Archdiocese, they wanted to believe that they were finally in the clear. They also recognized that were it not for the heroic efforts of the many friends and supporters they were leaving behind, they would most likely have lost everything, including their freedom, perhaps even their lives. Unfortunately, given Il Rossone's well-known propensity to pursue his many obsessions with unfettered abandon, there was still a real chance they would be followed and attacked. This left them with little choice but to rely on the captain's experience and guile to either avoid or repel any such ruthless endeavors.

Nicolo suddenly grabbed the feathered cap off his head and tossed it as hard as he could into the sea. "God damn it all!" he exclaimed. Obviously none of this was the cap's fault, but he wanted to destroy something – anything – and that was all he had on hand. The fact that it had been a long-treasured keepsake from his beloved benefactor, Maestro Piccini, was of no consequence at the moment. It had to go along with the rest of Genoa. He wasn't even sure what he was feeling - anger, despair, weakness, frustration, hopelessness – all, perhaps?

"It's hard to let go, isn't it, Nicki?" Michela lamented wistfully.

"Yes, it is. We're leaving everything we know, except for that which is ours alone. We still have that. No one can ever take that away from us, I swear. Besides, with any luck, this move might turn out to be the best thing we could ever do."

Michela sighed then reluctantly agreed. "You're right, my love, if we can survive the journey." She pressed forward and embraced him. "We'll make good of this. I can feel it in my heart. I'm just scared." And it was in that moment that the exiled newlyweds fully accepted that they had no choice but to move forward and step headlong into their future rather than mourn their losses and dwell in the past. The life they had known in Genoa was gone - forever. They let go of each other then turned around. Nicolo was planning, albeit with a bit of trepidation, to introduce himself to the deeply-hooded monk they had spotted briefly when boarding the ship, but he was gone, like a wisp of smoke, apparently having descended like a mole back down to the lower deck from whence he'd come. In light of his fleeting presence and unfamiliar garb, the monk seemed more than a bit mysterious to Nicolo, who had lately grown extremely leery of all men of the cloth, and most especially of this unidentified monk boarding in Genoa.

2

"Ah, Maestro Di Cottano, let me welcome you on board," Captain Zannaro greeted cheerfully.

"Oh, please, call me Nickolaus, my Saxon name. I must begin getting used to it now. And I'm afraid I am no longer Maestro. That honor was stripped away from me by the Genoan Archdiocese and the new guard at Saint Matthias."

"They may be able take your title, Maestro, but not your honor. From what I've heard, you've more than earned the admiration and respect of your peers and followers. Perhaps in Lubeck, you'll be appointed Kapellmeister." Nickolaus stared down at the deck and blushed, momentarily wordless. It was true that he sought, even craved praise and fame, but when it actually arrived, he inevitably felt tongue-tied and embarrassed. Ambitious yet shy, he usually wished he could step out of himself and watch the spectacle from afar. That way he wouldn't have to respond personally to the recognition that he secretly craved and had finally attained. He looked toward the aft castle deck then found his voice.

"I suppose it's possible, but I plan to steer clear of such commitments for the time being, maybe forever." Nickolaus pulled Michela forward. "Oh, forgive me, this is my lovely wife, Michela."

"Yes, we've met. Good day, Signora Di Cottano."

"I'm sorry. I knew that. I guess I'm just a bundle of nerves," Nickolaus confessed. "There's so much going on around here – crewmen everywhere, ropes, and sails, and cross ladders, and lookouts. How do you keep track of it all?"

"Well, fortunately I have several fine officers and a skilled crew to help take care of things for me. It is a bit much when I try to sail the ship by myself." The captain winked good-naturedly then glanced up toward the crow's nests. "Lookouts report," he shouted in a deep and convincing baritone voice.

"All clear, Captain," came three sequential reports from the front to the back of the ship.

The captain cocked his head slightly. "Splendid, then it looks as though we're in for some clear sailing for the time being. Please, allow me to invite you to the captain's table for dinner this evening, oh, and your son as well. He certainly seems to have taken to my first officer rather quickly."

"Yes, understandable, believe me," Nickolaus acknowledged. "Heinz Buxtaholda can be a godsend to a worried child." A bit confused, the captain squinted quizzically. "It's a long story, Captain. I'd love to share it with you some time, that is, if you're interested."

"By all means, I look forward to it."

Nickolaus turned his attention to the crew, many scurrying skillfully about the deck while others swung to and fro amongst the ship's rigging like squirrels in a forest. He shook his head in amazement. "It's a miracle you don't lose half your crew during these voyages. I can't even imagine the perils of such duties in heavy seas, or during a storm, or under attack, or if ... never mind." Nickolaus suddenly cut himself off, realizing he was extending his worries too far out, especially in front of Michela, who was already nervous enough.

The captain shrugged. "I must admit that it has been known to happen. I lost several members of my crew during one particularly devastating voyage, God forgive me. It's probably the greatest danger for sailors at sea. That's why we carry extra hands. It's not for their pleasure; I can assure you of that." Nickolaus continued to stare off in amazement. The spectacle seemed even more striking today than it had fifteen years earlier when he had endured his first sea voyage at the tender young age of ten - the miserable trip from Lubeck to Genoa just after his parents had died in the fire. Now, with the passage of time, he had experienced enough life and injury to imagine the pain of a bone-crushing fall to the deck, or hitting the side railing and being tossed overboard, or being swept out to sea in a storm, or the thousand other terrifying horrors that flashed through his highly imaginative, anxiety-riddled mind.

As he watched a sailor gracefully maneuver across one of the overhead rat trails, he was suddenly reminded of an old hornpipe tune he'd heard sailors singing down at the taverns near the harbor in Genoa. It was a bouncy, memorable little ditty - an old seafarer's tune, he supposed. He had even thrown it into one of his masses. No one knew, except perhaps a sailor or two who might have sensed something familiar. It was no wonder sailors drank so hard while on shore leave. After spending months in these conditions, who wouldn't? How did they do it, anyway? It seemed almost a miracle. Suddenly Nicolo was overcome with a pressing urge to compose something, nothing in particular, maybe a song or a chunk of a madrigal. Joy, anxiety, or melancholy usually induced him to compose. He supposed this time it was anxiety, or deathly fear, perhaps. Fortunately, First Officer Heinz Buxtaholda appeared just in time to distract him from his ruminations. At the commander's side stood Michela's fifteen year-old brother, Stefano, eagerly looking over everything as if he were a small child in a toy store. It was all new and exciting to the over-protected scholar, musician, and choirboy.

"Captain, reporting all stations trim. Shall we proceed as planned?"

"Yes, Commander, as planned. Perhaps you'd like to show our guests to their quarters and familiarize them with some of our rules and procedures. This is a whole new world for them. It's best they learn their way around sooner rather than later."

"Aye, Captain."

Nickolaus hesitated for a moment. "Captain, if you don't mind, I'd like to take a final look back before we lose sight of land." He couldn't tell whether he was already feeling homesick, or if he wanted to make certain with his own eyes that they weren't being pursued.

"Certainly, Maestro, Genoa is that direction." The Captain pointed astern, as the ship was still heading mainly due south. Heinz gathered Michela and Stefano and ushered them off to his quarters, which he had kindly granted them use of for the duration of the voyage. Nickolaus climbed the ladder to the aft castle deck where he made his way back to the stern of the ship. Once there, he grasped the railing and stared out across the water toward the Ligurian Hills that surrounded Genoa on the north. Carefully scanning the fading Genoan skyline, he managed to catch one final glimpse of Saint Matthias Cathedral, which overlooked the square where he had lived and worked for the past fifteen years. It was there that he had grown up, learned his profession, discovered women, explored life, and finally succeeded as Maestro Di Cappella. It was also there that Father Pietro - a corrupt, violent, child molesting priest; Father Raimondo – a betraying ex-comrade; Il Rossone, a vicious, local crime boss; and the enigmatic Archdiocese of Genoa had all conspired to destroy both him and his family. In the end they had failed, but the repercussions and scars resulting from the conflict would take a long time to manifest and heal. It was all Nickolaus could do to keep from screaming out at the world.

He leaned over the side of the ship and gazed downward into the sea. On this day it appeared so gentle and forgiving. Its soothingly warm, bright turquoise waters seemed to beg anyone in sight to pull off their clothes and jump right in. But when he stared straight into it, through its gleaming but deceptive façade, he could clearly envision the relentless dangers that lurked beneath its sparkling veneer. Forever dark and swirling, it lingered silently and patiently, waiting for any chance to ensnare its victims. And when a storm churned it into a frenzy, it was cruel and unforgiving. A ship and crew could disappear in minutes, sometimes without even a warning or a fight, never to be seen again. Nicolo knew all too well of its powers. Fifteen years earlier he had felt its cold, powerful talons reach up from the deep and tug at his legs with all of its might as it attempted to steal his young life for all of eternity. If Heinz Buxtaholda had not been there to wrest him from its grip, his existence would have ceased then and there. He jerked his head upward and shivered frightfully. "Heaven help me, what have I done?" he muttered pleadingly.

"Signore, the chief wants to know if you would like any of your family's personal items brought up from the hold?" Startled, Nicolo released an embarrassing chirp before reeling around to stand face to face with a young and sturdy yet somewhat effeminately mannered crewman.

"What the … oh, pardon me, what was that you asked?"

"Scusi, Signore, I didn't mean to frighten you."

"You didn't. Now please repeat yourself."

"Personal items, Signore, do you need anything brought up from your stores down in the hold? I'll be glad to retrieve them for you."

"No, not right now, perhaps later. By the way, what is your name, crewman?"

"I am Martinello, Signore, are you sure you don't need anything? It's not a problem."

"I said no. I'll contact the chief if I need anything." Nicolo had no idea who the "chief" might be, but he assumed that being first officer, Heinz Buxtaholda was in charge of cargo and stowage. He would ask about it at dinner. The crewman appeared confused.

"As you wish, Signore," retorted the young sailor curtly as he turned away and slipped down the ladder to the main deck. Momentarily troubled by the exchange, Nicolo seized one last opportunity to look back toward Genoa before heading off to find his family. While climbing down to the main deck, he happened to glance forward just in time to see the enigmatic monk intercept Martinello, grab him harshly by the collar, and then pull him close. After a brief but angry-looking exchange of words, the two men quickly disappeared through a doorway into the lower forward hold where most of the sailors slept.

Landing on the main deck with an awkward clump, Nicolo dolefully mumbled, "What on God's earth was that all about?" He shook his head. "This is going to be a long voyage."

# Chapter 2 – Accommodations

What a truly generous sacrifice it had been for the first officer to bestow his personal quarters to Nicolo and his family for the duration of the voyage. That said, they were by no means roomy or luxurious; in fact, the words cramped and spartan would have been more apt. On a positive note, they were located near the stern, uncommonly private, and isolated from the crewmen, who were housed below deck in the forecastle section, which was still better than most ships where crewmen were often left to make do out in the open on the main deck. Carrack ships were tried and sturdy to be sure, but they were also relatively crude, with poorly sealed decks and a sickening bobbing-cork stance that made them appear as though they might tip over at any moment. And this was more than mere appearance; many carracks had actually tipped over, particularly during strong winds or rough seas. On the other hand, they were bigger than the galleons that were steadily replacing them, and they were capable of handling more cannons while also packing the extra weight needed to hold the ship steady when the guns were fired. Furthermore, with their steep, bulging sides, carracks were very difficult to board during an attack, especially if the deck awnings were in place. They were, however, comparatively slow when heading into the wind, and they were well known for their lack of maneuverability. In addition, due to their relatively deep draft, they were much more likely to run aground in shallow waters than were the smaller caravels. Nicolo's old friend, Genoa's Harbormaster Angelico Di Mercadente, told him that sailing a carrack ship in rough seas or against the wind was like trying to steer a pregnant sow through a muddy pigsty. Christopher Columbus was reported to have referred to his carrack flagship, the Santa Maria, as a cow, though he later changed his mind about the virtues of carracks and even insisted on using them for all of his subsequent voyages.

In any case, this carrack, *The Paradise of the North*, was their ship, and they would have to trust her to carry them safely through their journey. Although she was beginning to age, she had been one of Lubeck's last great hanseatic carrack projects, and she was certainly a big one - nearly 130 feet from stem to stern and 35 feet across at the beam. She had been designed and built as a five hundred and fifty ton ship, but the captain often boasted that she could easily be coaxed to six hundred. Having been Captain Zannaro's ship for many years, he and his first officer had managed to design and install several enhancements, including changes to the masts, sails, and rigging, as well as modifications to the ship's basic floor plan, all of which had rendered the ship safer and more livable for both officers and crew. Success and respect can have their benefits, and Captain Zannaro and his first officer had earned plenty of both.

Seeking his family, Nickolaus passed through a bulkhead then climbed a few steps before traversing a dark, narrow hallway where he finally came upon the first officer's tiny cabin. He peered in warily through the doorway, wondering how Michela was faring with her unpacking. Stefano had already ventured off to find Heinz, perhaps hoping to learn more about navigating the ship, although it was typically the second officer, Chief Grumbach, who handled most of those duties. Nickolaus strolled in and placed his hands on Michela's shoulders then began rubbing gently. "Will it work? Will the three of us fit in here, my love?"

"It will be tight, but I think it's workable. I certainly can't vouch for its comfort, though." She shook her head. "That bunk sure seems narrow for the two of us, but there is a little dresser and a small desk built into the wall. You'll be able to compose if you should get the urge. And look here, the commander told Stefano he would have the privilege of using this odd contrivance." Michela pointed to a man-sized, puckered-up net slung between two ropes that were hanging from support beams on the ceiling. Nickolaus regarded it closely.

"Yes, it's called a hammock. Columbus brought them back from the New World. The natives have been using them there for centuries. Years ago, Heinz told me he uses them in rough seas because they sway with the ship and save him from hitting the floor."

"I've never heard of such a thing. Do all of the sailors have them?"

"I don't think so. They're still a bit of a novelty, and I think they require more space than is allowed most sailors. I'm not sure I'd like to get stuck in one of those. By the way, do you need anything brought up from the hold? A young mate just asked me if we needed any of our personal items."

Michela seemed confused. "Was it a strapping young lad?" She hesitated for a moment, "a bit ... girlish, perhaps?" Nicolo felt a momentary pang of jealously that his wife had taken such close notice of the physicality of the crewman. She continued. "It seems to me he'd be eaten alive out here among all these sailors, no matter how big he is." Michela shook her head back and forth, clucking her tongue as she imagined the prospect.

Nickolaus conjured up a similar image in his mind. "The voyage is young, my dear, and yes, I would say it was the same fellow. Calls himself Martinello."

"He was in here a few minutes ago. He asked me twice about retrieving our belongings. He certainly seems terribly interested in getting into our possessions, wouldn't you say?"

Nickolaus shrugged his shoulders. "Maybe he's just an eager young mate. I'll ask Heinz about him at dinner." Gazing into Michela's glistening blue eyes, Nickolaus realized that she seemed a bit pale. "By the way, how are your sea legs?"

"My what?"

"Your sea legs – how are you holding up out here at sea?"

"Oh, I hadn't a clue what you were speaking of, Nicki. This is all new to me. I must confess that I've felt lightheaded now and then. It's probably just the excitement, but I do worry that I'll be in for more difficult times when the seas get rough."

"Of that you can be certain, my dear, all of us can." Nickolaus pulled Michela close for a long hug, secretly concerned that she was already experiencing seasickness even in these calm waters. He released her then took one last look around their tiny new quarters. "Well, are you ready to find the captain's table?"

"I am. Please lead the way, caro mio." Nickolaus kissed her on the cheek then grasped her hand as they moved single-file down the narrow hallway and out into the waning sunshine that was still trickling across the main deck. The captain's cabin and lounge were located on the deck above theirs, just beneath the upper aft deck. Michela stopped for a moment and looked around. "There seem to be quite a few cannons for a merchant

11

ship, don't you think, Nicki?" Captain Zannaro had recently installed a pair of custom-made, two-pound falconette cannons at the front edge of the upper aft deck. Wheeled and mobile, they were held firmly in place by brackets and covered with canvass. Gun portholes had been cut and reinforced in several spots, and special tiebacks had been installed to hold the guns steady when they were fired. Less conspicuous but perhaps more ominous to Michela were the two much larger, six-pound cannons that were lashed to brackets on the main deck and also covered with canvas. Those could be readily rolled shipside if needed which, fortunately, had never been the case. The captain had prepared reinforced gun portholes and tiebacks for the six-pound cannons as well. In addition, he had arranged to have the sides of the ship painted by skilled Genoan artisans to make it look as though *The Paradise* was packing several more cannons on the deck below. Cannons and ammunition were cumbersome and heavy, so they did cost the ship valuable cargo capacity as well as a noticeable share of maneuverability. Carrying gunpowder was also extremely dangerous, so the choice to arm *The Paradise* had not been made lightly. The ship's owners had been reluctant to approve such unusually aggressive posturing; however, since Captain Zannaro almost always sailed without convoy, he insisted that his ship needed to appear as imposing as possible. In truth, her weapons were intended to be exclusively defensive, but from a distance, no one knew for sure. To Nickolaus, they seemed at once both portentous and reassuring.

"I'm sure the captain knows what he's doing. He has to be prepared to fend off attacks from pirates and …"

"What?"

"Never mind. Perhaps you should ask Heinz or the captain about it. Unlike me, they actually know what they're talking about."

Nickolaus knocked gently at the captain's door, which popped open immediately, as if the host had been lying in wait. It was the captain's steward, Mario Grimaldo, who saw to all of the captain's personal needs. Everyone called him Aldo. "Ah, Maestro, benevenuti!" The steward politely directed the young couple into the cabin and then showed them to their chairs. Both knew not to sit down until the captain had arrived, taken his place, and directed all to be seated.

"Ah, Grazie," Nickolaus replied as they took their positions, standing side-by-side while swaying gently back and forth with the motion of the waves. Aldo informed them in a surprisingly aristocratic manner that the rest of the officers would be arriving shortly. Most of the crew appeared to be of Saxon origin, but the captain always retained a Genoan steward and cook. It made him feel at home. Also, he tended to favor a good home cooked meal every now and then, and by home cooked, he didn't mean sour kraut and sausage. Although the crew's rations were far less appealing than those of the officers, Captain Zannaro had always insisted that the crew's food be wholesome and plentiful, at least to the extent seagoing circumstances permitted. His standards in that regard were superior to those of most captains of the day.

As they stood waiting, Nickolaus gazed around the room. It was a sizable area for such a ship, with two windows that looked out over the main deck. Unlike the rest of the vessel, the floor was smooth and neatly varnished. The interior finishes had clearly been designed and built by artisans with Italian sensibilities. The table and chairs were also clearly of Italian design and build. It appeared that Captain Zannaro, despite his well-earned, worldly reputation, had always kept his homeland close to heart and mind. Nickolaus thought of Heinz Buxtaholda's cabin, so stark and impersonal, almost as if he possessed no family, heritage, or motherland at all. Probably a Lutheran, Nickolaus joked to himself. Uncertain concerning proper etiquette at a captain's table, Nickolaus began to squirm a bit. He had taken all of his meals during his earlier voyage sharing treats and favors with the ship's cook, Tremonti, whom he had befriended despite disapproving looks from the crew. Now he was an adult and, by all fair measures, a successful Maestro, but he still felt like a child waiting to be scolded for some petty violation of etiquette.

A few moments later the silence and discomfort were interrupted by a bout of laughter from outside the cabin. Aldo slid silently across the room and quickly opened the door for the second officer, who had been sharing an off-color joke with one of the ensigns. "Aldo, my good man, are we all here yet? I'm god dam starved! Let's get that meal out of the galley and into my mouth before I pass out." He clumped impatiently across the room. "Well, where's the grub, my friend in waiting?" Second Officer Otto Grumbach, well into his forties, had taken on all the telltale signs of middle age – a spreading belly, balding head, graying hair, and a claimed libido far in excess of reality. He wore his baggy clothing sloppily and carried his thin, rumpled hair pulled back in a long ponytail. If he were a junior officer under inspection, he would have been chastised severely. Despite having served nearly fifteen years under the genteel and sophisticated Captain Zannaro, he was still tough-skinned and rough around the edges. Some even thought him an oaf.

The captain treasured Chief Grumbach not for his navigational skills with the instruments, though he was the best in the fleet in that regard, but for his near magical instincts that allowed him to sense wind, weather, tides, and direction with such striking accuracy that no one even considered questioning his guidance in such matters. Everyone assumed his skills were born of his Frisian heritage, or perhaps his youthful experiences navigating small boats through the Wadden Sea - trips that were rumored by some to have involved smuggling rather than just a young man's enthusiasm. But most of the crew simply considered him a gift from God, a heavenly nautical protector of sorts. As for Otto Grumbach, he loved his job, the sea, and Captain Zannaro with all his heart. Even so, his pursuit of pleasure and manly fulfillment while on shore leave was the stuff of legend. In fact, he often arrived for departure only at the very last moment and usually hung over, as had been the case on this voyage. Once on board, however, he was always sober and professional. It seemed a bit odd to many that a man of Chief Grumbach's talents and abilities had never earned his captain's stripes or even been promoted to first officer. Most people assumed that his crudeness had kept him out of contention, but the truth was that he had never sought a higher position. He was completely satisfied in his present station where he virtually commanded the movements of the ship - one of the most prestigious in the fleet - as if it were his own, but without having to shoulder the captain's burdens of responsibility. Most of the crew understood why the chief liked things the way they were, and they respected him for it. At times they just wished he were less of a lout.

"The captain and commander will be here shortly, Chief Grumbach. May I offer you a quick libation?"

"You bet, Aldo, but not too much. I'm still on duty."

"As you wish, Sir." The chief grabbed the mug from Aldo's hand and rapidly threw back its contents then slammed it back down on the table. A moment later, the captain, Heinz, and Stefano popped into the lounge area from what Nickolaus presumed were the captain's personal quarters. Nickolaus was quite surprised at how quickly Stefano had been brought into the fold, almost as if he were a senior officer.

"Ah, good evening to you all. I hope you are hungry. I understand Tremonti has graced us with a fine farewell repast of meats, breads, and vegetables gathered just today from the finest markets in Genoa. The fresh food won't last long, so let's enjoy it while we can." The captain sat down at his chair at the head of the table. "Please, everyone, have a seat. I want to welcome our special guests, Maestro Cottano and his family, to my ship. Let us all give thanks in advance for this delicious meal and for a successful and uneventful voyage. The Cottanos bowed their heads and waited for the blessing to begin, but that was it. It appeared the captain had little patience for religious ceremony, a trait his crew greatly appreciated.

"Excuse me, Captain, but did you refer to the cook as Tremonti?"

"Why, yes, Maestro, good old Tremonti has been with me going on fifteen years now. He arrived with Commander Buxtaholda. They'd both been serving on the same ship." Nickolaus turned to Heinz.

"Is it the Tremonti, my Tremonti?"

Heinz smiled. "The one and only. I couldn't leave him on our old ship. They hated him there."

"I sensed that to be so, but I could never figure out why."

"You were too young to understand at the time, Maestro, just suffice it to say that he is with us now and still pretty much the same, though a bit older and wider, I suppose."

Chief Grumbach chuckled. "Who amongst us isn't?" The captain scowled slightly.

"I'm truly surprised," Nickolaus remarked with a smile and an obvious bit of joy in his voice. "You two were like saviors to me on that voyage. I don't think I would have survived without you."

15

"You'd have been fine, Maestro," Heinz reassured him. "You can pay him a visit later on if you wish. He pretty much shuts down after dinner is served. Leaves all the clean up to his aid. What's that new man's name, the boy he brought on in Genoa, Martinello, was it?"

"I believe so, Commander," Aldo chimed in. "Are we ready for dinner, Captain?"

"Bring it on, Aldo," commanded the captain eagerly. The steward rapped on a side door, signaling for Tremonti to bring in the meal. The door opened to reveal Martinello holding a large wooden tray full of food. He was obviously uncomfortable and insecure.

"Put it down over there and then bring up the rest," Aldo ordered. The young man set the food down clumsily then quickly passed back through the doorway and disappeared. "I believe it is the young man's first job. With your permission, Captain, I am granting him some leeway."

The captain looked at Aldo a bit sternly. "I don't recall having approved that man." He turned to his first officer. "Heinz, did you bring him on?"

"No, Captain, I've never seen him before today. I thought Tremonti brought him aboard with your approval."

Nickolaus raised his finger into the air. "Captain, that young man came to both me and Michela wanting to know if we needed any of our things brought up from the hold."

"Yes," Michela added, "and he was quite insistent about it. He told me he was following orders from the chief." All eyes turned to Chief Grumbach.

"Don't look at me, Sir. I have no bloody idea who he is. I never saw him until a moment ago. I'll bet goddamn Tremonti brought the young prick aboard without any approval." The chief stared defensively around the table, certain that no one believed him. "Come on, now, I swear I had nothing to do with it. Besides, if you ask me, he seems like a bit of pretty boy for a seaman."

Once again, the captain glowered at the chief, this time for his impertinence. He turned to his first officer. "Heinz, would you please find out who he is and who approved his assignment. I don't want any dregs or idiots on board my ship. We've got some serious business going on here."

16

"Yes, Sir, I'll look into it right after dinner." Captain Zannaro seemed temporarily appeased.

"Well, Aldo, what do you have for us tonight?" The steward nimbly delivered a handsome evening meal of breaded veal lavished with a gently spiced white sauce, fresh bread, a mix of seasoned, pickled vegetables, and some fine Italian wine. Everyone ate heartily, although Michela seemed hesitant to join in.

"How do you find your food, Signora Cottano?" asked the captain.

Slightly embarrassed, Michela put down her spoon then daintily wiped her mouth. "Delicioso, tutti delicioso."

"Eccellente!" The captain smiled and resumed his meal. Michela continued to eat, but only very slowly and deliberately. She clearly had no appetite. Nickolaus assumed she was suffering a touch of seasickness. "Say, Stefano, you seem quite taken with our ship's operations. Ever given any thought to taking on a life at sea?"

"It's all very interesting and impressive, Sir, but I believe I intend to become a composer and musician."

"Ah, taking up the family business, eh? Well, there's no harm in that, unless someone wants you to work as some count's bureaucrat. That's what my father had in mind for me. He claimed it would take me places."

"Oh, please don't misunderstand, Sir, with all due respect, my love of music was a big part of me long before I ever met the Maestro. I've always wanted to be a musician."

"Well, then, it looks as though you ran headlong into the arms of destiny when you became a member of the Maestro's family."

"Yes, Sir, I would say so. A stroke of good fortune to be sure."

"Commander," Nickolaus jumped in, "do you mind if I ask how we managed to miss each other during my many visits to the ship through all of that loading."

Heinz smiled. "Not at all, except that I'm not sure young ears are up to hearing about it."

The chief gulped out a few jolly yucks of laughter along with little bits of his dinner. "I'll say, hell of a week, eh, Commander?" The captain shook his head back and forth in

17

frustration. He'd been trying to tame his second officer's boorishness and poor table manners for years, but the man seemed to be utterly immune to his efforts.

Heinz continued. "Chief Grumbach and I were enjoying our shore leave at the Bishop's villa up in the hills, courtesy of a longtime friendship. I really love it up there, except that it might have been a bit more pleasant had Otto not insisted upon bringing his special companion." Heinz glared at the chief in a manner of feigned contempt.

"Wasn't she great?" the chief crowed, jerking his eyebrows up and down in a common lascivious facial expression. "Oh, that Sophia, what a fine lady she is! Whoa, and she'll not give a second thought to putting out. I can tell you that right now! Picked her up right there on the main road off the wharf, like plucking a prize apple straight off the tree." Nickolaus suddenly choked on his food. Everyone turned in his direction to see if he was all right. He was obviously blushing. The captain quickly interceded.

"My God, Chief, you hauled a common whore up to the Bishop's villa? Have you no sense of decency, man?"

"What's the problem? The Bishop wasn't there. He and Pugno stayed down in Genoa."

"And that makes it all right? Were there any servants at the villa?"

"Well, hell yes, you don't think we'd take care of things ourselves, do you?"

"Don't you think they might share some of their experiences during your stay there with the Bishop?"

"Not if they're good servants. By my way of thinking, they should mind their own damned business."

"They work for the Bishop, Chief, not some sleazy hotelier."

"My apologies, Captain, but I still don't see what all the fuss is about."

"No, I don't suppose you do." The captain turned toward Heinz. "But I would expect more from my first officer."

"Sorry, Sir, he just showed up with her. What was I supposed to do?"

"How about sending her back to her street corner?"

"Look, Captain, I know what we … what the chief did was wrong, but the damage, if any, is done. I'll be more vigilant in the future, I promise."

"Well, see that are, Commander. Perhaps I should put some restrictions on the chief's shore leave."

"To hell with that," the chief mumbled under his breath.

"What was that, Chief?"

"Sorry, Captain, I garbled on some food."

The captain sat back in his chair and smiled. "Gentlemen, gentlemen, let us not forget our company this evening. Please, Maestro, forgive us. Ours is usually a private dinner. The conversations can be, shall we say, a bit raw on occasion." Nickolaus suddenly felt embarrassed by what may have been perceived as his somewhat prudish overreaction to the chief's casual man speak. In any event, he was certainly glad they had no idea what he was actually thinking about. He picked up his spoon and stared pensively down at his plate, poking at his food for a couple of minutes while picturing in embarrassing yet nostalgic detail his own special meeting down by the wharf with his Sophia, who he was virtually certain must have been the same woman. Michela gently patted him on the hand.

"Nickolaus, are you all right?" She crooked her head slightly. "You seemed lost from us for a moment. Is everything … the way we like it?" He knew she was referring to his mood swings and the odd behavioral twists they often entailed. It irritated him that she was always suspicious in that regard, even though he also realized that her insights were usually accurate.

"No, I mean yes. I mean it's nothing, really. I guess I was just reminiscing about home. I'll be fine. Just let me have a moment." Fortunately, Nickolaus promptly remembered the flow of the prior conversation. "Heinz, was that perchance the villa of Bishop Caravaggio, formerly of Saint Matthias?"

"Indeed it was, Maestro. You know, the Bishop speaks very highly of you; in fact, he made me promise to protect you and your family as if you were my own. He says that you are the most talented composer and musician he has ever known."

Nickolaus blushed, this time for more obvious reasons. "Well, I don't know about that, but I do know that I owe a great deal to the good Bishop. He has been a loyal supporter and protector of mine since I was a child. He means the world to me." The Maestro's unabashed praise was not delivered without some degree of ambivalence. Although he had promised himself that he would try to forgive the Bishop's many misdeeds and remember him mainly for all the good he had done, he had not yet been able to shake his anger and disgust over the Bishop's involvement in the conspiracy of silence that had allowed Father Pietro's pedophilic assaults to continue unabated for over fifteen years. In the end, Nickolaus had decided to let time temper his ultimate judgment of the Bishop.

Heinz continued. "In any event, Maestro, I promised him that I would protect you and your family, and that's exactly what I intend to do." Nickolaus smiled then bowed his head in a gesture of gratitude. A moment later, after a rapid knock at the door, Ensign Westfalen rushed in to report that a silhouette of a vessel had been sighted to the north. Captain Zannaro glanced over at his first officer.

"We'd better go check on that, Heinz. We've quite a bit to protect this time around."

"Captain, please forgive me," Nickolaus interrupted. "I had no idea our presence here would cause you so much trouble."

"Don't give it a second thought, Maestro." The captain hesitated for a moment before looking at the commander, who subtly nodded his head. "Suffice it say that yours are not the only exotic teas and spices on board this ship. Our mutual friend, Signore Albioni, has entrusted us with some of his special goods as well." It took Nickolaus a moment to realize what was being said. The captain was not just carrying the Cottano's gold and possessions, but also gold stores and perhaps other treasures of considerable value for the Bank of Saint George.

"Oh, I see. Well then, I guess we have common interests in the success of this voyage."

"That we do, Maestro. Now please sit back and enjoy your dinner. I must go up top to consult with Commander Buxtaholda and the chief." Stefano jumped up as if to join them. The captain raised his hand prohibitively. "Not now, son, this could be serious business." His ego bruised, Stefano slumped back in his chair, but after a few moments, he recognized that he'd been deceiving himself about his actual level of involvement in ship's affairs. He truly felt like an idiot. The captain carried on.

"Maestro, I'll keep you informed of ship's progress. And Stefano, I'll have the chief give you a few pointers on navigation when he gets the chance." Stefano perked back up and smiled. Nickolaus sat back down, nodded at Stefano, and then shoved another piece of apple tort into his mouth. What else he could do? He was utterly powerless.

# Chapter 3 - Moonlight on the Horizon

Captain Zannaro and the commander rapidly made their way up to the helm where they joined Hermann von Westfalen, the night watch commander. Having served Captain Zannaro for over five years, the senior ensign was highly regarded by both captain and crew. "What do you have for us, Mr. Westfalen?"

"Sorry for the untimely interruption, Captain. The aft lookout spotted a ship on the horizon, astern, and on a course that would suggest Genoa as a point of origin. We only picked her up because of the light from the full moon." There was, indeed, a full harvest moon setting quickly in the southwest, a brilliant apricot orb soon to be swallowed by the sea. "With that full moon behind of us, we probably look like we're up on stage to any ships astern."

"Yes, I see that. Perhaps we could use that to our advantage. Hermann, can you make out what she is?"

"She appears to be a caravel, lateen sails front and back, but I can't be sure. She's quite a distance back. It could be Gatardo's ship. That was the only caravel I saw docked in Genoa when we left. The rest were all fishing boats. Damn that Gatardo! I don't know why he hasn't been clapped in irons." Somehow, Silvestri Gatardo had acquired possession and clear title over his ship, which he had tauntingly renamed *La Notte Corridore* – The Night Runner. No one knew for sure how he'd managed to gain possession of her – a bet, extortion, piracy, perhaps - but she was universally recognized as his ship. Reputed to be a trader, smuggler, pirate, and mercenary, Gatardo swore allegiance to no one. For years, Genoan authorities had been searching for some provable offence to justify arresting Gatardo and confiscating his ship, but they had thus far been unsuccessful. They knew what he was doing; they just couldn't prove it. Whenever rumors or charges of misconduct surfaced, witnesses just seemed to disappear. Normally, the authorities would simply have taken care of the matter without bothering with any of the procedural hoopla, but Gatardo seemed to have some mysterious pull with the Spanish who, at the time, basically ruled Genoa from afar.

"Yes, Mr. Westfalen, I agree." The captain turned to his first officer. "Commander, under the circumstances, I believe we should treat that vessel as being hostile. Don't you agree?"

"Yes, Captain, no doubt about it. God knows what Gatardo has in mind, if it's even him. We don't even know who might have commissioned him. Hell, he might be on a mission of his own folly for all we know." The two officers stood silent, staring out toward the mystery ship, which neither could actually see. They trusted Mr. Westfalen's vision and judgment implicitly.

"Tell me, Heinz, do you think we're overreacting. It could just be another random ship passing in the night. Why does this one seem to bother us so?" They stared at each other for several moments.

"Captain, we've always followed our instincts in situations like this. I suspect we're both feeling the same thing. Given the timing and the nature of our cargo, I think that ship shadowing us this way is just too much of a coincidence." The captain nodded his concurrence. Cocking his head as he stroked his chin, Heinz blurted out, "Sir, I have an idea." The captain continued nodding.

"Yes, so do I, Commander. Are we thinking the same thing?"

Heinz turned to the captain and began speaking in a near whisper. "I recommend that we wait until the moon sets. As soon it's down, we'll head due southeast and hold that course for four hours. That's exactly the opposite of what Gatardo would expect. We'll hold still until morning and then head due west until we reach the coast. Then we'll sail southwest hugging the coast of Spain until we reach Gibraltar. Hopefully, they'll sail full speed along our former course, thinking they've somehow fallen behind us. Hell, we might even gain some offshore wind advantage. I suppose it's a gamble, but what do we have to lose?"

"Well, for one thing, the delay could cost us everything if we're sunk in some merciless North Sea storm when we finally get up there too late in the season. And don't forget, Gatardo is a wily one. I'm not so sure he'll fall so easily for our little ruse. On the other hand, I don't see any harm in giving it a try. I've no better ideas at the moment. All right, at the very moment the moon sets, extinguish any and all lights that might be visible from outside the ship. And keep things quiet. Then set a southeast course and hold it for two hours. Bring her to a full stop then lower the sails and send extra lookouts up top. We'll be stationed still and dark in the middle of trade and fishing routes. I don't want to be rammed while we're sitting on our hands. And make sure either you or Chief Grumbach are at the helm. I want this done right."

"Aye, Sir."


Nickolaus and Stefano finished their apple torts while Michela sat by silently. She had long since lost her appetite. With his mouth still full, Nickolaus garbled, "Would you two like to drop down and visit my old friend Tremonti, or shall we simply return to the cabin? I still can't believe he's here."

"Let's go," Stefano quickly replied. "Anything is better than trying to cram ourselves into that tiny cabin.

"Yes, I suppose so," agreed Michela unenthusiastically. She, too, could think of nothing better to do in their tiny, ship-bound universe. Besides, they were all worried, so the diversion would help them pass the time until they got word of the situation. Michela stopped then turned and stared intently at Nickolaus. "What did the captain mean when he said that ours weren't the only exotic teas and spices on board this ship."

Nickolaus leaned over and whispered into her ear. "He's talking about gold, and maybe silver or jewels. Ours is only part of the high value cargo he's carrying on this voyage."

Michela winced slightly then pulled away, feeling somewhat betrayed. "So we have more to fear than just retribution from the likes of Il Rossone."

"Yes, and I'm not sure I like it either. I know our fates are out of our hands, but we really have no choice. Either way, I think we're safer out here on our way to Lubeck than back on shore facing down whatever Il Rossone and his cronies at the Archdiocese had in mind." Although Nickolaus stated his case with assurance, he was not nearly so certain in his heart. Still, his intellect had convinced him that they had made the right choice in escaping Genoa, and it had certainly seemed like the only viable option at the time. Meanwhile, Stefano had been humming and thumping away while working out a fairly complex musical progression in his head, using the railing as if it were an imaginary keyboard. He already missed his music. So did Nickolaus.

Finding Tremonti meant a trip through a short, narrow corridor located one deck down from the main deck. There, Captain Zannaro had carved out a small kitchen area that included a hammock and small storage locker for the cook's personal use. Situated port and aft, just above the water line, the efficient little area included a small wood-burning stove that was used only during calm seas, and a sealed trapdoor that opened outward and allowed the cook to dispose of garbage directly into the sea without journeying up top. The design, which had continued to evolve over the years, was really quite ingenious, perhaps even patentable.

Nickolaus hoped to surprise his old friend – a bit of conceit, perhaps – but he wasn't quite sure how to reach the galley. Fortunately, a busy ensign happened by and agreed to lead the way. The narrow hallway, created mainly by stacks of crates and barrels of soft beer, hard cider, and food stores, was dark and unlevel, which made passage difficult. Once they reached the galley's open area, the ensign left the visitors to their own devices. A dim lantern stashed in the corner provided just enough shadowy light to see with. Within a few moments, Nickolaus spotted Tremonti slumped back and half-asleep on his hammock, his duties for the day having finally been completed. Nickolaus put his finger to his lips, motioning for silence, then stole over to Tremonti and tapped him firmly on the shoulder.

"Hey, where can a man get a decent meal around here?" Nickolaus bellowed. Tremonti jumped forward with a terrible start and would have no doubt fallen to the floor had Nickolaus not grabbed the side of the hammock just in the nick of time.

"What the bloody hell? Who the blazes do you think you are, God damn it?" Tremonti began foraging around for the large butcher's knife he kept nearby.

"Tremonti, Tremonti, I'm Nickolaus von Silberbach, your young friend from many years ago. Do you remember me? Tremonti?" Stunned and sleepy, the cook stared into Nickolaus's eyes for a time then turned around and sat up. Nickolaus grasped his old friend's hand.

"Nickolaus, yes, I knew you were on board, and your family, too. I was planning to look you up in the morning. Sorry, but I'm not worth a damn once I've finished my day's work. Hell, even the captain knows not to bother me." Tremonti rubbed his eyes and stretched. "But you're here now, so what have you to say for yourself?"

"I just thought I'd drop by to offer my greetings and to introduce my family." Blurry-eyed, Tremonti glared past Nickolaus and nodded at the two silent visitors cowering in the corner."

"It's all right, you two, I won't bite. Your man here just threw me a bit of a scare."

"Tremonti, this is my dear wife, Michela, and her brother, Stefano." Both stepped forward and muttered in unison, "Nice to meet you, Signore Tremonti."

"Signore Tremonti? Oh, bloody hell, you can just call me Tremonti. Do I look like anything more than a beggar's servant to you? And for God's sake, there's no reason to be afraid. I'm perfectly harmless, I swear." Tremonti grinned, exposing several chipped and broken teeth. Michela and Stefano both relaxed slightly then edged over next to Nickolaus. Under the circumstances, Tremonti might have come across as threatening to just about anyone.

Nickolaus's manner grew joyful and animated. "I can't tell you how surprised I was to find Heinz Buxtaholda on board, and now you. The coincidence is incredible. Heinz even loaned us his cabin to use during the voyage. I don't know where he's bunking."

"Probably slung himself a hammock up in the captain's lounge. It's roomier up there anyway."

"Tremonti, do you mind if I ask how Heinz ended up as first officer on this ship rather than captain of his own vessel?"

"Oh, he'll get there soon enough. It's just a matter of time. The captain's over sixty now; he's set to retire at the end of this voyage. I've no doubt the commander will be promoted to captain. You know this is the biggest ship in the southern merchant fleet. It'll be quite a feather in his cap. And he's damn well earned it, too. He's the best first officer in the fleet, and he's been more than patient about holding his place while he earns his stripes. It'll have been worth the wait, though. Good old Heinz, he's probably got another fifteen years, that is, if the sea favors his fortunes. Damn, he and Captain Zannaro are the best men

I've ever served with." Moved by Tremonti's loyalty and sentimental attachment to the commander, Nickolaus recalled how Heinz had risked his own standing by bringing Tremonti, a man of dubious reputation, with him to this new posting aboard *The Paradise of the North*. Nickolaus still wondered why a decent, dependable cook and seemingly harmless man like Tremonti would have been so rejected by his former crew.

What Nickolaus had no way of recognizing during his earlier voyage at the innocent age of ten, was that Tremonti favored men as companions, though he was suitably masculine for his crewmates and never obvious about his preferences. Still, despite his scrupulous discretion, the crew of his original ship had somehow learned of his sexual predilections and hated him for it, even though some of them undoubtedly shared the same preferences. It didn't matter; men were men, and sailors were tough men who sought women for company - period! They had also ignorantly assumed that Tremonti might attempt unspoken liberties with the ten-year old Nickolaus, which was why the crew had viewed the boy's relationship with the cook so suspiciously. Needless to say, their assumption that, because Tremonti preferred men to women, he would also be drawn to boys was as flawed as thinking that a man who favored women would also be drawn in a similar fashion to little girls. It was a common but absurd notion.

Once on board *The Paradise*, Tremonti had chosen to abstain from all paired sexuality while also making certain that he always behaved in a very manly fashion, even pretending to lust after women while on shore leave. All this had left him extremely lonely and, at times, desperate for companionship. Perhaps that was why he had so readily accepted Martinello's unanticipated assignment as his aide, something he had never asked for or consciously desired. Unfortunately, the young man's handsome build and soft mannerisms threatened the lonely cook's sincerest intentions to remain chaste. This scared him deeply, for he had long eschewed temptation, and he certainly wanted to avoid priming any of the damaging rumors that had destroyed his fortunes on his last ship.

"Tell me, Tremonti, how did Heinz end up serving with Captain Zannaro?"

"There's not much to tell. That old bucket you sailed on during your voyage south was due for the salvage yard. When Captain Ellstrom decided to retire, Heinz Buxtaholda suddenly became a sailor without a ship. He had already earned quite a reputation for himself, so he could easily have landed a good assignment. Captain Zannaro, who had been looking for a new first officer, just happened to be in port in Lubeck. They met up somehow and Captain Zannaro took him on right away. I don't really know many of the details, but for some bloody reason that escapes me, Mr. Buxtaholda wanted me to come with him. He said Captain Zannaro'd give his right eye for a first class Genoan sea cook. Well, I don't know about the first class part, but I am Genoan, and I am a cook, so I gladly joined the crew. I made a god dam new start of it, too. It's the best fucking thing that ever happened to me." Tremonti shrugged his shoulders, as if to apologize for his gratuitous use of salty language in front of a woman and a boy, though neither one was nearly so delicate as he imagined.

"You seem to be in pretty good stead for a cook," Nickolaus observed. Suddenly a tall shadowy figure flitted down the passageway and into the kitchen. It was Martinello.

"Signore Tremonti, may I have a moment?" It was the first time in his career that any crewman had ever referred to him as Signore. He loved it. "The monk is requesting some food and wine. He says he's feeling better now." It seemed both odd and annoying to Tremonti that Martinello had taken it on himself to serve as the monk's personal aide.

"What? Who the bloody hell does he think he is? If he doesn't eat with the rest of'em, he'll either go hungry or he can come down here himself and beg me for some leftovers. He's not some royal fucking nobleman, God damn it." Whatever trace of religion Tremonti might have picked up during his tumultuous childhood had long since disappeared. He'd seen an abundance of hard circumstances and spent plenty of time alone with his thoughts. Nothing about the church made sense to him anymore. Also, as time passed, he'd grown to view monks and priests with particular disdain, the higher-ups even more so, typically referring to all men of the cloth as "their royal fucking holiness." In this regard, Nickolaus and Tremonti shared fairly congruent religious outlooks, although each had reached their conclusions by way of

29

different paths. Nickolaus, however, did not necessarily share Tremonti's intense hostility though, admittedly, there had been times.

"Sir, I've spent some time with him. He deserves respect. I just want to take him some food and drink." Martinello stared pleadingly at Tremonti.

"All right then, boy, take him some food, but take him beer or cider. There's no wine down here and he doesn't deserve it anyway. And don't overdo it. There's nothing special about him. He might as well be a damned stowaway as far as I'm concerned."

"Aye, Sir. As you say, Sir." The four watched silently as Martinello gathered a few stores then disappeared back down the aisle way. For reasons unclear, none of them felt comfortable talking around the young man. Something about his demeanor just seemed to invite mistrust.

"I don't know why the captain brought him on, anyway." Tremonti grumbled.

"Martinello or the monk?" Nickolaus asked.

"Well, both, now that you mention it up. Captain Zannaro never accepts passengers, except in an emergency. I understand why you are here, but the monk? To hell with him! As for Martinello, I have no idea who sent him down here in the first place. He just showed up with some kind of letter from a priest. A hell of a lot of good that does me, I can't even read. I'm a cook not a damn scholar." Nickolaus had just begun pondering his next words when the ship suddenly lurched and swerved to the left, almost knocking the three inexperienced voyagers against the hull. Tremonti seemed unscathed, swaying gracefully with the abrupt, unexpected motion.

"What was that?" Michela muttered nervously.

"Not to worry, Signora, just a minor course change. A bit rough, I must say, and it doesn't seem to me that it's in the right direction, but then I'm only the cook. I just go where they take us."

"I wonder if the captain was forced to make a sudden course change in order to avoid that ship they were worried about?" Nickolaus speculated.

"May be, but you'd best stay down here with me for a while. Leave the captain and crew to do their business. You'll just be in the way up there." Tremonti pulled up a rickety old bench then leaned over and turned up the lantern. "Have a seat, mates. Tell me about yourselves. We've got some time." Peering around the small room, eyes as wide as owls, the three visitors slowly sat down on the bench.

"Perhaps it would be best if we were to remain here until there's some word from the captain or Heinz," Nickolaus suggested, as if it were his own idea.

"Aye, that'd be best," Tremonti affirmed, thrilled to share time with some friendly company for once.

# Chapter 4 – What's All the Ruckus?

Tremonti grabbed a jug of his special mystery brew and offered it to his guests. Everyone politely declined, except for Stefano, who was very eager to give it a shot. For the next couple of hours, Nickolaus and Tremonti shared fifteen years of times past. Michela and Stefano were quick to point out any puffing or perceived misreporting by Nickolaus and, on a few occasions, even offered their own somewhat differing versions of certain circumstances. Tremonti had plenty of his own tales to tell, many of which sounded menacing, harrowing, and quite unpleasant. The poor cook had clearly done some serious living.

After watching Tremonti enjoy a swig or two from his jug every few minutes, Nickolaus finally relented and took a few sips, and then a few gulps that he enjoyed immensely. It really seemed to take the edge off. Whatever was in the jug packed quite a wallop, which is probably why the cook's stories soon began to wander and overlap. Nickolaus, too, began to feel pleasantly relaxed, in fact, so much so that he failed to notice Michela lying sound asleep on the bench, rocking gently back and forth with the motion of the sea. Lying back on a half-empty sack of flour, a very sleepy Stefano was barely paying attention. For the moment, the young man felt safe and comfortable. Maybe it was the wine at dinner, or perhaps the several nips of Tremonti's brew that he'd secretly thrown back while no one was looking, either way, the boy loved the feeling and wished for more.

Tremonti suddenly grew silent, staring up knowingly at the ceiling. "We've come to a stop." Nickolaus felt nothing but the gentle sway of the waves as the ship continued bobbing up and down on the calm autumn waters of the Mediterranean. "They're pulling in the sails." Tremonti murmured.

Sensing nothing, Nickolaus whispered, "How can you tell?"

"I can just feel it. You come to know these things after a while. God, I'm tired. You'd be wise to take your family up to your cabin now. I've got to get some sleep. Damn, I'm really going to pay in the morning. I can feel it right now. Whew! Can you find your way, Maestro? I best not try to go anywhere. The captain will have my ass if he sees me drunk like this again. It really sets him off."

"Oh, we'll be fine. I think I know the way." Nickolaus jiggled Stefano's foot. "We're going to bed now. Help me with your sister." They woke Michela up then cradled her down the dark passageway, up the stairs, and then out onto the main deck. The sea air had cooled considerably. More striking was the near total darkness that had enveloped the ship, leaving the trio lost and disoriented. A moment later, a hand out of the dark suddenly grasped Nickolaus's shoulder.

"Maestro, allow me to accompany you to your quarters, and please be as quiet as possible." Nickolaus turned around. It was the same ensign who had helped them earlier, Kurt Grether.

"What's going on? Why is it so dark?" Nickolaus whispered.

"Never mind that for now. We need to get you off the deck. We're running dark and silent." Carrying a small, dim light, the ensign swiftly ushered the three guests to their small cabin where he closed the door and lit a lantern. "Sorry for the intrigue, Maestro, but we're hiding in the dark for a while, just in case. Keep your voices to a whisper and don't go back up on deck until someone gives you the word." The ensign pointed to a bucket hooked to the wall. "There's your … well, you know. Keep it hooked up if you don't want any spills. If you dare, you're free to find your way down the hall to starboard where you'll find the officer's seat of ease. But keep it quiet, and no lights." Nickolaus nodded as the ensign took his leave.

"Let's get you ready for bed," Nickolaus suggested as he began unfastening the numerous loops on Michela's dress. "Stefano, I think if you tug on that cord, the hammock will drop from the ceiling." Everyone made their preparations for bed then attempted to settle in for some sleep. Needless to say, the bunk was not at all hospitable for two adults, even though both were slimly built, but it was all they had, so they would have to make it work. It definitely gave new meaning to the term cozy. They decided to leave the lantern burning at a very low setting so they would know where they were when they woke up. Within a few minutes, Michela and Stefano had dropped off to sleep, but not Nickolaus. He was beginning to feel especially unsettled which, as usual, brought on an unwelcome spell of rumination followed by an attack of nerves.

In a way, the cramped accommodations provided some small element of security; however, the nervousness also made him want to keep moving, if only to wander around the ship for distraction and release. But he was imprisoned, encased, no, entombed in this tiny bunk, and Michela was sound asleep, so he would have to stay put. And then, just as he had anticipated, he began to feel the dreaded spears of anxiety and panic racing through his veins, those senseless, relentless spells of unfocused fear and foreboding that terrorized him so. He knew of no way to stop or control them. Oddly, when he was in one of his bright spells, the same phenomena filled him with excitement and energy. They made him feel strong, sometimes even invincible, but also sleepless. The dark times were different. When his spirits were low, the attacks spread through him like poison, seeking any vulnerable target they could grab hold of. Then, just as they seemed to be dissipating, another attack would strike, then again and again until, eventually, he would usually drop off to sleep. Fortunately, he'd not lately been suffering the gloom or despair of one of his dark spells, but he was certainly riddled with fear and anxiety. Everything he had come to know in his adult life was gone: his home, his position, his friends, and his beloved choir, even the familiar bells of Saint Matthias. He might have had a vague idea of where he was going and what he might find there, but for the most part he still perceived his future mainly as an intimidating threat. Oh, how he hated Father Pietro, Pope Paul IV, the Archdiocese, hell, the whole damned church. And then, when his thoughts turned to the upcoming voyage, he felt nauseous and vile, as if he might explode with anguish.

It was at times like this that he wished he possessed some outlet for his angst, some way to deflect or dilute his anxieties. Sometimes, he even wished he could pray like every one else, if only to escape into that magical mind zone where he might find freedom from the realities and responsibilities of life, perhaps even find someone or something to which he could transfer his fears and insecurities. If only there were some higher power he could turn to for hope and solace, as others did. But he had long since abandoned such beliefs, even though he often still wished that he could reach for them at difficult times like these. But for him, it would be like grabbing for a fistful of fog. How he missed that god he'd known and loved as a small child, always there, always his own, a deity so powerful that it could solve anything - anything, that is, so long as he was good and deserving. All he had to do was pray, worship, avoid sin, and stay on God's good side, then the merciful Lord would grant him protection and special favors, at least when he felt like it. Of course, such incidents of grace seemed to be granted, if at all, at the most random of times and circumstances and, it had appeared to the young Nickolaus, usually to the least deserving of people. How many truly good and faithful people had he seen left desperate and abandoned? Yet they still believed with all their hearts. Why, he always wondered. Why?

He had been suspicious of the faith contract from a very early age. It all seemed too convenient, too much like a fairy tale. It reminded him of other myths he had heard and refused to take seriously. He felt as though he should believe, but he didn't, and that made him feel guilty over his apparent breach. So when his parents burned to death in a freak and horrible house fire, and he was summarily dispatched to Genoa with barely a word of explanation, he was certain that it was all punishment for his lack of faith, indeed, his evil and heretical thoughts. Imagine the folly of a child's mind, trying to make sense over something so random and horrific. Considering what he had been taught in church, he felt he had no choice but to blame himself.

As time passed, he read, learned, and experienced life. As his intellect grew, doubt crept back into his mind, and his outlook slowly transformed until, once again, he came to understand that his initial impressions as a child had been both wise and true, at least so much as anyone can know. By age thirteen, young Nickolaus had again fallen away from the flock. He knew his agnosticism would lead him down a difficult and secretive path, but once he understood and was convinced of his beliefs, there could be no going back. None of it made any sense to him anymore, and he no longer believed in any of it. So here he was, left to his own devices, forced to rely on himself, humanity, natural circumstances, and probably a bit of luck, indeed, maybe even a lot of luck. Fortunately, within a few minutes, he finally dropped off into a fretful sleep.

Out on deck, the crew had brought the ship to a complete stop then set up station keeping. The sails had been lowered, but no anchor dropped. They had to be ready to move the ship at a moment's notice. A mild, northerly, offshore breeze was still pushing them slowly south, but not enough to cause any concern. Corsica, which they preferred to avoid, lay south-southwest. At dawn they would scan the horizon and, if clear, turn the ship around and head due west. They were proceeding under the assumption that the ship they had sighted was Gatardo's, and that he and his men had continued their pursuit along the normal course to Gibraltar. Gatardo's caravel could easily outrun and outmaneuver Captain Zannaro's gargantuan carrack, so the crew of *The Paradise* knew they would have to rely on trickery and stealth if they wanted to stay clear of her. On the other hand, odds of *The Paradise* blowing Gatardo's ship out of the water were fairly decent if it ever came to that but, wisely, the captain preferred not to take his chances with such a venture. He knew he was still vulnerable, and any battle would undoubtedly mean injury or death to members of his crew or, worse yet, his passengers, to whom he had come to feel a special duty of care.

While most of the crew had put down to sleep for the night, a dozen or so men were stationed on lookout. Orders were clear: dark and quiet – no exceptions – unless a ramming appeared imminent. For the time being, *The Paradise* appeared to loom silent and empty, like an abandoned ghost ship. All of a sudden, without so much as a creak of warning, a bright light shown out across the main deck. Someone had lit a poop lantern and set it for full illumination.

"What the bloody hell," whispered Ensign Fritz Fuhrmann, master of the forward lookouts. "Get down there and squelch that damn thing!" But since silence was still a paramount priority, the three sentries could only rush quietly to the light. The first one to arrive, Johann, grabbed the lantern and snuffed it out. Close to twenty seconds had already elapsed, which was nearly an eternity for an alert lookout searching the horizon from a pursuing ship. The three sentries grabbed the offender and shoved him forward into the forecastle's upper hold.

"What the hell's wrong with you, you stupid son-of-a-bitch?" growled Ensign Fuhrmann. "You heard the captain's orders. Who are you? Gregor, hurry up and light a candle. By God, I see some serious troubles in your future, sailor." But instead of unmasking a disobedient crewman, the sentries discovered the monk, his head and face still buried deeply within the hood of his robes. Johann grabbed the hood and jerked it back. Ensign Fuhrmann was livid. "Vater? Padre, what the hell … uh …what in heaven's name are you doing out on deck? How did you get hold of that damn lantern?"

"I was looking for the latrine. Do you mind?"

"Why yes, by God, I do mind. We have buckets and a pipe down there for that. Who do you think you are, traipsing around the deck while we're running silent? You're bunking down with the crew. You heard the orders. And how did you get hold of that lantern, anyway? For the love of Christ, you're either stupid or willful. I'm not sure which, but I don't think you're stupid, so what do you have to say for yourself?"

The monk slumped back, a bit of his ire exhausted. "I assure you, my son, I just needed to relieve myself. I'm sorry, but I can't share those filthy buckets with the men. I just can't. I'm getting older you know. Things don't work as they once did."

"Well, aren't we special, all clean and tidy, eh, like you're still in the monastery. Well you're not! You're on a ship, our ship, and you'll follow our orders. Padre or not, you'll do what you're told, or you'll be booted right off this vessel. Is that understood?"

"Yes, yes, my son, I will do as you ask. I didn't mean to interfere with your protocols. It won't happen again, I assure you. Now, could you please take me back down below?"

"Where are you bound on this voyage, anyway?" Fritz snapped brusquely.

"As close to Walkenried Abbey as I can get."

"Walkenried Abbey, where's that?"

"At Walkenried," the monk answered sarcastically.

"I don't appreciate your smart mouth, monk. Have you an appointment there?

"Why yes, my son." Fritz cringed at being referred to as "my son" again. He and Nickolaus shared the same aversion. "I am to be an instructor at a new academy soon to be founded there."

"You, an instructor? Of what, pray tell?"

"Ethics and secular commerce, of course." Fritz could barely hold a straight face.

"At a church school for young men? Ethics and secular commerce, are you serious?"

"Oh, you'd be surprised at what young men are capable of learning and doing, Ensign."

Fritz stared skeptically at the monk who, so far, had behaved mainly like a fool, though there was also something perceptibly deceitful about him. "You seem a bit simple minded … ah … provincial for those kinds of subjects to me – no offense intended." Inside, the monk was seething. At another time, he might have had Fritz killed for such insolence but, at the moment, he was in no position to complain about anything. The monk took a deep breath before releasing a long, malodorous sigh.

"Well, my son, you aren't exactly seeing me at my best. I prefer to travel simply and modestly, as Christ our Lord did. I could show you my commission if it would ease your concerns."

"No, no, never mind that, but you'd better follow orders from here on out." The ensign glared suspiciously at the monk then turned to the others.

"Johann, you and Gregor take him back to his bedroll. And you, Padre, will stay below until someone comes down to get you. Is that clear?"

"I promise, my son, I'll be no more trouble."

"Just the same, I'm sure Commander Buxtaholda will want to speak with you in the morning."

"Is that truly necessary? I believe I explained my predicament to you. Please, I'd prefer you share my little indiscretion with as few people as possible. I do feel stupid about it, you know."

"Is there a problem, Padre? Have you something to hide?"

"No, no, I just …well, no matter. I'll look forward to his visit. I know the safety of the ship is our greatest concern. God be with you, my son."

Fritz shook his head then turned to Gregor and Johann. "As soon as he's back in his bunk, return to your watches immediately. We'll need to be especially vigilant now."

From the far reaches of a confusing dream, Nickolaus slowly awoke. It took him a few moments to realize where he was. The room was almost totally dark, lit only by the dim light of the flickering lantern, which seemed to be down to its last few drops of oil. He had no idea how long he'd been asleep or even what time it was, but he could see that Stefano had abandoned the hammock. Whether that meant the boy had been unable to sleep, or had simply arisen for the day was a mystery. Nickolaus sensed that the ship was moving differently from when he had finally fallen asleep. The prior evening, he'd felt a gentle, back-and-forth bobbing motion. Now he sensed movement fore and aft that made it feel as though the ship were cutting through waves rather than just sitting on top of them. It also seemed to be listing noticeably to port, so he assumed that they were back under way and on the proper course.

He felt a bit stiff, having been pinned in and barely able to move by the slumbering Michela during the few hours he had managed to sleep. Still, stiff or not, his love was right there, pressing against him, her body moving back and forth with the waves, caressing his freshly awakened sensations. He relished her warmth, her softness, her seductive curves and crannies. Upon feeling his usual morning urges, he made himself even cozier, burrowing as deeply as possible into his lover's welcoming folds. To his delight, she stirred then sighed softly. She was awake, at least partially. She squeezed his hand, which had longingly found its way upon her breast. Still beneath the bed covers, she removed her pantaloons then squirmed closer and pushed against him, inviting him in. With no need for further coaxing, he quickly but gently found his way. Ah, perfezione! Everything was right with the world, just as it was meant to be - utter paradise.

He often moved swiftly in the morning, which was fine with Michela, as her motivation at that time of day was more a matter of loving cooperation than erotic involvement. On this day, however, she was very receptive, even eager in her sharing as her sensual rhythmic motions urged him to tunnel deeper and more intensely into her quivering lair. He obliged with great pleasure, yet something felt different this time. She seemed a bit shorter inside, as if overnight, either he had grown or she had shrunk. It was a new and surprising sensation. They had always fit together so perfectly, but now he kept bumping into the end of her tunnel. It actually hurt a little, so he altered his position a few times, but nothing seemed to change. It was as if something were blocking his path. No matter, though, for it felt wonderful anyway, and within a few minutes the matter had been settled. Afterwards, they both lapsed into a daze, with her still very tired, and him euphoric and once again drifting off to that extraordinary dream haze that seemed to engulf him at those special times. Sadly, the lull passed all too quickly as both soon realized they needed to move on. Neither wanted to budge, so they lingered a while longer, gently stroking each other, with each suffering silently through their own trepidations. Finally, she rolled over and hugged him tightly - more out of fear than tenderness - then they both struggled out of the bunk and prepared to find their way out onto the main deck.

Looking around more closely, Nickolaus discovered a pair of tightly closed shutters. He reached over and cracked them slightly, allowing a bright blade of light to pierce the shadows. Then he opened them all the way, revealing a small, stern-side window overlooking the sea. He and Michela stared at each other and smiled – a ray of light, a symbol of hope, perhaps? At the very least, their cabin would be a little more hospitable than they had assumed.

# Chapter 5 – Family Affair

Nickolaus and Michela were taken aback when they climbed out onto the main deck. The prior day's welcoming sun and warmth had given way to a menacing blanket of low-lying clouds that seemed to rake the sea with cold tines of dense fog. Fortunately, the surface of the sea was still pleasantly smooth while a steady breeze out of the east was generously filling the sails, propelling the ship rapidly toward the west. All was not gloomy, though, for several splashes of pale blue sky peeking through the overcast gave notice of the possibility that another bright autumn day might still be in store.

"I'm hungry," Nickolaus declared. "How about you, my love?"

"Oh, I'm fine, but we should find you some food." Nickolaus turned and glanced at his wife. She looked pale and tired again. He was actually surprised by her appearance, perhaps even alarmed. He gently brushed her cheek. It was cool – no fever – that was a relief.

"How are you feeling? You look a bit peaked. Perhaps we should try to find you some tea and biscotti."

"Yes, that sounds good. Maybe it'll give me some spirit. I feel so tired today. I don't know why. Maybe it was that early morning tryst." He smiled then kissed her on the cheek while patting her gently on the behind. She playfully brushed his hand away then kissed him back.

"You probably just need some time to adjust to the sea," he reassured her. In reality, he feared something more serious might be in the offing, though he knew not what.

"Ah, there you are. Good morning Maestro, Signora." It was Ensign Grether. "Commander Buxtaholda asked me to escort you to the captain's table for breakfast and a report on our progress."

"Yes, that would be excellent. Perchance, do you know where Master Stefano is?"

"Yes, Maestro." The ensign smiled and pointed up towards the forecastle deck where Chief Grumbach and Stefano were busy working with some instruments – a sextant, an astrolabe, or some other form of modern navigational device that neither Nickolaus nor Michela had any interest in. "He's in good hands with the chief, but I can't guarantee he won't pick up some of the chief's less savory habits. At least the chief's Genoan is pretty decent." Ensign Grether's Genoan was also quite impressive. Like the captain and Heinz, several members of the crew were multi-lingual, speaking German, Genoan, Frisian, and even bits of Spanish and Latin.

"Well, it won't be the first street manners he's ever experienced, I can assure you of that." Nickolaus was gazing across the ship when the mysterious hooded monk suddenly showed up on the main deck then began climbing to the upper forecastle deck, perhaps seeking a clearer view over the sea or, more likely, access to the seat of ease stationed on the starboard side between two rigging mounts. Nickolaus thought the spot looked almost farcically exposed to the elements, but he also figured that if you had to go, it was a better than using a bucket down in the hold. When the monk reached the top of the ladder and peered out across the forecastle deck, he spotted Stefano and the chief standing directly before him with their backs turned. He immediately ducked then retreated rapidly down the ladder to the main deck where he slid like a snake back into whatever hole he'd just crawled out of. "Well, he's certainly a bashful fellow," remarked Nickolaus.

"What's that?" Michela replied, staring off toward her brother.

"That monk seems to have been frightened off by the chief or Stefano, like a mouse caught in a light at night."

Ensign Grether shook his head. "That monk, he's a strange one. Last night he damn near lit us up like a lighthouse for everyone in the Mediterranean to see. Claimed he needed to use the latrine and couldn't find his way, so he took it upon himself to light up a lantern right out in the open. He knew the captain's orders. I don't know what he was thinking." The ensign's tone smacked of derision. "The commander is planning to pay him a visit this morning. Mr. Monk will have to straighten up or we'll put him off at Gibraltar. Captain Zannaro is doing him a big favor just by letting him on board. He's loath to take on passengers in the first place and then … well, except you, of course." The ensign blushed at his inadvertent slip of the tongue.

"It's quite all right, Ensign, we know we're a burden. I'm certain Heinz will set things straight with the monk. I've wondered about him too. He certainly seems to keep himself scarce."

"Probably used to the privacy of the cloister," the ensign suggested in a sarcastic tone. "Please, follow me, breakfast is waiting in the captain's lounge." Nickolaus and Michela felt a little embarrassed being treated like royalty, as conditions aboard ships, even trade vessels, were invariably strict and austere. The ensign opened the door and invited the Cottanos to enter. Ensigns Fuhrmann and Westfalen were standing silently against the wall, munching pastries and sipping hard cider. Both nodded politely as Nickolaus and Michela crossed the room.

"Ah, Buon Giorno," greeted Commander Buxtaholda, looking up from his work. "I trust your night passed without too much distress. There is some cheese and pastry over on the table. Aldo will see to some tea, or hard cider if you prefer. The captain will be here shortly. He wants to keep you informed of our progress."

"Well, this is certainly a pleasant surprise," Nickolaus declared, looking over the inviting breakfast spread. "Are all of these comforts customary?"

"First day out and a calm one at that," Heinz explained. "Consider this a special day. Conditions are seldom this hospitable."

"We'll take what we can get," Nickolaus noted with a smile. "Aldo, Do you happen to keep any biscotti around?" He placed his hand on Michela's shoulder, tilting his head toward her.

"Of course, Maestro, I'll see what I can do."

"Thank you, my good fellow." When Aldo stepped out of the way, Nickolaus noticed some maps and instruments scattered about on the table. With two windows open to starboard and one facing the main deck, the room seemed much brighter and inviting in the light of day. He believed he could almost feel comfortable there. He glanced at Heinz, who looked drawn and tired, as though he had slept very little during the night. It was the first time Nickolaus had ever detected any signs of vulnerability in the commander. He had always seemed invincible in the past, an impression most likely leftover from Nicolo's childhood experiences with the then much younger officer. Within a few moments, Aldo returned with a small plate of lemon biscotti, which he set down on the table with the other food. Having noticed Michela's paleness, he quickly brought her a chair before handing her a mug of tea.

"Grazie, Signore," she offered resolutely, as if to conceal how weak she actually felt.

A moment later, the captain arrived from the main deck with young Ensign Silvio Di Rufo, who came tripping through the doorway behind him. Silvio was a youthful, handsome lad, indeed, almost dashing, with a wasp-like build, ample wavy hair, and a neatly trimmed moustache. It seemed to Nickolaus that the young man bore more than a vague resemblance to the captain. Mr. Di Rufo managed several routine ship operations during the day and, despite his oft-bumbling incompetence, also served as a reasonably adept ship's surgeon when needed. Upon entering the room, his gaze fell instantly upon Michela, who glanced back at him while gently sipping her tea. He shuffled slowly across the room, his eyes still glued on Michela, whose uncommon paleness served as a mark of rare beauty. A moment later he bumped into the breakfast serving table.

"Oh, excuse me," he offered absentmindedly – to the table. Captain Zannaro looked askance at the young man before quickly introducing Maestro Di Cottano and his wife, Michela, the word "wife" being emphasized. Silvio immediately straightened his posture, stroked his moustache, then took off his hat and bowed to the couple. They, in turn, bowed their heads slightly, barely able to keep from snickering at the embarrassed young officer.

Captain Zannaro clumped a wooden mug down on the table like a gavel. "Good morning to all of you. Please eat and drink at your pleasure. Chief Grumbach is out confirming our new course, so I'll get started." Silvio began piling cheese and pastry on his plate, as if he hadn't eaten for a month. A disapproving glance from the captain seemed to wake him up;

whereupon, he just as quickly began disassembling the mighty feast he'd just laid out for himself. Once he was satisfied that he had properly adjusted his portions, he grabbed clumsily at a mug of soft beer, spilling its contents on both table and floor. Unable to quell his reaction, the captain stared toward the floor and shook his head in what could only be described as resigned acceptance of his officer's habitual inelegance. A few moments later, Silvio stepped over and stood directly next to Michela, at which point the captain responded by glaring at the ensign while cocking his head in a manner that told the young man to move on and find a more suitable place to stand. It was as if they were father and wayward son.

"As I was saying, I trust you are all doing well. We were a bit concerned last night after sighting what appeared to be a pursuing vessel, perhaps that of the infamous Silvestri Gatardo and his band of iniquity."

"You mean pirates, don't you," Silvio garbled through a mouthful of pastry.

Glaring down irritably at the ensign once again, the captain continued. "As I was saying, we took evasive action and then held still and silent over night. After seeing nothing this morning, we set course due west where we hope to sail close to the coast and pick up the down-slope northerly winds blowing off the mainland. This way we should make favorable time to Gibraltar while also staying off the main trade routes. Our actions may seem a bit overcautious, but there is a lot at stake here, so I see no harm in taking extra care. We've got a lot to lose in terms of both life and property. Commander, have you made our rules absolutely clear to the monk from Papenburg yet?"

"No, Sir, I will take care of that directly."

"Well, make damned sure he knows that we'll leave him high and dry in Gibraltar if he can't follow the rules. And have you clarified the situation regarding the new cook's assistant – what was his name – Martinello?"

"I'll get to the bottom of that after I deal with the monk, Sir."

"Good. I don't like leaving anything to chance under our present circumstances. We need to be at our very best, Heinz."

"Yes, Captain, I'll square things up right away." Heinz and the two silent ensigns departed, while Silvio remained, still chomping away at his breakfast. The captain took a deep breath then shook his head.

"Mr. Di Rufo, when you're finished, I'd like to have a word with the Cottanos, a private word, that is." Silvio, still chewing with his mouth stuffed full, nodded and mumbled his accord. The captain rolled his eyes. "Mr. Di Rufo, why don't you just take that with you?"

"Oh, I see, sorry Sir." He grabbed his mug then tripped out through the door onto the main deck.

"I'm sorry about that. It's really not as bad as it looks." The captain shook his head again, staring out the window at Silvio, who was barking out orders at the men while still holding a pastry in one hand and a mug in the other. "I should confess to you that he's my nephew, and that his commission here is somewhat of a family matter, more of a family favor, I suppose. But he's a lot better officer than he appears to be at the moment. For some reason, he seems to be distracted this morning." The captain smiled at Michela, who grinned back, confirming that she understood and accepted his unspoken apology. "Truly, he's a very loyal and devoted officer. I wouldn't put up with him otherwise, but he can be a bit trying at times."

"We thank you for the information, Captain, and for including us in your considerations. We know you're under no obligation to do so."

"Think nothing of it. I wish I could offer you something to help pass the time, but I'm afraid you're on your own. If you need any of your possessions brought up from the hold, feel free to contact the commander. And do be careful. It's just not safe out here for the uninitiated."

"Yes, we'll watch out and follow all the rules. What about Martinello?" Nickolaus asked.

"Oh, yes, Martinello, please steer clear of him until we find out who brought him aboard. He remains a bit of a mystery at present." The captain looked out toward the deck. "Well, I have some logs to fill out. Please let yourselves out when you are finished. Good day to you both."

"And to you as well," Nickolaus and Michela responded in unison.

# Chapter 6 – Oddities

The next few days passed without notable incident. It turned out that Martinello had come on board with the monk, who had immediately presented him to Tremonti, stating that the young lad had been received and accepted by Ensign Silvio Di Rufo. When asked, Mr. Di Rufo had no memory of the affair, but fearing that he might have missed something along the way, went ahead and approved the enlistment. Later, when questioned by Commander Buxtaholda, Martinello handily produced a Certificate of Culinary Apprenticeship from his parish as well as a special recommendation from a priest at the Genoan Archdiocese. Since everything seemed to be in order, the issue was deemed settled, though a stain of suspicion had definitely attached to the new cook's assistant. The monk, upon being confronted by Commander Buxtaholda, showed nothing but pure contrition and regret, promising, as if to the Lord, that he would follow all orders and ship's rules to the utmost. Although the commander left feeling generally satisfied, there was still something about the monk that made him uncomfortable.

As per the planned strategy, *The Paradise* slid along the south coast of France, taking full advantage of the steady northerly winds, which helped propel the ship at enviable speeds through calm and peaceful waters, past Cartagena, and then even more rapidly in a southwest direction down the coast of Spain toward Gibraltar. Progress slowed at night when the lack of sun and heat tended to quell the offshore wind flow. Fortunately, since they were sailing in Spanish waters and carrying the flag of Genoa, which at the time was a protectorate of Spain, they felt relatively safe. Still, they kept a close lookout for suspicious vessels, especially anything resembling Gatardo's caravel. In the end, while they did come in contact with several small fishing boats, none of them seemed to warrant any concern.

Slowly, the Cottanos began to adjust to their new living situation. Luckily, the placid autumn weather provided for unusually calm seas. Much to Nickolaus's relief, Michela soon began to perk up some; however, her appetite remained weak and she often complained of nausea, particularly in the morning. As the fresh food from Genoa dwindled away, they were forced to share in standard officer's sea faire: fish, cheese, hard tack, and beans which, although more nicely prepared than that of the crew, fell far short of Michela's fine cooking or the delicious offerings they had grown accustomed to at Edguardo's Restaurant in Genoa. Nickolaus quickly grew fond of the soft beer and hard cider that were readily available in place of water, which was highly prone to spoilage and contamination. In addition, the captain was most generous about sharing his personal stores of wine and brandy with his Genoan guests, as he truly enjoyed their company. Barely able to wash and certainly unable to bath, they soon began feeling dirty and decrepit. Stefano, on the other hand, felt surprisingly at ease, readily adjusting to his new surroundings. He even took up playing card games with some of the young pages burdened with the worst of ship's tasks, such as clean-up, deck swabbing, and bilge duty. The Cottanos' seaborne situation clearly constituted a stark hardening of circumstances compared to the soft, cultivated lives they had enjoyed in Genoa, but at least they found some comfort in making solid progress toward their new lives in Lubeck.

After a few days of maintaining a very low profile, the mysterious monk seemed to slip from everyone's mind though, occasionally, Martinello could be seen leaving the galley holding a tray loaded with food and drink, which he proceeded to carry across the main deck then down into the forward hold where the monk was bunking. Such personal service would never have been afforded to any regular sailor, so it was assumed that the intended recipient must have been the monk. On the other hand, since the monk dutifully complied with all ship's rules and orders after his dressing down, no one, including Tremonti, seemed to care much about his special treatment. Oddly, other than his quirky cameo appearance on the morning of the second day of the voyage, he was never again seen out on deck, although several sailors were heard complaining about his chanting, which they felt belonged in a church or monastery and not on board their ship. They could put up with his softly spoken Latin prayers, but the singing was too much. For them, a simple prayer or a short blessing was enough; besides, the chants were Roman Catholic and most of the sailors, to the extent they practiced any specific religion at all, considered themselves followers of Luther. For his part, Captain

Zannaro generally discouraged excessive practice of any faith on board ship, as he was intent on avoiding religious strife between men of either faith. The reformation, then in full swing, had cultivated neither amity nor tolerance among proponents of the various factions. In truth, however, the captain's official policy had only limited effect on the crew. Feeling both exposed and superstitious, the sailors let the monk sing his songs at will, just in case the Lord might seek to punish them if they turned out to have taken up sides with the wrong prophets. Then as now, superstition was a powerful and abiding force.

Early in the afternoon on the fourth day out, while climbing the ladder to the upper forecastle deck, Stefano happened to hear the monk's chanting spiraling up from the hold. The young man halted his climb and listened for a few moments, as his interest in musical affairs was keen. The doorway to the hold seemed almost to trumpet the chants, as if they were seeking any possible outlet through which to make their escape. After glancing down toward the hold, a passing sailor looked at Stefano then mockingly shook his head and rolled his eyes at the braying. Stefano nodded back. The monk's voice and articulation, though fairly accurate and experienced, were certainly not producing sounds that anyone would describe as pleasant. Stefano couldn't help but cringe at the missed intonations. Suddenly his ears perked up as the hair on the back of his neck began to sizzle. Both the voice and the tune seemed eerily familiar, indeed, very familiar. This was one of several tuneful chants that Nicolo had composed and then secretly slipped into Saint Matthias services as replacements for the old monodies that he had grown bored with. Then Maestro Di Cappella, Father Paolo, had never even noticed, since he seldom paid much attention to anything musical. On the other hand, Bishop Caravaggio, who recognized the switch almost immediately, invited young Nicolo to his office to express his genuine pleasure over the distinctive new music before happily granting his formal approval of the changes. He, too, had grown tired of the old chants – and of Father Paulo.

That musical coup had been Nicolo's first success at replacing some of the worn out traditional music with one of his radical new compositions - at least that was how he viewed the achievement. In truth, irrespective of any technical musical considerations, the new chants were tuneful to the point of being memorable; delivering the kind of melodies almost anyone could hum or whistle. As a consequence, they had quickly become popular with the priests, the choir, and the congregation. That being said, they had never been performed beyond the walls Saint Matthias. Both Nicolo and the Bishop had deemed them to be proprietary, that is, their own protected artistic property. As such, it was a virtual certainty that Nicolo's chants could never have made it into any monastery, nor would any monastery ever think of replacing the old tried and true monodies with something new, since the ancient chants were still revered like sacred relics.

Stefano listened again, this time very carefully. There was no doubt about it; this was one of Nicolo's Saint Matthias chants, and he would certainly know, having sung it countless times as a member of the church choir. Whoever was chanting down in the hold had spent time at Saint Matthias masses. With his interest in the mysterious monk ignited, Stefano quickly backed down the ladder and headed straight across the main deck to report his discovery to Nickolaus.

He knew just where to look. Nickolaus and Michela had been passing their afternoons seated out on the main deck, taking in as much sun and warmth as possible. Michela spent most of the time resting up, while Nickolaus had taken to composing whatever he could eke out between the ups and downs of the undulating waves. He had set to work on a series of three madrigals, a form with which he had very little experience; however, being highly motivated, he decided to put aside virtually all considerations of proper form and style and just compose whatever he felt like. In other words, he was improvising – one of his greatest musical strengths. He knew what he wanted to say and how he wanted it to sound, but getting it all down on paper was another matter. Just as often, the young couple could be found standing shipside at the railing, admiring the schools of dolphins that kept returning to swim alongside the ship, skipping in and out of the water while chasing each other, almost as if they were playing games. The dolphins' antics were both curious and mesmerizing, and it even appeared as though the beasts might actually be communicating amongst themselves.

Stefano found his sister sporting a wide grin as she perused one of Nickolaus's completed pages of music. This must have been something different. Perhaps he had finally plied his hand at a bit of musical comedy. Whatever he was working on, he was staring straight ahead, as if in some sort of trance, while at the same time, scribbling musical notes onto a piece of paper that he'd had Tremonti tack to a board so that it wouldn't blow away in the wind. Stefano almost hated to interrupt.

"Maestro," Stefano blurted out excitedly. "I think there's something you need to hear."

"Yes, I know. I need to hear my music on a harpsichord, but since that isn't going to happen soon, you may as well share your news with me."

"Your chants, I heard your chants being sung down in the hold. I'm sure it must be the monk."

"You heard my chants? How can that be?"

"They're yours; I know them well. They're yours for sure. I'd put a wager on it."

"A wager, eh?" Nickolaus stared down at the deck for a moment. "You know, I could have sworn I heard one of the sailors whistling my fourth monody this morning. Those idiosyncratic twists in that melody are unmistakable. I assumed it was just coincidence, or maybe that I'd picked the tune up from an old sea song somewhere." Nickolaus climbed up out of his perch and kissed Michela on the forehead. "All right, Stefano, let's go find out what you heard." Michela smiled up at them, squinting painfully through the sunlight.

"Don't get lost," she warned facetiously.

"We'll be careful," Stefano promised as they headed off toward the bow.

At the very same moment, Ensign Grether rushed into the captain's lounge to report that a caravel resembling Gatardo's ship had been spotted to the southeast, running on what appeared to be a direct intercept course. Still quite distant, no flags or colors could be identified, but the ship's profile looked ominously familiar. Captain Zannaro and Heinz departed at once to take a position on the rear quarterdeck where they could get a first-hand feel for the situation. On their way, they passed directly by Nickolaus and Stefano without speaking so much as a word.

As they trekked across the main deck, Nickolaus began humming the tune of his fourth monody. Stefano offered up the

53

harmony. Just as they were about to reach the hold, Commander Buxtaholda bellowed, "Ship approaching to port. Prepare for evasive maneuvers!" A volley of additional orders involving sails and tiller movements followed immediately. At the first command, Nickolaus and Stefano both stopped in their tracks then swung around to see what was going on. It was as if a hidden crowd had suddenly taken possession of the decks, masts, and riggings of the vessel. Sailors were scrambling and climbing about on every corner of the ship, not randomly, but with purpose and precision. The nature of the orders, which had been delivered in German, mainly escaped Stefano, but Nickolaus had a pretty good idea what was going on. Their ship was either being pursued or attacked. In any event, he knew they had to make their way back to Michela and get her to a safe place; however, the instant they turned around, they were grabbed from behind by Ensign Grether and propelled briskly toward the rear of the ship. "Come, Maestro, you and Stefano must take refuge in the captain's lounge immediately."

"But Michela, we have to find Michela."

"We've got her, Maestro. Please, just do as I say." Ensign Grether pushed Nickolaus and Stefano rapidly across the deck, somehow directing them along a path that allowed them to bypass the various riggings and other protrusions that blocked the way. A moment later, they spotted Michela being led hurriedly off the main deck into the captain's lounge. Within a few seconds, Nickolaus and Stefano joined her, whereupon she immediately threw herself into her husband's waiting arms.

"What's happening? I heard the man in the crow's nest yelling very loudly." The report had been delivered in German, so Michela had only perceived the urgency of the cry from its alarming tone.

"We're either being chased or attacked," Nickolaus informed her. "I'm not sure which, but I'm sure we'll know shortly."

"Please, Maestro, you must all sit down over there." The ensign pointed to a bench that backed to a wall that bolstered the center of the ship. "You'll be safe here. This may end up being nothing, but just in case, you'll need to remain here." The trio immediately sat down on the bench as directed, though Stefano seemed far more curious than concerned. He wanted to join the crew out on deck; in fact, he even jumped back up from the bench.

"Sit down," Nickolaus snapped. Stefano looked up at Ensign Grether, who was anxious to get back to his regular duties.

"The Maestro is right. Stay where you are – none of this is child's play." His ego badly bruised, Stefano dropped back down onto the bench as if he had been punched in the stomach. Ensign Grether quickly disappeared onto the main deck, latching the doorway behind him.

Captain Zannaro was at the helm, helping Chief Grumbach ascertain both ships' precise trajectories. In the meantime, Commander Buxtaholda had taken charge of defensive operations. *The Paradise* had been sailing southwest across the Alboran Sea just off Spain's Costa del Sol. The Rock of Gibraltar was visible on the horizon, but still a way's off. The captain believed that if they sailed at full speed, they should be able to round the horn first and then seek refuge at the nearest port on the east side of the Bay of Gibraltar. But was there really a threat? The ship certainly looked like Gatardo's, and since it appeared to be racing toward them at flank speed, the only reasonable choice was to assume that its intentions were hostile.

Fortunately, *The Paradise* did have one small advantage. The captain knew his fully loaded carrack would normally suffer a substantial speed disadvantage compared with the caravel; however, in this case, he had a brisk tailwind pushing him down the coast, whereas the approaching ship was moving in from the southeast, sailing almost directly against the wind. *The Paradise* definitely had a decent chance to win the race. It was also true that if the two ships should happen to meet in conflict, *The Paradise* stood a better than average chance of prevailing. Either way, it was unusual to see Captain Zannaro take on such a highly defensive posture. It was almost as if some unforeseen force had spoofed him. Perhaps it was the rare presence of passengers, or maybe he just didn't want to miss his chance to make it home where he could finally settle back into his well-deserved retirement and enjoy the fruits of his life's labors. After such a long and successful career, it would have been a damnable shame for him to go out losing his ship for the first time in his life.

Back in the captain's lounge, Nickolaus still had his arm wrapped around Michela's shoulder. She shook her head. "I'm obviously no sailor, but why are they so certain that ship is headed in our direction or intending to do us harm. It could just as easily be an innocent merchant ship passing through Gibraltar. The straits are narrowing - wouldn't we expect to come across more ships? I know I've seen a lot more seagulls flying overhead. We must be getting close to fishing boats or settlements. Don't you agree, Nicolo?"

"Very astute, my love. Your logic is superb, and your ideas have certainly crossed my mind as well, but the truth is that we just don't have any say in the matter. Besides, I'm prone to trust the captain's intuition. He's been doing this for a very long time. We're just passengers along for the ride."

"I suppose so, but I do hope they don't do something stupid and get people killed for no good reason. You know, one of those preposterous, manly honor contests."

"You do understand - men and their overblown egos — the abiding constant throughout all time. I've never been the best judge of character, but I sense that Captain Zannaro has grown beyond those sorts of foolish antics. Heinz, too. We'll just have to hope for the best."

"I'd sure like to see what's going on out there," Stefano grumbled.

"I'm not sure I like being in the dark either," agreed Nickolaus, "but we have to stay put for now. The last thing they need is to have their attentions diverted worrying about us."

"Yes, yes, I know," conceded Stefano. A moment later Tremonti slid in through the service door holding a jug of hard cider and a plate of his delicious sweet biscuits with raisins.

"I thought I'd join you up here. I can't bloody stand to be stuck down there in that miserable little galley pit at times like this. One goddamned cannonball in the wrong place and I'd be swimming with the fish." Tremonti handed around the jug, inviting everyone to share in a swig or two.

"Thanks for those uplifting words of confidence, Tremonti, that's just what we needed to hear."

"Sorry, Maestro, I just tell it like it is."

"Of that I am certain, but candor isn't always the best course."

56

"What's that you say about our course?"

"Never mind, I'm just glad you and your biscuits are here, my old friend."

"Me too."

# Chapter 7 – Race to the Rock

Up top, all sails and rigging had been configured for maximum speed. Simultaneously, the two main deck guns were made ready and rolled into position. Meanwhile, Chief Grumbach had drawn the captain a triangle displaying the relative courses of the two ships as well as his estimates of the applicable wind speeds and directions facing each ship. Using the point of Gibraltar as the acute angle, *The Paradise* was traveling on the long base, while the approaching ship was running along the hypotenuse of the same right triangle. *The Paradise* clearly had the distance and wind advantage so, with any luck, they would round the point of Gibraltar first where they would then be in relatively protected waters. Fortunately it was still early afternoon, so the offshore winds were expected to remain at least stable, if not increase slightly. Unfortunately, with their eyes trained almost exclusively on the big rock and the approaching ship, the lookouts failed to notice a small fishing boat anchored in their path until they were almost on top of it. The occupants of the smaller boat must have been either asleep or oblivious, since they took no evasive action whatsoever, all of which seemed quite odd in light of *The Paradise's* overwhelming size and presence.

"Vessel off the starboard bow!" shouted Chief Grumbach from the helm. "Tiller hard to port." The chief knew his action would slow the ship down a bit as well as temporarily send it off in the direction of the pursuing caravel, but he had no intention of sacrificing an innocent vessel when it might be so readily saved. Or could it? The tiller had been moved as ordered, but the ship barely seemed to be changing course at all. The chief had suspected as much. With *The Paradise* so heavily loaded and moving at such a high speed, she would not be so willing to change direction – like a sow in the mud, he kept reminding himself. Even the wind refused to cooperate, suddenly tossing strong easterly gusts at them as they approached the Strait of Gibraltar.

One of the deck mates had commenced ringing a warning bell as soon as the chief issued his alert but, so far, there had been no response. The smaller boat remained motionless, as if it were an empty derelict. Soon *The Paradise* drew close enough that the crew could even see down into the boat. Then, just as a collision seemed inevitable, *The Paradise* managed to change course just enough that she was able to avoid a direct impact. Instead, she only grazed the small boat, resulting in a loud bump followed by a hideous scraping noise as the smaller boat slid along the starboard side of the larger ship. Chief Grumbach and the captain both peered over the side, watching nervously and cringing at the sound. On the other hand, what seemed like a mere shudder and some racket to those on board *The Paradise* sounded more like Armageddon to the two fishermen in the smaller boat, who had been lying peacefully under a tarp taking their afternoon siestas. Shocked and dazed, they jumped up and began scrambling about their boat in terror, seeking any possible means of escape from their grave predicament. However, within a few moments it was all over as *The Paradise* cruised away at full speed, leaving the smaller boat rocking sickeningly back and forth as its occupants stood violently waving their fists and screaming their most potent epithets at the top of their lungs.

Mr. Di Rufo, who had been watching the oncoming collision with dread, immediately commenced waving at the two fisherman while shouting, "Perdedor, perdedor," which he had once been told by a sadistic bar companion meant "forgive me, forgive me." Those words, however, as they had done in the tavern, just seemed to make the fishermen even angrier. As it turned out, Mr. Di Rufo's bar mate in La Coruna had been setting him up for a beating, as the proper apology would have been *perdoname*, which meant sorry, rather than *perdedor*, which meant loser. Young Ensign Di Rufo had barely escaped with his life in La Coruna, while his bar mate had barely been able to keep from exploding with laughter. Apparently, Mr. Di Rufo never realized that he'd been the butt of a dangerous joke.

In a more apt response, Ensign Westfalen quickly began shouting, "Perdoname, perdoname," at the passing craft in an effort to soothe relations with the outraged fishermen. He then turned to the his ensign and explained, "Very nice, Mr. Di Rufo, you just called them a bunch of losers," at which point the embarrassed young officer hung his head in shame then disappeared into the shadows.

The chief quickly ran back to port to assess the more pressing situation – the approaching caravel. "Tiller hard to starboard," he ordered, attempting to restore the ship's original course and regain its slight advantage. Perhaps he had underestimated the speed of the approaching caravel, or maybe *The Paradise* wasn't quite as fast as he had hoped for; either way, the challenger was moving in on them in a hurry.

"Otto?" the captain groaned, glaring over at his second officer.

The chief shook his head. "Sorry, Sir, I did my best. There's only so much I can do." By then, both ships were rapidly approaching the point of Gibraltar; however, it now appeared that they might round the point virtually simultaneously, which was not at all what they had hoped for.

"Chief, do we know who that is yet?"

"It sure likes Gatardo's ship to me, but I can't make out her flag or colors. She is hanging some kind of banner, though, but I'll be God damned if I can make out what's on it."

"Well then, Chief, let's find someone who can." Frustrated, the captain shouted down to Commander Buxtaholda, who was busy supervising men and weapons on the main deck. "Heinz, can you make out that banner she's flying?"

The commander peered off into the distance. "There are red markings on a white background. I've never seen it before, but they're flying it high. Wait a moment, Sir, I'll be right back." A few seconds later, the commander reappeared, leading Nickolaus to the port railing. "What do you make of that banner?" Nickolaus stared so intensely that he thought his eyes might pop out. "Well, Maestro, can you read it?"

"Hold on a minute. I won't swear to it, but I think it's a Bishop's coat of arms."

"Yes, Maestro, yes, the red on white. I hadn't considered that. Do you recognize it by any chance?"

"I'm afraid ecclesiastic markings aren't exactly my specialty," Nickolaus replied a bit sarcastically. He wrapped his hands in a circle around his face then continued staring across the steadily narrowing gulf between the two ships. "Wait, wait!

61

Damn, that looks like Bishop Caravaggio's insignia. I've seen it many times. Now I'm almost certain of it – it's quite unique."

"This must be some kind of trick? Why on God's good earth would the Bishop be chasing us down in Gatardo's ship? This makes no sense at all. Come, Maestro, follow me, let's go up and talk to the captain." The two men promptly made their way up to the helm.

"You'd better have a damned good reason for bringing him up here," scolded the captain.

"Sir, Nickolaus is almost certain that our pursuer over there is flying a banner displaying Bishop Caravaggio's coat of arms."

The captain stared incredulously at his first officer. "How can that be, Commander? The chief is virtually certain that it's Gatardo's ship."

By that time, the crews of both ships could almost see each other. All of a sudden, Gatardo's ship began changing course. "Captain, she appears to be running parallel now."

"Yes, indeed she does. Hold on a moment, Commander, they're raising some kind of white flag. Good God, what the hell is going on over there? There's a knight standing on deck waving a sword back and forth, and I believe he's shouting at us. I don't understand - a knight waving a sword along with a flag indicating his intent to yield? What do you make of that, gentlemen?" The inquiry was met with complete silence. The captain glanced down toward the main deck at Ensigns Di Rufo and Grether, both of whom shook their heads.

Nickolaus found the whole scene odd and confusing, but as he continued trying to make sense of the situation, something about the knight suddenly struck a familiar chord. Once again, Nickolaus stared hard across the breach then he shuffled back and forth trying to gain a better view. "No, it's not possible. This just can't be. I must be seeing things. How could...?"

"What, how could what, Maestro?" Heinz asked insistently.

"If I didn't know better, I'd swear that was my old friend, Marco. He has an odd habit of swinging his sword around like that. I think it's something he learned in battle training as a tactic to destroy the enemy's confidence or scare them off. Hell, I don't know, something like that." Nickolaus continued to gaze at

Gatardo's ship. "I'm almost certain of it now; that has to be Marco in uniform. Hold on a moment." Nickolaus placed his thumb and finger in his mouth then let loose with an intensely shrill whistle that carried a distinctive tune. "Listen carefully," he cautioned. Sure enough, almost immediately a very similar shriek with a slightly different tune resounded. Nickolaus whistled over another shrill calling, which was again answered almost instantly. "That's Marco, no doubt about it, Captain. I don't know exactly what he's doing, but he would never betray us, of that I am absolutely certain. And now that we're closer, I can almost guarantee that the banner they're displaying is Bishop Caravaggio's coat of arms."

Captain Zannaro paced back and forth a few times. "Heinz, what do you make of this? What's he up to?"

"I can't say, Captain, but I think we should tread cautiously and not be too aggressive. I don't think we can justify any sort of preemptive attack." Privately, Heinz was surprised by the captain's intensely defensive posturing on the matter. The threat level just didn't seem to warrant such a hostile response.

"Affirmative, Heinz, I agree. For the time being, we'll stay on course to Gibraltar, but we'd better keep a damn close watch on our shadow over there. Stand ready to take evasive action the instant I give the order. We don't want to be caught off guard." The captain turned toward the main deck. "Steady as she goes, men." Shortly thereafter, Gatardo's ship began moving away. With Captain Zannaro's cannons staring them in the face, they had wisely decided to give their quarry a bit of distance, lest their intentions be either misunderstood or blown out of proportion. In addition, the tangle of winds and currents surrounding Gibraltar made for a tricky affair when rounding the horn, making it best to keep to a safe distance between ships. Highly perplexed, the captain turned to Nickolaus. "Maestro, what do you make of this? Do you have any idea why the Bishop would send Gatardo's ship and your buddy Marco across the sea to chase us down? This is damn peculiar, I tell you. I've not seen anything like this in … well, ever."

"I can't imagine, Captain. I'm neither a sailor nor a strategist, but it seems to me that they've either been sailing around looking for us, or they left a day or two behind us. You said their ship is faster than ours. Perhaps that ghost ship on the first night out was nothing more than a coincidence, or maybe it was just an innocent ship passing in the night. Either way, none of that explains what Marco and that ship are doing here now, sailing under the Bishop's banner."

"Maestro, tell me, is it possible you've been granted some form of reprieve or immunity? Maybe the Archdiocese came to their senses," Heinz proposed. Nickolaus grinned and shook his head. "Yes, I see your point, Maestro, they'd never admit they were wrong about a damned thing, would they?"

The captain shrugged his shoulders. "Well, Gentlemen, they're here for some reason. As I said, we'll take safe harbor once we round the horn. I assume we'll find out then what they're up to."

# Chapter 8 – Emptying the Bilge

Rounding the horn was always risky. Winds and currents were erratic and unpredictable. Tides could play an even bigger role. Fortunately Captain Zannaro had made the journey so many times that he knew exactly what to expect and how best to deal with it. Add in Chief Grumbach's legendary skills and sailor's intuition and it barely seemed a challenge anymore. Still, if there were storms, prudent ship captains would hold back and wait for calmer seas and friendlier weather. Temporarily at ease, the captain turned to Nickolaus. "Maestro, perhaps you should return to your wife. Comfort her and let her know what's going on. I imagine she's in quite a state by now. This is no fine place for a woman."

"Of course, Captain, I'll go to her at once. She was quite worried when I left her." Nickolaus descended from the bridge then quickly made his way to the captain's lounge, almost colliding with Ensign Di Rufo, who was pacing back and forth across the main deck with his face turned downward. Once inside, Nickolaus found Michela and Stefano seated calmly at the table, playing cards, one of several games of chance that Stefano had picked up from his new friends aboard ship. "Ah, my love, it's good to see you so calm." Nickolaus immediately set about explaining their situation, but neither Michela nor Stefano seemed particularly interested, which was good. Stefano stood up and stretched.

"You know, Maestro, we never did determine who was chanting your monody down in the hold. Do you think we should look into that before we reach port?"

"Ah, yes, the enigmatic monk, he slipped my mind in all the excitement. Perhaps we should have one of the ensigns accompany us. I don't want to step on anyone's toes. Let's go find Ensign Grether; he seems eager to help. Michela, are you comfortable remaining here with Tremonti?" The ship's cook looked crestfallen, thinking the Maestro didn't trust him alone around his wife.

"Oh my, yes, please go ahead," she replied without hesitation. "I'm sure Mr. Tremonti and I can find some way to keep the game going without Stefano." She grinned slyly. Tremonti perked up and smiled, relieved that she felt safe around him and even wanted to continue their card game. He would never have admitted it, but he truly missed close, congenial human companionship, especially with a woman in a situation where he felt no pressure to engage her in a romantic or sexual manner in an attempt to impress the other crewmembers. The cook waved the two off then picked up Stefano's cards and turned his attentions to Michela.

"Please, Signora, you must call me Tremonti. There is no Mister Tremonti about it, just plain old Tremonti."

"As you wish, plain old Tremonti, proceed if you dare."

"No wagering, Tremonti!" Nickolaus admonished facetiously with a smile.

"Yes, Sir, Captain."

Upon exiting the captain's lounge, Nickolaus and Stefano ran directly into Ensign Grether, who seemed to be in close conversation with a still dejected Ensign Di Rufo. Mr. Di Rufo had trouble maintaining a decent level of self-confidence in the first place, so whenever he made one of his many feckless blunders, it usually took him a while to recover. For the most part, he tended to mope about the about the ship for a spell; however, occasionally he would take to verbally abusing lesser members of the crew. For some reason he felt as though he might recover his sense of authority if he acted particularly aggressive and puckish toward those beneath him. Needless to say, such tactics were completely ineffective, usually causing only more damage to his already shaky command authority.

As soon as Ensign Grether noticed Nickolaus and Stefano approaching, he stepped away from Mr. Di Rufo, saluted, and then stated loudly but awkwardly, "Thank you, Sir, I'll get right on that." Unable to conceal his surprise and confusion, Mr. Di Rufo saluted back before muttering something unintelligible and then walking off.

"Maestro, Master Stefano, I'm not sure you should be out on deck like this. Is there something I can help you with?" Ensign Grether seemed truly concerned but also a bit distracted.

"Ensign, I was wondering if you might accompany us to the forward hold to investigate an oddity?"

"An oddity, what do you mean?"

"Earlier, just before our encounter with the other ship, Stefano heard our not-so-friendly monk passenger chanting a monody that he really shouldn't be familiar with. We're highly curious to discover where he picked the chant up. I'm sorry, but it's a bit hard to explain. Let's just says that it's a matter of professional urgency. That being said, I have no desire to interfere with ship's business." Nickolaus stared quizzically at Ensign Grether.

After a quick survey of the ship's situation, the ensign reluctantly consented. "I'm not sure what you mean by professional urgency, but I will agree to escort you to the forward crew quarters so long as circumstances remain stable. Be prepared, though, I'm not sure you'll like what you find there. I must warn you in advance that it's no fine hostel."

Nickolaus held his open hand out toward the forward quarters. "Agreed, Ensign, you lead the way." Ensign Grether glanced off toward Gatardo's ship as the threesome traversed the main deck. When they reached the forecastle, the ensign pulled open the door, peered in warily, then stepped in to take a quick look around. Finding nothing remarkable, he moved forward then told Nickolaus and Stefano to follow him in. Stefano had been there before and knew precisely what to expect. Nickolaus, on the other hand, had thus far been spared the grittier details of a sailor's life aboard ship. At first, he nearly recoiled from the stench of sweat, dirty bedrolls, and unpleasant latrine residues. Empty of crew, the room was dark and disorienting, but after a brief period of mouth breathing and sensory acclimation, Nickolaus took his time searching thoroughly around the room. It certainly seemed that no one was there. He turned to Ensign Grether. "Where else could he be? Are there any other places he might hide or … be keeping himself?"

"We don't really trust him, Maestro. Commander Buxtaholda ordered him to remain here where he couldn't do any damage. He should definitely be here and nowhere else." While the three men stood staring at each other, wondering where to look next, they heard a faint rustling followed by a thump from beneath a clump of blankets in the rear portside corner of the room. All three swung around. "Who's there?" shouted Ensign Grether. Silence. "I said, who's there?" Again, nothing. "All right, mister, if I have to come over there and drag you out, there'll be hell to pay. Now show yourself!" Still - nothing. And with that, Ensign Grether, who had clearly run out of patience, grabbed a grappling hook and charged across the small room to the corner where he dropped the hook onto the heap and ripped the blankets back.

Nickolaus and Stefano couldn't resist stepping over to take a look. "What the hell is going on here?" barked the ensign. Lying deep in the shadows was Martinello, his breeches pulled down awkwardly around his ankles. Another man, the monk, was lying down, facing the sidewall of the ship with his robes drawn up over his torso. The two men remained utterly still and completely silent, except for the occasional shallow breath necessary to sustain life. Ensign Grether poked at Martinello with the grappling hook. "Hey, you, get up, I say, get up now. And you, Mister Monk, pull down those robes and come out of there. Ach, mein Gott," the ensign exclaimed disgustedly, looking away as the tumescent Martinello stood up then hurriedly pulled up his breeches. The monk, however, refused to move. The frustrated ensign poked at him with the grappling hook. "You, mister holy one, get up out of there or I'll pull you out with this hook. Do you understand? Move it! God, I can't believe my eyes. What the hell is going on here?"

Finally realizing there would be no escape from his predicament, the priest rolled over, then sat up and revealed himself. "Father Pietro?" Stefano muttered hesitantly.

"You, Pietro, God dammed Pietro! What the hell? My God, man, I can't believe this!" Nickolaus was truly shocked. He turned to Ensign Grether. "This is Pietro, the disgraced, defrocked, homicidal, child-molesting, common thief formerly of Saint Matthias." He turned back toward the villainous priest. "How in the hell did you get in here and what in the name of God are you doing? What a bastard you are!" Nickolaus turned white and began pacing back and forth, panting frantically. "I can't believe this is happening. Who do you think you are? Oh my God!"

Stefano suddenly realized that Nickolaus was falling into the throws of one of his attacks, one of his infamous panic attacks. The harder he breathed, the more lightheaded he felt which, in turn, made him breath even harder. His thoughts flew everywhere and nowhere. He was afraid he was going to die, but at the same time, almost wished that he would, if only to be over with it all. He would then grow sweaty and nauseous before being overwhelmed by an intense desire to find an escape, an escape to anywhere, alas, an escape from his own frenzied emotions. Stefano had witnessed the attacks several times before, but he'd never quite figured out precisely how to deal with them. On the other hand, he also knew that whatever this ungodly phenomenon was, it usually didn't last all that long.

"Maestro, Maestro, you're doing it again. Stop pacing. Stop breathing so hard. Come with me now, we must get out of this stinking dungeon."

"What, no, no, I'm not going to miss this. Ensign Grether, I want this man placed under arrest immediately." The Maestro's antics were so extreme and out of character that Ensign Grether, who felt both trapped and responsible, knew he had to do something quickly.

"Stand up, monk. Well, what do you have to say for yourself, you and this … this boy strumpet of yours? My God, man, a priest and a boy, on my ship, what the hell is wrong with you?" Pietro slowly climbed to his feet, allowing his robes to slip back down around his ankles. For a few moments he appeared to be confused, perhaps even a bit contrite, but then an evil smirk crossed his face. Having seen the same sickening expression on Pietro's face before, Nickolaus knew things were about to turn ugly.

"I have no idea what you're talking about. This young dog threw me into that corner and tried to rape me and smother me under those blankets. I tried to fight him off, but … but I lost consciousness. When I woke up, you were poking at me with that hook of yours. Arrest that heathen. He's a rapist and a sodomite, probably even a deputy of Satan. Search him, I'll bet he bears the mark of the devil. Go on, search that little pissant."

"Oh, search yourself, Pietro," shouted Nickolaus. "I already witnessed this very same miserable act of innocence at Saint Matthias. You'll not get away with it here either, you degenerate bastard." Ensign Grether's glare bore straight into Martinello, like a carpenter's awl.

"Are the monk's claims true, cook's mate?" Martinello stood frozen in his tracks as his eyes flitted back and forth between Ensign Grether's piercing glare and Pietro's harrowing gaze. "Well, speak up, man, did you attack this monk as he claims?"

"No, sir, we were under the blankets seeking extra protection from the cannon balls."

"What cannonballs? Are you serious, extra protection from the cannonballs? Do you honestly expect me to believe that?" The ensign thought about it for a moment. "Oh, bullshit! You two were down there going at it like a couple of man whores. Don't deny it, boy. You were still spiked up when I pulled the blankets off."

Martinello's eyes began flitting back and forth again, seeking either asylum from Ensign Grether or direction from Pietro. "I ... I don't know what to say, Sir."

"The truth, son, only the truth will serve you now." Martinello stared at Stefano for a few seconds, then at Nickolaus, then he thought back, remembering his first encounters with Father Pietro at Saint Matthias, the subsequent abuses at the bathhouse, and how it had all changed his very perception of life. His words suddenly poured out.

"I'm here for Father Pietro. I'm his servant and protector. I do everything he asks of me – everything – just as it should be. I love him and he loves me. He is mine. He is my father and my lover, God's gracious gift to me alone. No man could ask for more."

"Well, obviously the young lad is demented," protested Pietro. "He has no idea of what he speaks. Why, he's imagining things that aren't there. Poor lad, he's taken leave of his senses. Please, let us not shun him, but offer him our gracious pity instead. He is but a lost soul now."

"Stow it in the bilge, Pietro. You're a liar," Nickolaus yelled, still panting away. "He's one of your trophy boys from the bathhouse, isn't he? Isn't he?"

"I'll shut that prick mouth of yours, if it's the last thing I ever do, dandy man." Having finally been pushed over the brink, Pietro suddenly crouched as though he were going to lunge at Nickolaus. But it was not to be. Before he could manage even one step forward, Ensign Grether reached out with the grappling hook and punched the priest backwards then leveraged him against the floor by placing his foot down hard on the shocked priest's abdomen.

"Come now, monk, behave yourself. Are you not a man of God? Well?" Pietro remained dead still, refusing to speak or move. "You know, the captain and Commander Buxtaholda will be very interested to hear of all this." Pietro squirmed, trying to break free. "Oh, no you don't, priest, lie still," the ensign commanded, pushing down even harder with his foot while positioning the grappling hook right up next to the monk's neck. "Stefano, please go find Ensign Westfalen and ask him to bring a couple of men with him. Tell him I issued the order."

"Aye, Sir," Stefano answered assuredly, suddenly feeling like a valued member of the crew again. "I'll be back at once."

Within a minute, Ensign Westfalen flew into the crew's quarters with three stocky sailors – brothers, in fact - who the crew jokingly but respectfully referred to as the Teutonics. Because of their unusual height and rare muscular heft, Helmut, Erik, and Ludwig usually served as master rigging mates, but when the need arose, they were also called upon to serve as guards, soldiers or, on occasion, generalized muscle. They were loved but also a bit feared by the entire crew. The Teutonics spoke mainly in a north Frisian dialect, which was actually more English than anything else, and were quite spare even with that, except among themselves and Chief Grumbach with whom they shared their beloved homeland. Many of the crew suspected that the Teutonics were actually descendants of ancient Norsemen, but no one had ever dared ask them about it. Obviously, referring to North Frisian Norsemen as Teutonics made no sense at all, but somehow their actual surname of Terpstra had slowly warped over time into Teutonic. Such are the mysteries of nicknames. Perhaps given their close-knit brotherhood, they seemed more like an order of knights than just three members of a hanseatic shipping crew. At any rate, the captain's orders for double rations of food and drink for his loyal Teutonics were accepted by the crew without complaint.

Followed by Ensign Westfalen, the Teutonics marched straight across the crew's quarters, ducking their head, of course, then halted beside Ensign Grether awaiting his orders. "Gentlemen, please take these two vermin out of here and lash them to the mizzenmast. I want them detained and exposed but out of the way. Make sure they don't block ship's business."

"Aye, Sir," the three answered in unison.

"Erik and Ludwig, you handle the monk. Lash him up especially tight. He's a bit of a handful. Martinello, you do understand that it's in your best interest to be honest with us, don't you?" The troubled young man stood silent for a moment, obviously scared and ambivalent.

"I'll do my best," he finally mumbled.

"Good, because it might save you life and limb. All right then, men, get that bilge filth out of here."

# Chapter 9 – Ambivalence

Nickolaus and Stefano followed the entourage out onto the main deck. Relieved to be back in the sunshine and fresh air, Nickolaus began to regain his wits almost immediately. Once his breathing returned to normal, he elatedly told Stefano, "We must tell Michela of this right away. She'll be ecstatic. She's been silent about it, but I know Pietro's freedom to roam about at will has been worrying her ever since he escaped his exile at Certosa Di Pavia."

"What about Pietro, shouldn't we be there to tell the captain of his crimes?"

"There will be plenty of time for that; besides, I already told the captain and Heinz much of what happened in Genoa while we were still in port. Michela's peace of mind is more important to me at the moment. I imagine she's had her fill of Tremonti by now. We need to go rescue her." Stefano nodded as they hurried across the main deck to the captain's lounge. Still totally engrossed in their cards, Michela and Tremonti barely even looked up when Nickolaus and Stefano stepped through the door, beaming with excitement.

"Michela, you'll never guess who we just found in the crew's quarters?" Stefano blurted out. Michela laid her cards down then stood up and stretched.

"Let me guess, some sailors?" Stefano's grin faded away.

"No, sister. You won't believe this, but that miserable Father Pietro has been stowed away in the sailor's quarters throughout this entire voyage – there, the whole time, right under our noses." Michela glanced back and forth between Stefano and Nickolaus then stared directly into her husband's eyes.

"Nicolo, is this true? Pietro is right here on this ship - with us? You can't be serious?

"Yes, we are, and he is, and he is ours, or I should say Captain Zannaro's, since it is his ship."

"Has he been clapped away in irons or, better yet, tied up in chains and tossed overboard?"

"He's being lashed to the mizzenmast as we speak."
Michela rushed over and draped her arms around her husband.

"Oh, thank God! I've been afraid of that monster returning ever since he escaped. What a relief, Nicolo, what a blessed relief! Will there be justice this time? God forbid, they aren't going to let him go free again, are they? They aren't going to allow him to be sent off to holiday in some hillside monastery, are they? I won't allow it! He deserves his just comings this time."

"Be still, my love. I do not yet know what is to become of him, but I'll do everything in my power to make sure that he never threatens anyone again. Truthfully, though, I can't guarantee anything. His fate is out of our hands."

"Oh, Nicolo, you have to make sure he's gone forever. I can't live being haunted by that beast any more, wondering when or where he might show up, or what poor innocent he might have in his filthy clutches."

"I know, I know, we'll put him away. I know we can, just have faith."

Heinz made his way to the mizzen deck as soon as he was summoned. When he arrived, he found the priest and Martinello lashed to opposite sides of the mizzenmast. "Well, what have we here, Ensign Grether? I understand you netted a rather sickening catch."

"Yes, Sir, caught'em havin' their way with each other under a pile of blankets in the crew's quarters. I'd hazard neither one of them is who he claims to be."

"Is that so?" Heinz stepped around the mast and poked Martinello in the thigh with his boot. "So, you're no cook's mate, eh? Nor much of a man either, I hear." Martinello sat dead still, staring down at the deck planking. "Well, let's make this easy, son, I don't want to hurt you. You're too damn young and pretty for that kind of thing." Everyone snickered. "Why don't you just tell me what's been going on here, how you got on to this ship, and what your story is with the monk. Come now, son, make it easy on yourself. We'll treat both of you fairly, you have my word."

"Hold your tongue, boy," Pietro grunted from the other side of the mast. "Our affairs are none of their business. They're just trying to scare you. We've done nothing that's any of their fair concern. They're just looking for scapegoats. I'm a man of God; do as I say and you'll be righteous with the Lord. I promise."

"Scapegoats," the commander protested irritably. "Silence, monk, speak only when spoken to or I'll have you gagged." Heinz turned away from the two prisoners. "Helmut, unlash Martinello from the mast and take him to the crew's quarters. Keep his hands tied and hold him there until further notice. You, monk, sit there and ponder your miserable future. And by the way, it wouldn't be wise to irritate Erik or Ludwig. They can be very ill-tempered." Heinz winked at the Teutonics then headed off to inform Captain Zannaro of what had happened.

Upon being apprised of the unusual situation, the captain shook his head. "Most rare, Heinz, most rare, indeed," then he scowled, "but we don't have time for this right now. We can't afford the distraction. Just hold them where they are until we get around the horn and drop anchor in Rosia Bay. I'll attend to them after that. We're heading north into the bay right now. Our sword and banner-waving friends are still with us, but they seem to be keeping their distance."

As it happened, tides favorable to northern progress up the Bay of Gibraltar were helping to combat the offshore winds, which tended to push them southward. Carracks like *The Paradise* weren't known for their upwind prowess, while caravels, with their trimmer hulls and lateen sails, were comparatively adept. However, it seemed not to matter, as *La Notte Corridore,* having located her quarry, appeared to be satisfied just keeping *The Paradise* in sight. Her crew's intentions were anyone's guess.

None too soon, Chief Grumbach proudly navigated *The Paradise* into the relative safety of Rosia Bay. Despite an absence of manmade piers or moorings, Rosia Bay was an excellent natural harbor and a popular stopping off place for ships needing repairs and supplies. In fact, the sight of two handsome Spanish galleons holding port in the bay was just what Captain Zannaro had been hoping for. Thankfully, there they were in all their glory, with cannons and crew on full display. Shortly thereafter, Heinz skillfully piloted the ship to within close vicinity of the Spanish ships then gave the order to drop anchor. No one would dare attack them now. Nonetheless, feeling either unabashedly innocent or boldly confident, Gatardo slid his ship in right next to *The Paradise* and dropped anchor barely more than a stone's throw away. Captain Zannaro signaled for his cannons and crew to remain ready. "What the hell are they up to, Heinz?"

"I have no idea, Captain, but she doesn't seem to be particularly hostile."

"Why the hunt then? Why chase us down like some renegade pirate ship?"

"I'm not sure it was a chase, Captain. Maybe she wanted to catch up with us for reasons that are friendly, perhaps of purpose or benefit to us. We should stand strong, but also remain patient and cautious, Sir."

"Your reason and temperament are quite impressive, Heinz. You know, and I'll say this again, you are more than ready to take over this ship when I hang up my captain's hat."

"Hold on, Sir, those two men are back out on deck waving their banner. One of them is Nickolaus's friend, Marco. The other man doesn't look much like a crew member, and I don't see Gatardo anywhere." After waving the banner for a short period, Marco released his end and then cupped his hands around his mouth.

"Hail, Captain Zannaro and the crew of *The Paradise of the North*. I am Marco Di Caniglia and this is my comrade, Vincenzo Di Guidatore. Speaking on behalf of Bishop Giovanni Di Caravaggio of Genoa, we seek permission to come aboard."

"Captain, Nickolaus confirmed that the banner carries Bishop Caravaggio's coat of arms, and there is no sign of Gatardo or any armed men. I recommend we grant his request. That may be the only way we'll find out what this is all about."

"Do you see any unreasonable risk, Heinz, perhaps a trick or some form of pretense?"

"Maybe, but it seems like something we could control? We have plenty of guards on board and two Spanish galleons at our side. What would they dare try?"

"I agree. I'll go aft and stand with Chief Grumbach while you arrange to have them come aboard on the main deck. And have the Teutonics stand with you when our guests arrive."

"Sorry, Sir, I have the Teutonics guarding the cook's mate and the monk."

"Someone else can handle that. We need to show some muscle from the outset. And please arrange to have Nickolaus standing nearby as well; after all, they are his friends."

"Aye, Sir, right away."

Back in the captain's lounge, Nickolaus and Stefano were enjoying honeyed biscotti and hard cider when Tremonti abruptly dropped his cards and jumped up. "Damn, I need to start gathering up some supper or I'll have a gang of angry sailors on my ass. God damn it, and no Martinello to help out either. I suppose I'd better get to it then. Say, Stefano, how about giving your old friend Tremonti a hand down in the galley? I'd be most grateful for your help." Stefano glanced at Nickolaus, who shrugged his shoulders.

"I'm your man, Tremonti, you lead the way." The two stepped through the narrow service door then headed down to the galley. A moment later, the door to the main deck swung open, revealing a hurried Ensign Grether.

"Maestro, the commander needs your assistance out on the main deck, right away, please." Nickolaus glanced over at Michela with a look of panic on his face. She, in turn, cocked her head slightly, not quite sure why he was hesitating.

"Yes, Ensign, he'll be right with you, if you could just wait outside for a moment." Ensign Grether nodded then bowed slightly as he backed out and closed the door behind him. Michela stepped over and placed her arm around her husband's shoulder.

"What is it, Nicki? You look panicked. Is everything all right?"

"Michela, this is all too much for me. It's absolutely … overwhelming to say the least. I'm sorry, but I'm just not cut out for all of this hostility and turmoil. I'm a composer and a musician, not a prosecutor or a diplomat. I'm in way over my head here, and I refuse to bring on another one of those crazy attacks like the one I just had. I'm staying right here. They'll just have to get through this without my help."

"I understand how you feel, but you know you can get past all of that if you just put your mind to it. I've seen you do it many times before. I know this is an uncomfortable situation, and not anything either of us could have anticipated, but you have to step forward. I mean this with all of my love and respect, but you're acting like boy Nicolo again, the person you left behind months ago. We need Nicolo the lionhearted, the leader who took down Father Pietro and then stood up to Il Rossone and the Archdiocese. Maybe that Nicolo, my Nicolo, just stepped away for a moment, but we need him, you, my husband, back, right now." No one else would have dared admonish Nickolaus so outspokenly, but Michela, who knew her husband very well, had needed on past occasions to pull him back into adulthood. This was another one of those times, and he would ultimately thank her for it. Still, her candid remarks and blunt call to action struck him like a slap in the face in the heat of the moment.

"What? My God, you sound like Loretta. Is this the way a loving and respectful wife properly addresses her husband? I think not."

"Well, this is not the way a petty and fearful wife addresses an angry and controlling husband, but I am not that wife, and you are not that husband. Nicolo, you know what you have to do. You just need to pull yourself together and do it." She stared at him resolutely while he sat motionless, staring at the floor, feeling both angry and challenged. His first impulse was to run into the captain's quarters and slam the door, though he knew it would be both childish and futile. After seething in silence for a brief spell, he suddenly realized she was right, once again. They had been through this before. He took a deep breath then stepped over and kissed her on the forehead. Before leaving, he turned around and gulped down nearly half a mug of hard cider, perhaps seeking a bit of mental fortification. Michela shook her head disapprovingly. "Oh, Nicki, do you really think that's going to help?"

"Sorry, my love, I've got business to attend. Will you feel safe staying here alone?"

"Of course, now on your way, Lionheart, I'll be fine."

# Chapter 10 – Joint Venture

Nickolaus stepped out into the bright, mid-afternoon sun then set out for the mizzenmast. "Excuse me, Maestro, the commander needs you over near the docking rails to attend the boarding of our guests from Gatardo's ship." The ensign pointed toward Heinz, who was talking with Erik and Ludwig. A couple of additional crewmates stood by, waiting to help the approaching visitors climb on board.

"Oh, thank goodness, I was afraid I was being called upon to confront Pietro again." Ensign Grether looked a bit confused for a moment.

"Later, perhaps, but right now we need you to greet your friend Marco and his companion. We thought you might enjoy the occasion. The commander, in turn, would appreciate hearing your impression of their motives."

"What a relief. I'd be thrilled to greet my old friend Marco, and I can promise you that their mission is a righteous one."

"Let's hope so, Maestro, but we would also hope that you would view the situation from the standpoint of our ship and the crew's safety. No doubt you can read his intentions better than anyone else here."

"Intentions, what do you mean? He is what he says he is."

"Yes, but the captain can't depend on that. He needs to be sure this isn't some form of elaborate ruse."

"From Marco? Are you kidding?" Nickolaus snickered briefly, but then, not wishing to insult the ensign, quickly corrected himself. "Yes, Ensign, I see your point. I'll be most vigilant, I assure you." Nickolaus bowed slightly as he approached the commander, who appeared to be openly relieved by the Maestro's presence, as he would no longer be singly charged with judging the nature and character of total strangers.

"Ah, Maestro, please stand over there while we board our guests. When I nod, you may approach and greet your friends. I'm sure all will go well."

"Aye, Commander," Nickolaus replied, as if he were a member of the crew. As the small boat drew up, Marco threw out a line, which the deck mates then used to snug the dinghy against the hull of *The Paradise*. Once the boat had been secured, crewmembers leaned over the side of the ship and pulled the two visitors up and over the railing onto the deck of *The Paradise*. Heinz bowed respectfully while the two Teutonics saluted half-heartedly.

"Welcome aboard *The Paradise of the North*," the commander greeted solidly. The two visitors saluted, then immediately began scanning the deck, sizing up their situation. A huge grin spread over Marco's face as soon as he spotted Nickolaus, who waved and smiled back. Marco nudged his companion in the side, who then also turned and faced Nickolaus. It was Vinny, by God. The two visitors moved forward as if they were planning to head straight away to Nickolaus, but the Teutonics quickly stepped up and blocked their way. Marco instantly realized his breach of protocol and stood down. "Commander, we have important information to share with you and your captain. May we have a meeting as soon as possible?"

"May I ask the nature of your business?"

"Yes, it concerns a passenger you took on board in Genoa. We believe he may be a dangerous fugitive." Heinz glanced at Erik and Ludwig as the three of them smiled.

"Ah, yes, you must mean the monk and his companion, Martinello."

"We know of no Martinello, but with your permission, we would like to see the monk as soon as possible. And be forewarned, he can be prone to violent outbursts. He is not who he appears to be." A few moments later, the captain arrived from the helm.

"Good day, Gentleman, I am Captain Zannaro. I hope your transit and boarding went without incident. What can we do for you?"

Marco saluted like a soldier then handed the captain a large, splendidly decorated jug of fine brandy. "Yes, Captain, my name is Marco Di Caniglia. I represent Bishop Giovanni Di Caravaggio of Genoa. I have in my possession a Writ of Arrest and Extradition for one Peter Von Papenburg, long known in

Genoa as Father Pietro Di Zancanaro of Saint Matthias Cathedral. And that marvelous jug of fine spirits is a gift to you from Captain Gatardo for not trying to blow him out of the water. He told me to inform you that he respects and appreciates your restraint." The captain stared at the jug for a moment, nodded, smiled, and then handed it to Ensign Grether.

"Well, Marco Di Caniglia, your arrival is both timely and convenient, as it seems we happen to have one Peter Von Papenburg presently lashed to our mizzenmast."

"Yes, and he is quite the belligerent son-of-a-bitch, too," Heinz threw in pointedly. Somewhat peeved by the comment, the captain glared at his first officer momentarily then continued.

"So we appear share joint interests in dealing with this rather unsavory situation."

"Unsavory?"

"Yes, it seems members of my crew caught the monk having … shall we say … forbidden relations with his young companion, Martinello, in the crew's quarters. What's more, your monk has breached several ship rules and has, at times, seriously endangered the welfare of this ship. I've not quite been sure what to do with him, though I had tentatively decided to drop him off in Gibraltar. Now, however, having realized who he actually is, that option is no longer on the table. That would clearly be wrong, considering all of the shameful and malicious criminal acts he committed in Genoa. Honestly, I don't know what I was thinking when I granted him passage without thoroughly checking him out. He seemed so simple and harmless, and his German was flawless, not even a hint of an Italian accent. It never occurred to me that he could be Nicolo's Father Pietro. I must be getting careless in my old age. As for Martinello, he just seems naïve and perhaps a bit disturbed. May I see your official paperwork?" Marco handed over the arrest warrant, which had been scrolled up and stored in a finely crafted, metal canister bearing the coat of arms of the Duke of Papenburg. The captain unrolled the document and read it carefully, then handed it to his first officer.

"That figures," mumbled Heinz, handing the scroll back to the captain.

"Well, Signore Di Caniglia and …"

"Vincenzo Di Guidatorre, Captain, but please call me Vinny."

"Yes, as I was saying, if you two gentlemen will come with us, we will happily introduce you to our wayward passenger." The captain held his hand out, directing the two visitors toward the monk.

"God damn it, I knew it," Marco exclaimed gleefully. "We've got that bastard dead to rights now. Let's go, Vinny." The Teutonics stepped aside and allowed Marco to approach Nickolaus. The two old friends embraced and slapped each other on the back. "Nicolo, my good man, it's nice to see you alive and well. How is your dear Michela faring?"

"Good, we're both good, if not a bit shaken and confused. It's nice to see you as well, Marco, but I haven't the slightest idea what you're doing here."

"Well, let's go see if we can't clear up some of that confusion." The contingent proceeded to the mizzenmast where they stepped directly up to Pietro who, seated facing west, was forced to stare upward, directly into the sun in order to see who was approaching. For a moment, Marco just stood there, rapping the warrant's decorative metal canister against the palm of his hand, as if he were preparing to smack a misbehaving child. After a few moments, Pietro managed to identify his inquisitors.

"Well, it looks like somebody invited the fool brigade over to pay us a visit," Pietro sniped, sporting his trademark smirk. Vinny moved toward the monk, but Marco subtly held his eager companion back.

"Fools, eh, we'll see about that, but fools or not, we have a valid warrant of arrest and extradition for you, Mister Monk." Marco bent forward and bopped Pietro on the head with the metal canister. With his hands and feet tightly bound, Pietro could do nothing but squirm and glower.

"I don't recognize your jurisdiction. You have no authority here. This ship is registered to a Holstein consortium in Lubeck, so you can take your warrant and stow it up your ass, my son,"

"Yes, Herr Papenburg," Heinz interjected self-assuredly, "that may be true, but this ship is also a member of the Hanseatic League, as are our associates in Papenburg, so I'm afraid your doorway out has just slammed shut for good. I assure you that we

82

have complete jurisdiction over this matter." Smiling, the captain could barely keep from laughing out loud at his first officer's astute legal reasoning.

"We'll see about that, Captain. You do realize that I have the complete backing of the church, don't you?"

"Which one?" challenged Heinz. "I'm quite certain the Duke of Papenburg and most of the members of the Hanseatic League are loyal to the Lutherites now, not to your Pope, so I'm afraid your Roman connections won't help you here, my son."

"Besides, Pietro, you no longer have any pull with the Church of Rome," Nickolaus chimed in derisively. "They have about as much use for you as for an overflowing commode." The entourage laughed heartily.

"Do what you will, but I warn you, you'll pay for it in the end. I am still a servant of our Lord Jesus Christ, and he avenges his apostles, I can assure you of that. You'll all burn in the perpetual fires of hell."

The captain looked at Heinz, then at Nickolaus, and then shook his head in disgust. "Well, be that as it may, you'll still be treated like any other man aboard this ship, Padre. You are in no way above the law here." The captain stepped back and crossed his arms defiantly.

Marco turned to the captain. "Sir, I have a proposal for you. In addition to the writ of arrest and extradition I showed you, there is also this Notice of Bounty, which I didn't get a chance to share with you. If you would agree to transport the prisoner to Papenburg and allow Vinny and me to stay on board in order to guard and deliver this man to the Duke of Papenburg, I would be willing to share half of the bounty with you. The reward is quite substantial - fifteen hundred gold florins."

"Hmm, I see. He must have really done some evil to the Duke's interests. That is quite a generous reward; however, this would all be most irregular. You know I'm only the captain of this vessel. The monk is correct, this ship is owned by a prestigious and honorable shipping consortium in Lubeck. I'm not sure how they would feel about having their Mediterranean flagship used as a prison scow."

"Captain, with all due respect, it wouldn't be like that at all. You would simply be providing consent and transportation. The owners would have nothing to lose. We would take full responsibility for the care and delivery of the prisoner and, hopefully, you would be sufficiently generous to front us enough rations to get by on. I know Bishop Caravaggio as well as the Maestro and his wife would be most grateful to have this matter handled properly." The captain stared searchingly at Heinz and then at Ensign Grether.

"We'll have to take this under advisement, Marco Di Caniglia. Also, we still need to deal with Martinello, Pietro's servant and ah … travelling companion. Would you be willing to take him off our hands as well?" Marco glanced at Vinny then back at the captain.

"Well, Sir, we really have no legal authority to hold him for anything, but we would certainly be willing to help keep an eye on him for you, if it would help out."

"Yes, I understand, and to be honest with you, I am prone to grant the young man some degree of leeway under the circumstances. I suppose we'll just have to see whether he's cooperative or not." Marco and Vinny both nodded their approval. The captain continued, "Well then, allow us to ponder the matter for a time. Meanwhile, if you could go have a conversation with Martinello, maybe you can figure out what he's actually doing here other than digging his spoon into the wrong porridge. Ensign Grether, will you kindly conduct our guests to Martinello in the crew's quarters?

"Aye, Sir, this way, Gentlemen."

"Marco," Nickolaus called out. "I'm going to find Michela. Perhaps I'll see you later at dinner." Vinny shrugged his shoulders indecisively. Marco's thoughts, however, had already turned to interrogating Martinello. In the meantime, Nickolaus made his way to the captain's lounge where he found Michela lying sound asleep on a blanket draped over the bench. She had been eerily tired of late, which worried him no small measure, but at least she was relaxed enough to fall asleep, and this made him happy. Still, he knew she would be awakened all too soon when Aldo began preparing the room for the officer's evening meal. Temporarily stymied, Nickolaus dropped back into the captain's chair and poured himself another generous mug of hard cider, which he seemed to be growing increasingly fond of. As he drank, he gazed lovingly upon his pale and exhausted wife. "God,

I hope I can keep you safe," he muttered drowsily. Within a few minutes, he fell asleep.

# Chapter 11 – Disposition

As late afternoon crept in at the foot of the great rock known as Gibraltar, the sailors of Rosia Bay settled into their evening routines. Cooks and mates everywhere were busy pulling together meals for the officers and assembling proper rations for the crewmen. As desirable as it might have been, shore leave was not possible here, as Rosia Bay lacked both docks and viable leave facilities. Besides, there was always work to do as well as strict order and discipline to be maintained.

Nickolaus awoke with a start. Under the circumstances, he could hardly believe he'd managed to doze off at all, but now that he had, he felt half-witted and sickeningly dizzy. He sat still briefly, looking on in a daze as Aldo set out dishes, eating utensils, napkins, and candles. Officers hungry for their late day meal would be arriving shortly. The diligent steward trusted, albeit with a bit of trepidation, that Tremonti would arrive on time with the food and drink. Aldo's trust was generally rewarded though, occasionally, usually due to excessive alcohol consumption, Tremonti would miss the mark and show up late or, even worse, with an ill-prepared meal. Either failure irritated the officers no end. Nonetheless, the captain continued to tolerate his cook's lapses because he loved the Genoan cuisine that Tremonti was so adept at creating from very meager resources.

Michela sat up with a start and looked around. "What's going on? I fell asleep." She blinked her eyes several times, feeling stunned and woozy.

"Yes, I know." Nickolaus replied groggily. "I hope we didn't miss anything important." He shook his head rapidly back and forth, as if he were a dog waking up from a long slumber. "Would you like Aldo to fetch you some tea?"

Michela smacked her tongue around in her dry mouth then tried to lick her lips. "Yes, I suppose, or maybe some cider. I'm really parched."

"How about some wine?" Nickolaus suggested, eagerly eying the cask of Chianti that Aldo was just then setting down on the table. Michela rolled her eyes.

"Aren't you becoming a bit too comfortable with that? It's not like you, Nicki." Nickolaus glared at her for a moment then slumped back. She was right and he knew it. He could feel it too. He was often drawn to spirituous beverages, even though he knew their unpredictable effects on him were usually harmful. He believed it had something to do with his moodiness, as did Doctor Schicchi, who had always insisted that he should avoid them as much as possible, which he usually did.

"It helps with my nerves. You know how anxious I get."

"Maybe for now, I suppose, but you know it's bad for you, and you shouldn't get used to it." Nickolaus said nothing as he pulled himself up and walked over to the window. He stared out onto the main deck.

"Here they come." he announced quietly. It was obvious from their boisterous, backslapping demeanor that the officers were happy and relieved that the immediate crisis had passed. Nickolaus thought he heard some ridicule directed at Mr. Di Rufo regarding his verbal blunders toward the fishermen, but it all seemed to be in good fun. The ship and crew had performed admirably, even if the danger had ultimately turned out not to be real after all. Nickolaus swung open the door to the captain's lounge and welcomed everyone in.

"Ah, Maestro, good to see you've got things squared away," greeted a beaming Captain Zannaro. "Is your wife properly settled?"

"Indeed, she's fine, and most relieved as well."

"Excellent! Shall we take our places and raise a toast to victory, such as it was?" Everyone smiled as they grabbed up a mug then shoved them all together with a sloshing clunk.

"Cheers to victory and safe returns!" They all shouted in unison. The captain motioned for all to be seated.

As always, Aldo had the food, drink, and place settings ready and waiting. It was the most joyful and relaxed dinner Nickolaus had experienced since leaving Genoa. The crew's sense of relief was obvious and invigorating. Everyone ate heartily, except for Michela who, once again, could only manage an occasional peck at her food and a few gulps of tea. No one really took much notice – not even Nickolaus.

When everyone was finished, the captain clanged his knife against the side of his mug. "Gentlemen, given the change of circumstances, I would like to open the table for suggestions as to our proper course of action." The room instantly fell silent as all faces turned toward the captain. Captain Zannaro always welcomed input from his officers, but they all understood that he would ultimately make any final decisions. They were properly satisfied with the arrangement, which was far more inclusive than most ship hierarchies.

Chief Grumbach clumped his mug down on the table. "Do what you will with your guests, Sir, but do it bloody fast. That goddamn weather up north is turnin' on us as we sit here. I can feel it. We haven't any time to dally, Captain." No one else would have dared speak up so bluntly, but the chief's exceptional talents and uncluttered outlook had earned him a certain license that no one else shared. In most cases, his unique brand of clarity was much appreciated.

"Noted, Chief Grumbach, so let's get this done and move on at the first outgoing tide in the morning." The captain nodded at Heinz, his preferred lotesman. "Now, suggestions, please."

Ensign Grether pulled forward in his chair and proposed somewhat acerbically, "I say we turn the monk into a castrato and leave him here to sing for the Spanish. And make damn sure they know just who he is and what he's done. They won't play around with him." He glanced around the table looking for support for his rather outlandish and, hopefully, facetious suggestion, but no one really took him seriously. Ensign Westfalen cocked his head a bit and then smiled.

"Come on now, Kurt, you just can't rid yourself of the image of that monk and Martinello going at it like a couple of crazed rabbits." A few chuckles passed around the room.

"Well, if you'd have seen what I did, you might feel the same way," responded Ensign Grether defensively, feeling a bit abandoned. The Captain raised his hand into the air.

"Hold on, please. I understand your feelings, Kurt, but you know I always insist that we act as civilized men on board this ship. I don't think your suggestion quite falls within the spirit of that philosophy."

"No, Sir, I suppose not."

Heinz jumped in. "And I don't really care what they were caught doing in the crew's quarters. They didn't hurt anyone, and God knows I've seen worse. My main concern is that I don't trust that monk. He's trouble. I think he had something specific in mind when he fired up that poop lantern, and I don't believe it was intended for Gatardo's ship, especially now that we know the nature of Gatardo's mission."

"What are you saying, Heinz?" the captain probed.

"I'm not sure, but I'm highly prone to want him off this ship - period. I don't know, maybe he has cohorts, or maybe he has some hidden plan in action. Who the hell knows? I may be overly suspicious, but I just don't like him here. At the very least, he's too much of a distraction, and possibly a lot worse."

Nickolaus could hold his tongue no longer. "Forgive me for barging in on ship's business, Captain, but what about Marco's arrest warrant and the bounty. With all due respect, we can't just let that wild animal loose again and hope the Spanish deal with him properly. I swear he'll be back abusing his priesthood and grabbing at little boys before the week is out. Do what you need to for the ship - that is entirely your domain, and I respect that - but please don't let Pietro loose. He needs to be held as a dangerous prisoner and then tried and punished accordingly."

"Amen to that," Michela added with conviction and a single nod.

"What about Tremonti's man, Martinello? I don't think he deserves to be in the same boat as the monk," offered Mr. Di Rufo, who was inclined to feel empathy toward those he considered weak or put-upon, even if those were the very same people he tended to abuse when he felt like he was under personal attack. "What crime has he committed?"

"I'll tell you what he's done," garbled Chief Grumbach, "he stuck his ..."

"That'll be enough, Chief," snapped the captain, rolling his eyes toward Michela.

"Well, I just wanted to ..."

"I said I don't care about any of that," Heinz repeated, obviously a bit annoyed. "I'm just concerned over the safety of our ship and crew."

"Well said, Mr. Buxtaholda. Anyone else?" The captain looked slowly around the table. "All right then, we're taking them both with us, along with Nickolaus's two friends, who will be responsible for keeping the monk properly restrained and under constant guard. For the time being, Martinello will be free to serve his post as cook's assistant so long as he gets nowhere near the priest. If he does, he'll be confined. Heinz, I want the crow's nests manned at all times with our best lookouts. Keep them sharp and attentive. I don't know if this is the wisest or safest path, but it's the one I've chosen. Are there any questions?"

"How much coddling shall we afford the monk, Captain?" asked Ensign Westfalen sardonically.

"Not very damned much, Ensign. I'll leave that up to you and your conscience. Alive and in one piece will be good enough, but I don't want to see him abused. He's my charge, and on this ship, we treat men like men, not beasts, even if he is one.

"Aye, Captain, I'll defer to his two guards. I should probably stay out of it unless he steps out of line."

"Wise choice, Ensign, your restraint will be appreciated."

"Thank you, Captain," Michela blurted out appreciatively. "The idea of Pietro running free sickens me." Everyone turned toward Michela, who suddenly looked frighteningly pale.

"That's quite all right, Signora, I believe it's best for all concerned."

Nickolaus stood up. "Perhaps we should retire to the deck, my dear. Some fresh air might help clear our heads"

Yes, yes, Nicolo, you're right, I'm sure." The Maestro helped Michela up then they both stepped outside into the cool evening breeze.

"Captain, she doesn't look at all well," remarked Heinz worriedly as soon as they were gone.

"I know, Heinz, and there's a long, probably rough voyage ahead, but we can't leave them here, so we'll just have to hope for the best. Make sure they have everything they need. They and their belongings are the most valuable cargo on this ship right now, so let's make sure we get home safely."

"Aye, Sir, as always."

# Chapter 12 – Up Hill and Against the Wind

Ebb tide arrived just before dawn, which was the perfect time for *The Paradise* to pull up anchor and head out toward the open sea. Passing through the Strait of Gibraltar was always a tug-of-war between tidal flows in and out of the Atlantic as well as the variable wind and sea currents, which changed with the seasons and even the time of day. There were times, however, when everything worked in a ship's favor, which made for a pleasant and scenic passage. By providence, this was one of those days. Once again the Cottanos were spared from some of the more difficult challenges of life on the sea.

Nickolaus and Michela woke up soon after the ship set sail. Stefano had already headed out to begin his day. Michela was still tired and queasy, so Nickolaus donned his coat and shoes then headed out onto the main deck where he found the crew hard at work raising and adjusting sales. Heinz Buxtaholda was at the helm, handling the tiller as per Chief Grumbach's directions. Nickolaus looked over and noticed that Gatardo's ship was nowhere in sight. Having decided not to tempt fate, Gatardo had slipped out of Rosia Bay before first light so as to avoid any unwelcome Spanish inquiry. He knew they probably considered him a pirate.

Despite the fact that he had originally decided to avoid Pietro altogether, either curiosity or that certain schadenfreude that inhabits all of us compelled Nickolaus to seek out his nemesis. He headed aft where he ran into Ensign Grether. "Ah, Maestro, you're up early this morning. Is there anything I can do for you?"

"Yes, thank you, Ensign, could you direct me to my two friends, Marco and Vinny?"

"Ah, the monk keepers, eh? One of them is in the forward cargo hold watching over the priest. The other is up on the forecastle deck, catching some fresh air and taking his ease."

Nickolaus climbed to the upper foredeck and found Marco walking straight toward him.

"Marco, we didn't get much of a chance to talk yesterday. How on earth did you manage all of this?"

"Manage all of what?" Marco seemed a bit distracted, or pained, perhaps.

"The arrest warrants, Gatardo's ship, the pursuit – so fast – how did you manage?"

"Well, I couldn't pass up a chance for a good adventure. You know that as well as anyone. I ask you, my boy, do I really look like a livery driver to you?"

"No, I suppose not, but you threw us quite a scare. We thought you were pirates coming after our …" Nickolaus lowered his voice, "very special cargo."

"We weren't too thrilled having to throw in with Gatardo, but the Bishop had very strong feelings in the matter, and Gatardo's ship was the only one available. The Bishop paid dearly, I promise you that."

"Perhaps with his soul."

"You know, if truth be told, I'd say Gatardo the man isn't quite as bad as Gatardo the reputation, at least from what I saw. I'd also have to say that his crew is a bit rough, although they do work well together. That being said, I sure wouldn't want to meet up with any of them in a dark alley."

"And the arrest warrants?"

"That's a good question. I think the Bishop may have had them squirreled away in a drawer for some time now. Once he and the harbormaster figured out that the monk aboard your ship might actually be Pietro, they knew they had to do something quickly. That's when the Bishop suddenly and somewhat mysteriously came to be in possession of the arrest warrants. God only knows why he's been protecting Pietro all this time." Marco grimaced then slapped his sword a few times.

Nickolaus shook his head, feeling both sadness and regret. "I don't know either. The good Bishop can be maddeningly unpredictable. At times he seems like a great and benevolent leader whose body has been possessed by some kind of evil spirit, namely, Pietro. I don't know what power that man has over him, but it's bitter and poisonous. I suppose it doesn't matter anymore. Bishop Caravaggio is out of my life now, and he sent me off with one final attempt at redemption on his part. I wish him the best."

"You're more forgiving than I am, Nico. Say, would you like to visit poor, miserable Pietro down in the cargo hold? We've got him tied to a beam. I'll tell you this much, he's still got a hell of a lot of spirit left in him. He acts like he has some kind of foolproof escape plan hidden under his robes. Personally, I think he's delusional." A look of concern crossed Nickolaus's face as he considered Marco's words.

"You'd be wise to inform Heinz or the captain of any suspicious behaviors you notice. That Pietro is a wily one - you can count on that. You should tell them what you just told me."

"What's that?"

"That Pietro isn't treating his future as a lost cause. He should be feeling pretty damned hopeless right now."

"Maybe he's just a petulant bastard."

"Oh, that goes without saying, but maybe there's more." Staring off into the distance, Nickolaus scratched his head. "I suppose I could bear to see his ugly face once more, if only to see him tied up in disgrace."

The two friends climbed down off the forecastle deck and descended into the cramped darkness of the forward cargo hold. It felt as though they had entered a dank, gloomy underworld. Vinny was dozing on a stool with his neck wedged back against a bulkhead. When Nickolaus and Marco arrived, he teetered forward with a clump then stared up with a startled look on his face. "Sorry, I was just resting my eyes."

Nickolaus smiled. "It's good to see you, Vinny. How are you getting along without your horse and carriage?"

After a moment of confusion, Vinny nodded then mumbled, "I suppose I'll live. I'm not sure, Nicolo, I think I miss the land more than the beasts, but I'll adjust. I always do." Despite his claim, Vinny had been the Bishop's driver, single, and living in the same tiny flat for over twenty-five years. Adaptation was not something he had a lot of experience with. Nickolaus nodded understandingly then looked down at Pietro, who stared straight ahead, absolutely deadpan. He suddenly shifted and looked up.

"Well, my son, it looks like your dreams have finally come true. You probably think you have me right where you want me, huh? We'll see whose side the Lord takes. Rest assured, my son, this isn't over. You'll rue the day you crossed paths with me." Nickolaus knew the double "my son" references were intended to annoy him; more importantly, it was clear that for some reason, perhaps a secret plan, Pietro still held on to hope that he would ultimately perfect his revenge.

"You well know that I already sorely regret the day we met, Pietro. God knows I wish I'd never seen or known of you at all. But now that I have, I'll be glad to see you spend the rest of your rotten life at hard labor, splitting rocks in some hellhole quarry. And even that is better than you deserve." Pietro suddenly swung his leg out wide and hard, apparently attempting to kick Nickolaus's leg out from under him. Startled, Nickolaus jumped back, as though Pietro were a snake. Marco grabbed a nearby orange and pitched it into the priest's gut like a cannon ball.

"There, have some breakfast, monk, and shut the hell up. Vinny, Nicolo and I are going up to speak with the captain. I'll be back shortly. Don't be too easy on our dear monk."

Sailing north into the open waters of the Atlantic was not quite the experience Nickolaus had expected. Except for a few brief periods, land usually remained within sight, even if only barely visible. According to Heinz, sailing north in autumn was like balancing on a beam. If the ship remained close enough to shore, the offshore water currents actually pushed the ship northward; however, it was also necessary to stay a certain distance out to sea in order to minimize exposure to the northerly offshore winds blowing against the ship. Whatever the secret, Chief Grumbach knew exactly how to exploit it. Still, the ebb and flow of the tides along with the constant changes in wind direction meant suffering the zigzagging effects of near constant tacking, which led to a bobbing ship that was almost constantly leaning away from the wind. No one liked it, especially not Michela, who suffered horribly from seasickness.

With comparative ease, the ship sailed rapidly up the coast of Portugal, rounded the northwestern tip of the Iberian Peninsula, and then proceeded to La Coruna in Galicia – now the north coast of Spain - where they offloaded several large cartons containing fine silk and a near priceless collection of various spices. Those were quickly replaced by five very heavy, sturdily clad, unmarked trunks, as well as fifty slatted crates filled with oranges headed for the Hanseatic States. The crates of oranges were carefully stacked around and over the trunks, leaving what appeared to be an innocent shipment of near-ripe oranges. The crew had no idea what was in the trunks, and no one asked. In light of his past experiences at La Coruna, Mr. Di Rufo decided to stay on board ship so that he could, "Watch over things."

Nickolaus, Michela, Ensign Grether and Ludwig of the Teutonics went ashore but remained in the harbor district. Needless to say, terra firma never felt so wonderful to the land-loving Cottanos. Before reaching port, Nickolaus had decided he would try to have Michela seen by a physician if at all possible. He even hoped that he might stumble upon a practitioner of his Genoan doctor's caliber though, in his heart, he realized that such expectations were merely distant dreams. He never mentioned his intentions to Michela because he knew she would refuse, as she still claimed that she was fine and healthy, just a little seasick. He realized she might be right, but feeling certain that there was something more going on, he asked Ensign Grether to find him some sort of reasonably reliable medical practitioner. Naturally, he feared that language might be a problem.

After wandering around for a while, Ensign Grether directed the group down a narrow street lined with an assortment of businesses primarily selling seafaring gear and cheap libations. Near the end of the lane, the ensign suddenly stopped and directed Nickolaus and Michela into a small shop named *Rosina's*. Stefano and Ludwig were assigned to watch the doorway. "What is this place?" Michela asked suspiciously, glancing around at every corner of the eclectically furnished, dimly lit room that vaguely reminded her of their apartment in Genoa. A slim, dark-complexioned, middle-aged woman came out of the back room and slid quietly forward.

"Maestro, allow me introduce you to Rosina Di Fortunato, fortune teller, midwife, astrologer, and healer of both mind and body." Rosina bowed her head slightly then held out her hand, as if to be kissed. The ensign bent over and kissed her hand, then turned to the Cottanos. "It's all right, she's Genoan, and she's the only healer in La Coruna that I know to be trustworthy." Rosina nodded and smiled appreciatively at the ensign's complimentary introduction.

"What's going on here?" snapped Michela, obviously annoyed. Nickolaus stared nervously at his wife then back at the ensign before sighing with exasperation.

"Ensign Grether, did you not understand my request, a physician for Michela?"

"I did, Maestro, and here she is. This is by far your best option in La Coruna." Rosina smiled and nodded once again in her singular manner that seemed practiced yet quirky. "Signorina Rosina, this is Maestro Nicolo Di Cottano of Genoa and his wife, Michela." Rosina smiled and held her hand out in greeting. Nickolaus shook her hand timidly while Michela remained barricaded behind her husband.

"So, you have come to my studio to have your fortunes read, eh, always an excellent idea before crossing the sea." Nickolaus shook his head in disbelief.

"No, no, there must be some misunderstanding. We aren't seeking our fortunes." Rosina cocked her head then took a closer look at her three visitors.

"Well, you don't seem to need a midwife, so how can I help?" Rosina pulled her silken garments more tightly around her slender body. Ensign Grether stepped forward.

"It's Signora Di Cottano, Madam. She's not been feeling well of late. Her husband is worried." Rosina glanced warmly at Nickolaus then stepped slowly around him, took hold of Michela's hands, and then gazed probingly into her eyes. Next she stared upward and began squeezing Michela's hands gently and rhythmically while swaying back and forth.

"So what have you been feeling, my child?"

Michela stared down at the floor for a moment, embarrassed but also intrigued. "All right, I'll play along. I'm very tired – more than I've ever been, and I'm nauseous and sick – often, even when the sea is calm, and I have no appetite. And my moods are ... peculiar. It's hard to explain."

"Ah huh. And how long since you suffered your last blood curse, my child?" Michela suddenly came to attention. Ensign Grether blushed and glanced up at the ceiling.

"I don't know for sure. A while, I'd say." Rosina leaned over and placed her hand on Michela's lower abdomen then thumped the back of it with her fingers. She abruptly straightened back up.

"My dear, you are with child. I can feel it. Do you not feel it, too?

"What! How can that be?"

"Oh, it's quite simple, my dear, couples have been managing it without even trying since the dawn of time."

"I know, I know, but I …"

"You are with child, my dear, like it or not. The matter is not up for discussion. I can feel these things. The mighty deed is done." Michela sighed deeply then smiled slightly and turned to her husband. Wide-eyed, Nickolaus stared intently at his wife then grinned.

"Amore Mio, is it true? Do you know; is it true?" Nickolaus gently grabbed Michela's shoulders then wrapped his arms around her and swallowed her in a tight, passionate hug. It all made sense to him now - the fatigue, the disproportionate seasickness, and the changes he had felt in her feminine natures. Both of them suddenly turned back toward Rosina. "Are you certain, Signora?" Nickolaus asked.

"As certain as I am that the sun will come up in the morning, my children." Nickolaus turned and stared questioningly at the ensign.

"Don't ask me, Maestro. We've never carried an expectant mother on board, or any woman at all for that matter, but I can't really see that you have any choice. We can't leave you here." Rosina stepped forward and took Michela's hands.

"Perhaps now would be a good time to have a reading, my child. Please, step over to my table of fortunes and have a seat." Michela glanced at Nickolaus, who shrugged his shoulders.

"I don't really see any harm in it. Do you want to?"

"Oh, come, come, my children, both of you, you must let me read your fortunes. It will help you decide what to do. What could be the harm?" Rosina circled around Michela, put one hand gently on each of their backs, and then ushered them over to her lavishly decorated *Tabla de Fortunas*. She lit three candles then poured a dab of spirit water from a shiny metal bottle onto the table in front of each chair. "Please, sit and grasp hands, my children. Our charmed circle of spiritual forces will capture the essence of your futures." Nickolaus rolled his eyes. It reminded him of many of the church ceremonies that he'd always privately ridiculed; nonetheless, he winked at Michela and she winked back, then they played along, if only for a bit of fun.

"Close your eyes and think only of good thoughts – nothing divine - just of goodness." Nickolaus and Michela closed their eyes, but then immediately opened them back up, just a slit, to watch the proceedings. Rosina bowed her head forward then thrust it upward toward the ceiling. Her eyes opened and then immediately rolled up into her forehead, as if she were searching the inside of her brain. Her hands began to quiver slightly as she shifted restlessly in her seat.

"I see a powerful beacon of love and respect emanating from this couple – a young love both strong and abiding. But I also see turmoil and change from every corner of the cosmos. You are entering a very tumultuous time in your lives. There will be challenge, struggle, and strife, perhaps even defeat. What's this? I sense an evil spirit, a twisted fiend, a dark and wicked demon who seeks to envelop you, perhaps even swallow and destroy you. Beware of this beastly imposter who cloaks himself beneath a shroud of holiness, for he bears the stigma of manipulation and deceit. Watch him! He will devour you and yours if you do not defend against him. You must protect yourselves from both him and his malevolent army – all of you must!" She suddenly wrested her hands free then wrapped them around her chest, gasping at the horror of her own prophecies. At last she took a deep breath and opened her eyes. "It is done. You are with child, my dear, but its delivery will not be any easy one, and the road to that deliverance will be fraught with many dangers. Feel confident that you may succeed if you follow the right path, and be certainly wary, my children; but most of all, trust your instincts - all of you must trust your instincts, for they will guide you." She stared pointedly at Nickolaus who continued to squeeze Michela's hand. He wondered how Rosina had managed to light upon something so close and relevant with such remarkable accuracy. He knew it had to be a trick, but it was a damned good one. "And now, you, young ensign, it is your turn. Sit and hear your future, or do you prefer the astrologer's tale?"

"As much as I would like that, I'm afraid we must be getting back to the ship now. We depart at ebb tide, first thing in the morning. I'll return soon, next visit for sure." Rosina began to object, but Nickolaus and Michela both stood up. Nickolaus began fumbling for a pouch in his frock coat.

"What are your charges, Signora Rosina?"

"That is up to you, my child. It is for you to judge the value of my services." Nickolaus fidgeted around then handed Rosina several ducats, which in his mind constituted an amount appropriate for an unrestricted session with a quality female escort. It was the only standard he could relate to under the circumstances, as his own Doctor Schicchi had never charged him at all.

Rosina bowed graciously. "Thank you, Maestro, your generosity is most appreciated." She smiled and nodded at Ensign Grether for having brought in such a well-paying customer then she turned to Michela. "Remember, my child, you must eat well, avoid hot peppers and shrimp, and treat yourself with gentle love. Your baby will feel it. And to all of you, anytime you're in port, feel free to come by. I'm always here. And be sure to tell your friends and loved ones." The three customers thanked her then quickly departed, setting off for the ship in virtual silence, each deeply absorbed in their own thoughts. Nickolaus wrapped his arm around Michela's shoulder. He was cautiously excited; she was surprised and scared; Stefano was confused and thirsty; and the ensign was busy trying to figure out how to raise the captain's concerns over the Pietro situation without citing a street-side soothsayer as justification for his heightened alarm. Ludwig took up the rear, wishing he had been given the chance to have his fortune told; instead, he was invited to join the entourage for a quick libation at the ensign's favorite La Coruna tavern. They would need to be careful, though, for they had no desire to commit any "Rufo's" in this part of town.

# Chapter 13 – Raz de Sein?

Stefano's reaction to the news of his sister's pregnancy was pure ambivalence. Nickolaus was Stefano's acting father figure. Michela served both as his sister and, when necessary, a mother figure. At first, Stefano wasn't even quite sure what relation he would be to the baby. And he, too, was very much concerned over taking Michela out on the open sea when she was with child. In his mind, Stefano felt excited, embarrassed, worried, and confused, though his only show of emotion was that of polite acceptance.

The captain barely flinched upon hearing of Michela's condition. "Ah, such a lovely couple, I'm surprised it took so long."

"Begging your pardon, Sir, but I don't believe it works that way. It seems to me that ugly couples make at least as many babies as attractive ones." The captain shook his head then turned to his young ensign.

"Yes, I know, Mr. Di Rufo, I was only joking."

"Oh, sorry, Sir."

"Go ahead and make the appropriate preparations for this … joyful event, whatever that might entail." He smiled at the confused young ensign, who obviously had no clue what to do. "Well, your guess is as good as mine, Silvio. You're ship's surgeon, aren't you?"

"Aye, Sir, I'll get right on it," he mumbled hesitantly before heading off to find Heinz, hoping that the senior officer might be able to provide some insight into how to proceed.

As soon as Silvio was out of earshot, Ensign Grether brought up his renewed concern over keeping Pietro on board, suggesting, "I have a sense that our spiteful monk still has unfinished business in the works." He dared not mention the source of his heightened distress, as he knew the captain to be a logical and pragmatic man. Not surprisingly, the captain already held serious misgivings of his own.

"We'll be careful, Kurt. There's much at stake here – even more than usual. I'm going to keep the extra spotters up top.

Speed is paramount now. It's only a matter of time before the autumn storms move in up north, if they haven't already. Any other suggestions, Ensign?"

"Just caution, Sir, extreme caution."

There was plenty of excitement at the captain's table that evening, most of which revolved around Michela's condition. There were also a few tales to share from the officers' brief stints ashore – some a bit sordid, but nothing extraordinary. There simply hadn't been enough time to do any real damage. After a while, the captain turned his attention to the Cottanos, taking on a very serious, paternal air. "You must consider your options carefully. You can choose to stay here in La Coruna where you should be safe, or you may continue your voyage with us. It is my belief that you would be safe aboard *The Paradise*; however, I cannot guarantee it, nor can I speak with any wisdom regarding how well you might tolerate the conditions. Needless to say, we've never carried a pregnant woman on board, and Ensign Di Rufo is the closest thing we have to a ship's surgeon. But I must also warn you that you might not reach Lubeck for quite some time if you don't continue on with us. So if you have a legal deadline to meet, be advised of the consequences of remaining in La Coruna." The captain took a gulp of wine then gazed intently at both Nickolaus and Michela. "So, what say you?"

Nickolaus turned to Michela, who smiled and nodded her head. "If you don't mind, Captain, we'll continue on with you. I'm sure I'll be fine. There must be many months ahead before I deliver. In the meantime, I'll just do my best." The captain turned to Nickolaus, who cocked his head and shrugged his shoulders.

"She has the final say, Captain, so it looks like we'll be staying on with you."

The captain hesitated then nodded. "Good, I think you've made the right decision. We'll be leaving port first tide out in the morning. I should warn both of you that our voyage thus far has been the smoothest of sailing. Don't count on that continuing, especially as we approach the North Sea."

As soon as Nickolaus and Michela reached the privacy of their tiny cabin, they held each other in deep embrace. Both felt scared, thrilled, and utterly powerless; worse yet, there was no one to whom they could turn for advice or comfort. They were alone. What should have been a momentous occasion had, instead, left them lost and worried. After a few minutes, they lay down side by side upon their narrow bunk. Michela began sniffling, then quietly weeping. Nickolaus wrapped his arm around her.

"Micki, my love, you'll be fine. I know you must be feeling shocked and confused – I know I am - but I have no doubt that we'll find our way through this. I suppose we really shouldn't be too surprised that this happened."

"I know, I know, Nicolo, I'm not even sure what I'm feeling. We are so lucky, and I am truly happy at our good fortune, but I am also afraid for our future. How will we survive? This is such bad timing. Why did you do this to me when we were so vulnerable? We should have resisted your urges until the time was right. You know we should have waited. Heaven help me, Nicolo, sometimes you're so blind to logic and reason." Nickolaus suddenly realized that such passionate outpourings were completely out of character for his notoriously levelheaded wife. Given the nature of his artistic persona and his oft-erratic mood swings, it was usually her keeping his emotions aligned and focused; however, this time she was the one who seemed to have slipped off the road. In a way, it reminded him of those certain times of the month during which he had learned to tread gently and carefully around her. This turmoil, he decided, must be a manifestation of a similar phenomenon, induced on this occasion by the tiny baby she was nurturing within her womb. He tenderly grasped her hand and caressed it soothingly with his thumb. After a while, they both fell asleep to the gentle rocking of the ship.

As had been the case at Gibraltar, the Cottanos were abruptly roused from their sleep in what seemed like the middle of the night by the customary cacophony that arises from any great sailing ship as she leaves port. Her course was set almost due north into the Bay of Biscay. Another ship left port right behind her, but proceeded northwest, as if destined for the Isle of Erin. The spotters kept close watch until she fell below the horizon. Once again Ensign Grether expressed his continued anxiety to Heinz, who admitted that he also felt uncommon concern over the situation. "Just keep your guard up, Ensign, and come straight to me or the captain if anything strikes you afoul."

The Bay of Biscay offered much greater resistance to *The Paradise's* northern progress than had the Mediterranean Sea or the Portuguese coast. As they lost sight of land, the sea grew taller but less choppy. Short bobbing waves transformed into high swells, which in some ways seemed less threatening; however, they were definitely far more sickening. As he had done during his earlier voyage, Nickolaus took refuge from his seasickness by positioning himself high upon the aft quarterdeck, staring out across the horizon.

Michela, on the other hand, was sentenced to wander back and forth between their small cabin and the captain's lounge where she seemed to find some small measure of solace and stability. Nickolaus felt horrible for her and did all he could to comfort her, but there was really nothing to be done. Sympathetic crew members suggested several sailors' remedies, all of which she tried, but nothing seemed to help, except for a mysterious sweet concoction that Tremonti whipped up for her in the galley. Nickolaus thought it smelled mainly of brandy and orange juice, but Michela liked it, and it seemed to relax her a bit, so he encouraged its use and even had Tremonti set him up with several batches of his own.

Oddly, the miserable conditions seemed to inspire Nickolaus to work on several new musical ideas that he could only write down in short spurts without being overcome by seasickness. Since beginning the voyage, he had accumulated a growing collection of partial compositions that he intended to finish sometime later, perhaps even order into some sort of thematic compilation. Interestingly, for the first time in his life, none of them had anything to do with church or religion. For reasons unknown, he no longer felt an inclination to create any more of the adored and revered church music that had driven his entire youthful career. That said, it was his magnum opus, *Michela's Stabat Mater*, that had led him to seek maximum musical expression by means of an accompanied solo voice rather than through the extended exhibitions of a cappella choral counterpoint that were the mainstay of church choirs everywhere. Even though he lacked the proper training to undertake such a striking musical departure, he embarked upon it anyway, blending

106

his scattered knowledge of madrigal writing with his own version of legato vocal writing, creating what sounded to him like a perfect musical fusion. He was well aware that he had overestimated the value of his compositions before, and with no way to actually hear the music he was writing, he lacked any reliable method of gauging its quality, effect, or viability. Moreover, how it looked to him at any given moment in time depended on his mood, which tended to change all too frequently. Michela occasionally hummed a few bars and complimented him on its beauty and originality, but her distracted attention was usually cut short by her condition, at least that's what she claimed. Despite her lack of formal musical training, Nickolaus implicitly trusted her judgment, realizing that she was likely to be biased in his favor.

Stefano seemed much less affected by the onslaught of waves, scampering about the ship as if he had spent his entire lifetime upon the seas. He was particularly taken with Chief Grumbach who, at this point in the voyage, seemed to be virtually in charge of the ship. On several occasions, the captain and Heinz had guardedly asked the chief about cutting through La Raz de Sein, a perilous shortcut off the western point of France. Because it was so hazardous and unpredictable, ships almost universally avoided it by making a hundred mile detour to the west, usually fighting stubborn and opposing winds and currents. The chief seemed somewhat resistant though not completely averse to the possibility. "We'll see when we get a bit closer, eh, Captain," or, "I'd rather not chance it unless we have to," or, "I'm not getting a good feeling for it right now, Sir." Then he would stare straight into the captain's eyes to gauge his reaction.

"I've never seen you so unsure of yourself, Chief, are you losing your confidence?"

"Captain, I'm surprised you take passing through that briar patch so lightly, especially after the last time."

"God Damn it, Chief, you don't need to remind me. Keep in mind, those sailors' lives were my responsibility, not yours. Those men were fooling around when they knew better. We all know La Raz de Sein is a goddamn maelstrom, and they chose to hang up there on the foresail riggings showing off for each other in direct violation of my orders. We have rules against that for a reason."

"I understand that, Sir, but Mannheim didn't deserve it. He was just doing his job."

"Chief, are you going soft on me? We've been through this before. Mannheim was an innocent bystander. His tragic loss still haunts me, but this is the life we've chosen. It's dangerous. We all know that when we sign on. Come on now, Chief, what is it? There's something else."

"I don't know, Sir, maybe I'm losing my magic, or maybe I'm just getting old, but something just doesn't feel right. I can't say what is."

"Well, we're all getting older, Chief. Listen, I respect your vigilance as well as your occasional humility, but let's wait until we get a bit closer before deciding. Maybe we'll have a better perspective then. You know I trust your judgment. You're the best damned navigator in the fleet and you know it."

"Aye, Sir, whatever you say."

Two days later when the moment of decision finally arrived, the chief and Heinz burst out of the captain's lounge and headed up to the helm. Both officers looked very worried. Nickolaus and Michela happened to be out on deck at the time. Nickolaus, violating his self-imposed rule against intrusion, hastened across the deck. "Gentlemen, is everything going as hoped for?" The chief ignored him. Heinz scowled.

"Not now, Maestro, not now." The gruff response struck Nickolaus like a slap in the face.

"Pardon me, Heinz, I shouldn't have …"

"Never mind, Maestro, it's not you. We'll discuss it later." Heinz proceeded directly to the helm to speak with Ensign Westfalen and the chief.

"Nicki, come here and leave them alone," pleaded Michela. "They don't need you bumbling around in ship's business." Nickolaus turned around. His wife motioned for him to return to her. "Come on, Nicki, let's go find Stefano." He shook his head from side to side, impishly resisting his wife's obviously sensible suggestion. He turned back around and glared up toward where Heinz had been, but the first officer was nowhere in sight. After a few moments, he realized that he was behaving like an impudent child - again.

"I'm an imbecile," he muttered to himself. "Scusate, my love," he said sheepishly before walking over, grasping her hand, and then heading off to find Stefano. Unexpectedly and somewhat annoyingly, their search led them to Pietro's makeshift brig. Stefano and Marco, who were engaged in a lively conversation, jumped up when they entered the room. Pietro was sitting down, lashed to a support beam, half asleep, and appearing none too healthy. Marco barely looked any better, though his spirits seemed high and his speech quite animated. It sounded as though he might have been recounting another exaggerated war story - one of his favorite pastimes.

"Nicolo, my boy, what brings you down into this hellhole?" Marco blurted out.

"The better question, Master Stefano, is what brought you down here? As I recall, the captain, Heinz, and both of us asked you to stay completely away from Pietro. You've no reasonable need for any contact with that … that dung heap lying there. Do you remember? I know you do."

"Maestro, please, your anger is unwarranted," insisted Stefano. "I was only curious. I wanted to see just how far he'd fallen." Stefano glared at the monk. "I'd say pretty low."

Michela shook her head. "You know, Stefano, I don't think it's possible to fall from the deepest pit on Earth. Have you spoken to him?"

"I asked him if it's all been worth it."

"And what did he say?"

"He said he didn't know. He's not in the grave yet, so he couldn't say for sure who'd come out on top. What do you suppose he meant by that?"

Marco shook his head. "I don't know. He keeps rambling on about getting even. Commander Buxtaholda and Ensign Westfalen have questioned him a couple of times, but he's totally lock-lipped about what he has in mind." Nickolaus stepped over and poked Pietro in the hip with his foot.

"You sorry son-of-a-bitch, you always have to be in control somehow, don't you? This bluff, or whatever it is, just keeps them all guessing, doesn't it? Well, you're stuck now, you bastard." Michela stepped forward and gently placed her hand on Nicolo's wrist.

"Nicki, please, Stefano's here - we should try to set a proper example."

"This is as proper as I can be under the circumstances. Frankly, I'm surprised that it bothers you so, considering the grotesque transgressions your family has suffered at the hands of this devil. I think they ought to beat him half to death, throw him overboard, and then let the sharks finish him off. Even that would be a light sentence." Michela scowled at Pietro, shaking her head back and forth in disgust.

"You may be right, Nicolo, but with our pain being so deep and personal, we should try to be a little more restrained in front of Stefano, don't you think?"

"Oh, don't hold back on my account!" Stefano exclaimed. "I think he's nothing but a pile of human garbage. As far as I'm concerned, he deserves whatever he gets."

Marco nodded approvingly. "I couldn't agree more, my boy, but Vinny and I have to keep him alive in order to earn the full bounty."

"All right, all right," Nickolaus conceded, poking Pietro with his foot once more. "We've got better things to do than stand around here next to this rubbish. Come, Stefano, I'd like you to look at some music I've been working on. Maybe it'll divert our thoughts from this waste of skin."

Pietro looked up slowly, as if awakened from a trance, then stared Nickolaus straight in the face. "You'll get yours – all of you will. As God is my witness, I'll have my revenge."

Marco kicked the bottom of Pietro's foot. "Shut up, monk, or you'll miss another meal." Pietro lowered his head, as though he'd been broken again. The Cottanos quickly made their way up to the main deck. They had taken only a few steps when a cry bellowed out from the forward crow's nest.

"Ship off the port bow - forward crow's nest reporting - ship off the port bow. Heinz immediately shouted downward into a tube that led to the captain's quarters. Seconds later, Captain Zannaro tore out of the captain's lounge, as if it had been set on fire.

Ensign Westfalen stepped forward and reported excitedly, "Port bow, Sir, ship sighted off the port bow." The captain and

Heinz ran across the main deck and shot up the ladder to the forecastle deck.

"Second ship sighted off the port bow, Sir. Now there are two of them," yelled the forward watchman from the crow's nest. Ensign Grether was already stationed at the port forecastle railing, straining his eyes to see anything he could. The captain and Heinz joined in, though neither had good enough eyesight to match the challenge. As it turned out, even the young ensign could barely make out the blurry tops of the two sets of masts and sails bobbing in and out of sight. Contrary to protocol, Ensign Grether jumped onto the rigging and climbed up to the crow's nest where he had a higher vantage point above the mist. The captain and Heinz stared up anxiously as the ensign and crow's nest watchman, Willy, stared out intently over the ocean, sharing opinions on what they were seeing.

"Ensign, report. Ensign, what do you see?" the captain shouted.

"Hold on a moment, Sir, I'm coming down." Ensign Grether scurried down the ladder and rigging as if it were his regular assignment. The captain and Heinz met him at the bottom. "There are two of them, Sir. According to Willy, they came out of the northwest then turned due east, heading straight for us. My estimate is that they will catch up to us in about three quarters of an hour at present courses and speeds."

"Then they must be coming after us," declared the captain. "There can be no other reason for them to pursue a course in our direction. There's nothing east of here but rough seas and an empty coastline with a thirty-foot tidal range. Ensign Grether, you remain here and keep track of things. The commander and I will hasten aft to consult with Chief Grumbach." Heinz glanced at the captain.

"La Raz de Sein, Sir?"

"It's up to the chief, but right now, I'm pretty damn sure it's our best hope."

"Aye, Sir, then let's do it."

# Chapter 14 – Bold or Brash

La Raz de Sein is a perilous ocean narrow that passes between the Isle of Sein and the Pointe Du Raz on the western tip of Brittany. A very tall tidal range, wicked currents, fickle winds and tides, and craggy rock formations that jut up out of the sea like ship-hungry predators make this stretch of ocean nothing less than a sailor's nightmare. Chief Grumbach was already hard at work gauging the tides and currents, feeling the wind and air, and calculating the ship's best course and sails. Although he had originally counseled against taking the shortcut, he also understood that conditions had changed, so he was going to be forced to take it anyway. He was fairly certain he could do it, but it was going to be brutal journey. On the positive side, given the hellish conditions, he figured no other captain in his right mind would try to follow them through.

Like a medieval battle scene, a volley of carefully chosen orders shot across the decks like arrows. Sails were turned, raised, lowered, and riggings secured. Sailors seemed to be flying around everywhere. As soon as everything was in place, Chief Grumbach and an apprentice navigator set the tiller precisely where they wanted it. Almost immediately, the ship began turning to the northeast, then due east. The chief well knew that he had to enter the strait at exactly the right moment, angle, and pitch. He had used his most skillful calculations in directing the approach, but now he was relying primarily on instinct. The actual crossing would depend on his intimate knowledge of dealing with anything and everything that might be encountered along the way. He would simply have to do his best, which had always been good enough in the past.

Nickolaus and Michela headed warily toward the captain's lounge where Tremonti met them at the door. "Mr. Buxtaholda ordered me to secure both of you here with Stefano and me. I am to stay with you and not allow you leave unless there's a … well, never mind, we'll all be safe. Follow me." Glad to be ordered out of the fray and free of his kitchen duties, Tremonti directed the Cottanos into the lounge and offered them seats. He sat down and pulled a deck of cards out of his pocket. "Anyone interested?"

Pale and petrified, Nickolaus fretfully declined. "No, no, you go ahead. I've got better things to do." Michela knew when to leave her husband alone, so she sat down next to Stefano who proceeded to shuffle cards like an old pro.

Tremonti sat down on the bench. "I was gonna show you how to play, my boy, but it looks like there's no need for that." Stefano smiled shrewdly, shuffled some more, and then dealt. "I see you've done this before, Steffy. I may have my work cut out for me."

"Please, Sir, I prefer to be called Stefano."

"Well, nobody calls me Sir, so you can call me Tremonti." They both nodded.

Nickolaus wandered over and stared out the small, soon-to-be shuttered window. The tumult of the raging sea immediately caught his eye and sent a shiver down his spine. The water was swirling around in all directions, harboring several mysterious forces, all competing to wrest control of the ship, which appeared, nonetheless, to be moving forward against what seemed like an invincible, opposing current. He could also sense that the ship was tacking against the wind. So how, he wondered, could the ship still be drawing closer to several monstrous clumps of stone that looked as if they were clawing their way out of the sea like famished beasts. "Who in the hell dreamed this up?" Nickolaus moaned, turning to Tremonti with a look of horror on his face. "Have they ever done this before?"

"Too goddamn many times, Maestro, but we've always made it through. The chief knows his way around, but it's still a miserable ride." Tremonti stood up and stepped over to a mysterious chest that had previously drawn Nickolaus's curiosity. The cook swiveled a metal clasp loose then pulled open the lid. "Say, how 'bout some of the captain's special brandy? I don't think he'd mind under the circumstances, at least as long as I don't drink any." He held up an elaborately decorated jug and waved it around. "What say you?"

Nickolaus needed no more prompting. "I'm in, my old friend. Michela?"

"Ah, come on, Signora, it'll help settle your nerves a bit."

114

"Oh, all right, I suppose it might help. And how about a little snort for Stefano, too? We might as well all go down happy." Tremonti filled three small mugs from the trunk then shrugged his shoulders and filled up a fourth. He raised his cup.

"To life," he toasted.

"To long life," they amended before throwing back a slug or two.

Captain Zannaro took his usual emergency position at the very front of the bridge where he could focus on the big picture while also shouting out orders to every quarter of the ship. His first officer and chief navigator were stationed at the helm, piloting the ship with the help of a couple of tiller mates. "What's that look I see on your face, Chief?" Heinz asked worriedly. "Is this going to work?"

"Aye, Sir, but it's going to be goddamn close, and rough as hell, too. I told you things weren't quite proper for a safe passage. The tides are right, but the current isn't as strong as I'd hoped for, and we've got a bit of a crosswind." The chief and two sailors tugged hard at the tiller. "I'd say we got in here at the last possible moment."

"It really doesn't look that bad out there, Chief. What am I not seeing?"

"Looks can be deceiving, Commander." A vast shower of seawater suddenly sprayed across the deck, almost knocking one of the tiller mates down. A moment later another more forceful cascade hit. "We're being tugged toward those rocks over there and I'm not even sure why. Hold on Mr. Buxtaholda." The chief cupped his hands then shouted out orders for several strategic adjustments to the sails, which the crew responded to promptly and precisely. He then made a slight adjustment to the tiller before ordering several additional changes to the sails. Shortly thereafter, the waves that had been smacking so hard against the starboard side of the ship seemed to lose a bit of their punch. A few moments later, the ship appeared to rise up out of the water and turn in mid-air, almost as if it were twisting on its own axis. Within a few minutes, despite the violent resistance of the wind and sea, the ship slowly started moving away from the rocks and then forward through the ferociously turbulent waters of La Raz de Sein. "Hold her steady," the chief bellowed. Heinz took a deep breath, as it now appeared they might succeed after all.

Ensign Grether suddenly showed up at the helm. "Commander, one of the pursuing ships is attempting to follow us through the strait – a caravel – still no colors."

"Are you kidding me? They're out of their bloody minds!" the chief yelled, turning around and raising his head like a turtle peering up out of its shell. "My Lord, those fools must be goddamned obsessed with catching us. Well, no fuckin' matter now 'cause they haven't a chance in hell. We barely made it through ourselves for Christ's sake. Look at that, now they're trying to follow our trail and it's all turning to shit. That'll never work, you stupid bastards!" the chief screeched, as if they could actually hear him. He knew what was coming for them and couldn't help but feel the tragedy of their predicament. They were destined to suffer badly.

"Stay sharp, men, steady as she goes," shouted the captain from his perch, attempting to keep the sailors' attentions on their own duties rather than staring off at the imminent destruction of the pursuing ship, which was already faltering badly. At first, she seemed to be following *The Paradise's* route, but her captain and crew lacked the experience and knowhow to execute the chief's life-learned navigational adjustments, so instead of joining forces with the winds and tides, as the chief had done, they were waging a hopeless battle against a slew of mysterious vectors they neither recognized nor understood. Obviously out of control, they began listing badly to port, then sliding helplessly, closer and closer to the giant crag of rock that was bearing down on them like Satan's promontory. Then, with a great heave and a thunderous crash, the mystery caravel smashed violently against the point, her hull splitting wide open as she scattered broken masts, shredded rigging, and shattered men onto the piercing rocks and out upon the ruthless swells of the raging sea. All hopes of saving the doomed sailors quickly evaporated for, as big and cumbersome as she was, *The Paradise* had found the sweet spot and was sliding through the chaotic waters of La Raz de Sein like a kayak over rapids. There would be no rescue mission for those lost men. It would be suicidal to even try.

"Damned fools," growled Heinz. "By the way, Ensign, did you see what happened to the other ship that was following us?"

"She vanished into the mist, Sir, heading due west. The captain believes they are planning to sail the west loop around the Isle of Sein and then try to chase us up the channel. We'll see, Commander."

"Yes, I suppose we will, and all too soon, I fear." A few moments later, Captain Zannaro stepped back to the helm.

"Good sailing, gentlemen! Chief, are we in the clear?"

"Not yet, Sir, but the rough part is over." The captain took one last look back and then shook his head.

"Those must be pirates chasing us – no colors, no flags, nothing."

"Not much sense, either," Heinz added bitterly.

"Perhaps not, but as soon as that second ship rounds the Isle of Sein, she'll be right back on our tail, and I know she's faster than we are."

"Beggin' your pardon, Sir," the chief broke in, "but who says we have to run straight up the channel. If the water's smooth enough, why not head due east and hide out near Mont St. Michel for a bit. They'll never look for us there. They'll just keep running up the channel trying to catch up with us."

"And risk those tides?" Heinz protested. "I don't want to end up high and dry and lying on our side."

"The tides are very high right now, Commander. I can find a passable channel and shelve her during low tide if we have to. We'd be fine; I'm sure of it."

Captain Zannaro shook his head. "No, no, there's no time for that. I appreciate the suggestion, Chief, and it does offer some appeal, but we can't keep running away from those bastards. We'll head east then north. They're not likely to anticipate that. If they do, we'll just have to face them down." Heinz and the chief quickly turned toward the captain, both startled by such an unusually bold move.

"You surprise me, Captain," ventured Heinz. "With our cargo and passengers, you must know that what you're proposing is pretty risky ... Sir." The captain glanced at the chief, who nodded his concurrence.

"Maybe so, but with the chief navigating those shallow seas, we'll have the upper hand. I've made my decision. As soon as we clear La Raz, sail due east at your best safe speed. Keep me informed, Gentlemen."

"Aye, Sir," Heinz and the chief sang out in unison.

As soon as the ship began to settle down, Nickolaus staggered over and opened the window shutter in the captain's lounge. Stefano immediately jumped up and ran over to join him. The craggy sea rocks were no longer in sight, and the once sickeningly swirling sea had calmed down enough to allow the ship to sail without the risk of turning on her side at any moment. Shaky and nauseated, Nickolaus turned to Michela. "How are you faring, my love?"

"Not so well, I feel awful," she complained, which her lilywhite color readily confirmed. She nodded her head toward Tremonti who, having thrown back three or four extra slugs of the captain's special brandy, was slumped back and snoring heavily. The burned out cook simply couldn't resist the spirits. "Nicki, is he in trouble?"

"I suppose so, but it won't be the first time. The captain will probably tear him up and down a bit and then send him back to the galley. Tremonti has a good heart, but like all of us, he also has his weaknesses. The captain knows that, and since he relies so much on Tremonti's cooking skills, he'll let it go." Stefano headed off toward the door.

"I'm going out there. I've got to see what's going on."

Nickolaus shook his head. "No, you won't. You'll stay right here with us until someone tells us it's safe. This is just the kind of situation that leads the captain to resist accepting passengers in the first place. You'll just be in the way; besides, Tremonti told us we were ordered to stay right here." Nickolaus looked over at the passed out cook and shook his head again. A moment later the lounge door flew open as the captain and Heinz barreled into the room.

"Maestro and family, how are you doing?" the captain inquired, glaring over at Tremonti. "What's with him?" he snapped scornfully, noticing one of his favorite jugs of brandy lying sideways on the bench next to his soused cook. "Oh, for God's sake, not again. I told him the next time this happened, he'd be out of a job. Damn him." The captain shook his head disdainfully.

Heinz stepped over and nudged the cook's thigh with his boot. Tremonti slapped at the boot then turned his head away. "I'll get to it in the morning," he stammered groggily.

"You'll get to it now, Mister."

"What the hell … oh, Commander, it's you." Startled, Tremonti jerked his head up and stared straight ahead, cross-eyed and confused. "I did as you asked, Sir. See, Nickolaus and his family are still here, safe and sound, just as you ordered."

"All thanks to your valiant efforts, no doubt," Heinz scolded. "How many times do we have to go through this, Tremonti? Why, I ought'a …"

The captain placed his hand on the Heinz's shoulder and glared angrily at his cook. "Never mind, Commander, we'll deal with this later. We've got more important issues to contend with at the moment."

"Aye, Sir. Tremonti, see if you can stagger back down to the galley and get to work. And everything better be perfect this evening, or you'll be swimming ashore." Tremonti quickly slid through his special doorway to the galley and disappeared. He knew he'd just barely dodged an ugly dressing down, or perhaps worse. Not only had he breached his duty, but he'd also embarrassed the captain, which was probably the worst thing he could do.

The captain turned to Heinz. "Sorry about the summary orders up there, but I suddenly grew sick of running. It makes me feel like a coward. And frankly, I don't feel like wallowing through those damned mud flats around Mont Saint Michel either. A captain should never appear indecisive before his men. Don't you agree?"

"Yes, Sir, not a problem. I understand completely. The men will gladly go wherever you lead them." Looking straight at the captain, Heinz rolled his eyes and tilted his head slightly, indicating the presence of the Cottanos.

"Yes, Commander, I am aware." The captain stepped over and faced Nickolaus directly. "As you know, Maestro, we just passed through La Raz de Sein, which is somewhat of miracle under the circumstances. There were two ships chasing us, both of which were unidentified and presumably manned by pirates.

One of them tried to follow us through La Raz but was smashed upon the rocks. The other, probably now racing around La Sein, no doubt intends to catch up with us and then try to capture us. They know if they sink us, the treasure they seek will be lost. I don't know why they are so obsessed with having us, but for some reason they seem pretty damned intent, as if they know what we have on board. My ship and these men are my first responsibility; however, you and your family are just as important to my way of thinking. At least a third of the value of our cargo is yours, so I feel as though I owe you some explanation as to our upcoming course of action."

"Me? Captain, with all due respect, I barely have the wherewithal to know one direction from the other. Our destiny is in your hands - surely you know that. Lord knows I can hardly keep from following Tremonti into the bottle. I'm a mess and Michela is as sick as a dog, poor girl. I appreciate your honesty and consideration but, please, you must do as you see fit without undue concern for our interests. We trust you and your crew implicitly. Obviously we'd rather make it through – with our belongings – but only you know how best to accomplish that."

"Maestro, please, ease your worry. I was only going to ask if you would consider being dropped off at Mont Saint Michel. Although there could be some risk, it might be worth our holding up there for a couple of days while you disembark. Then we could continue on our way without you having to incur any further risk to your lives. Understand, of course, that it would all depend on the tides and the weather."

"Leave us where? At Mont Saint Michel? Where would we go from there? What would we do with ourselves, and our property?"

"Ah, Maestro, with your musical prowess, I'm sure they would gladly take you in and find a place for you. You'd probably step up their choir by at least ten notches."

"I appreciate your kind words, Captain, but it's a lot more complicated than that. I have certain legal duties to attend in Lubeck." Nickolaus glanced over at Michela's worried face, then at Stefano, who was still itching to get out on deck. "Michela, what say you?"

"Don't ask me. I just want to be on land, if only for a spell, to rid myself of this terrible sickness. You must decide,

Nicki, I'm too weak right now. Just do what you think is best for us. I will abide by your decision and make my way as best I can." Nickolaus looked over at Stefano, who nodded his acquiescence.

Staring hard at the floor, Nickolaus shook his head in anguish. "Damn. Well, there it is, Captain. I say we continue on with you. We must reach Lubeck before the end of November if I am to claim the Silberbach Estate within the required vesting period. We can't wait until spring. Please make your decisions as if we weren't here. We'll do whatever is necessary to survive."

"As you wish, Maestro, but you must realize that you will always be a high priority for us so long as you are on board this ship. That is as it should be. And, for what it's worth, I think you are once again making the right decision."

"I have to ask, Captain, why did you even offer us a choice?"

"I wanted you to have the opportunity to avoid the remainder of what could be a very rough and dangerous voyage. Mont Saint Michel is probably the last viable drop off point before the toughest part of the journey. That said, I think your decision to stay on is a wise one."

"I hope so, Captain. The wellbeing of my family is the most important thing in my life. I hope my judgment here isn't tainted by selfish material desire."

"I doubt that, Maestro, but only you can answer that question for certain."

"Tell me, Captain, is it safe for Stefano to be out on deck now?"

"I'd say so, at least for the time being, but we'll be watching closely. That mystery ship could show up at any time - or maybe never – there's just no telling."

Heinz placed his arm on Stefano's shoulder. "Come on, I want to show you something."

# Chapter 15 – Mud Flats and Lowlands

The waters smoothed out nicely as the ship headed east. Michela asked to be taken to her cabin where she lay down and dozed off. Nickolaus sat in the gloomy quarters and stared at her for a time, feeling guilty and sick at heart over the perilous situation he'd placed her in. He was sure she resented him, but he was wrong. She had no such feelings at all. She accepted their circumstances completely and was ready to follow him anywhere. It was the weakness and nausea she resented – not Nickolaus. Nonetheless, he felt like waking her up and, once again, apologizing profusely, even though he knew she was always irritated when he did so. On several occasions she had made it crystal clear that she felt he was diminishing the value of their love and partnership when he went on that way. Still, it seemed to relieve his guilt, if only slightly and temporarily, when he apologized. She thought to herself, but never said aloud, that it reminded her of boy Nicolo who, despite having generally been vanquished, still seemed to reappear far more often than she preferred.

Nickolaus stood up and slid silently into the hall then made his way out onto the main deck where he drew up against the railing and stared down broodingly into the rapidly darkening waters. He knew they were cold, murky, and undoubtedly inhabited by all sorts of treacherous sea creatures, yet he was still drawn to the inviting promise of comfort and respite in those mysterious, swirling depths. He hated himself. He felt tiny and scared, as if he were drowning in stormy waters hopelessly deep over his head. And as he stared into the sea, alone and wallowing, a sick desire to see it all end crept over him, just as it had in the past. A quick drowning would remedy that. He imagined himself sinking peacefully into the water, deeper and deeper, until all light and sensation vanished. There, in the depths, he would be at rest, neither feeling, nor thinking, nor sensing anything for all of eternity. Everything would be to him just as it had been before he was born – total and absolute void - no cold, no pain, no fear, and no anxiety - just complete and utter nothingness – oblivion! It all seemed so consoling.

Surely Heinz would see to his wife and Stefano, and they would always have his more than ample fortune to live on. He realized they would be sorely hurt and profoundly damaged by the experience, possibly forever, and that they would never forgive him – nor should they - but he wouldn't have to deal with that either. It all made for the perfect solution. He lingered for a while, trying to imagine exactly how it might feel. It was a dark and lonely sensation, and he felt a lump forming in his throat as he wiped a tear from his eye. It suddenly struck him that perhaps he was not so comforted by such a bleak and meaningless ending after all. There were things about this life that he treasured and would most certainly miss. Had he been simply fooling himself all along? And then, ever so slowly, reason began to wash over him, and he remembered just how sickeningly selfish he could be. He hated himself for being so callous toward the pain his friends and loved ones would suffer from his suicidal death. Ah, if only he were alone and not responsible for these dear people he had brought along. If he were by himself, he could just leap overboard without consequence. No one would know the difference and it wouldn't matter. He would be gone, and that would be that, in the blink of an eye. He relished the thought.

As time passed, he slowly began to realize that his suicidal wanderings were all part of the same misguided, egotistical fantasy that he so often conjured up as a mental escape, a secret pathway to evade his pain or, at the very least, provide a seemingly credible distraction from his struggles. In truth, he knew that he had to face up to the situation as it really was. Michela and Stefano were there at his behest, and they needed him, and he needed to step up and face it like a man, not like boy Nicolo. "Oh hell!" he grumbled to himself. "How many times am I going to have to dredge up the same miserable muck before I can just let it go once and for all? God damn me!" He smacked the sides of his head with his palms, soundly and painfully, then he clenched his fists and punched himself firmly in the thighs, which hurt a lot more than he expected. His ears were ringing and he was trembling. "Grow up, little boy, you son-of-a-bitch." He was suddenly furious with himself, which wasn't necessarily a bad thing. Under the circumstances, anger accorded him far more strength and peace of mind than did misery and despair. Then, just as he was preparing to slam the railing with his fists, he heard footsteps shuffling up behind him.

"Have you taken your evening meal, Maestro?" Startled and embarrassed, Nickolaus reeled around to find Tremonti staring him straight in the face.

Shaken, Nickolaus stammered, "I beg your pardon?"

"Your dinner, Maestro, did you and Signora eat?"

"No, I forgot. Michela is napping. I'd say she is best left alone."

"Well, how about you, Maestro? Come on down and I'll whip something up for you. I saw Stefano eating with the chief up at the helm. Follow me. I swear I won't bite. Besides, you look like you need some company, and maybe a lick of the spirits, too."

"That's probably the last thing I need, but I wouldn't refuse if you offered. You lead the way, my good man." As they headed toward the galley, the cook suddenly halted in his tracks then swung around.

"It's none of my affair, Maestro, but I know what you were thinking back there."

"I beg your pardon?"

"I've seen it before, that blank look in a man's eyes, the dark blue emptiness, as if they've already escaped from this world into the one down there."

"You know, Tremonti, I do have blue eyes. I was born with them."

"Aye, but it's more than that and you know it. Hell, I've been there myself, too goddamn many times. Trust me, Maestro, you need harbor no shame on my account. I just beg you to reconsider. When all of this is past, you'll wonder what in the hell you were thinking; besides, it doesn't work the way you think. The moment you jump, you'll be sorry you did. I know - I've heard it from sailors who've been rescued. Every damned one of them was glad we pulled them up from the bloody drink. Come now, Paesano, let's go down to the galley and drink to happiness and good times."

Deeply touched by Tremonti's wisdom and concern, Nickolaus followed along, making every attempt to squelch the hot tears welling up in his eyes. A moment later the cook spun around once again and took hold of his shoulders. "Be kind to yourself, Maestro, you know I love you." Squinting, Nickolaus tilted his head and looked questioningly into Tremonti's bloodshot eyes. "Oh, for God's sake, man, I didn't mean it that way." After staring off into space for a few seconds, Tremonti turned away and continued on toward the galley.

Nickolaus pondered the image for a few seconds then remarked, "For a moment I thought you'd conjured up a new meaning for the phrase whipping something up in the galley." Tremonti thought about it for a moment before laughing awkwardly.

"Don't you ever tell anybody what I just said, Maestro, those bastards might take it the wrong way."

"That conversation was between you and me, Tremonti. It will forever remain our private moment."

"I thank you for that, my friend." Just as Nickolaus reached the doorway to the galley, Michela appeared at the landing. "Where have you been, Nicki? I awoke in fear for you, but you were gone. I had a terrible dream that you were falling farther and farther away from me, and I couldn't reach you. It was dark, and cold, and everything was wet. Are you all right?"

Nickolaus gently took hold of Michela's cold, clammy hands. "I'm fine, a bit troubled perhaps, but I'll be all right. We'll talk later. Are you hungry?" Michela gazed deeply into her husband's eyes.

"I wouldn't object to a little something, maybe some hardtack and ale."

"Follow me, Signora," invited Tremonti. "I'll get you fixed up right away. Forget the hardtack, I've still got some pastry left over from La Coruna. I was saving it as a treat for the captain, but he won't miss what he doesn't know about. It may be a bit stale, but it's still tasty." The trio made their way into the darkened galley where Tremonti turned up the lantern, rustled around a bit, and then laid out a small feast of pastry, hard cheese, and cider. The Cottanos sat down on the bench and started eating while Tremonti flopped back onto his hammock. His day was finished. Nickolaus stared off into the darkness while Michela concentrated on her food, which she found unusually tasty.

"I thank you for your counsel, Tremonti. I don't know what comes over me at times. It's like I'm sinking into the mud with nothing to grab hold of." Nickolaus reached over and patted Tremonti on the knee.

"Never mind, Maestro, you'd have done the right thing. I just happened along."

"Perhaps, but just the same, I'm glad you were there."

With a mouthful of pastry, Michela quietly garbled, "Is there something I should know about, Nicki?"

"No, everything is fine. When you're finished, we should retire to our quarters and get some sleep, my love."

"Yes, let's do that."

When Nickolaus and Michela emerged from their cabin early the next morning, it was as if their world had been transformed overnight. As late autumn had fallen into place, a chilling cold and rapidly vanishing sun had slowly become the order of the day. On this night, however, a dreary, smothering fog had enveloped the ship, as if a great force had draped a cold, wet blanket over the entire world. Secretly despairing, Nickolaus felt it most of all, almost turning around and returning to his cabin. Instead, he decided to move forward and forge through breakfast as best he could. Michela immediately sensed her husband's halting reluctance, but decided not to make anything of it. Sometimes she thought he tried to use his dark spells as a tool to gain sympathy or attention. She was wrong. He had almost no control over them whatsoever.

Early that morning, the captain had ordered the chief to set a course east and north that would carry them as rapidly as possible toward the Wadden Sea while still remaining within easy reach of the tidal flats where, every twelve hours, the power of the tides drew the shore waters out into the open sea, laying bare hundreds of square miles of sand, mudflats, and shallow sea channels. It was a spectacular phenomenon that had to be seen to be appreciated – land and sea alternately occupying the same space. Many on the crew felt the course was an odd choice but, as always, obeyed orders without question or hesitation. Heinz and the chief knew exactly what the captain had in mind, as he had employed the same tactic once before.

Sitting stooped and silent throughout breakfast, Nickolaus picked stingily at his food, drank a spot of tea, and then quietly took his leave, presumably to use the seat of ease. The morning's gloomy setting seemed to have darkened everyone's mood, so no one but Michela noticed her husband's waning spirit. This was a relief, since she knew how much he worried that people might misconstrue his various eccentricities. She ate her meal slowly while sharing a disjointed conversation with Ensign Di Rufo who, in his clumsy attempts to impress her, only made himself more boorish than usual. Worse yet, he kept leering at her recently expanded breasts whenever he thought she was looking the other way. She chose to ignore him.

After a while, she grew concerned over her husband's absence. Was he sick? Had he fallen overboard in the fog? Then she began wondering what he and Tremonti had been discussing when she fell upon them the evening before. She patted her face with her napkin then stood up abruptly, which left her swooning dangerously. Fortunately, as she slumped toward the oblivious Ensign Di Rufo, Heinz managed to reach over and cushion her fall so that she landed softly at the ensign's feet.

"Pardon me, Signora, are you all right?" asked Heinz worriedly as he gently helped her to her feet.

"Yes, yes, I'll be fine. How silly of me. I just don't seem to be myself today."

"You do look a bit pale, Signora, perhaps I should help you back to your cabin."

"Yes, Mr. Buxtaholda, please do." The first officer ushered Michela out of the captain's lounge onto the main deck. She stopped and turned. Weakened, she confided, "Heinz, I'm worried about Nicolo, and now he's disappeared. I'm not sure what to do." Her knees buckled once again.

Heinz tightened his grip. "Come, I'll get you settled in your cabin and then I'll find Nickolaus. How far could he have gone?" He smiled at Michela, but she was in no mood to brook any humor. They climbed through the doorway, traversed the short passageway, and then pushed open the cabin door, which they found slightly ajar.

"Nicolo!" Michela exclaimed. "What are you doing here?" The Maestro stared up at his wife and Heinz with a droopy, forlorn look on his face. "Nicolo?"

"Maestro, are you well? Is there anything I can do for you?" Heinz sensed that something was wrong, but had no clue as to what.

"No bother, Heinz, I just need to rest. I'm feeling tired and a bit ragged this morning." Heinz glanced at Michela.

She realized what was going on. "Thank you, Commander, I am familiar with this. He should be fine after some rest. Sometimes he strains under too much pressure." Nickolaus glared at his wife. He felt she had revealed too much. "Perhaps we'll come out later and take in some sun should we be so lucky as to see any today?"

"Yes, I see, it's quite all right. I'll check on you later. Rest peacefully, both of you." Heinz closed the door quietly then headed back out onto the main deck. Suddenly he remembered what he had read on the paperwork that accompanied Nickolaus on his original voyage from Lubeck to Genoa fifteen years earlier. Now it made sense to him. Nickolaus was suffering the effects a dark humour; he could be a danger to himself. So being a man of caution, he wisely decided to station two young fog spotters in positions that would enable them to see anything unusual in the vicinity of the doors leading to and from the Cottanos' cabin. Saying nothing of his reasons, he simply ordered the sailors to, "Keep a close watch on things, men."

Warily gauging her crestfallen husband, Michela sat down on the bunk with a sigh, then brushed his cheek softly with her hand. "What's wrong, my love?"

Nickolaus sighed as well. "There's too much going on in my head right now but, mainly, I'm sick at heart.

"Concerning?"

"Concerning everything. It's just all too much. I can't believe the danger I've put you and Stefano in."

Michela had intended to pour out a comforting dose of empathy but, instead, she shook her head in frustration. "This again?" she protested, barely managing to catch herself mid-eye roll. "How many times do we have to go over this? You know this is just another one of your dark spells. It's too bad we can't get our hands on some of Dr. Schicchi's coffee. That always seemed to cheer you up a bit. How about some sun or, better yet, a nice pouch of Johanneskraut? Do you suppose anyone on the ship has some Johanneskraut?"

129

"It's possible, I suppose, but I doubt it; besides, everyone knows what it's used for. They already think of me as some crazy eccentric."

"So what. You're an artist. That's what they expect of you. We all do."

"Seriously, is that how people view artists and musicians?" Nickolaus seemed simultaneously surprised, slightly relieved, and somewhat irritated by the suggestion.

"Well, I certainly can't speak for everyone, but much has been spoken of it, and I believe it to be fairly common lore. Remember your friend Di Lasso? From what you told me, he has it worse than you do, and look at how famous and respected he is."

"Ah, yes, my old friend Orlando, I'm surprised you remembered him. I wonder how he's doing? I so miss our conversations."

"I'm more concerned with how you're doing. You know, Nicki, I have an idea. You need to work. You need to get up and do something constructive. Compose some music, organize the music you've been working on, arrange it, something, anything but lying around in here moping. You know it only makes you worse. We've been through this before."

"It isn't that simple, and you know it." He stared up at the low hanging ceiling, as if it might hold some special vision of enlightenment. She knew him as well as anyone, yet not even she had come to comprehend the true depths of the despair he felt when he was in one of his darkest moods. She really had no idea how often he thought about death and suicide during those periods. She had no idea that, at least in theory, his own life meant so little to him, and that he viewed the suicide option as an important escape mechanism that was as much a part of him as his arms and legs. Admittedly, he had always assumed that he was crazy, but so what, he was who he was, like it or not. And besides, he felt he had no choice in the matter. He turned and stared directly into her eyes.

She opened her hands then tilted her head. "It may be simpler than you think, my love. Just give it a try. Put yourself to work and stop worrying about every awful thing that might happen to us. Stop stewing in your own misery. Do it right now.

Forget all your worries. Come on, Nicki, for me, you could at least give it a try. What could be the harm?"

He rubbed his eyes then placed his hands beneath his thighs and stretched. Still and silent, he thought for a moment about what she had just said. All of a sudden he grabbed a peg on the wall, pulled himself up, and then put his arm around his wife. "You're right, my dear, you're absolutely right. That's exactly what I'll do."

"Perfect." She smiled and nodded her head assuredly.

"But what about you, my love, how are you holding up?"

"Oh, I'm fine. I just need some rest, though a bit of time on solid ground certainly wouldn't hurt. Soon enough, I hope."

"Yes, yes, let's look forward to that. In the meantime, I shall set to work completing my three madrigals. I suppose we could ask Heinz about the Johanneskraut. There might be some on board somewhere. Just try to keep it as quiet as possible. It's our business and no one else's."

Michela slumped back on the bunk. "Yes, of course, Nicki, I'll make a point of it after my nap. Perhaps you could go up and work in the captain's lounge. It's too cold and dark out on deck. I'm sure they wouldn't mind."

"Agreed, my love." Nickolaus bent over and kissed his sleepy wife on the cheek, gathered up his music portfolio, smiled, and then slipped out through the small doorway. When he reached the main deck, he stopped for a moment and looked out over the ocean. Cheery on the outside, he still felt miserable on the inside, and still somewhat drawn to the lifeless finality of the sea. A moment later, one of the fog sentries stepped forward.

"Watch your step, Maestro, it can be very dangerous out here in all this dampness."

"Yes, thank you, crewman, I'm off to the captain's lounge. I'll be careful."

# Chapter 16 – Channel Hunters

Nickolaus stepped into the empty captain's lounge where he sat down at the command table and began composing. For two days he worked almost obsessively, which was by no means an easy task. As the *Paradise* moved north and east through the English Channel, she encountered ever-mounting tides and turbulence. Michela felt as if she were certain to die from her constant seasickness. Nickolaus and the crew tried to help her as best they could, but there was no cure for her condition under the circumstances. She suffered immensely. Desperate with fear and concern over her health, Nickolaus demanded to know when the storms might end and the sea stop churning. "I'm sorry, Maestro, but there are no storms here. This is life in the channel. Do you not remember it from before?" Heinz was right. Nickolaus had blocked many of the memories from his previous voyage through the channel where, narrower and shallower than the surrounding seas, powerful and opposing tides, currents, and wind forces often whipped the sea into a ferocious and unpredictable fury. It seemed a miracle that any ship ever made it through.

Late during the first evening, Nickolaus heard that a light had been spotted off the starboard bow. The sighting, which he interpreted as a pursuing ship, sent him scurrying over to their cabin to check on Michela, who he found resting quietly during one of the sea's relative calm spells. Awash in fear, he rushed back to the captain's lounge where Ensign Westfalen calmly informed him that the light was nothing more threatening than a celebratory autumn bonfire on one of the Channel Islands. Still, in Nickolaus's mind, this also represented a very grave danger, as these waters were home to a thirty-foot tidal shift, which meant that *The Paradise* and her crew were liable to be dashed upon a jagged coastal escarpment at any moment. Grinning ever so slightly, Ensign Westfalen assured him that Chief Grumbach knew exactly what he was doing, that the ship was safely in a channel, and that the island was farther away than it looked.

A few moments later, Captain Zannaro and Heinz stomped in from the cold. Heinz casually pushed Nickolaus's papers out of the way then grabbed a rolled up map and spread it out on the table. Two heavy candles were placed at each side. A few minutes later Chief Grumbach clumped in, still fidgeting around trying to secure his trousers. "Glad you could join us, Chief," the captain greeted sarcastically.

"Aye, Sir, did you miss me?"

"About as much as a dog misses fleas."

"Aye, Sir, but I promise I'll not bite ye."

"Glory be to that, Chief, now show me where we are." The captain leaned over and perused the map closely; however, his near vision was no longer as reliable as it had once been. Struggling, he turned to Nickolaus. "Could you lend me your candles, Maestro?" Nickolaus slid his candles over then shoved the sheets of music into his leather portfolio. He sat back down and tried to slip into the shadows. "You're welcome to stay, Maestro. This concerns you as much as the rest of us."

Quickly and with the precision of a supernatural navigational instrument, the chief dropped his finger directly on their exact location. "That's it, Captain, and we're heading almost due northeast, so that's our prospective course." The chief slid his finger back and forth over the map. "It's not the quickest route, but we'll get there."

"And the weather?"

"It feels good for now, but at this time of year, things could turn ugly fast. You know that as well as I do."

"Well, blazes, Chief, we've got to quit treading water and get ourselves up to Papenburg before all hell breaks loose." The captain seemed unusually agitated, as if he sensed something ominous in the wind. Heinz leaned over and pointed at the map.

"As I see it, we can either head straight up the channel on the normal trade route, or we can scoot up through the Wadden Sea. The channel is faster, but ..."

"Yes, I know, that damned caravel," the captain grumbled, "and she's liable to have company by now if she hails from Helgoland as I suspect." The chief stepped up to the map and thumped his finger down hard on their position.

"We can head up the channel as far as possible then take her due east into the Wadden Sea. When the time comes, we'll be right there at the Ems River." The chief looked straight into the captain's eyes and nodded, repeatedly poking his finger up and down on the Ems River inlet. The captain straightened up and stared off into the distance for a moment then back toward Nickolaus, whom he looked right through.

"Forget the Ems, Chief, we've got to get this ship up to the Elbe as quickly as possible. Can you recalculate to that objective?"

"Aye, Sir, right here." The chief ran his finger across a slightly different course several times.

"Do it, Chief. Heinz, double the watches and keep me informed. If anyone sees anything, I want to know right away, day or night. And men, I want our best possible speed. Is that clear?"

"Aye, Sir."

Both officers rushed out into the night and began issuing orders. Captain Zannaro dropped down next to Nickolaus with a groan and a sigh. "Just between you and me, Maestro, I'm getting too old and tired for this." Slumped forward and staring down at the floor, Nickolaus nodded in empathy. He was pleased that the captain felt free to confide such a deeply personal and potentially image-damaging admission to him.

"Me too," commiserated the twenty-five year old Maestro.

The new course allowed for markedly speedier progress; unfortunately, it also ushered in a gross heaving of the ship that would have made the dead cringe. Even the crewmen - generally accustomed to such effects – found themselves seeking relief from the sea's unyielding onslaught. The chief insisted that conditions would soon improve, but that didn't really matter, since every minute seemed like an hour to those who were suffering. Somehow Michela, having surrendered herself to the magical effects of Tremonti's special tonic, lay sound asleep for several hours. Nickolaus was not so lucky.

Late the next morning, the ship turned fifty degrees to starboard, heading as due east as winds and currents would permit. Although the frothing havoc on both ship and sea continued, at least there was some prospect that conditions might soon improve. When Nickolaus went to check on Michela, he found her awake but looking appallingly ill. She buried her head in his chest and let out a long, haunting moan followed by another that sounded even more agonizing. The cabin had taken on an utterly fetid smell, so he cradled her out onto the main deck for some fresh, albeit, cold and misty air. A young sailor immediately rushed over and pushed them brusquely into the captain's lounge. "Sorry, Sir, captain's orders," the crewman explained firmly though apologetically. "You could be washed overboard in a instant out there. Don't go out again without assistance ... ah, Sir."

"I understand. It's quite all right. Thank you," replied Nickolaus calmly as the crewman slammed the cabin door closed behind them. Nickolaus warily sat the now trembling Michela down on the bench then helped her lean back against a cushion he had positioned against the wall. Somewhat in shock, she took several deep, labored breaths before she finally recognized where she was. In this relatively light, clean, and airy room, she felt an immediate sense of relief, almost as if she had just been released from a horrible dungeon. She stared up gratefully at Nickolaus, who leaned over and kissed her tenderly on the forehead.

"What is to become of us, Nicki? I cannot tolerate one more hour of this misery or I will most surely die." She hiccupped and then gagged a bit. Not having eaten for over twelve hours, there was nothing in her stomach to cause much trouble. On the other hand, she was growing weaker by the minute. Nickolaus assumed that the baby must also have been suffering; however, his beloved Michela was always his first concern.

"I believe that if all goes well, we might be able to set foot on solid ground within a day or so. No guarantees, but that's what Chief Grumbach implied." The chief had made no statements that would suggest such a prospect, but Nickolaus felt like he had to say something encouraging, and there was always that possibility, no matter how far-fetched. Michela sighed deeply and then smiled, just slightly. Nickolaus had buoyed her, if only for a short while. "We should try to get some liquids into you."

"I don't think I can swallow any more of Tremonti's potion."

"No, I mean some tea or cider. You need something to keep you and little Johann going."

"Johann?"

"Well, we'll need to name him something, won't we?"

"What makes you think it's a boy? Besides, I had been thinking of naming him something more Genoan, like Ludovico." Nickolaus detected a slight glint in his wife's eyes and realized she was joking around – another positive sign. He played along.

"Hmmm, Ludovico, that does have a nice ring to it, doesn't it?" She fell for it.

"Indeed, like a clay bell being struck by a brick. Are you serious, Nicki?"

"In a word, no. Boy or girl, we'll be living in Lubeck. We should not handicap our child with an Italian name. In German, that name would be Ludwig."

Michela grimaced slightly. "Oh, I see. Well, in that case, Johann might be an excellent name for a boy after all, but I'm not at all certain we should decide on a name until we see the baby. He may not look like a Johann. And you know, there's just as much chance that it will be a girl."

"In my heart, I kind of wish it would be a girl," Nickolaus admitted.

"What? And forfeit all those God-given rights of primogenitor?"

"There should be plenty of time for that, my love."

"Hold on, you expect me to go through this again? I have serious doubts that I will make it through this time."

"You're a strong woman, Michela, a lot stronger than you think. If anyone can do it, you can. Anyway, we're really only borrowing trouble, aren't we?" She nodded as he swallowed a hefty gulp of hard cider. "So, what would you like to drink? Any food, per chance?"

"I'm really thirsty, Nicki. Is there any tea?"

"I'm at your service." He poured her a mug of tea, still warm from earlier. She grabbed the mug and drank from it thirstily, as if she had been wandering parched in the desert for a week. "Oh my, not so fast, give yourself a chance to let it go down." She pulled the mug away from her mouth, swallowed, and then sat back with a look of warm satisfaction. He watched

137

her closely, fearing the worst, but she seemed fine for the moment. Then, just as he began pouring himself another mug of hard cider, the ship suddenly bumped, then lurched, and then bumped again – hard. He lost his balance and fell back against the wall, but then managed to grab onto the bench, which saved him from hitting the deck. A moment later, deep vibrations, guttural groans, and hideous grating noises spread throughout the ship as if something had driven a great stake into its core. The two stared in horror at each other then slid together and embraced tightly.

"Nicki, what's happening?"

"God only knows, but it can't be good." The sound of rapid footsteps, harried yelling, and assorted clunking noises poured in from the various decks. Michela's fingernails dug into her husband's shoulders as she gripped him as hard as she could. He wanted to cry out in pain, but managed to restrain himself in order to comfort her and appear strong.

"Nicki, tell me what's going on!"

"I don't know for sure, but it feels as though we may have hit bottom. Maybe we're traversing one of the channel walls into the Wadden Sea."

"It's not an attack?"

"I don't think so. There's been no cannon fire or sharp, evasive moves."

"Then we're safe?"

"I told you, I don't know, but I'm sure when someone is free, they'll come and tell us. Even if it's not an attack, there's nothing particularly safe about striking bottom." He immediately regretted his last words.

"What? Are we going to sink?

"No, no, we'll be fine. This ship is made of the strongest timbers, and Chief Grumbach is a fine navigator and pilot. I'm sure it was just a brief aberration." Nickolaus had absolutely no faith in the validity of his statement, but he spoke with absolute confidence just the same. A few moments later, the ship jiggled back and forth a few more times to the tune of some additional scraping noises.

"Nicolo, what's happening to us?"

"You stay here and hang on. I'll step outside and see if I can find out what's going on."

"Don't leave me here alone!"

"No choice, my dear, no choice. I'll be right back." He passed through the cabin door onto the main deck. The presumed panic from a minute earlier had been replaced by an orderly row of sailors stationed along each side of the ship, all bearing oars or poles.

"Keep your eyes peeled, men," Heinz shouted. "Yell out if you see anything – anything at all."

"Aye, Sir," they responded like a trained chorus. A moment later Heinz spied Nickolaus.

"Maestro, are you and your bride all right?"

"Yes, at least so far. What's happening?"

"No worries, Maestro. The chief tried to put her into the channel before the tide was quite high enough. We'll be fine now. Go back inside and comfort your bride. And you might want to keep a tight grip on something solid. There could still be a few more bumps."

"That doesn't exactly inspire confidence," Nickolaus noted, but Heinz was already headed to the bridge. Nickolaus then returned to the captain's lounge where he assured a highly skeptical Michela that everything would be all right.

"Chief, I can't believe you hit bottom," Heinz complained as he approached the tiller.

"I never claimed to be perfect, Commander. I've not come in here this late in the season before, and you know how these channels shift around." The chief was obviously peeved, mostly at himself. Heinz slapped his second officer on the back.

"Come on, Chief, I'm just playing around with you. We're over the rough spots now, and under the worst of circumstances. You're a regular miracle worker, Otto." The chief smiled then ordered a few gratuitous adjustments to the tiller, just to appear even more masterly.

"I wouldn't say we're clear yet, Commander. You know how fickle these waters are."

"Yes, but if anyone can get us through, it's you. And hopefully, we'll be safe from any pursuers now. No sane captain of any ship of substance would ever follow us in here."

"I'm not so sure, Commander. A few of those Helgoland pirates have just as much experience as I do in these waters, and someone sure as hell has a god dam obsession with chasing us down. Remember, they followed us into La Raz de Sein like a ship of fools." Heinz stared glumly out to sea for several seconds, feeling a bit less secure than he had a few moments earlier.

"I hadn't really thought of that, Chief."

"I'm not saying they will. I know I wouldn't come in here under these conditions unless I had a damned good reason. And you know, before it's all over, we may well end up being sorry as hell for daring to come in here ourselves. This is no place for the tenderhearted, Commander, I'll damned well warrant you that"

"Do your best, Chief, that's all we can ask. Anything you need?"

"A hearty mug of grog might hit the spot, Commander." The chief suckled his lips. Heinz shook his head.

"I bet it would. I'll see what I can do."

# Chapter 17– Not on my watch!

After sailing several unnerving hours through the twisting channels of the Wadden Sea, *The Paradise* dropped anchor for the night. The officers all agreed that it would be foolhardy to attempt traversing the sea's shallow, tide-driven waters without the full benefit of bright light and a high tide. It was essential for both the lookouts and the pilot to have a clear view into the water, even if it was often murky from the shifting sands. The ship's best lookouts were stationed up top in the crow's nests where they had a panoramic view of the water's changing colors as well as occasional sightings of the actual hard borders of the channels they were sailing through. The reality was that no one of prudent mind would ever try to finesse a ship as large as *The Paradise* through waters of this nature. "This is not child's play," the chief was oft heard to say. "Best say a damned prayer if that's your way, my boy," he would suggest to any sailor around him when things got particularly sticky.

Needless to say, so far north and so late in the season, daylight hours were already in short supply. Moreover, since perilous winter storms were not uncommon for that time of year, it was sheer luck that the weather had remained clear and lightly breezy; in fact, it was unusually warm and pleasant for the date. Their good fortune seemed to holding out.

Most of the first night was spent during the ebb and flow of low tide, which was unusually high due to the relative positions of the moon and the sun. High tide was nearly turning by the time light was sufficient to make safe passage over the shallow waters. Even then, there were serious risks. The tide might recede faster than expected, or underwater ridges might be encountered. As low tide approached, channels could suddenly end or become too narrow or shallow to navigate, or an unexpected breeze could blow the ship off course. It was also important to keep a sharp eye out for that rare channel that was either deep enough or sufficiently susceptible to grounding to sustain them through the low tides. The size and relatively deep draft of *The Paradise* made this quest exceedingly challenging. In some cases, it might even be necessary to position the ship against a channel wall in such a way that it would be supported when the tide fell too low to keep the ship floating and upright on its own. It was a dangerous game. Worse yet, an unexpected storm or gale could spell the end of the whole affair. Under existing conditions, the chief estimated that it would take at least two days to traverse the Wadden Sea safely and enter the deeper, more reliable channels that led to the Elbe River.

For two harrowing but marvelously successful days, the ship sailed northeast across the Wadden Sea. Speed was briefly good during peak high tides, but then slowed as the tides ebbed and flowed. Low tide brought on an entirely different seascape that required the chief to concentrate almost entirely on keeping the ship in a channel deep enough to stay afloat in. When low tide and nighttime approached together, the chief would find a deep spot in the channel then drop a shallow anchor. There was no safe sailing in the treacherous sea of mud during the night. Even during the day, speeds would slow to a near stand still when the ship encountered a headwind during low tide, as tacking safely in the narrow channels was virtually impossible. During those periods, they had no choice but to stand by patiently and accept whatever forward progress they could manage. Fortunately, this only happened twice – both times at the lowest of tides.

Ensign Di Rufo thought the whole idea was crazy, but kept it to himself. Although he had been trained as a navigator, he had no real idea of how to pilot a ship over such long distances of shallow, tide driven waters – few people did - and he had never served aboard a ship undertaking such a rare and dangerous journey. Nevertheless, he took his duties very seriously, marching up and down the length of the ship, maintaining a near constant vigil over the entire horizon. Several times each afternoon, he would grind to a halt on the port side of the rear quarterdeck and stare off intently into the waning afternoon sun. Then, shielding his eyes with his hands while gazing intently into the glare, he would suddenly call another lookout over to join his search. Sometimes he would even enlist Stefano who, due to his sister's near constant seasickness and

Nickolaus's unusually nervous demeanor, had taken to keeping himself as isolated as possible from his family. After repeating his odd display of sighting contortions, Mr. Di Rufo would elbow Stefano in the side and whisper, "There, right there, see that shimmering on the water. What is that? It all looks like a lumpy field out there to me."

On one such occasion, Captain Zannaro stepped in to explain. "It is a field, Silvio. We're heading into low tide. As the water recedes, it flows out through the mud flats. That shimmering is the sun reflecting off the rivulets as they stream out with the tide. Have you never been through the Wadden Sea?"

"You know I haven't, Sir. I've been through mud flats before, but never in such a vast, open expanse as this."

"It is amazing, isn't it - many hundreds of square leagues of sea disappearing and reappearing every twelve hours. It never ceases to amaze me."

"How do you keep track of the channels, Captain?"

"Well, I just … I don't, Silvio, Chief Grumbach does, with the help of instinct, experience, and whole lot of damn good fortune."

"That's not exactly encouraging, Sir."

"Nor should it be. We'll be lucky to get through this in one piece. This is a big ship with a deep draft sailing through preposterously shallow seas. If it weren't for the exceptionally high tide right now, we'd be perched here high and dry. Of course, we'd have never ventured in here in the first place under any other circumstances, but I think you get the idea. We really ought not be here at all, but …" The captain shrugged his shoulders then raised his open hands toward the sky. "We do that which is demanded of us."

"Aye, Sir, then may good fortune be with us all." Silvio turned around and headed off to continue his lookout duties.

Stefano squinted his eyes until they were aching. "You know, Captain, I realize that Mr. Di Rufo is prone to seeing phantoms out there on the mud flats, but I have to admit that this time there's something out there I haven't seen before. It's fleeting, but I'd swear I keep seeing a flock of birds, or clouds on the horizon, or …"

"Or perhaps a set of sails? Keep your eyes trained on that position, son." The captain turned toward the main deck then cupped his hands around his mouth. "Mr. Westfalen," he shouted, "I need you up here right away." Within seconds, the ensign joined the captain and Stefano on the rear quarterdeck. Everyone stared out intensely, trying to fashion all sorts of makeshift visors and telescopes with their hands.

"I do see something out there, Captain, but I'll be damned if I know what it is," reported Ensign Westfalen.

"Crows nests report!" The captain shouted. Silence.

"Crows nests report," bellowed Mr. Westfalen, as loudly as he could muster. Everyone looked up.

"Aye, Sir, ship to port. Hold on, I'm trying to estimate distance and bearing. There's a lot of glare out there. Hold on." The lookout peered down as if to yell out his findings but, instead, decided to scramble down the mast to deliver his report in person. "Captain, it's a caravel. It looks just like the one that was following us back at La Raz de Sein. She's sailing in a channel that moves toward ours. I suspect the channels will eventually meet up, but I can't really see well that far out."

"Well, damn, then it's a race to the finish unless someone runs out of water. "How's the tide, Chief?"

"Still going out, Captain, I'd say about an hour or so 'til we're stuck."

"Can we clear our channel?"

The chief stared up into the sky while making several calculations in his head. "I'd say the odds are about fifty/fifty, Sir."

"Is that a calculation or a guess?"

The chief thought about it momentarily. "It's a calculated guess, Sir, and that's the best I can do. These channels are constantly changing. I'm hopeful, but I can't guarantee a damn thing."

"Yes, I know, Chief. I'm just pulling your leg a bit."

"Aye, Sir, but I can tell you that we have a better chance than they do. Ours is the main channel; theirs is a lesser branch. Then again, as I said, these damn things are constantly changing. You know as well as I do that no one sails these big ships through these channels unless they've got a damned big set of balls." The captain scowled, feeling a bit under attack.

"Well, be that as it may, Chief, like it or not, we're here, and we dare not push her too hard. It's essential that we maintain sufficient maneuvering room in this channel."

"Aye, Sir, I'll take her wherever you tell me. You know that." The captain nodded his forgiveness.

"Chief, please tell me we've reached the Elbe River Delta."

"Aye, Captain, that much I can pretty much say for sure. We're still a ways out from the mouth, but when the tide flows back in, we can sail straight up the river."

"That is if we can manage to get there in one piece."

"Aye, Captain, but that's mainly up to you, me, and a hell of a lot of damn good fortune." The captain nodded at the chief then sent the lookout back up to the crow's nest to resume his search.

"Willy, as soon as you see anything, and I do mean anything, immediately and directly report it to me, Mr. Buxtaholda, or the chief."

"Will do, Captain," Willy confirmed before scaling back up the mast."

"Now for some superbly good luck," the captain grumbled to himself. Just then, he noticed Nickolaus standing back in the shadows, having witnessed the entire exchange. "Ah, Maestro, perhaps you and Stefano should collect your wife and set yourselves back up in my lounge for a while. Things might get a bit rough, and I want to know exactly where everyone is."

"I shall do so immediately, Captain. I know we're in the best of hands. Come, Stefano, let's find Michela. I suspect she's in the cabin. Stefano promptly disappeared over the edge of the quarterdeck, landing on the main deck with a thud. Nickolaus shook his head in amazement then turned and slid down the ladder to the main deck, more than a bit pleased at how adept he, too, was becoming at seafaring, but also frightened to his very core over what he imagined might next be in store for them.

Just as they were approaching the cabin, they ran into Michela exiting through the bulkhead door. Despite the fact that she had obviously just awakened after a long sleep, she looked refreshed and even a little pink. Nickolaus brushed aside a rogue lock of hair from her forehead then embraced her and kissed her gently on the cheek. She pulled him close and held on tightly for several seconds. "Hello," she said quietly.

"Buon giorno, my love," Nickolaus whispered back. "Are you all right?"

"Oh, I'm fine, a bit tired but very glad to see you." She pulled away and stared sleepily at Stefano. "Has he been behaving himself?" Stefano shook his head at being treated like a child.

"He's been both an officer and a gentleman," Nickolaus declared like a proud father. He turned and smiled at Stefano, who was both pleased and slightly embarrassed. "In fact, he may possess the best eyes on the ship." Stefano started to object. "He made sense out what he spotted across the mud flats before anyone else." Michela was genuinely impressed. "Unfortunately, I'm afraid what he spotted isn't good news. The captain has asked us to take up temporary residence in his lounge again." Nickolaus expected Michela to be annoyed or frightened by the news, but she was past all of that. Instead, she trudged forward, opened the door to the captain's lounge, and then motioned everyone in. Like obedient children, Nickolaus and Stefano climbed through the door without saying a word. Aldo was busy tidying up, which he often did to distract himself from his worries.

"Ah, the Cottanos, how are you doing today? Care for some refreshments?"

"Oh, how kind of you," Michela replied, "I would love some. I'm exceptionally hungry." Nickolaus was very pleased by what appeared to be his wife's improved appetite. She stepped over and began eyeing the food leftover from breakfast.

"Aldo, the captain sent us in here to hold up for a while. It appears there may be another hostile ship approaching." Nickolaus glanced over at Michela, fearful of her reaction, but she seemed surprisingly unconcerned. Stefano stared back and forth between the two of them to see who would prevail, as if it were a quarrel.

A troubled look clouded Aldo's face. "Oh, I see. Well then, perhaps I should clear the center bench to provide a safe place for you to sit." Aldo began nervously scooping things up, including the food.

"Wait," pleaded Michela, "I need some of that."

"Ah, yes, Signora, most certainly." He handed her a clean wooden bowl, which she immediately filled with hard cheese, one of Tremonti's special sweet cakes, and a small orange left over from the ship's docking in La Coruna. Then he handed everyone a mug of hard cider before disappearing into the captain's personal quarters. Michela sat down on the bench and began munching away. Twenty seconds later, Tremonti burst through the hidden galley door.

"What the bloody hell – not this again! I'm getting damned sick of these chases. I don't think I've seen this much diddling around in ten years of sailing. Oh, sorry, I didn't see you sitting there. Never mind me, I was just giving the captain an earful while he couldn't hear me."

"It's quite all right, Tremonti. We seem to have brought aboard more than our fair share of trouble."

"Oh, pay me no heed, Maestro, I didn't mean anything by it. You know I've got a big mouth."

"No, no, you've every right to be annoyed. It's quite possible that whoever that is out there is primarily interested in catching up with me and my belongings. Someone may have tipped them off to my plans and the cargo we brought with us."

"Maybe so, but this isn't just about you. We have a lot more valuable cargo than just your ..." Tremonti went silent. They looked at each other and nodded just slightly, affirming their mutual understanding of all that the ship carried. Ensign Grether unexpectedly shot in from the main deck.

"Oh, good, I just wanted to make sure you're all here. The captain and Mr. Buxtaholda were quite concerned." He quickly began to retreat.

"Please, hold up a moment, Ensign," garbled Michela, still chewing on one of Tremonti's sweet raisin cakes. At just that moment, a flurry of orders echoed in through the door. "What's happening out there?" she demanded.

"Not to worry, Signora, we'll inform you as soon as there's something to ..." The ensign's words were cut short by an abrupt, severe bump followed by a deep scraping noise emanating from the port side of the hull as the ship shuddered to a halt. "I'll be back soon," promised the startled ensign, hurriedly escaping onto the main deck.

"All stop," shouted the captain. "Chief?"

"That's it, Sir, we've lost the tide. We're grounded here until it comes back in."

147

"But I thought you said … never mind, belay that question. Aspect, Chief?"

"She's still partially afloat, but we've got her banked in order to keep her stable. She'll rest upright against the channel wall. I've made sure of that."

"Stuck?"

"I'd say not."

"Thank you, and well done, Otto." The chief smiled, highly pleased by his captain's astute recognition of the near miracle he'd just performed in banking the ship tilted but upright in a relatively stable stance with so little warning. "Do you see the other ship?" the captain yelled up to the crow's nest.

"Just her masts and sails, Sir, but she still seems to be moving."

Mr. Di Rufo stepped up to the captain. "She's got a shallower draft than we do, Sir. Do you think she'll clear her channel?"

"How the hell should I know?" growled the captain in an unusual display of misdirected anger.

"She won't," the chief declared. "No way, Sir, I'd stake my life on it."

"I'd say you just did, Chief, we all did." The officers and a couple of sailors stepped over and began staring out across the mud flats toward where they assumed the other ship was traveling. The captain shook his head. "You don't suppose they'd ever try to make it over those mud flats on foot and attack us right here, do you?" Everyone pondered the possibility in silence.

"That would be an act of sheer lunacy," Heinz proposed when he arrived at the helm to join the other men. "I doubt if there would be time even if they ran at full stride; besides, we'd see them coming and blow them all to hell with the cannons. Can you imagine trying to run that far through all that mud?"

"Thank you, Heinz, I was just thinking out loud. But now that you mention it, this would be a good time to make sure the falconettes and ammunition are in order. I want to be ready to fire those little cannons at a moment's notice. Also, break the big guns free so that we can use them for ballast when the tide comes back in. I want this ship ready to sail and shoot as soon as she's clear." Heinz dashed back down to the main deck to oversee the unlashing of the main cannons. A few moments later the captain

148

ordered Ensign Di Rufo and two crewmen to climb down into the mud to check for any damage to the hull and look for anything that might potentially hang the ship up when she refloated and ascended the channel wall. Though obviously a bit miffed by the messy assignment, Silvio climbed down to the main deck where he ordered a couple of sailors to gather up the equipment they needed to complete their charge.

"I wouldn't wear those fine boots down into all that muck, Mr. Di Rufo," warned Heinz lightheartedly.

"Ha – ha – ha," Silvio laughed sardonically as he tossed a wad of gull droppings over the side railing. "Sir, we could sure use your help down there. You know this ship better than anyone."

"As inviting as that sounds, Mr. Di Rufo, I think I'll pass, but I will assist you as soon as we break these cannons free." Still, despite Heinz's recommendation, Silvio followed the two sailors down the ladder and into the mud wearing his dress boots. All three hit the sea floor with a splat. Fortunately, the sandy mire was much firmer than it looked; even so, in short order, their shoes and the bottoms of their breeches were coated in mud. Teeming with insects and various crustaceans, the Wadden Sea mud flats were relatively hard and stable due to the pressure of the water as well as constant erosion from the ebb and flow of the tides. The men inspected the ship as carefully as possible without coming too close to the edge where they might slip into one the breaches and get penned in. There, they could easily be badly injured or even drown.

After thoroughly examining the hull, the only structural concerns they had to report involved several trim boards that might have imbedded too deeply into the channel wall. Below those protrusions, the hull was theoretically smooth enough to slide freely up the wall when the ship refloated. "Let's check her again and then climb back on board, men," Mr. Di Rufo ordered with uncommon authority. He liked being in charge of an important mission, even if he did feel a bit insulted at having to tromp around in the mud like a farm animal.

Heinz and Ludwig held the ladder secure as the inspection crew climbed up and out of the mud. As soon as Silvio and the two sailors crossed the deck and sat down to remove their muddied boots and breeches, an eager swabbie showed up to scrub the decks to a state of spotlessness. Satisfied with Mr. Di Rufo's report, Heinz jokingly complained to the ensign about the sorry state of his uniform. "How are you supposed to command men looking like that, Mr. Di Rufo? What do you think this is, a pig sty?"

The young ensign smiled. "I'll get on it right away, Sir."

"Well, see that you do." Heinz slapped Silvio on the back as the muddied ensign headed off toward his bunk to don a clean pair of shoes, socks, and breeches, the dirty ones having been left to a cabin boy to clean and polish. Glancing down at the young lad, Heinz suggested, "It would probably have been fairer to send those filthy things down to that damned priest and have him clean them off with his own spit and robes."

"Oh, God, that's disgusting!" Silvio exclaimed. "Better to throw them out with the bilge water." They both laughed. Silvio stepped back over to Heinz. "By the way, how's the old creeper doing, anyway? You're in charge of him, aren't you, Sir?"

"I'm afraid so. He's surviving. We're probably treating him better than we should. From what I've heard from Nickolaus, it's more than he deserves. He gets enough food and water, and Marco and Vinny drag him out to use the crapper a few times a day and to catch a bit of sun when it's there. I have to confess, I feel kind of sorry for Martinello. He keeps showing up with food trying to see that miserable monk, but they just throw him out. He's like a lost puppy. All he really did was end up being in the wrong place at the wrong time when he was a kid. Now he's, well, whatever he is. He's far too loyal to that damned priest if you ask me. Hell, maybe they're even in love." Silvio let out an awkward giggle. "I know, it doesn't make any sense to me either, but those two men seem to want what they want. To be honest, I'm considering having Martinello released back into our custody when we reach port. He's a hard worker and loyal to a fault. It's too bad he's sacrificed so much for that wretched priest. Reformed, he'd make a pretty damn good ship's mate to my way of thinking. We'll just have to keep him away from Tremonti, eh?" Heinz elbowed Silvio, who only looked confused.

"Sir?"

"Never mind, just report to the helm as soon as you're done cleaning up."

"As you wish, Sir."

# Chapter 18 – Stuck in the Mud

"The mist is clearing, Sir," Ensign Westfalen reported. The captain stepped up to the port railing and stared out over the sea.

"Crow's nests report," Heinz shouted. Willy scaled rapidly down the mast while those below looked on admiringly. The lookout was so skilled and balletic that it seemed as though he had been specially born for the task.

"Sir, she's still there. I can't be sure, but I think she's right where she was. Her masts are straight upright, so I'd say she's either floating or grounded like we are, but probably floating."

"Maybe she's just waiting to see what we do," the captain conjectured. "They've got to know we wouldn't stop moving voluntarily."

"Captain," Mr. Di Rufo volunteered, "I'm thinking that rather than taking off as soon as we're clear, we should hold off a while to keep them guessing as to our status."

"Now why would we do that, Silvio, what would be the advantage?" Heinz challenged. Everyone stared skeptically at Mr. Di Rufo.

"We'll be moving toward darkness as high tide approaches. If we hold still, perhaps they'll think we're truly grounded or even disabled. If they hold pat, and we come into a good wind and current and then take off as quickly as possible in the dark, maybe they won't see us, and then, just maybe, we'll be able to beat them to the mouth of the Ems."

"Ems, Mr. Di Rufo? Remember, we had to bypass the Ems and go straight to the Elbe," reminded Ensign Westfalen. Silvio looked both hurt and befuddled.

"All right then, the Elbe, that's better anyway. The water should be deeper, and we can pick up as much speed as possible." Silence ensued. "By the way, I don't think Vinny and

Marco are going to be too pleased about missing the Ems and their reward."

"That's their misfortune," Heinz replied. "We've got more important things to worry about; besides, I don't think they'd mind too much under the circumstances."

"Hold on, we need to stop and think about this for a minute," advised the captain. "Let's assume our ship is going to float and clear the channel wall. If they start moving right away, we'll set sail and make the best possible speed toward the main channel and hope that we can beat them. If they don't move, we'll assume they're either stuck or waiting to see what we do. At that point, we'll quietly raise the anchor but take no visible action, perhaps even shift some weight around so we look a bit lopsided in the water. As long as they hold still, we'll set up to reach flank speed as quickly as possible – full sails, oars, everything we've got. With any luck, we can pick up a decent pace before they even know we're moving."

"Begging your pardon, Sir, but you're making a lot of assumptions," cautioned Heinz.

"Such as?"

"The winds, the currents, and the intentions and abilities on board that ship."

"And a full moon sitting directly overhead," the chief added.

"I see your point, Gentlemen, and I agree. I certainly understand your concerns, but we're making so many assumptions because there's so much we don't know, and so many possibilities to contend with." The captain turned to Silvio, "Mr. Di Rufo, thank you for your suggestion. You've the makings of a fine officer. Anyone else, ideas?" The captain glanced around at the other officers. "All right then, let's make ready. And make sure we've got several good pairs of eyes scouring the landscape at all times, just in case whoever the hell they are decide to defy all reason and try to launch an attack across the mud flats. I know it's a ridiculous proposition, but they seem to be motivated in the extreme, so let's be prepared."

"Aye, Sir," the men answered as they headed off to fulfill their duties. Captain Zannaro generally welcomed his officer's input, but once he had made his decision, he expected his orders to be carried out faithfully. He had never been disappointed in that regard. This time, however, the situation was so fluid that his orders were more like a maze of contingencies than a clearly directed pathway. Even in his own mind, he wasn't completely sure what he had just ordered. He stole over to the chief in whom he held complete personal confidence.

"Otto," he whispered, "you know I hold your judgment in high regard. Does this plan make sense to you?" The chief looked around to see if anyone was within earshot. He had already ordered the tiller mates off to eat and sleep while the ship was grounded. He and the captain were alone. "Be honest, Chief."

"It's a bit confusing, Captain, but I don't know what else I'd suggest. We'll just have to wait and see. Do you mind if I make a personal observation, Sir?" The captain nodded reluctantly.

"Go ahead, Chief."

"With all due respect, Sir, I've never seen you so unsure of yourself. I don't know if it's because this is your last voyage before retirement, or whether you're just tired, or what, but I think the men can feel your hesitation. They're not used to it, and neither am I. Do you feel it?"

"Does it show that much?"

"We've been together a long time, Captain, so I'm sure I see it more than the rest of the crew. I suspect they have only a rough sense that something's not quite as it should be."

"Well, damn, Chief, you're probably right. By God, I don't have the faintest idea what's come over me." The captain pulled closer. "I'm not even sure if you know how much gold we're carrying, but I can tell you that it's enough to fund a decent-size kingdom for a few years. I'm not sure why the hell I agreed to take so much on, but the Bank of Saint George seemed intent on getting it out of Genoa. I don't know, maybe they're afraid of that god dam new Pope." The chief smiled. He appreciated it when the captain dropped ranks and spoke in his idiom. "To be truthful, we've never really been in this kind of position before. I'm playing it by ear to some degree. Compound that with my sense of personal duty toward the Maestro and his family, and I … hell, I don't know, maybe I'm just getting old, perhaps too old to captain this ship."

"Oh, you are getting old, Sir. We're all getting old, but I'd choose to follow your orders before anyone else's I've ever served with. We'll get through this, Captain. I may be a bit rough around the edges, but I damn well treasure my reputation as a navigator and pilot. I'm going to make sure this works out. To hell with those bastards, whoever they are!"

The captain slapped the chief on the back in a manly gesture of recognition and brotherhood. "That's the spirit, my good man! I'm going downstairs to have some tea and cookies. Maybe I'll even nap for a few minutes. Call me back up if you see anything going astray. And thanks for the advice, Chief, I'll make certain I don't reveal any more signs of weakness." The chief smiled again then dipped his head in affirmation.

"You've got it, Sir." The captain departed the bridge then disappeared into the lounge where he was startled to find Nickolaus and his family. He had hoped to be totally alone for a few minutes; more importantly, he had no desire to face any questions, especially since he lacked any specific or reassuring answers.

"Ah, Maestro and family, so good to see all of you. Our condition is stable and … uh … solid. We'll be fine. I'll tell you more later on. Right now, I've got to go check some charts." The captain stepped into his private room and closed the door. He halted and took a deep breath. Exhausted, he poured himself a mug of lukewarm tea and then, in a departure from his customary stayed and steady demeanor, unbuttoned his collar and flopped down in his captain's chair. Privately, he thought of it as his personal throne, though he would never have shared that outlook with anyone, as he was basically a humble man and certainly wanted to be seen as such. "God, I'm tired," he muttered to himself. He laid his head back, closed his eyes, and sighed deeply. "I should have turned the ship over to Heinz for this one," he bemoaned quietly, shaking his head in frustration.

He stood up and turned the back of his chair toward the door, then sat back down and stared out the rear of his ship through a small open window. He sighed again then closed his eyes and conjured up an image of his beloved wife standing out in front of their stone captain's house in the Ligurian Hills above Genoa, waving to him as he trudged up the final steep hill to their porch. Once there, they embraced lovingly before disappearing into the cottage to share a spell of the marital love that they so missed during his long absences. Admittedly, the woman of his reverie was far more reminiscent of the slender, youthful maiden he had married at age twenty-two than the finely burnished woman she had matured into over the years. And it was that fresh, young beauty that he still fantasized about when they had sex, which in the natural progression of life had grown increasingly rare. He still loved her deeply, even more so than when he was young and often treated their relationship frivolously, but their love was different now, less about lust and infatuation, and more about history and familiarity. He loved what she had become and respected her immensely for all the loneliness she had endured over the years. He sighed deeply once again, as he so yearned to be with her during such trying times. However, as he sat pondering the matter, his mental image of her seemed to revert back to the beautiful young maiden he'd been so raptly taken with so many years earlier. He relished the notion for a few minutes before finding himself squirming uncomfortably, suddenly tumescent. "Good God, I must miss her more than I thought," he mumbled as he adjusted himself. He took a deep breath then shook his head in bewilderment. "Lord have mercy, what the hell has come over me? I've got duties to attend to for God's sake."

His ruminations were brought to an abrupt end when a rapid series of bumps and jolts rocked the ship, along with a distressing ruckus of crunching and scraping. The incoming tide was refloating the ship. The captain cringed and shook his head at what sounded like a gang of miners with pick-axes hacking away at the hull of his ship. An agitated knock at the door immediately followed. "Coming," he shouted. He quickly jumped up, readjusted himself, and then straitened his uniform. "Action, not despair, you old fool," he admonished himself before pushing through the door like a man possessed. It was Ensign Grether. "Are Buxtaholda, Westfalen, and the chief on the bridge?"

"Aye, Sir, the chief sent me down to get you. He says the ship is refloating." The captain glared at the ensign for a moment, wondering if the junior officer thought him an idiot – of course the ship was refloating - but he wisely decided to let it go. The ensign was simply following orders.

"Thank you, Mr. Grether." The captain tipped his hat at the Cottanos as he charged through the lounge and out onto the main deck.

Michela, still munching on one of Tremonti's raisin cakes, casually commented, "Now there goes a man with a mission."

"I certainly hope it's a successful one," replied Nickolaus fretfully. Stefano started out the door, but Ensign Grether instructed him to have a seat and stay indoors until further notice.

Out on deck, everything appeared remarkably calm as the captain made his way to the helm where his officers were waiting for him. "Is everything prepared as ordered, Mr. Buxtaholda?"

"Aye, Sir, as soon as we're clear, we can either sail or not sail at a moment's notice. The hull has cleared the channel wall. Pretty smooth, eh? The tip of the anchor is the only thing holding us in place."

"And the mud flats are clear for sailing?"

"About another half hour, Sir," advised the chief.

"Well then, all we can do is wait and see what happens."

# Chapter 19 – Mud Bath

The ship was completely clear and free to sail just as dusk receded into night, though with a nearly full moon halfway up in the sky, there was still plenty of light to go around. With the moon positioned overhead between the two ships, all of the exterior lanterns on board *The Paradise* had been extinguished in the hope that she might blend in with the shadowy, rolling waves of the sea. As of the last sighting, the mysterious caravel had not moved from its previous position. In the meantime, the captain had been pacing around the bridge for almost an hour, quietly demanding near constant reports from every section. During one such rotation, upon reaching Chief Grumbach, he suddenly stopped and, without any drama, ordered his pilot to prepare to set sail at once and move as rapidly as possible toward the main sea channel into the Elbe River.

"You know, Sir, we don't actually know where the main channel into the Elbe is running right now. It's not that easy to find during the clearest daylight hours, and now, well, I ca ..."

"Chief, I thought you were nearly omniscient in these waters."

"Sorry, Captain, I don't know what that means. I will say that I can fairly well tell when I'm nearing the channels if I can feel the currents, but there's no way to spot them at a distance, especially not in the dark."

"I know, Chief, I'm just poking your ribs a bit. Am I correct in assuming that you have a fairly good take on the bearing and approximate distance to the channel?"

"Not precisely, Sir, but I have a pretty good idea where the mouth of the river lies. If we were to head due northeast, we'd likely end up in the channel and reasonably close to the mouth of the river. But since the main channel heads in east by southeast, we'll have to sail slightly past the mouth of the river before we actually reach the channel. We can't head straight for the mouth, or we're liable to end up grounded."

"Is the water deep enough yet to allow for free sailing?

"I think so, but we could still strike a high spot in the mud flats. If we do, there's a risk of damaging the hull or even getting stuck. Having said that, my best estimate is that we shouldn't expect either."

"Then do it, Chief, choose your heading and sail at the best possible speed."

"Aye, Sir, you've got it." The chief turned and quietly issued a slew of new orders. Within moments, sailors were scurrying about the decks, raising sails, securing the riggings, and re-centering the cannons. Shortly thereafter, the anchor was pulled up, clinking and clanking as though the town crier had thrown his bell off a balcony. "Keep that damned thing quiet, men, everyone in the whole bloody sea will know right where we are." Almost instantly, the ship took off at a good clip, pushed along by a rising tide and a modest but steady breeze blowing in a favorable direction.

The captain peered out toward what he believed to be the last known position of the caravel. "I have a feeling our pirate escort over there is also on the move, and probably headed in the same direction we are. That's what I would do if I were them."

"Aye, Sir, I wouldn't be surprised." The chief suddenly tugged hard at the tiller, as if he were trying to break it off. "Hold that tiller tight but give it some slack, men, let her float a bit. I felt some resistance. We're running through some damn shallow waters. Hell, the rudder may even be digging into the mud. Nothing good can come from that."

Ensign Westfalen stepped up and tugged gently at the tiller. "Chief, how can you tell we're sailing in shallow waters? Do you possess some sort of divine sensibility?"

"I'd like to make such a claim, Ernst, but I'd be lying. Do you feel the ship slowing down a bit?" Everyone stood totally still for a few seconds, trying to sense any change in speed.

"Yes, by God, what is that, Chief?"

"Is there an arrowhead shaped wake pattern behind the ship?"

"Yes, that too, but what does it all mean?"

"When the hull comes close enough to the sea bottom, it begins pushing the water down against the mud. The resulting resistance slows the ship down and also creates that angular wake pattern off each side of the stern." Mr. Westfalen was staring at the chief as if he were a total stranger.

"Chief, how do you know this? You sound like a university maritime engineer."

"I learned it as a kid. I've seen boats running at full sail come to a complete stop without even touching the bottom, even with a good wind. Anyone who regularly sails these shallows learns to recognize it early on. It's a matter of successful seamanship. The wordy explanation comes by way of my first captain in the service. He was a stickler for using just the right words. He damn near drove me crazy until I managed to master the proper language. You know me; I'm a simple man of the sea. Now, steady as she goes, men."

For a couple of hours, *The Paradise* bobbed lightly across the high-tide waters of the Wadden Sea, that is, as much as a fully loaded Carrack can lightly bob over anything. As the third hour progressed, the moon rose steadily higher into the sky until it was almost directly overhead. The increased light came as a mixed blessing. The crew could see more of what they were doing and where they were going, but it also tended to make *The Paradise* more visible to the other ship. Willy suddenly appeared at the captain's side, having climbed down from the crow's nest in total silence. "Captain," he whispered. The captain and Mr. Westfalen both startled slightly.

"Damn, you're good, Willy. You could have snuck up on us in broad daylight. Now, let's hear your report."

"Captain, I think I'm seeing land to the northeast and possibly a few spatters of light, maybe some fires. I can't be sure. In this light it could also be a fog bank or clouds."

"Clouds with lights?" the chief grumbled.

"Well, there are always thunderstorms, Chief," countered Mr. Westfalen.

"Good spotting, Willy," commended the captain. We may be on the right course after all. Any sign of that other ship?"

"That's the other thing, Sir, I'd swear I keep catching glimpses of something off to the northwest. I just started seeing it when the moon got high enough. It could be a ship, any ship, or those bastards who've been chasing us, or maybe it's just a flock of birds passing through."

"Well, we certainly won't count on that. Thank you, Willy, now get back up there and keep a close eye out. If you spot a ship again, try to estimate its distance and bearing. I know it's dark, but do your best." The captain nodded his approval as the lookout scaled back up the mast. "How are we doing, Chief?"

"Good speed, Captain, but we'd better make the main channel into the Elbe within the next hour or we're going to run out of water. I can feel the tide ebbing now, and we're having to fight some current."

"Will we be able to sustain this rate of progress for a while, Chief?"

"I think so, but she'll start slowing down pretty soon. I can't say how much. We've still got favorable winds, but the tides and currents are starting to turn against us. It's hard to be certain of anything in these waters at night, but if we don't make that main channel soon, I'm going to have to start looking for another side channel. I'd hate to be grounded out here in the middle of one of these mudflats."

"Amen to that, Chief. Do what you can. I'm going forward to speak with Heinz."

On his way across the main deck, the captain ordered Ensign Grether to check on the Cottanos and assure them that everything was fine. "But Sir, I thought …"

"Just do it, Ensign. Please, just reassure them - the less they know, the better."

"Aye, Sir."

Upon stepping into the captain's lounge, Ensign Grether found Nickolaus sitting next to a large mug of hard cider, busily scribbling out notes and musical symbols while tapping out time and rhythm on the side of the table with his fingers. He was so engrossed in his work that he barely even noticed the ensign's arrival. Michela was lying down, snoozing on the center bench using a rolled-up blanket as a pillow. Stefano was standing up, staring anxiously out the window trying to figure out what was going on. Ensign Grether nodded at Stefano, who immediately slipped across the room to complain that he was going crazy being cooped up in the captain's lounge when he could be helping out on deck.

"Are you hungry? You must be hungry, Master Stefano."

"What? Yes, but I'm more concerned with what's going on out there."

"Ah, yes, the captain asked me to reassure all of you that everything is under control. There's nothing to worry about." Nickolaus looked up from his work and took a large gulp of hard cider.

"You don't sound all that convinced."

"Right now, all is well. We'll see about later. In the meantime, Maestro, do you mind if I take Stefano with me to go look for Tremonti? He's been roaming around the ship passing out hardtack and cider to the crew while they're standing these long shifts."

"Is it safe?"

"As safe as it is in here, I suppose."

Nickolaus stared pensively at Stefano. "Well, he's pretty much a grown man; he can make such decisions on his own. Heavens, you've got bilge boys younger than he is. Have at it, Stefano, but obey the officers."

Stefano was at once pleased with his freedom but also annoyed that Nickolaus even thought of it as an issue. He considered himself generally free to do as he pleased. "You lead the way, Ensign," Stefano proposed in a masterly fashion, not even bothering to look back at Nickolaus or Michela as he headed toward the door. However, instead of taking the roundabout way across the main deck, Ensign Grether directed Stefano into the secret galley passageway where they stole through the dark, labyrinthine staircase that unexpectedly made a ninety-degree turn half way down, and then descended through a constricted tunnel into the galley. Stefano felt as though he had just been pushed through the deepest section of an ancient catacomb.

"God, I hate that thing," Stefano gasped breathlessly. "Tremonti already drug me through that twisted nightmare once."

"It's just one of Captain Zannero's personal projects. Quaint, isn't it?"

"That isn't exactly the word that comes to mind. I was thinking more along the lines of sickening."

"Yes, I suppose so, but you get used to it after a few passes. It's hell in a storm, but it keeps the cook off the deck and ensures that the officers get their food."

"I think I'll take the regular passageway next time, Ensign Grether."

"Please, call me Kurt."

"Hey, what are you sons-a-bitches doing in my galley?" Tremonti barked angrily, tromping down the shadowy, narrow aisle of his kitchen confines. "Oh, Ensign Grether, I didn't recognize you. Sorry, Sir."

"Never mind, Tremonti. I brought Master Stefano down here for some food."

"Please, not Master Stefano, just plain Stefano." Tremonti began sifting through his stores looking for something a bit more appetizing than hardtack and cider. The rare task of providing food on the move had led him to abandon his typically well-ordered routines.

"Ah, here are some of my sweet cakes and some hard cheese. In fact, there's quite a bit of it here. Oh, damn, this is the officer's setting. I better get this up to the captain's table before the officers arrive and give me hell. God dammit, I knew I'd forget something."

Ensign Grether placed his hand on Tremonti's shoulder. "At ease, my good fellow, they're all still up on deck. Just take it up to the lounge and set it out, and do it quietly, please."

"Yes, Sir."

Kurt nodded at Stefano and then motioned him down the dimly lit aisle. "Come with me out onto the main deck. Let's get you some air." Thrilled at the opportunity, Stefano quickly headed off through the galley toward the open air.

"I thought I was supposed to stay in the captain's lounge unti …" Suddenly, a series of rumbling bumps knocked all three men against the hull. Kurt grabbed Stefano's arm and pulled him upright.

"Damn, the ship's hit a mud ridge. It's either a high spot or the tide is receding faster than we expected. "Everything under control there, Tremonti?" Kurt shouted back, pushing rapidly forward without waiting for a response. "Let's get up top and find out what's going on."

When they reached the main deck, they found sailors hustling about in every direction, turning, raising, and lowering sails. Some were busy pulling out oars and setting them up, while others were tying up slack rope from the riggings. Even Marco and Vinny were out on deck lending a hand. Kurt ran over to Heinz with Stefano in tow. "What's happened?"

"We're running out of sea. The chief is pretty sure we're approaching the main Elbe channel, but the tide is ebbing faster than he expected and the wind has turned against us. We've got to make that channel or we'll be lying out here on the mud like a beached whale."

"What do you need me to do?"

Heinz thought about it for a moment. "Take Stefano up to the forward quarterdeck. We need the best eyes available up there looking for that channel. Just tell him what to look for."

"Aye, Sir, but what about the captain's orders to secure him in the lounge."

"These are extraordinary circumstances, Ensign, necessity must prevail." He looked straight into Stefano's eyes. "Are you up to the challenge, son, it won't be safe or easy?"

"Just show me the way, Sir." They darted across the main deck then climbed the ladder to the forward quarterdeck where they pushed up the steep incline to the very bow of the ship. Ensign Fritz Fuhrman was in charge. His calm appearance belied an internal state of panic.

"What's he doing up here?" Fritz asked gruffly while smiling at Stefano.

"Commander Buxtaholda suggested we use him as a spotter. He's proven that he has exceptional eyesight. Just tell him what to look for."

"Look for? We can't see a damn thing in this light. Then again, I suppose we might as well give him a try." He turned to Stefano. "Look for anything – a dark splotch, different wave patterns, a visible current - anything that looks different from what we're in. Tell me if you see anything – anything at all - but keep your voice down. We're still trying to sail as quietly as possible. Ensign Grether will secure you to the railing so that you don't go flying overboard if we hit anything. He'll show you how the quick-release knot works. Are you sure you're up to this, young man?"

"Hell yes, umm, Sir." As Stefano watched Ensign Grether tie him in place, he thought of Pietro imprisoned below, lashed to a support beam. Here they were, both tied to the same ship not thirty feet apart – one doing his best to save the ship, the other looking for any way he could to sabotage everything. And who was it that considered himself a man of God? Stefano spat over the side of the ship at the mere thought of the miserable priest.

Only a few minutes had passed when *The Paradise* began shuddering in an odd fashion, as if someone were applying carriage brakes to the ship itself. The irregular jerking motions pushed Stefano uncomfortably against the railing. He knew why he had been secured in place.

"Keep a sharp eye out, men, we've got to find something in a hurry," implored Ensign Fuhrman in a hoarse whisper. Along with two young sailors and an older seaman who had been with the ship for many years, Stefano carefully scanned the horizon, searching for anything and everything. Through a series of surges and shudders, the ship continued moving east by northeast.

Back at the helm, the chief and his crew were working feverishly to keep the ship moving at all. The telltale arrowhead wake pattern was on full display, spreading ominously backward off each side of the stern. The chief was also preparing to deploy oarsmen if necessary, just to keep the ship moving at all. It was the closest he had ever come to beaching a ship on the open mud flats - an embarrassing calamity he was determined to avoid.

"Sir," whispered Stefano, "there's something in the water ahead. It's darker than the water and keeps disappearing then reappearing, and I'd swear it's moving." Stefano pointed off in the direction of his sighting. The other men scoured the horizon.

"I don't see a thing, Sir," reported the others, one at a time.

"There it is again," Stefano reiterated. "Right out there, maybe a hundred yards or so." Ensign Fuhrman stepped up to the railing and stared out toward where Stefano was pointing. The other men had mainly been looking farther out into the sea. It disappeared again. Suddenly there were two mysterious dark mounds moving through the water, and then they were gone. "There, did you see that? What is that?"

"Well, I'll be damned. That, my boy, is a pair of whales. I'd swear to it. How in the hell did you see those?"

"I think I noticed a few splashes first."

"Way out there?"

"Yes, but what does it mean?"

"It means we've found the channel. Those whales are heading out to sea before they get beached. Somehow they're able to find the channels in the dark. If you listen closely enough, you might even hear them wailing. It's like magic."

"Whales?"

"Yes, my boy, most likely sperm whales. They swim south through the North Sea in October and November heading for warmer waters. I've seen'em before, even saw a few hung up on the mud flats once. God knows how easy it is to lose your place out here in these tidal waters. I suppose it's the same for them, but they're far better navigators than we are, dolphins, too."

"Kurt, have you got a fix on those whales?"

"I sure do, Fritz."

"Run aft and show the chief where they are in case he hasn't already spotted them."

"You've got it, Fritz, any other messages?"

"Yeah, tell'em Stefano made the find."

"Will do," Ensign Grether acknowledged just as the ship experienced several abrupt, ricocheting bumps and another obvious speed reduction. As Kurt rushed across the main deck, jigging and jagging back and forth, several men were already dropping six oars into the water. The three Teutonics, each with an assistant, were in charge of three of the oars, while six other sturdy sailors handled the remaining three.

Ensign Grether dashed to the helm and informed the bridge officers of Stefano's discovery. He pointed directly to where he thought the whales had last been seen – by then about a hundred and fifty yards off the port bow and headed out to sea. "Well, son of a bitch," marveled the chief, "there they are. Now why didn't we see those beasties?"

"It was Stefano, Chief. Heinz sent him forward to help with sighting and somehow he managed to spot them."

"Well, good for him ... and good for all of us, by God," proclaimed the captain. For Christ sake, how in the hell are we going to make it that far in this water? We're damn near scraping bottom already."

Options were limited. With the wind in their face and the keel riding only inches above the mud, they had neither the time nor the space to undertake any broad tacking strategies. They would have to make do as best they could. Hence, as soon as the tiller had been set for the straightest possible course, the oarsmen were ordered to drop the oars into the water and do whatever was necessary to keep the ship moving forward - no matter what. Finally, in order to eliminate as much wind resistance as possible, all the sails were either dropped or moved into neutral positions. Shortly thereafter, four more oars were lowered into the water with every free hand available lending their weight to the push.

At first, the efforts proved successful; however, as the ship slowly picked up speed, it met with increasing resistance from the additional pressure of the progressively shallower water being forced down harder against the seabed. Worse yet, every few seconds or so, the keel would nick a high portion of the mud flats, which only served to slow the ship down slightly more with each mushy blow. Despite the setbacks, each of the strong and well-trained men threw all they had into every pull until the ship finally seemed to break free, as if someone had pulled up the anchor at the same moment a strong wind had filled the sails. Still, their work was by no means done. As soon as the entire ship was safely in the channel, the chief ordered the tiller handle pulled hard to port in order to facilitate a sharp turn to starboard. Simultaneously, Heinz directed the oarsmen to make commensurate rowing adjustments so that the hard turn to starboard could be completed as quickly and smoothly as possible, as there was no way of knowing just how wide the channel actually was. "A sow in the mud," the chief mumbled to himself.

By the time the ungainly ship had been properly turned and settled, it appeared fairly certain from the dark silhouettes of the low-lying landmasses at the mouth of the river that they were in the main channel and most likely on the proper course to enter the Elbe River when the tide and currents improved. Everyone settled back momentarily for a well-deserved breather, everyone, that is, except Willy, who, being an exceptional lookout, continued carefully scanning the horizon. "Oh, hell," he grumbled under his breath. "Yo, ship to aft," he shouted down insistently. "I say, ship to aft!"

"Well, I'll be damned," the captain exclaimed. "Why am I not surprised? I knew those bastards were shadowing us. Distance and bearing, Willy?"

"It's dark, Sir, but I'm estimating about a quarter of a league, and she's bearing right up our ass … ah, stern, Sir."

"Do you recognize her?"

"I can't say for sure, but it's a caravel and it looks just like the one that split off from us at La Raz and then showed up in the flats. I can't make much out, but she seems to be standing still."

"That's odd, isn't it Chief?"

"I'm afraid not, Captain. With these headwinds, and the tidal flow out, and the current from the river channel pushing us seaward, we're actually moving backwards."

"What?"

"Yes, Sir, we're being pushed seaward toward that damn ship."

"Can we row our way forward?"

"We could try, but I wouldn't count on it. I say we'd be better off anchoring ourselves in the channel and holding her in place until either the wind changes or the tides and currents are in our favor. You'd row the men to death trying to push this behemoth forward under these conditions."

"All right then, do it, but I want that anchor as shallow as will hold us in place, and I want this ship ready move at the first possible moment." The captain rushed down to the main deck to address his first officer. "Heinz, our pursuer is half a league behind us. Can they reach us with their cannons?" Heinz had more experience dealing with cannons and battle strategy than anyone else on board. He had even served in a sea battle during which his ship was nearly sunk, and it was he who had supervised the acquisition and supplying of the customized two-pound falconette cannons that Captain Zannaro had purchased from a Portuguese arms trader.

"It depends on what they're packing, Sir. Shooting from that distance is quite a toss. They'd have to have perfect accuracy or a bounty of good luck to hit us. Still, if they've got a six or eight pounder on board, they might be able to drop one right on top of us without more than a few seconds notice. Honestly, Sir, I just don't know, but it's certainly a possibility."

"What about those big fellows?" The captain pointed to his own six-pound cannons that had already been re-covered with canvas and strapped back into place on the main deck – one facing in each direction.

"They're as close to ready as we can make them. Just roll them forward, secure them in place, load, aim, and fire, but we'd have to position ourselves nearly broadside to that caravel. Frankly, Sir, in this channel, I don't think that would be advisable, especially under the present circumstances. We'd have to present our full side aspect to their guns, and our forward progress would be kaput."

"Just as I feared, Heinz, thank you." The captain stared off into space for about twenty seconds, as if he were consulting an invisible oracle. "Heinz, let's get this ship ready for battle, but do it quietly."

Ensign Di Rufo, who had been overseeing the oarsmen, stepped forward and spoke with uncommon stridency, "Captain, how can we know of their intent? They may just be on the same course as we are. Should we risk innocent blood on our hands without knowing?"

"Does that seem reasonable to you? For Christ's sake, Silvio, they've been chasing us for days; this sure as hell isn't a social call. It's that same goddamn ship, no flag and no colors. In these waters, a ship that size would carry either a flag of state or a hanseatic banner. They've got neither. They're pirates, dammit, probably some of those bastards from Helgoland. Just look at how well they've handled these waters."

"Aye, Sir, of course you're right. I'm sorry I spoke out of turn."

"You didn't, Silvio, I said your thoughts were always invited, but you've still got a lot to learn. Now where's Ensign Grether?"

"He's back up front with Stefano and Ensign Fuhrman." The captain contemplated for a few moments.

"Well, we may as well leave them up there for now. That's as safe as anywhere else on the ship at this point. Silvio, go to my lounge and make sure the Cottanos are firmly situated against the main center bulkhead. Even if that ship fires from astern, I suspect they're as safe there as anywhere. And make sure Tremonti keeps passing out food and drink, even if he doesn't want to. You know how he sometimes cowers under threat. God, I hope he isn't drunk again."

"No, Sir, he's been carrying out his duties like a man possessed. Hard to believe, isn't it?

"Well, good for him, I may have misjudged him."

"What do I tell the Cottanos, Sir?"

"Tell them the truth as you see fit. Just be gentle and don't overdo the details. Hell, improvise. I'm assigning you as my personal liaison to the Cottanos. You're in charge of that duty now."

"Aye, Sir." Silvio felt proud to be directly representing the captain, but the assignment was actually just a way for the captain to rid himself of his nephew's presence and, at the same time, save himself from having to deal with the distraction created by his passengers.

In the meantime, officers and sailors alike set about in earnest, tightly securing all of the equipment and window shields. The port facing main deck cannon was rolled shipside, shoved through the gun portholes, and then secured firmly in place. The makeshift gun crews, including the powder boys, who were actually re-designated bilge boys, were quickly called to order and given a brief but critical review of the most dangerous aspects of handling the ammunition and loading the cannons. It was a very dangerous undertaking. *The Paradise* was not a ship of war, nor had her crew been selected or prepared for battle, though they had been trained and drilled to a fair extent in the loading and firing of the cannons. Attacks from pirates and other nefarious forces against merchant ships were fairly common, especially against ships that carried no defenses. Most merchant ships just surrendered, as that was usually the safest strategy, but the captain and Heinz had decided early on that they weren't going to be pushed around so easily. Naturally, they would surrender if conditions warranted, but they had also striven to make sure that they were never among the defenseless.

"That other ship is still holding her place, Chief," Willy shouted down from the crow's nest.

"As are we, thank God," the chief mumbled, having successfully anchored the ship in place for the time being. The

169

exhausted chief dropped back on a makeshift chair he'd fashioned out of a few odds and ends from around the ship. He had been on continuous, high-demand duty for over eighteen hours. "Ernst, please take the helm for a few minutes. I've got to rest a bit before I fall over. Damn, I'm getting too old for this." He sighed heavily as he leaned back and closed his eyes. Even though he, too, was exhausted, Ernst Westfalen eagerly stepped forward and grabbed the tiller, immensely proud to be put in charge.

# Chapter 20 – Dead Reckoning

Ensign Di Rufo found Nickolaus and Michela sitting on the bench that backed to the center bulkhead in the captain's lounge. Michela, wide awake and looking unusually perky, was stroking the back of her husband's neck. Slumped over and pale, he appeared to be gravely ill, as if death were barely more than a heartbeat away. An expression of serious concern crossed Silvio's face. Michela smiled. "Don't worry, he'll be fine. He's just having one of his spells."

"But he was fine earlier. Oh, I see," he replied, having absolutely no idea what she was talking about. "The captain asked me check on you and give you a report on our status." Nickolaus and Michela both stared up at him somewhat suspiciously. "We've made it into the main sea channel that leads to the mouth of the Elbe River. At present, we're just waiting for the tides and currents to turn in our favor, then we'll sail straight up the Elbe to Hamburg."

"Then that's it? That's all there is to it?" Michela smiled and let out a big sigh of relief.

Nickolaus hesitated then asked skeptically, "And that ship that was chasing us?" The hair drew up on the back of the Silvio's neck. How could he answer honestly without alarming his passengers? Temporarily speechless, he decided on the truth.

"They're still with us, about half a league back, but they don't seem to be moving right now. I'd say we're both equally stalled by conditions beyond our control."

"So we're just supposed to just sit here and wait to be sunk?" The ensign was taken aback by the derisive cut of Nickolaus's tone.

"Nicki," Michela scolded, "he's just performing his duties. None of this is his fault. He's just telling us how it is. You do want to hear the truth, don't you?" She smiled at the ensign, instantly evoking an oddly warm feeling in the lonely young man. "Forgive my husband, he tends to see only the worst of things during perilous times like these. It's just his way. It's nothing personal." Nickolaus glared at her for a moment before reconciling himself to the accuracy of her explanation.

"She's right, Silvio, I apologize. What is the outlook?"

"I don't know. Everything is in limbo right now. If we're lucky, we'll just sail into Hamburg. If they attack us, I suppose anything could happen. But we are preparing our defenses, and we certainly aren't helpless. We may even have more guns than they do."

"Oh, great, that's just wonderful, truly stupendous," Nickolaus groaned, "an artillery battle at sea - with pirates no less. How could that possibly go wrong?" Michela squeezed her husband's hand.

"Nicki, please."

"Sorry, Silvio, I just meant to say that this isn't a good place to be, is it? Be honest."

"No, I'd have to say not, Maestro, but with daylight coming on, we'll soon be able to get moving, so there's certainly good reason to be optimistic. Captain Zannaro doesn't believe they'll follow us up the Elbe, and I tend to agree. They'd face almost certain capture up there. I'm sure there's an army of ship owners and hanseatic merchants just itching to get their hands on whoever that is out there chasing us. In fact, a friendly ship could come along at any moment and help us out. The seas are calm, so fishing boats are undoubtedly moving out to sea as we speak. There is hope - there truly is." The ensign suddenly felt better himself, having devised a reassuring scenario of encouraging possibilities in the process of consoling the Cottanos. He was truly impressed with himself. Perhaps the captain was right after all; he did have the makings of a good officer.

"Thank you, Silvio," Michela said assuredly. "We feel much better now." Nickolaus nodded then slumped back against the wall. He suddenly pulled forward.

"Where is Stefano?"

"My God," exclaimed Michela. "I forgot all about him. Ensign, do you know where Stefano is?"

"He's fine, safe, and happy as can be. He was the one who located the river channel in the distance by spotting some whale movements in the dark. It was really a nice piece of work. None of the other men saw a thing. This is the second time he's served us bravely. You should be proud. He's presently up on the forward deck with the other men, enjoying his achievement."

"Good for him," lauded Michela. "It'll help build his confidence. God knows he was going crazy stuck in here." Nickolaus nodded and smiled approvingly, as he was actually quite proud of Stefano's courage and accomplishments. Deep down, Nickolaus wished that he, too, could show more grit and determination. With nothing further to report, Ensign Di Rufo bowed slightly then turned and departed.

"Nicki, perhaps you should go back to your music. When you were busy, you seemed happy."

"I'm tired, but I suppose you're right." Nickolaus stood up and shuffled back over to the captain's table where he sat down, adjusted his papers and pen, and then proceeded to stare off into space. After a few moments, he poured a sizable dose of brandy into the mug that he'd formerly had filled with hard cider, then downed a hearty gulp, or two, or three. Michela shook her head disapprovingly but said nothing.

Meanwhile, the captain and his first officer were out on the main deck, leaning back against one of the big cannons discussing potential battle strategies. "Heinz, if we get into it with that ship, do you think we should untie the priest and hold him elsewhere. Heinz grimaced and hissed slightly before speaking. He felt much less tolerance toward Pietro than the captain did.

"I don't know why. He's lashed up front with two decks of ship overhead. How safe does he need to be? It's your call, Captain, but I say leave him be."

"It seems to me that keeping a man lashed down like that during a battle at sea would violate his rights as a human being, even if he is a loathsome bastard."

"I guarantee he'd not be the slightest bit concerned about you if the roles were reversed."

"I've no doubt about that, Heinz, but I feel an obligation to maintain a certain level of common decency on board my ship at all times."

"I suppose you're right, Captain. I'm sorry, but that rotten priest just fills me with contempt. However, you are the captain, so if we come under fire, I'll send someone down to untie him. But he still has to be kept under guard, and we'll have to keep Martinello away from him. I don't trust those two together. I think that priest has some kind of fanatical hold on the boy."

"By the way, where do they keep Martinello?"

"I think he's mainly down in the galley setting up food and drink for Tremonti to carry out to the men. Do you want me to find out for sure?"

"No, no, don't bother, we've far more important matters to deal with."

"As you wish, Sir." Heinz stood up and headed off toward the front of the ship. The captain stiffly pushed himself forward then limped toward the bridge. He was old and tired, and he knew it. When he reached the helm, he found Ensign Westfalen proudly piloting the still immobilized ship. The chief was lying back sound asleep against the aft mast, snoring peacefully.

"All is quiet, Sir," Ensign Westfalen declared in a whisper, not wanting to wake the chief, since he would most likely want to take back control of the tiller. The captain looked down at his overworked second officer.

"He deserves all the rest he can get. I think there's going to be an ugly race when the tide comes in which, if I'm not mistaken, should be in about half an hour or so. Maybe we'll see a peek of light soon, too." A few moments later Tremonti showed up with some sweet cakes, hard cheese, and tea that he'd prepared especially for the captain and other bridge officers. "Ah, thank you, Tremonti, I'm looking forward to a real meal if … when we reach port, not that there's anything wrong with your galley meals."

"You and me both, Captain, my nerves are a wreck waiting this damned thing out."

"Well, I'm not sure this should be comforting, but it won't be long now." The cook set out his offerings then quickly retreated below deck. The captain and Ensign Westfalen spent several minutes munching on Tremonti's snacks while the chief and several sailors assigned to tiller duty slumbered as best they could. It was an oddly tranquil interlude, punctuated by the dim waking of daylight and the sounds of birds calling out their morning songs as they passed by overhead on their way out to feed. Smooth and serene, the sea itself seemed to be waiting patiently for the lull of low tide to give way to the inevitable rush of the tidal flow. "Sleeping like babies, aren't they, Ensign?"

"If you say so, Sir, but I suspect they'd rather throw themselves overboard than hear you say that."

The captain chuckled. "Yes, I suppose so." Both men smiled, momentarily at peace in their own thoughts. A distinctive scuffling from above drew their attention. "This can't be good news," the captain muttered. The two men watched as Willy scampered down the mast like a squirrel being chased by an unwelcome suitor.

"They're moving, Captain, and they're moving in our direction. I can't say how fast, but it's fast enough that I can see it with my own eyes. And I'm almost certain they're in the same channel as we are."

"Oh, hell, the incoming tidal flow must have reached them first. Well, no matter, it'll be here momentarily. We've got to get this ship moving right now." The captain stepped over and jiggled the chief's shoulder. "Otto, Otto, wake up! They're on the move."

The chief stirred, then opened his eyes and looked around. He sat dazed for a moment until he realized where he was and what was happening. "They're on the move, Sir?"

"That they are, Chief. Let's get this tub moving as quickly as possible."

"Aye, Sir." The chief jumped to his feet as if someone had set a fire under him.

"Ensign Westfalen," the captain barked, "go down to the main deck and tell Commander Buxtaholda the move is on – pronto. Then run forward and give Ensign Fuhrman the same message. Tell both of them I want this ship ready to sail at flank speed up the channel toward the mouth of the Elbe by the time you get back here. We'll issue the necessary orders. And make sure they know that we're still trying to sneak out of here if we can."

"Aye, Sir," the ensign confirmed, rushing off.

"Chief," the captain ordered firmly, "I need that anchor up and this ship moving as fast as you can make it happen."

"Give me a minute to check conditions, Sir. I've got to know where we stand." The chief ran over and stared intently into the water, attempting to gauge currents and flows. Then he

175

looked up and searched for any hovering sea birds. He knew from experience that they almost always hovered facing the direction from which the wind was blowing. Unable to spot any birds, he wet his finger and held it up in the air, nodded his head, then returned to the tiller. Once there, he formed a box with his hands then stared off toward the mouth of the Elbe, moving his hands from side to side as he settled on a course. Finally, he took a brief but intense look upward toward the stars, which were rapidly fading in the new day's light. With the sailors now awake and reasonably alert, he began systematically issuing a precise series of orders, some to be carried out on the bridge, others to be sent forward to direct the rest of the crew. Times like these were the reason Chief Grumbach had never sought a promotion. He basically ran the ship and everyone knew it, though he was always humble and beholden to his captain and first officer. He knew his rightful place in the official scheme of things, but he also felt possessed of a secret authority over the whole process. His perceptions were spot on.

Within a few minutes, the men had raised and secured the anchor, this time making barely a sound in the process. Simultaneously, sails were raised, turned as ordered, and riggings set. The strongest oarsmen dropped eight oars into the water and began rowing as if they were trying to keep the ship from running over a waterfall. *The Paradise* suddenly surged forward as though a team of powerful horses had been prodded into action pulling at the bow.

"Aye, that'll get her moving, by God. What say you, Captain?"

The captain shook his head in amazement. "You've certainly got a way with her, Chief. Now let's see if we can beat that damned pirate ship."

"Aye, Sir, that'll be the real test. She's smaller and more maneuverable than we are. They also had benefit of the tide before we did.

"Well, give it all you've got, Chief."

"You know I will, Captain." And that is exactly what he did, and the crew, too, more than even they thought possible. Nevertheless, after several exceptionally long and agonizing minutes, Willy shouted out the words no one wanted to hear.

"They're gaining on us, Sir, and quickly, too." The captain turned to Ensign Di Rufo.

"Silvio, go find Marco or Vinny and take them with you untie the priest. See to it that he's kept under very close guard."

"But Sir, Marco and Vinny are both manning the oars."

"Well then, find someone else, maybe one of the Teutonics. Just get the job done, Silvio."

"Aye, Sir, I'll do my best, but I ..." The captain had already turned away. Flustered, the young ensign hesitated for a moment then headed off, looking none to sure of himself but determined to carry out the captain's orders one way or another. The captain, also none too confident, suddenly stepped forward and bellowed out a truly rare call for a merchant ship. "Battle stations! Man your battle stations!"

Instantly, Heinz and several sailors tore to the stern where they quickly pulled the canvas covers off both of the two-pound falconettes, unlashed them from their moorings, pushed them hard against the railing cannon ports, and then tied them securely in place with the strong ropes that would absorb the back force from the powerful recoil when the cannons were fired. The powder boys arrived a few moments later, carrying powder, swabs, wads, cannonballs, and a firing stick. Under the close supervision of Commander Buxtaholda and provisional gunner's mate, Theo Gluckmann, the cannons were loaded slowly and carefully; thereafter, a protocol of constant aiming and re-aiming was commenced. Even working with only the dawn's early light, it was readily clear to the officers and crew just how quickly the officious caravel was gaining on them.

"Captain, I know we're in range of their guns now," Heinz warned. "I don't understand why they haven't fired on us."

"Be careful what you wish for, Commander, it just might come true," warned the chief.

Boom! A huge blast of fire and smoke burst forth from the caravel. Boom! Again.

"Incoming!" shouted the captain. "Take cover if you can." A few seconds later, a thudding splash stung the water midship, about thirty yards to port, then another, forty yards to port and astern. "Chief, angle to starboard but keep us in the channel. Sacrifice as little speed as possible. Damn, those were close."

"Close, indeed," Heinz agreed, "but I believe those were intended as a mere tap on the shoulder. They're just trying to get our attention. Six pounders, I'd guess. Those will do some serious damage if they hit us."

"No kidding, Heinz. Damn, this is just what I suspected. They want us whole. They're trying to scare us into stopping. Bastards! Wait. Hold on a minute. They think we're running unarmed and defenseless. They think we're just going let them sail on up and board us without a fight." The captain glanced at Heinz and then at the chief, who both nodded their approval. "Well then, by God, let's show them just how badly they've miscalculated." Moments later, for the first time in his career, Captain Zannaro ordered his men to fire their cannons at another ship. After about thirty seconds of frenetic final preparations, and an order for everyone to cover their ears, they let loose with their falconettes. Boom, Ba-boom! *The Paradise* rocked back and forth just slightly. Heinz had fired both two-pound falconettes directly at the bow of the pursuing ship. No warning shots warranted for those bastards, he reckoned. Everyone watched anxiously, hoping for a big hit. Splash – a miss. A moment later, splintering Crash! The second cannonball struck the starboard side of the caravel's bowsprit, ricocheted off, and then smashed through the shipside railing, taking several chunks of rigging with it into the water. Cannonballs of the day carried no explosives, so no immediate detonations or fires were in the offing.

Despite having been warned and prepared, the men's ears were left ringing painfully. Heinz immediately ordered his gun crew to reload the cannons and check the tie-downs. They complied quickly, even though the cannons were still sizzling hot from having just been fired. Reloading a hot cannon was dangerous for even the most practiced of gun crews, which these men were definitely not. After taking exceptional care, however, the two falconettes were ready for action in commendably short order.

The crew watched closely, waiting nervously for the next volley, but silence prevailed. In truth, the blow to the pursuing ship had been far more damaging than first appeared. On the way down, the collapsed rigging on the caravel had gotten tangled up in its cannons, leaving its gun crew in a temporary state of terror and disorganization, which, in turn, had seriously delayed reloading. Aggravated on multiple fronts, Captain Zannaro decided not to wait. "Fire!" He shouted, raising his fist into the air. Boom – Boom! The two falconettes blasted again. Smoke and firing debris shot across the stern once more. The ship seemed to shake more violently this time as the falconettes recoiled farther back then before, tearing viciously at their tie downs. The effect was both shocking and disorienting to *The Paradise's* merchant ship crew.

Firing almost directly astern offered *The Paradise* a critical advantage over the caravel, which had to turn partially to broadside in order to fire her forward cannons, an action that cost her speed and made for a much broader aspect for *The Paradise* to fire at. This time around, Heinz's aim was more accurate. The first cannonball struck midway down the starboard side of the caravel's hull before splashing harmlessly into the water. The second shot, however, smashed directly into the lower starboard side of the forward mast before bouncing off and rolling helter-skelter across the deck, and then straight through the port side railing into the water. Panicky screams were heard, giving the distinct impression that men had been hit in the process.

"Nice shooting, Heinz," praised the captain.

"God, I bet they're really in a rage now," shouted the chief. "But at least they're not gaining on us anymore."

"They're getting ready to fire again," Willy yelled down from the crow's nest.

Boom – Boom, then Pop – Crash - Explosion! The caravel's first two cannonballs were on their way, but the third cannon had badly misfired then exploded, wreaking hellfire and destruction over everyone and everything in its vicinity.

"Incoming!" shouted the captain, as did Fritz Fuhrmann from the upper forecastle deck. There really wasn't much to do except to duck, hide and, maybe, pray.

CRASH! The first incoming cannonball struck the stern dead center, breaking, splintering, and then lodging in the rear hull, precisely where the center bulkhead provided extra support. CLUNK – CLANG – CRASH! The second cannonball struck *The Paradise's* center mast, and then bounced off and struck one of the ship's big cannons before ricocheting across the deck into the forecastle, somehow managing to miss every one of the several people in the vicinity, though two men were seen lying on the deck.

"God dammit!" shouted Heinz. "Well, that cannon's done for."

"Westfalen," the captain shrieked, "get down there and bring me back a damage report – right away."

"Yes, Sir," the ensign responded with a quivering voice.

"Load'em again Heinz," ordered the captain.

"Already on the way, Sir, but these cannons are almost too hot to handle, and we've got to reinforce those tie downs or these guns will blast right across the deck. Watch yourselves, boys, we don't want to be nursing any burns." Under Mr. Gluckmann's skilled supervision, the men loaded the cannons like veterans while a couple of riggers swiftly re-lashed the cannons to their tie downs. Heinz, with the assistance of Willy from above, directed the final targeting. This volley really needed to hit its mark.

In a few minutes, Ensign Westfalen returned breathless. "No significant damage to the ship, Sir, but we dare not fire that big cannon that got hit by the cannonball. Ensign Grether says it looks cock-eyed to him. I'm not sure what that means. It looks normal to me, but it seems to have been knocked loose from its stanchions."

"It's out of the game," shouted Heinz. "It's not trustworthy in that condition."

"And the cannonball that lit into the forecastle?"

"Rolled across the crew's quarters and rammed through the hull just above the water line. It's a good thing the men weren't in there. And Sir, that room is totally empty of people."

"What? Where the hell is that damned priest?" The captain's face flushed red with anger.

"I don't know, Sir, there's no one in there. Didn't you tell Silvio to take someone with him to untie the priest?"

"I most certainly did. Where is Silvio? Did anyone see what happened to him?"

"Sorry, Sir, I didn't think to ask."

"Well then, go find him – find all of them. I don't like the sound of this. Silvio has his own ways at times, but he always follows orders. Christ almighty, we don't have time for this right now. We should have thrown that God damned priest off the ship when we had the chance."

"Captain," Willy yelled from above. "We're starting to pull away from the caravel. Their forward sail is drooping. I think the rigging we took out may have disabled them. Also, they have to turn every time they fire on us."

"Good, maybe we can get into the Elbe before they catch up with us. I know they won't follow us in there."

"Maybe so," agreed Willy, "but I'm pretty sure I see them reloading their cannons."

"Captain!" exclaimed Heinz, pointing across the ship to the starboard side of the forecastle deck. "What the hell is going on over there? It looks like that damned priest has a grip on Silvio, holding some kind of knife to his throat." Three sailors were holding at bay, while Fritz Fuhrmann, tightly clutching a grappling hook, was attempting to reason with Pietro.

"Those liars promised they would take me with them," Pietro screeched, his eyes bulging out grotesquely along with the veins on his bright red forehead.

"Who, who promised they'd take you with them?" the ensign shouted back.

"My men in Genoa, they swore I'd be taken off this godforsaken ship before they were finished with you."

"Well, what in the hell gave you the fool idea that you could trust the word of a pirate?" Fritz inadvertently took a step forward.

"Stay back, man, or this poor half-wit won't live to take his next breath." Pietro feigned a slicing motion across Silvio's neck then doubled down on his grip. Blood began to trickle.

"Damn, I can't leave the bridge to go deal with that," the captain bellowed, very much out of character. "What a maniac! God, I hate that son-of-a bitch priest!" He stomped his foot then turned back to his first officer. "Heinz, aim those fucking cannons at that caravel and blow that God damned ship out of the water. Do as much damage to those miserable bastards as you can." The captain suddenly clutched at his chest then swung back around toward the forecastle deck. Pale, light-headed, and gasping for air, he screamed, "Fire, I say fire!"

"You've got it, Sir." After a few moments of final targeting adjustments to account for the shifting distances, Heinz gave the final order to fire. Boom – Boom – then a second later - Boom – Boom - the caravel fired her cannons back. "Damn!" yelled Heinz.

"Incoming!" roared the captain, as if the crew didn't already know. Up front, Fritz Fuhrmann was well aware that the cannons were about to be fired at any time, but Pietro had no idea; furthermore, the priest had no notion that the other ship might also fire their cannons at precisely the same moment. So when it happened, Fritz jabbed the startled priest on the shoulder as hard as he could with the grappling hook. Staggering backwards in pain, Pietro lost his grip on Silvio, who immediately tore over to the other side of the deck, grabbing at his neck the whole way. From there, he slid down the ladder to the main deck where, stricken with terror, he took shelter under the deck overhang. With only seconds to spare, each man took cover as best he could. At that instant, life and death depended almost entirely upon the random spoils of chance.

No one saw precisely what happened next, as every sailor on board both ships was totally occupied trying to shield or cover himself as best he could. As for the caravel, the first cannonball tore through her sails and rigging before striking the mizzenmast then veering off into the water. The second cannonball landed on her main deck, shot through several men, and then smashed through the portside railing into the sea. As for *The Paradise*, the first cannonball slammed through the shipside bulkhead of the upper forecastle, shredding and spraying splintered wood in all directions, then continued through the cabin before smashing through the outer hull into the sea. The second cannonball crashed through the forward quarterdeck inner railing, hit the base of the foremast, then ricocheted directly starboard where it violently and quite pointedly struck Pietro in the chest and shoulders, first crushing, then punching his mangled carcass through the rigging before sending several bleeding chunks of flesh splashing unceremoniously into the water below. Plop, plop … ka-plop!

After several miserably tumultuous seconds, Captain Zannaro managed to regain his composure then attempted to assess the situation as best he could. The chief stepped forward. "Orders, Sir?"

Straining to catch his breath, the captain slowly grumbled, "Get this damned ship out of here and up that river as fast as you can. That caravel is in no condition to follow us now."

"Aye, Sir, we'll give it everything we've got."

"Ensign Westfalen, are you hurt?"

"No, Captain, shaken but not injured. How about you?"

"Never mind me, Ernst, just go get me a damage report as quickly as possible." The captain reeled around, still grabbing at his chest. "Heinz, hold off on the reload. I think we're in the clear now."

"Good thing, Sir, those tie downs are ripped to shreds. We wouldn't dare fire either one of these falconettes the way they are. We do still have the one six pounder down on the main deck if we need to fire something. I'll go down and check on it – make sure it's still usable.

"All right, but let's try to sail our way out of this if we can. We've suffered enough damage for one day." And with that, the captain, still gasping for air, staggered over and collapsed onto the chief's perch.

# Chapter 21 – Sow and Ye Shall Reap

Dear old Father Pietro in all his sanctimonious splendor had spent years preaching to his minions about the hazards of incurring God's righteous and powerful wrath. Alas, it seemed that he had finally proven his point. Fritz Fuhrmann was the first man to reach what was left of Pietro's mashed torso, contorted and twisted through the shredded rigging. Apparently the cannonball's impact had decapitated the poor bastard, sending his head flying across the deck where it landed rather fortuitously in a nearby latrine bucket. Marco and Vinny arrived moments later, fearful that the source of their bounty may have been mangled beyond recognition and then blasted out to sea. They joined up with Fritz Fuhrmann to inspect the serendipitous casualty.

"Well, my God, will you look at that?" Marco marveled.

"Now that's something you don't see everyday," added Vinny, pushing at the bucket with his foot, causing the head to roll over and fall out onto the deck. All three men jumped back. "Damn!" Vinny exclaimed as one sailor flew over to the side railing and sent his breakfast soaring out into the sea. "Where's the rest of him?" Marco pointed toward the bloody mess tangled up in the rigging. "Oh, Lord, that's not going to make for much of a corpse now, is it?"

Marco shook his head. "Jesus Christ, man, at least show a little respect for the dead."

Stefano stepped up and peered down at the now permanently defrocked priest's head. He turned pale and had to sit down on a nearby coil of rigging. "I don't imagine Nicolo will be too broken up over this turn of affairs," he muttered. He looked up searchingly at Marco for a moment, then smiled and chuckled awkwardly before taking on a more serious countenance once again. He shook his head and stared off into the distance. Having never before seen anything so strikingly gruesome during his young and protected life, he had no idea how to react. The scene was at once totally revolting yet profoundly satisfying.

There could have been no better justice for the man. Marco and Vinny both shrugged their shoulders. What could they say?

"Dieter, go find me some canvas for a shroud so we can wrap this mess up and get it off the deck." Fritz turned to Marco. "I assume you'll be wanting to take it with you in order to claim your bounty from the Duke."

"Yes, yes, by all means, thank you." Marco turned to Vinny. "We certainly aren't going to want to keep that around for long." Vinny nodded and smiled, as did Stefano. As repulsive as it was, it also seemed slightly amusing – perhaps a coping mechanism. Marco, Vinny, and a couple of sailors stepped over to begin scrapping off what was essentially human jelly from the rigging. All four stepped back in disgust.

"Maybe just the head will be enough," Marco suggested sheepishly.

"Maybe so," agreed Fritz, "but we still need to have that rigging cut and cleaned so we can repair it. Have at it, boys, it's your trophy." Fritz held his hand out, as if he were inviting them into his office, which technically he was.

A moment later, Ensign Westfalen arrived to gather information for his damage report of the front section of the ship. Pietro's head was still lying undisturbed on the deck. "What in the hell is this?"

"That is what is left of the priest," Fritz reported matter-of-factly. "Their last cannonball punched right through him and cut him to shreds. The rest of him is hanging out over there in the rigging." Ensign Westfalen somehow managed to gag and snicker at the same time.

"Damn, that has to be the most grotesque thing I've ever seen."

"Yea, me too," seconded Fritz.

"Anything else, anyone have any damage to report?" Ensign Westfalen scanned the crew.

"You'll need to check the cabin in there," Fritz suggested. "One cannonball blew right through it. I haven't looked in on it yet."

"All right, I'll check it out. Carry on, men." Ensign Westfalen pulled his collar up over his nose then stepped down gingerly into the crew's cabin.

Back at the bridge, Captain Zannaro was still slumped back in the chief's special seat against the mast, panting heavily. The pain in his chest was beginning to subside somewhat, but he still felt frighteningly short of breath and increasingly panicky. As soon as the commotion cleared, the chief noticed the captain lying back, looking pale, sweaty, and fretful. He quickly shouted several orders to the crew, all aimed at achieving maximum speed into the Elbe River, then turned his attentions back to the captain. "Sir, are you all right? You don't look well at all." He swung back around and cried out frantically, "Find Ensign Di Rufo immediately and send him to the bridge. Pronto!" Ensign Di Rufo had spent time at university in Milan where he had begun a program of medical studies. Unable to keep pace, he resigned and, at the urging of family, joined Captain Zannaro on *The Paradise*. His formal training may not have amounted to much, but at least he had an interest in helping the sick, and he had been exposed to some aspects of modern Italian medicine. Plus, he was actually smarter than he appeared at first glance.

Ensign Grether found Silvio still curled up under the ladder, shaking and nearly despondent. He grabbed the ensign by the shoulders and pulled him up. "Silvio, we need your help up on the bridge. The captain has taken seriously ill. We need your medical advice. Pull yourself together, man."

"What? What's wrong with the captain?" Silvio slowly began to regain his senses.

"I don't know. Maybe it's his heart. You've got to come and take a look at him."

"All right, I suppose I can do that." Still dazed, confused, and bleeding a bit, Silvio glanced around haphazardly in every direction. Ensign Grether grabbed him by the arm and drug him across the main deck then pushed him up the ladder to the bridge.

"Get with it, my good man, the captain needs your help right away." As soon as Silvio noticed that everyone was staring at him with worried faces, he snapped out of his befuddlement and ran straight to the captain.

"Uncle Ami, what's wrong?" He grabbed the captain's wrist and methodically slapped the upper side of it several times. Then he grasped it tightly between both hands, creating a flattened hand sandwich. The motion carried no diagnostic value

187

whatsoever, but it seemed to impress the crew. Silvio thought he remembered seeing physicians doing it back in Milan, though he couldn't actually remember why. Still pale and breathing erratically, the captain reclaimed his hand and clutched at his chest again."

"Here, Silvio, right here." The captain pointed at the center-right region of his chest. "I've had this pain before, but never this bad. It even hurts up into my shoulder. I'm sure it's nothing. I probably just pulled something climbing up the ladder so quickly. I'm not getting any younger, you know."

"Yes, you're probably right. Now lie there and rest for a few minutes." Silvio suspected that his uncle's heart was the culprit, but he had no way of knowing for sure, nor did he have any idea what to do about it. The captain reached up and grabbed his nephew by the collar.

"Silvio, go find Aldo and tell him I need my medicine. Tell him it's in the apothecary jar Dr. Schicchi gave me in Genoa. He'll know what you're talking about. He's probably in my cabin hiding under the desk. That's where he keeps himself during times of peril. Hurry, Silvio."

"Yes, Sir, I'll be right back." Silvio bounded off the bridge onto the main deck, and then tore through the lounge into the captain's chamber. There, he found poor Aldo curled up in a ball under the bureau, just as the captain had predicted.

"Is it over yet? Is it safe to come out?" The steward stared up wide-eyed from beneath the desk.

"Yes, Aldo, it's safe now. Get out from under there, we need your help right away."

"Me? What can I do?"

"The captain is having bad pain in his chest."

"Oh, no, not again. The doctor warned him about this. Oh, I'm sorry. I'm afraid I said too much. That was between the captain and me."

Silvio looked up pensively at the ceiling for a few moments, recalling a couple of similar incidents with the captain that suddenly began to make sense. "I don't care about that right now. He says you know of a certain medicine from a Dr. Schicchi in Genoa."

Aldo stood up and pulled open a drawer. "Oh, yes, I do have that in here somewhere. Hmm, let's see. Ah, here it is."

"What is it?" Aldo looked closely at the jar.

"I don't know. It has A. Zannaro written on it. I think this symbol here is Dr. Schicchi's personal trademark. Now what did he call this? Oh my, let me think. Oh yes, it's written down here on the bottom of the jar, Composto di Salice e Digitale. As I recall, he said it was a mix of herbs, and flowers, and bark. I'm supposed to make a tea of it – a strong tea. The captain's never tried it. He claimed he wasn't sick enough to drink any mysterious potions made of grass and weeds."

"Well, I'm afraid he has no choice now. Let's get that potion brewed up right away, Aldo. There's nothing I can do for him. I'm good at bandages, stomachaches, and maybe even splinting a broken bone every now and then, but this is way beyond my abilities. I haven't a clue what to do." Silvio shrugged, forgiving himself. "Well, be that as it may, bring that up to the bridge as soon as it's ready, and make it quick." Silvio rushed back through the lounge, tipped his hat at the Cottanos, and then shot out onto the main deck where he nearly ran headlong into Heinz, who was also heading up to the bridge. "Sir," he acknowledged as they made their way to the bridge together.

As senior officer, Heinz reported first. "Captain, they're turning, but they aren't going anywhere fast. We've the perfect chance to drop a few of those six pounders right on top of them, maybe finish them off. Sir?"

Silvio stepped forward. "Commander, the captain has taken very ill. He needs to rest."

"What? Captain, were you hit?" Captain Zannaro pulled himself upright then waved his arm around in gesture meant to dispel concern.

"No, no, I'm fine. I'm feeling much better now," he claimed, grimacing.

Heinz continued. "Captain, I believe we should finish those bastards off right now, while we have the chance. They're limping away like a man with a broken leg. They certainly deserve whatever they get."

"Can't you see he's ill?" Silvio insisted forcefully. "He needs to rest."

"It's fine, Silvio," the captain mumbled as assuredly as he could, sympathetically waiving off his newly self-confident nephew. He pushed himself slightly more upright against the mast and then leaned forward, groaning in pain. No matter how hard he tried to hide it, he was obviously still in great distress. "Heinz, I understand your desire to finish them off. By all rights, we would certainly be justified in doing so, but we are a merchant ship, not a ship of war."

"But Sir, if we finish them off, word will spread far and wide. They'll think twice about attacking this ship in the future."

"Perhaps, but it might just as easily paint a big, bright target on our backs. Brinksmanship is a dangerous game to play, Commander, you never really know how your posturing is going to be perceived or reacted to. The last thing we want to do is precipitate an all out war between the Helgoland pirates and the Hanseatic League. I don't think anyone wants that. In the end, we might be cast as villains rather than heroes. Fair or not, they're getting away with it this time. I'm sorry, but that's it, I've made my decision." The captain slumped back against the mast once again, still sweating profusely, breathing heavily, and obviously exhausted. "And now, I'm going to go below and rest. In the meantime, Commander, you're in charge until further notice. Take good care of my ship and crew."

"Aye, Sir," Heinz agreed hesitantly, looking around at the crew and feeling more than a bit confused. He'd never seen the captain in such a physically weakened state before. He seemed so old and frail that he was almost unrecognizable. Still, Heinz understood that the captain was counting on him to follow orders faithfully, and he had every intention of doing just that.

Silvio and a nearby sailor hoisted the captain up then helped him down to the main deck and into his cabin. As soon as they walked through the door, Nickolaus and Michela jumped up and ran over to help. "What happened?" Nickolaus asked. "Here, let me help you."

"The captain has taken ill," Silvio advised. "Aldo, is the medicine ready?"

"Yes, I just now finished it. Bring him in and sit him down on the bed." Nickolaus and Michela followed the trio into the cabin. Nickolaus took note of Dr Schicchi's trademark on the apothecary jar sitting on the desk. They sat the captain down on his bunk where Aldo poured the medicinal tea into him, at least as much as he would drink.

"God almighty, that's vile," the captain protested.

"That's pretty much expected of Dr. Schicchi's elixirs," Nickolaus remarked jokingly.

The captain nodded his acquiescence; nevertheless, despite a myriad of sour faces, he managed to force down as much of the woodsy smelling elixir as he could stomach. "God help me, this simply doesn't taste like something a man ought to be drinking." Silvio took the mug and set it down on the desk.

"Now, let's see how that settles. Just sit still for a few minutes until you burp, then lie back and rest."

"Yes, Sir," the captain replied weakly before smiling slightly.

"Dr. Schicchi is my doctor, too." Nickolaus added. "He'll fix you up if anyone can."

"I know, Nickolaus, I know." The captain lay back, sighed heavily, then closed his eyes and turned his head away. "Please, everyone but Aldo leave. I need to rest now. I feel so very tired."

# Chapter 22 – Aftermath

The crew of the wounded but able *Paradise of the North* sailed proudly into the mouth of the Elbe River just before nine in the morning on November 15, 1555. The weather during their voyage had been remarkably kind for so late in the season, almost shockingly so. They had been extraordinarily lucky in that regard. Their current speed was pleasantly brisk due to the incoming flood tide and a favorable tailwind off the North Sea. Sailing on a south by southeast heading, *The Paradise* was aimed directly toward the rising sun, which had already begun burning off the thick morning fog still hanging low over the cold autumn waters of the Elbe. The pirate caravel that had chased her across the Wadden Sea was gone, reduced to little more than a remnant of history past from an ugly encounter soon to be remedied by a relaxing period of shore leave for the crew and an extended layover in Hamburg for repairs to the ship. Other than some bumps, bruises, abrasions, minor burns, scratches, three broken fingers, a sore back, and one sprained ankle, the only souvenirs of note were the crew's memories of some harsh and vivid moments - no doubt destined to become the stuff of family legend - and a defrocked priest's head stashed below deck in a tattered canvass bag.

As soon as they felt certain the danger had passed, Nickolaus and Michela joined Stefano on the forward quarterdeck to enjoy the sights and smells of land and safety. By the time they arrived, Pietro's remains had been scraped up, stowed in a bag, and taken below. It had been a grisly task, but not without a bit of emotional reward for all of those who had grown to hate Pietro both personally and symbolically. Despite their heroism and great fatigue, Fritz had insisted that the courageous powder boys - having already been demoted back to mere swabbies - thoroughly clean and scrub the deck until it revealed no signs of Pietro's ghastly dénouement. Temporary repairs to the upper deck railing and rigging were already in progress; however, the more extensive damage to the crew's cabin below would have to wait.

Michela stepped over and stood next to the men who were busy repairing the rigging. "So, this is where the old goat met his maker, eh?" A look of satisfaction crossed her face. "That's a great weight off my mind. We won't have to worry about him crawling up out of the slime anymore." A sailor that understood Italian snickered at Michela's exceptional candor and unusual lack of feminine inhibition. "Don't you agree, Nicolo?"

"I do, my love. I imagine he went out quickly, probably never even knew what hit him."

"What difference does it make? I say he deserved worse than he got. Rotten bastard!" She stared down angrily at the splintered ship railing, as if the miserable priest were still tangled up in it. "And how fitting, taken out by his own kind – murderers and thieves - except I doubt any of them are nearly as vile as he was."

Nickolaus nodded halfheartedly. For some reason, he felt a twinge of guilt over the priest's untimely death. He understood the nature of Pietro's many wicked crimes, though not their full extent, and it was he who had turned the malevolent priest into the authorities in the first place and then fought for the fullest possible prosecution and punishment for his crimes. Nickolaus fully believed that his actions had been both just and proper yet, somehow, he still felt partially responsible for the wretched priest's fate. Michela, on the other hand, shared none of her husband's ambivalence. Pietro had murdered her father in cold blood, molested God knows how many innocent boys, and pocketed vast sums of ill-begotten monies from loyal church followers, all while physically and emotionally threatening nearly everyone who ever came in contact with him. He was an evil monster and Michela hated his guts. Despite her genuinely good and peaceful nature, there would never be any room in her heart for forgiveness of that despicable beast. Never!

Nickolaus grasped Michela's hand. "You're right, my love, he deserved what he got, loathsome son-of-a-bitch!" Still, in his heart, there remained a small measure of inexplicable guilt that he would probably always carry with him. "Time to move on," he declared out loud, but mainly to himself.

Ensigns Di Rufo and Grether had taken up vigil in the outer lounge after being asked to leave the captain's quarters.

Aldo remained with the captain in case he needed any assistance. "I don't like the looks of this," Silvio confided to Kurt. "Aldo said the captain has had attacks like this before. At sixty-two, he's reaching the age when anything can happen. I hope he's all right. Maybe it's just exhaustion. He's been under a lot of strain lately."

"I'm sure that's all it is," agreed Kurt. Neither believed it.

Heinz took command as ordered. The ship was squared away and temporary repairs were commenced immediately. "Chief, can we make it into Brunsbuttel Harbor before the tide ebbs?"

"Brunsbuttel? Maybe, but the tide is turning on us right now and there's barely a breath of wind. I think we might be safer staying in the channel and anchoring down until the next flood tide arrives. For some reason, this ship is handling like a bloated sow. Besides, it'll give everyone a chance to rest up a bit. Why, are you still worried about that damned pirate ship?"

"No, no, they're gone. I'm certain of that. I'm more concerned about getting the captain to a doctor."

"In Brunsbuttel, that podunk little burg? Silvio and Tremonti are probably a better bet than anyone we might find there. Sorry, Sir, I forgot that you grew up in a small town."

"No, you're probably right, Chief, I'm just so worried about him. He looks like a ghost. It's not like him."

"I know, Commander, I sense it, too. It's goddamn troubling for sure."

"Sense what?"

"You know ... oh, never mind."

"No, Otto, what?"

"Well, I think it's bad. I've seen men taken down like this before. They usually die, especially at his age." The chief hung his head, feeling guilty about his frank assessment. "Sorry, Sir, just thinking out loud."

"No, it's all right. I respect your honesty. I know we're both very fond of him." Heinz stared pensively up the river. "Can we make Hamburg by tomorrow, Chief?"

"We'll get there, I swear, one way or another we'll get there by tomorrow ... unless something gets in the way. You never know for sure what's waiting around the corner."

"No truer words have ever been uttered or sung, my friend. By the way, Chief, you've been up almost twenty-four hours straight, maybe more. I'm ordering you off duty to go rest until the next flood tide arrives. Mr. Wand can take the helm until then. Ernst, go find Mr. Wand and bring him up here to the bridge. I think I saw him taking a bit of a snooze down on the main deck. Oh, damn, that reminds me, we'll have to have those cannons looked at in Hamburg."

"Begin' your pardon, Sir, but you've been pulling hard for at least twenty-four hours yourself. You look dead tired … Sir… Commander."

"I know, Chief, I'm planning to indulge in a bit of rest myself. "Willy," Heinz called up to the crow's nest, "I'm sending up a relief man for you. As soon as he gets there, climb down and take a rest until the next flood tide arrives. That's an order!"

"You'll get no argument from me, Sir."

"Mr. Westfalen, when you go to retrieve Mr. Wand, please bring Bruno with you. He's going up to the crow's nest."

"Aye, Sir, I'll be right back."

Having finally arrived in the Germanic states for good, the Cottanos decided that they would henceforth hail by the name of Silberbach, Nickolaus's birth surname.

Although Nickolaus and Michela slept only sporadically during the night, they were both wide-awake and energized by the prospect of reaching Hamburg. They would still need to arrange for overland transport between Hamburg and Lubeck as soon as possible if they were to complete their journey in time to meet their legal deadlines. Nickolaus had only nine days remaining to reach Lubeck and file his acceptance of the Silberbach Estate in person with the Duke. Consequently, the timing would be very close, unless he chose to go alone by hired carriage and leave Michela and Stefano in Hamburg to oversee the arrangements for the property transport. The shipment would need to be subtle, not conspicuous, and extremely well protected. The gold stores of the Bank of Saint George also had to reach Lubeck as quickly and safely as possible, so it was likely that the two shipments would be carried in tandem. While this was somewhat of a relief to the Silberbachs, it also opened up the possibility of excessive delay, which would send Nickolaus off to Lubeck by himself, or perhaps with a companion or two.

For now, the Silberbachs were headed back to the captain's lounge where they hoped to scrounge up a bit of food. Once there, however, they found no food; instead, they were promptly but gently hustled away by Silvio, who wanted the captain to rest undisturbed for as long as possible. Nickolaus and Michela stood out on the main deck for a few moments trying to decide what to do. The already ship-shape deck was nearly empty, as all but the most essential crewmen had been sent to rest.

"I'm hungry," complained Michela. "I swear my stomach is eating itself up."

"Me too," added Stefano.

"Shall we go down to the galley and see what Tremonti can stir up for us?" Nickolaus suggested.

Stefano shrugged his shoulders. "Why not?" In the meantime, Michela was already climbing through the doorway to the gloomy passageway that led to Tremonti's galley.

Humored, Nickolaus shook his head and chuckled. "She definitely wants what she wants, no doubt about that."

They made their way through the shadowy passageway, guided only by the dull glow of Tremonti's galley lantern. The grind of heavy snoring permeated the entire corridor. They found the galley in a complete state of disarray, with food stores scattered everywhere, the floor sticky and wet with spilled cider and beer, and Tremonti either sleeping very soundly or, more likely, passed out on his hammock. Apparently the stress of prolonged service under such hazardous conditions had induced him to overdue with the spirits again. Even in his drunken stupor, the wayward cook was still clinging firmly to one of Captain Zannaro's prized and potent jugs of fine brandy.

"Poor Tremonti," sympathized Michela.

"Poor Tremonti, indeed," Nickolaus countered. "If they find him like this, he'll have hell to pay."

"Even after all he did?" Stefano argued. "He spent almost the whole time during the chase and battle passing out food and drink. He went everywhere. I didn't think he had it in him. The crew was certainly grateful."

"Well, in that case, perhaps Heinz will be as forgiving as you are. Besides, I'm not sure how soon the captain is going to be up to drinking his brandy." A sudden stirring in the corner startled the trio. "Rats?" Nickolaus speculated.

Stefano squinted into the dark. "I suppose so, in a manner of speaking, it's Martinello."

"So that's where he's been keeping himself. He must have been helping Tremonti with the rations. I was wondering if he had anything to do with Pietro's escape."

"Highly unlikely. When the battle seemed imminent, the captain sent Ensign Di Rufo off to untie Pietro"

"Why, for God's sake?"

"The captain thought it would be the humane thing to do. The ensign was supposed to take someone with him, but he couldn't find anyone, so he decided to do it by himself. In the process, Pietro overpowered him, grabbed his dagger, and then took him hostage. That's how Silvio ended up on deck with a knife to his throat just before Pietro was blown to shreds by the pirate ship."

"You don't say. Well, that was certainly fortuitous. Was poor Silvio injured?"

"Just his pride. Ah, yes, and a long cut to his neck, but it wasn't deep."

Nickolaus nodded then smiled. "He's a lucky man, isn't he? I suppose we were all supremely lucky. Now let's find some food and get up top. It smells like piss down here."

"It really does smell bad, doesn't it?" agreed Michela. "Like bilge water, or worse."

"I don't think this feels right," Stefano cautioned. "We'd better go find Commander Buxtaholda and report this right away. This may be more than spilled cider on these deck planks."

"What do you mean?" Nickolaus questioned nervously.

"Never mind, Maestro, just grab some food and drink if you want it, and let's get out of here. I think they need to check this out and get these men out of here right away. The ship may be taking on water. Now let's go!"

# Chapter 23 – Waterlogged

As soon as the Silberbachs reached the main deck, it was obvious that something serious was going on. Exhausted men and boys were darting about the ship in all directions responding to a multitude of urgent of orders from their superiors. "What happened?" Nickolaus yelled to a hurried Ensign Grether.

"We're taking on water – slowly – but we're definitely leaking somewhere. We've got the bilge boys and some extra crewmen manning the pumps at full tilt as we speak. Sorry, Maestro, no time, have to move on."

"Wait," shouted Stefano, "Tremonti and Martinello are passed out down in the galley. Someone needs to go down there and bring them out. They're too much for us to handle."

Ensign Grether quickly scanned the deck. "Helmut, Erik, go down to the galley and pull out Tremonti and Martinello. Right away!"

Helmut glanced at Erik and snickered. "Ha, Tremonti and Il Piccolo Concubino passed out down in the galley, eh? I bet that was something to see … ha, ha, ha …"

"That's enough, Gentlemen, just go down there and get them. And cut back on the bawdy jokes, eh."

"Yes, Sir, where should we put them?" Erik asked.

"Anywhere on the main deck, just put them somewhere out of the way. And hurry."

"Aye, Sir." The big men immediately lumbered off toward the galley.

"Il Piccolo Concubino?" Nickolaus cocked his head quizzically.

"Yes, I'm afraid so, Maestro. The men seem to have assigned Martinello a nickname."

"Yea, pretty funny, isn't it?" Stefano snickered.

Nickolaus shook his head disapprovingly. "Crude and unwarranted, if you ask me, but why not Die Kleine Konkubine?

"They wanted to make sure he knew exactly what they were calling him, you know, to make him suffer. It's really quite obnoxious to be honest with you, but what can I say?" Unable to contain himself any longer, Ensign Grether chuckled then headed off toward the captain's lounge.

"Thank you, Ensign," Stefano called out.

Nickolaus glanced around the deck. "Why do you think the ship started leaking - cannonball damage?"

"I don't believe we were hit in such a way that would have compromised the hull below the waterline."

"Good God, Stefano, you sound like a seasoned naval officer."

"I'm wondering about all that scraping we heard against the bottom of the keel when we were passing over that last section of the mud flats just before we reached the river channel. That could really have overstressed the hull. Ensign Fuhrmann was gritting his teeth and grumbling and swearing the whole time."

"I think we should find our way to the captain's lounge," suggested Michela. "We're only in the way out here."

"Speak for yourself," countered Stefano. "I'm going up front to find Ensign Fuhrmann."

"Oh, I don't think so," Michela objected. She glanced questioningly at Nickolaus, who shrugged his shoulders and then nodded his approval. Michela acquiesced. "Never mind, Stefano, go ahead, you might as well help out the crew rather than sitting around on your hands in there with us. Just take care of yourself."

"You know I will," he yelled back, bounding across the main deck before leaping up the ladder to the forward quarterdeck.

Michela shook her head. "He'll probably end up a ship's officer. He certainly seems to love it out here."

Nickolaus grasped her hands. "He's lived such a narrow and protected life up until now. He may just be thirsty for some adventure. He is a young man, you know. The sea offers a unique and exciting life, but it's also dangerous, and it definitely offers very little opportunity for a composer or musician. With his prodigious musical talent, I doubt if he would be content living his life at sea for very long. I must admit, though, I can certainly see the superficial appeal of being out here among the living, the truly living, rather than being cooped up with all of those holierthan-thou stuffed robes that I've had to contend with in my world."

"Nicki, I never knew you felt that way. You never complained about it in Genoa."

"I know. To be fair, I didn't realize how much I hated certain aspects of my life until I moved on. There were certainly many things and people that I loved back in Genoa, but I felt stifled there, smothered, even imprisoned by all of the rules and traditions. Too much church, I suppose. You know how I feel about all that hocus-pocus. To be truthful, I doubt if it will be any different in Lubeck. I've heard the Lutherans maintain ruthless control over their church musicians and composers. And they're none to liberal when it comes to trying out new musical ideas either, just hymns and chorales, hymns and chorales." Nickolaus mockingly wagged his head back and forth.

"Surely it's not all that bad, do you think? I had hoped Stefano might have a fulfilling future in music ahead of him here. He's so gifted."

Nickolaus tenderly took Michela by the elbow and led her toward the captain's lounge. "That he is, my love, that he is. Your dreams for him are entirely possible, but he did grow up thinking and doing the Genoan way. He may or may not adjust. Besides, who says his music has to have anything to do with the church? Well, whatever happens, we know he's smart and resilient."

"I suppose you're right," Michela conceded. As soon as they stepped into the captain's lounge, Heinz waved them over to the bulkhead bench and motioned for them to sit down. Aldo was stretched back in the captain's chair with his eyes closed.

"We've got a bit of a problem, Maestro. Both of you will have to remain here until we get things under control." Heinz went back to measuring charts then scribbling out computations for what appeared to be some sort of mathematical problem. He gracefully scrawled out a curly-q, punctuated it with a hard poke, then jumped up and nudged the steward gently on the foot. "Aldo, I'll be up with the chief if anyone comes looking for me. Take care of the captain." Aldo groggily opened his eyes then sat forward.

"Yes, Sir," he answered with conviction. However, as soon as Heinz left, he turned to Nickolaus and Michela and asked what he'd been ordered to do.

"Hmm, let me see," Nickolaus replied. "If anyone wants to know, Heinz is up with the chief. You're supposed to take care of the captain, and …"

"And is there any good food around here?" Michela interrupted impatiently.

"Sorry dear," Aldo explained, "there's nothing left here or in the captain's room, and I'm afraid Tremonti seems to have disappeared. I'm sure he'll show up with something for dinner in a while."

Nickolaus shook his head. "I wouldn't count on it. The last I knew, Helmut and Erik were hauling Tremonti and Martinello, both of whom are drunk to the gills by the way, up out of the flooded galley. I'm not even sure if there's any edible food left on the ship."

"Oh my, that will certainly make for a cranky crew."

Nickolaus clucked his tongue. "A sinking ship and hungry sailors – not exactly the recipe for smooth sailing, eh, Aldo?"

"Well, Maestro, I believe Mr. Buxtaholda may have decided to put in at Brunsbuttel after all. The ship is in trouble and the captain isn't getting any better. The commander seems to feel from his calculations that Hamburg is too far to push the ship in its present condition. Now with this food problem, I'm quite certain he will put in to port as soon as possible."

"Brunsbuttel? Aldo, I need to talk to the commander right away." Nickolaus kissed Michela on the forehead then tore off to find Heinz, who was up on the bridge conferring with the chief about putting in at Brunsbuttel.

"Chief, I ask you again, do we try to fight the tidal currents, sail immediately, and risk taking on more water, or do we wait it out until the flood tide pushes us in?"

"Sir, we've got a little bit of wind at our back right now. We might be able to push her forward slowly, but I recommend we wait half an hour or so until the tide has flattened, then we raise the sails and get this sinking ship on the move. I don't want to fight that current. It might just force more water through the damaged hull."

"All right, Chief, I'll leave you in charge of calling the time and issuing the orders. Let me know as soon as we're ready to get moving. I'm going down to check on the bilge pumps - see if we can't make this soggy tub a little lighter on its feet."

"Aye, Sir, the lighter the better, she's moving like a wagon through a swamp right now."

"Yes, I bet she is, Chief."

"Commander," Nickolaus called out breathlessly when he arrived at the helm. "I need to speak with you right away."

"Later, Maestro, there's a lot going on."

"Just tell me, Heinz, are we putting in at Brunsbuttel?"

"I believe so ... no, I'm certain of it. Why do you ask?"

"Because if we're going to complete our journey overland, Brunsbuttel may be the perfect place to dock. Unlike Hamburg, the route from Brunsbuttel to Lubeck lies entirely within the state of Holstein. My estate is right outside Lubeck. I believe it may be the safest and most certain way of getting there on time."

Heinz thought about it for a moment. "Yes, but Hamburg would be a much shorter overland journey. We could transfer the important cargo to a different ship, perhaps a barge, and then complete our trip to Hamburg.

"But that would take a lot of extra time for loading and unloading, and we would still have to go overland from Hamburg to Lubeck, most of which passes through Holstein anyway."

"What about all those Duchy passage fees and taxes? There must be a handful of little kingdoms in Holstein right now. They could suck us dry by the time we get where we're going."

"Normally I would agree, but I happen to be in possession of a special transit document from the Duke. My consigliere in Genoa gave it to me just before we set sail. According to him, it grants my family and possessions free passage through all of Holstein and even into Lubeck. I don't know if it will actually work as described, but it does bear the official royal stamp of King Christian III."

"Are you serious? Such a pass actually exists?"

"Apparently so, I have it stored with my affairs in my ... in your cabin. It certainly appears to be legitimate."

"Such a document would be extraordinary. But would it grant free passage for the bank's gold that is also to be delivered to Lubeck?"

"I don't know. Do you believe they would actually try to bleed you of hanseatic money that is clearly bound for the Bank of St George?"

"I have no idea. I've never tried anything like this before. I've spent my life as a mariner, not as a coach and wagon man."

"Well, who says the authorities would have to know? We could transport all of it as if it were mine. I'm sure we would need to make a few contributions here and there to smooth the process along, but that shouldn't be too painful. Does the bank's gold come in the form of trademark-stamped bullion or simple gold Florins? Our gold is held in the form of gold Florins."

"I don't know; we'd have to look." Heinz shook his head at the thought of arranging such a challenging and unusual undertaking. "You know, such a load would require transporting a very large concentration of wealth over quite a distance through the hinterlands. It would be like a giant treasure chest on wheels. And those roads can be of very poor quality, especially in the rainy season, which is already upon us. We would certainly need very heavy protection."

"Or very good camouflage," Nickolaus countered.

"Either way, it would be a serious undertaking to say the least. To be honest, this all sounds very risky and tentative to me." Heinz glanced around impatiently then turned to Nickolaus. "Look, we'll have to consider this later. Perhaps the captain will have an opinion on the matter. Right now, I'm going below to check on the pumps. We've got to make it to port before we can plan to do anything else."

"Agreed, Commander." Nickolaus shook Heinz's hand.

"Once we're docked, we can figure out the rest." Heinz turned to the chief. "Carry on as we discussed, Otto. Get this tired old lady into port."

"Aye, Sir," he responded firmly. Heinz and Nickolaus rapidly descended to the main deck where the commander headed below into the hold. Nickolaus, teeming with rediscovered confidence - temporary or not - and greatly relieved to be nearly back on land for good, made his way into the captain's lounge to speak with Michela. Alone and dozing, Aldo slowly lifted his head from the table and stared bleary-eyed at Nickolaus.

"Your wife is in with Ensign Di Rufo tending to the captain," he mumbled. He pointed his thumb behind him then dropped his head heavily back down onto the table.

"Good man, Aldo, as you were." Nickolaus smiled as he slowly peeled open the door to the captain's chamber, looked around, and then stepped in quietly. Michela was seated on a small stool beside the captain's bunk, gently massaging her patient's hand in a manner that Nickolaus was very much familiar with. She often used the same technique to help calm him down when he was having one of his spells. Silvio put a finger to his lips to indicate silence then directed the Maestro back out to the lounge where they spoke in whispers.

"I think the captain is delirious. He stirs every now and then, and calls out for his wife, Clarita, but he also mumbled something about the children."

"I didn't know he had any children."

"He doesn't, well, at least none that I know of, though I believe him to be a faithful husband."

"If he's delirious, he could be thinking or dreaming of anything. I don't know about you, but when I'm really sick or have a bad fever, I dream all sorts of crazy things, sometimes over and over. I hate it."

"Perhaps you're right, Maestro, but he hasn't yet regained consciousness that I know of. I'm very worried."

"Give him some time, Silvio, and be patient with him. He's only been out for a few hours. God only knows what has befallen him. Stay with Michela; she's very good at nursing the sick and wounded. I'm going to try to scrounge up some food and drink. As far as I know, Tremonti is passed out on the main deck, and it is he who would know where any spare food might be stored. With any luck, we'll be into Brunsbuttel in a of couple hours." Nickolaus headed out onto the main deck. "I'll be back when I've found something."

As soon as Stefano saw the inlet to the docks at Brunsbuttel, he tore off the upper forecastle deck to find Nickolaus and Michela. He was certain they would want to share the satisfaction and exhilaration of finally putting into port for good. He was right. He found Nickolaus in the captain's lounge, snacking on a variety of odds and ends with Silvio, Kurt, and

Aldo, who had finally awakened and managed to scrounge up some food. "Where's Michela?" Stefano asked excitedly.

"She's in with the captain. He's stirring a bit. At least he seems to know where he is now," Silvio reported, clearly relieved.

"That's very good news. Is there any chance Michela might be released to come share our arrival in port with Nickolaus and me?"

Ensign Grether jumped to his feet. "Oh, most certainly, the captain will be fine for now. We're very grateful for all she's done. The captain has been very much comforted by her efforts." Aldo stepped into the captain's chamber to relieve the tired looking Michela from her self-appointed nursing duties. She shuffled out, yawned, and then stretched. Nickolaus stepped over and hugged her tightly.

"We're here, my dear, at Brunsbuttel. We made it back to land, and this time for good, I hope."

"Brunsbuttel? I thought we were going to Hamburg."

"No longer, Signora," Ensign Grether quickly interjected. "The ship is taking on too much water and must be docked and repaired here. We could not make it to Hamburg,"

"But Nickolaus, we have to get to Lubeck."

"I know, my love. We'll get there in time. For now, how about the three of us get out on deck and ride this ship into port?" She thought about it for about half a second then grabbed his hand.

"I'd love to, Nicki, by all means, let's go." They scrambled up to the forecastle deck where Ensign Fuhrmann assigned them to a relatively safe and guarded position next to a high railing and some rigging.

"I'd rather you be tucked safely away in the captain's lounge," he advised. "It's liable to get a bit rough up here when we pull up to the tidal dock, but I suppose you might as well stay up here for the time being." They thanked him then grasped hands and stared out eagerly at the many passing sights that seemed to be personally welcoming them to port.

Entering the harbor at Brunsbuttel was both joyful and revealing, as the thrill of a harrowing voyage at long last complete was slowly but surely overtaken by the sobering recognition of the grim realities of their new home. This was no bright autumn day in Genoa. Instead, the late afternoon air was cold, breezy, and damp, despite the presence of a shimmering, low-hanging sun. Rather than the towering, darkly forested Ligurian Hills that framed the gently rising slopes of Genoa, they were surrounded by endless acres of austere flatlands barely rising above the waterline, along with lonely stands of gray, leafless trees bordering long-since harvested fields and barren tidal lowlands. The grasses were still green, but there was nary a flower in sight. As they passed by the town waterfront into the harbor, the differences grew even more striking. In place of the orange-roofed, bright stucco buildings that graced the tiled streets of Genoa, they spotted narrow, cobbled alleys lined with dark, rustic, wooden structures covered with thatched roofs. Admittedly, there was a certain Saxon charm about it, but it also felt eternally gloomy, as if autumn and winter might last all year long. Nickolaus had thoroughly warned his family of the stark contrasts they would find in the lands up north, but actually being there and seeing the genuine item brought to life made it real for them. No matter, though, they no longer had any choice in the matter. This would be their home now, and they would have to adjust to it and make the best of it. Besides, it might turn out not to be so bad after all.

As they approached the tidal dry dock, the distinct scent of northern wood smoke filled the air. A few moments later, inviting whiffs of steaming sausages, fresh kraut, and baked apple strudel began wafting across the deck of the ship. It was time for the midday meal. The crew perked up immediately. For most of them, this was the smell of home, and it was close. They had just survived what would probably be the most treacherous voyage of their lives. Next would come a welcome and well-deserved period of rest and recovery. Everyone was more than ready.

As the docking grew imminent, Ensign Fuhrmann ordered the Silberbachs down to the main deck where they would be more secure. Nickolaus and Michela had no objection, but Stefano resisted. He was curious to watch what was certain to be a rare and complicated mooring procedure. After a bit of coaxing and cajoling, Fritz finally agreed to allow Stefano to remain on the forecastle deck. The two had grown quite chummy. Nickolaus and Michela looked at each other and shrugged. "Have at it, Stefano," Michela relented as she and Nickolaus climbed down to the main deck.

Once again, a litany of orders began flying around the decks as the sailors sought to steer the ship to a safe and gentle stop, perfectly aligned, and in just the right spot. It appeared as though they were trying to steer the ship into a huge wooden box that had been left open at one end. Nickolaus was extremely concerned that the ship might not fit at all, but after several pokes with the oars, adjustments to the rudder, and an advantageous push from the incoming tide, she slid right into place, suffering little more than a couple of bumps and a thump. There she would stay until repairs and upgrades were complete.

"I'm confused," remarked Stefano to Ensign Fuhrmann. "How can we keep the ship from sinking when it's still floating in ten or twelve feet of water?"

"Ah, the water is there now, my boy, but when the tide ebbs, this dock box will be as dry as a bone. Then we'll close those lock gates at the seaside end, and when the tide returns, the ship will stay high and dry, save for a bit of seepage that we'll pump out. As soon as the keel is resting firmly on the bottom, they'll brace the ship with timbers so she stands upright and secure. Quite clever, isn't it? In some ways, it will be easier here than at Hamburg because the tidal range is greater here."

"Amazing!" Stefano was truly impressed.

As soon as the gangplanks were set in place, Nickolaus, Michela, and Stefano descended onto the pier. Each brought their important personal belongings with them. At Michela's insistence, they immediately headed to a nearby inn for a meal and drinks which, in Brunsbuttel, meant steamed pork, sour kraut, some sort of twisted-up, baked dough called a bretzel, and plenty of beer. Feeling both famished and celebratory, they all ate and drank heartily.

Still aboard *The Paradise*, Ensign Grether woke up Captain Zannaro then sat him up at the side of his bunk. The captain seemed to be feeling slightly better, but still complained of a nagging cramp in his chest and of feeling mortally tired. Even so, he demanded to be taken out to the main deck so that he could check on his ship. A moment later, Heinz showed up, hoping to find the captain well enough to approve certain essential operations. At that point, all orders for supplies and repairs would need to be signed off by the captain himself, as he was still the ship's official commanding officer. "Get me out of here, please," the captain demanded feebly.

"Aye, Sir," Silvio agreed dutifully.

Assisted by Heinz and Kurt, the captain stepped out onto the main deck and scanned his ship. After several seconds of confusion, he grumbled, "Heinz, where are we? What the hell did you do to my ship?" Simultaneously humored and somewhat annoyed, Heinz held back several sarcastic responses that flooded his mind. "Well?" the captain insisted.

"Sorry Sir, here, come this way." They half walked, half carried the captain across the main deck then down the gangplank. "It seems we didn't actually escape the mud flats unscathed after all. It appears we damaged a section or two of the hull near the keel and started taking on water. With your incapacity and my need to keep the ship from sinking, I decided to put in to dry dock at Brunsbuttel. We can discuss the details and our future plans later. For now, let's get you to an inn, so we can put you to bed." Upon reaching the pier, the captain turned around and surveyed his ship. He winced uncomfortably, either for himself or the ship, perhaps both.

"Any casualties?"

"Just a few bumps, bruises, sprains, and burns - nothing that won't heal, Sir."

"Well, she still looks in tact to me, Heinz, very commendable. Good job! Now get me to a bed somewhere before I pass out." Heinz and Silvio rushed the captain to the small inn situated just off the pier. Aldo followed up shortly with some of the captain's clothing and, perhaps most importantly, his medicine. Ensigns Grether and Fuhrmann were left on board with several crewmen to watch over the ship and make certain that its new home was pumped dry as soon as the tide ebbed and the dock gates were closed and sealed.

After an hour or so of hearty eating and Nickolaus downing his fourth and already one too many beers, Heinz and Silvio joined the Silberbachs in the dining hall for some much needed food, spirits, and relaxation. Nickolaus was in an unusually cheerful and friendly mood, even acting a bit drunken at times. When the barmaid came around asking for orders, Michela nodded a very certain no when asked if Nickolaus might want another, and since he had yet to empty the mug in his hand, he let it go without objection. He knew he'd already had too much.

As soon as the officers sat down, Nickolaus began pressing them about plans for the trip to Lubeck. "I don't think we want to talk about that here, Maestro," Heinz responded firmly, glancing pointedly around the room, indicating the possibility of eavesdropping ears.

"Oh yes, Heinz, you're right, of course."

"I can tell you that I discussed certain mutually beneficial possibilities with the captain when we brought him in and put him to bed. He referred me to an old merchant friend of his right here in Brunsbuttel, a man he knows to be able, willing, and trustworthy."

"That's a relief. I imagine it could be quite difficult to make such complex arrangements in a strange land such as this."

Slightly irritated, Heinz shook his head. "There's nothing particularly strange about this land, Nickolaus."

"Sorry, I just meant …"

"As I said, that's enough for right now. We'll discuss it later."

# Chapter 24 – Danish Wagon Train

"Too bad there's not a nice, deep river between here and Lubeck," Heinz lamented. "It would certainly save ships and sailors a hell of a lot of time and misery not having to sail around Jutland with all that extra distance, the passage taxes, the storms, hell, the perils of piracy. It's really quite a burden, you know." He shook his head in frustration.

"There's no use wishing for something you can't have," counseled Chief Grumbach. "Maybe some day there'll be a canal, but not today. In the meantime, you know what you have to do." Heinz winced as he turned around and surveyed the line of wagons that had been carefully assembled for the trip to Lubeck. The transports had been disguised as food and produce carriers and then bannered as *Hanseatic Overland Trade Transport*. Loaded at night using only sailors from *The Paradise*, the discreetly packed trunks of gold had been completely surrounded by the Silberbach's household items and several conspicuously stacked crates filled with the oranges they had picked up in La Coruna. It all looked very pedestrian. Along with his most reliable wagons, the captain's merchant friend, Herr Gunter Buhl, had dispatched his most trustworthy drivers and several armed escorts on horseback. He had also lent the caravan his customized patrol carriage, known across the land as Herr Buhl's Sonderwagen which, along with its driver Johann Ghent, Erik of the Teutonics, and gun master Tjaard Hansen, carried a selection of various handheld weapons, ammunition and, most importantly, a wagon-mounted falconette cannon. The heavily built Sonderwagen brought up the rear of the column. The two other Teutonics were stationed in the second and fourth wagons.

Marco and Vinny had also been commissioned to ride in the first two wagons, as each boasted of both teamster and fighting experience. Much to their chagrin, they had been forced to temporarily suspend their quest for the bounty on Pietro's head when they discovered that the leadership in Papenburg was hopelessly in shambles. They also feared that their proof of Pietro's death, which consisted of his rotting head and a few personal belongings, might not be sufficient to prove their claim to whoever the ruling leader of Papenburg ultimately turned out to be. Furthermore, if the leadership ended up changing hands, the bounty offer might no longer be valid anyway. As additional evidence, Captain Zannaro, Heinz, and several ensigns had signed a formalized document stating that they had all witnessed the man, who they knew with absolute certainty to be Father Peter Von Papenburg, being split apart and scattered in several directions by a direct hit from a cannonball while on board their ship. Marco and Vinny hoped that the combination of the document and Pietro's personal belongings, including his signature Bible, would be ample evidence of their success. The head, of course, would never have made it to Papenburg in any sort of tolerable or recognizable condition.

Herr Buhl had also loaned the convoy his roomy, comfortable, and somewhat lavish coach for Nickolaus, Michela, and Stefano to ride in. That coach was positioned in the middle of the column. Captain Zannaro, who seemed to have accomplished at least a partial recovery, was remaining behind in Brunsbuttel to oversee the repairs and upgrades to *The Paradise*, which he had every intention of returning to Genoa on as soon as possible. Once there, he planned to rejoin his wife and retire in their captain's house in the Ligurian Hills for as long as nature would allow. He continued to use the medicine Dr. Schicchi had prescribed for him, and it seemed to be helping, but it wouldn't last forever, and the provincial doctor in Brunsbuttel had never heard of it, or anything like it. The medicines he recommended were little more than witch's brews. Heinz planned to make further inquiries in Itzehoe, which was a regional capital on their route across Holstein; otherwise, he hoped for better luck in Lubeck.

The exhilaration Nickolaus had experienced upon his arrival in Brunsbuttel was still hanging with him, though it took him a whole day to recover from the monumental hangover he tied on during his first night of drinking at the tavern. After chasing several beers with an unknown number of brandies, he had to be carried upstairs to his room where he slept for over twelve hours. When he finally managed to drag himself out of bed, it looked as though death itself had taken over his body. Finally, by late in the day he was beginning to feel half human again, just in time to head off to the tavern. First, though, he had to attend a meeting with the officers in the captain's quarters.

Stefano, on the other hand, had spent almost the entire day observing and even helping with work on *The Paradise*. He was far more interested in the technical aspects of the repairs, which he approached as if he were an actual shipbuilding engineer, than he was in the day-to-day seafaring considerations that seemed far more important to the seamen. Fortunately, his deep immersion with the crew during the voyage had left him with a fairly decent working knowledge of conversational German and even a bit of competence with Frisian. And the more time he spent around the crew, the more fluent he grew. He seemed to be a virtual language sponge. Michela, however, was not so fortunate. Nickolaus had hoped to familiarize his wife with as much German as possible during the voyage. Needless to say, her condition as well as the nature of the trip itself had left him very little time to teach her much of anything. Her German would have to wait.

During the day, a thick, saturating fog had blown in from the North Sea. With temperatures barely into the forties and daylight from the low-lying sun scarcely able to pierce the deep fog, the weather had cast a hauntingly dark pall over all of Brunsbuttel. It was an entirely new experience for Michela and Stefano. Even Nickolaus was hard-pressed to remember the deeply affecting nature of such damp, penetrating cold. He just wanted to curl up next to the crackling fire at the inn and down a cup of spirit-warming brandy. Just the same, he made his way to the captain's room where he was invited in to sit with the officers. Herr Buhl, a noble gentleman of magisterial presence, appeared to be in charge. Nickolaus immediately perceived Herr Buhl as a man who commanded both respect and power in this small but important provincial community. The men welcomed Nickolaus then continued on with what was, by then, a very nearly completed conversation. A wagon convoy would be arranged, set up the following day, and then loaded that night. They would leave bright and early the morning after next. The plan didn't allow much time, but they were certain they could succeed nonetheless.

As soon as the meeting adjourned, the heavy drinking commenced, at least for Nickolaus. And heavy drinking it was, for the next thing he knew, the morning after next had arrived, and while it was certainly early, it was by no means bright, as the murky fog that had rolled in from the North Sea two days earlier continued to hang over Brunsbuttel like a drapery of gloom. Still, it was time to depart – ready or not.

A bit peeved, Heinz sent Ensign Grether back into the inn to retrieve Nickolaus and his family. Just inside the front door, he found Michela and Stefano all but dragging Nickolaus across the dining hall toward the front door. The Maestro had once again guzzled far too many sweet brandies the night before. Someone had also made the mistake of introducing him to both peach and apple schnapps, not an ideal proposition for a man with an eager sweet tooth and a burgeoning penchant for spirits. By the time he'd been laid out in bed, he barely knew who he was and cared even less.

Michela managed to remain calm despite a bitter combination of fear and anger that she found overwhelming. She also felt helpless, which really put her in a foul mood, at least in her own mind. She wasn't sure what worried her more: the upcoming journey, or her husband's new fascination with alcohol. Just as they reached the doorway, the innkeeper's wife rushed over and handed Ensign Grether a pouch of food and drink for the Silberbachs to take with them. This was fortunate, since Nickolaus had barely even managed to dress and get out the door that morning, let alone eat any breakfast. Michela thanked the frau graciously then pushed her husband through the front door and out into the waiting cold.

"Don't worry, Signora, he'll be fine," Ensign Grether assured her. "A lot of men overindulge after a long journey at sea, especially a voyage as tough as this one."

"Perhaps, but this is not like my Nicolo at all. He generally avoids drinking altogether. It interferes with his moods. But be that as it may, Ensign Grether, I thank you sincerely and wish you the very best. You've been of great comfort to all of us." She wiped a few tears from her eyes.

"My pleasure, Signora, and farewell to you, Master Stefano." The two young men shook hands then touched shoulders.

"Perhaps we'll meet again, Kurt ... uh, Ensign Grether."
Stefano smiled.

"I'd enjoy that, my good man, and Kurt will be fine.
There is no chain of command between us now. We are friends
and comrades."

Upon reaching their carriage, the Silberbach's were
surprised but pleased to find Captain Zannaro out of bed, fully
dressed and, despite both Silvio's and Aldo's strenuous
objections, standing outside in the cold waiting to offer his
personal farewells. Though rarely sentimental, the captain had
insisted on coming out for the Silberbachs, as he assumed they
would not meet up again in this lifetime. A moment later,
Tremonti came around from the rear of the carriage where he
had been working on some provisions.

"I left some stores in the back for you, Maestro. Please,
come around and let me show you." Not all that quick-witted at
the moment, Nickolaus obediently followed Tremonti around to
the rear of the carriage where the cook stepped up and hugged
him. "Nicolo, you know I love you. You've treated me more like
a true friend than anyone else in my entire life."

"You are a true friend. You are dear to me, Paesano."
Nickolaus patted Tremonti gently on the shoulder before
stepping back, suddenly feeling a little awkward.

"You know, Nicolo, I've had some experience with this
type of thing. Don't let it get the best of you. You don't need it.
I've witnessed men like you before. You're letting a monster get a
hold on you that you may never be able to break free from."

"Tremonti, my good fellow, what in God's name are you
talking about?

"The spirits, Nicolo, the spirits. I watched you on board
ship and during the past few days in port. You have to stop
drinking while you still can. It's a special danger to a man like
you. I can tell. I think I could have done away with that poison if
I'd have done it when I was a young man like you, but now ...
well now, hell, I'm helpless against the beast. It cries out to me
whenever I see it. I crave that burning feeling in my gut, and the
warmth and joy it gives me when I've finally had enough, except
there's never enough, and there's always a tomorrow. Look at me,
Nicolo, I'm a mess. I'm hopeless. But you, man, you still have a

215

chance. I know you have your fears and your worries and, uh … your moods, but this isn't the answer, believe me, it's just another demon to battle. Please, Nicolo, swear off the spirits now, today, before it's too late."

Stunned by Tremonti's sincere concern and rare eloquence, Nickolaus tilted his head and gazed intently into his old friend's life-worn, bloodshot eyes for several seconds, trying to think of what to say. A moment later, the spell was broken by the clatter and thudding of men on horses – the mounted guards arriving. "Honestly, Tremonti, I hadn't thought about it as being a problem." Nickolaus nodded and blinked, affirming a new awareness of the situation. "Perhaps I have been short-sided in this regard. I shall give your advice serious consideration."

"That's all I ask, Nicolo, nothing more. Now you take care of yourself … and your fine family, too."

"I will. I promise. Addio, my old friend." Nickolaus nodded then turned and retreated quickly back to Michela and Stefano, who were still sharing farewells with the captain and some of the ship's other crewmen. After hugging the captain, Michela partially released him then gently rubbed his hand for a few moments, just as she had done to comfort him on the ship.

"Take care of yourself," Michela implored with tears in her eyes.

"I'll be fine, dear," he insisted, tugging his uniform back into place with his free hand. "Don't worry, it'll take more than a little chest pain to put me out of service. I thank you for your kind assistance. It meant a lot to me." He lifted the hand that she had been rubbing his palm with and kissed it tenderly. She bowed slightly then quickly turned away only to find Tremonti staring her forlornly in the face. She grabbed him and hugged him tightly, then stepped back and handed him an ornately drawn deck of cards she had acquired at the inn. "These are for you to remember us by, Mr. Tremonti. And thank you for the delicious sweet breads. Thank you for everything." She stood up on her toes and kissed him peckishly on his grizzled cheek. He blushed then wiped away a single tear. Stefano, who had been speaking with Chief Grumbach, turned around and shook Tremonti's hand, thanking him with great sincerity.

Nickolaus stepped up and firmly grabbed the captain's hand. "Thank you for your patience and understanding. Hell, thank you for everything. I can never repay you."

"Yes, yes, you can, Maestro, you truly can. Just make it safely to Lubeck, rebuild your life, take care of your family, and then turn out some of that beautiful music you're so well known for. I shall tell Angelico of our stories when I get back to Genoa. He and your father were very close. It is good that you've returned to your native home. Angelico will be most pleased."

"Board up," ordered Heinz. Nickolaus hastily but firmly shook Chief Grumbach's hand then, along with everyone else, scrambled up to claim a spot and make it as comfortable as possible. Beyond town limits, the roads would be rutted and bumpy, so no one was expecting a pleasant ride. Searching for a hospitable place to sit down, Nickolaus discovered that someone had used several blankets to fashion a well-cushioned spot to lie down on in the back seat of the carriage. Nickolaus felt truly warmed by such a considerate, personal undertaking. He immediately offered it to Michela, who smiled and nodded back at it.

"That's for you, Nicki. The captain said Tremonti made that up just for you." Tears welled up in Nickolaus's eyes – tears he could barely hide as he realized that this was what Tremonti had been working on just before coming around from the rear of the carriage when they first arrived. For a moment, he considered jumping down to embrace his old friend again, but then wisely thought the better of it. He waved feebly at Michela then lay down on the blankets with his face turned toward the rear. He knew he should be thrilled to be on his way; instead, he felt beat up and sick at heart.

As soon as the wagenmeister, Anton Mogensen, confirmed that everything was in place, he gruffly shouted out the final order that sent the wagon convoy on its way. Incoming travelers had reported that the roads were still in very good condition – probably due to the exceptionally dry autumn. On the other hand, several people arriving during the previous week had reported hearing rumors of attacks by highwaymen, though none of them had actually seen any evidence of such activity. The wagenmeister estimated that the trip to Itzehoe would require five to seven hours, depending on conditions. The convoy would need to travel slowly - barely faster than a walk - due to its excessive weight and the necessity of protecting the harpsichords. They had also teamed the horses lightly, hoping to avoid revealing any clues as to the exceptional weight they were carrying. As soon as they started moving, even at their very conservative pace, it became readily apparent that the journey was going to be cold and bumpy. The wagons also tended to rock back and forth due to the ruts in the road, especially the Silberbach's carriage, which was more softly sprung than the others. Needless to say, the endless rocking motions were not at all welcomed by either Nickolaus or Michela, both of whom had less than solid stomachs at the time. Nevertheless, after a short while, Nickolaus forced himself to get up and join Michela near the front of the carriage.

"Feeling a bit better?" she asked.

"Yes, I suppose." He gazed out at the passing scenery for a few moments. "No, not really. I just thought I'd spend some time with you. I miss you."

"I'm glad you joined me, Nicki. What did Tremonti have to say? I saw him giving you an earful."

"Did you put him up to that?"

"What?"

"You know, about the drinking."

"No, certainly not, although I am worried about you."

"So you did put him up to it?"

"No, I said I didn't and I meant it. Whatever he said to you, he said entirely on his own. I wouldn't have someone else do my bidding for me. I was just waiting until we left town to bring it up, or maybe not at all if it eased up a bit. You know it's not good for you, especially with your condition. Haven't the last three days been miserable for you?"

"Yes – and no – I don't know. I love it and hate it at the same time. It feels great when I'm drinking, and it makes me forget most of my troubles, but then it wears off, and I wake up feeling like hell. I've always avoided it in the past. You know that."

"What did Tremonti say to you?"

"He told me to stop drinking right now or I may never be able to stop, that I could easily end up just like him – never able to say no to it."

"Sounds like very wise advice to me." Nickolaus took hold of Michela's hands.

"I'm sure it is, my love. To be honest, I don't know what has so drawn me to it during this trip. It just seems to call out to me. I can't explain it."

"Perhaps you don't have to. The trip is almost over. Just stop and it won't be an issue anymore. It's that simple."

"I'm sure you're right, and that is my intention, I assure you."

"I'm not judging you, Nicki, I just want you to take care of yourself. It's your choice to make. I need you, the real Nicolo, not the silly, half-witted noodle you become when you're drunk. Do you understand?"

"I do, my love."

After about an hour and a half of rocking and bumping, the convoy pulled over and stopped in a clearing by the side of the road. By that time, Nickolaus and Michela had both fallen into a near trance-like state. Stefano jumped right down and headed off for the tall grasses.

"I wonder why we've stopped?" asked Michela.

"Probably to rest the horses and give everyone a chance for relief," Nickolaus speculated.

"Ten minutes," the wagenmeister yelled out, "and not a moment longer." The wagons emptied by shifts, overseen by the mounted guards, who also took turns exiting their mounts. Both Heinz and the wagenmeister insisted that the convoy be actively guarded at all times. Having finally developed a touch of hunger, Nickolaus rooted through the pouch of food and drink the inn had given them. He offered Michela some delicious looking swirled pastries with fruit in the center, which they ate voraciously before washing them down with some of Holstein's finest hard cider. After what seemed like the shortest of interludes, the break was over and they were back in motion.

A couple of hours later, the caravan left the Dithmarschen region and entered the Steinburg district where the city of Itzehoe was located. Contrary to what Heinz had feared, border stops with demands for passage fees or transport taxes were nowhere to be found. Heinz was duly relieved until Anton informed him that there would be a stop at the Stor River Bridge in Itzehoe. "That's where they get you, Commander, at the bridge. You want over the river, you pay the proper tolls and the bridge is yours." Heinz's frowned. "Don't worry, Commander, they know me there, and with your man's passage document from King Christian, we should be fine."

"I certainly hope so," Heinz replied worriedly. After traveling another ninety minutes, the convoy unexpectedly slowed to a snail's pace. A disabled wagon with no draft animals in sight was blocking the road almost entirely, although it would have been possible to get around it with some degree of difficulty. Vinny, riding in the forward wagon, ordered Heinz to signal the wagenmeister to stop the convoy immediately. It looked to him like a perfect set-up for an ambush. Having served as both driver and bodyguard for Bishop Caravaggio, Vinny had developed an acute sense of awareness over such matters, and he was always on guard.

"Are the men and weapons ready to defend?" Heinz asked Anton.

"All but the cannon, but it is always ready to be loaded." Vinny spoke Genoan, Latin, and decent Spanish, but barely a word of German or Frisian, so Heinz did all of the talking.

"Send a horseman up each side of the road and have them check carefully for everything - horses, people, anyone hiding in the bushes, anything suspicious." Vinny was taking no chances. Back in the second wagon, Marco had already drawn his sword and laid it down beside him on the driver's bench. Neither man would step off his wagon until the safety of the convoy had been secured.

"It may just be a broken down wagon," Anton suggested peevishly. "Tell your driver this is a safe district. They keep tight order around here."

"Just the same," Heinz insisted, "I'd rather be sure."

"It's your convoy, Commander," Anton relented, begrudgingly sending a mounted guard up each side of the road, just as Vinny had recommended. Although both men proceeded slowly and appeared to be cautious, Vinny was not at all convinced they were being as thorough as they should be. Near the disabled wagon, the horseman on the right suddenly stopped. He stared into the brush for a several seconds, exchanged words with someone, then turned around and rode back to the wagenmeister.

"Off to the side of the road in the tall grasses, there are two men, a woman, a couple of children, and a tent surrounded by their belongings. They say it's their wagon blocking the road."

"They're probably stranded, waiting for someone to help," Anton suggested.

"Let me send a couple of my men up with your horsemen to check things out," Heinz proposed, turning to Vinny. "Vinny, do you want go forward and see if you can get a sense of things?" Vinny nodded, applied the wagon's brake, and then climbed down. Heinz shouted back to Helmut and Erik, who spoke both German and Frisian, and ordered them to join the entourage. Not sure what was going on, Nickolaus jumped down and then helped Michela climb off the wagon as well. Stefano, who had been riding with Marco in the second wagon, also jumped down and walked back to talk to Nickolaus. Suddenly people were at risk.

"Let's rest for ten minutes while we check this out, then we'll get moving again," Anton barked crossly. "Keep a sharp eye out, men, we aren't in a very defensible position right now." Having developed a strong familiarity with wagons and tools while serving as an army carpenter's assistant in Corsica, Marco decided to examine the situation for himself. He jumped down and sheathed his sword, but when he began walking toward the stalled wagon, Anton snarled, "Hey, where the hell do you think you're going? You need to stay with your rig."

Marco pointed ahead. "I'm going up to take a look at that broken wagon. Maybe we can fix it."

Heinz translated the statement to Anton, who shook his head defiantly. "Tell your man we aren't a charity service; we're a convoy. Leave them be. Someone will eventually come along and help them out."

"Sir, on the sea we don't leave ships or men in distress to fend for themselves."

"How about pirate ships?" Anton countered acerbically.

Heinz tilted his head and glared at the wagenmeister, confused about what he was referring to. "I have no idea what you're talking about. These aren't pirates; they're a family of travelers."

"Well, this isn't the sea, Commander, but since it is your convoy, I suppose this time I'll let it go." Anton brusquely waved Marco forward then rode back to the rear of the column where he began talking quietly to one of the mounted guards.

Marco stepped forward and inspected the stalled wagon carefully, shaking and poking at various things here and there. "The hitch yoke is jammed. I think we can fix it, but I need some help from the Teutonics."

"How long?" Heinz queried.

"Maybe half an hour." Heinz made some quick computations in his head.

"Do it, Marco. There's still plenty of time to get to Itzehoe. We're spending the night there anyway. Can you do it with just Ludwig and Helmut? I want to leave Erik back in the Buhlswagen just in case.

"They'll do. I just need an iron lever and a mallet."

"I'll ask Anton about it, but he'll probably just dish me up another ration of horseshit."

"No doubt, but that's his problem."

"Yes it is. I'll get you what you need, Marco. Just do the job quickly, and if anyone complains, refer them directly to me." Heinz rounded up Ludwig and Helmut, who were both fairly handy as well, and sent them forward to work with Marco. After stretching a bit, Erik rejoined gun master, Tjaard Hansen, at the rear of the Buhlswagen.

"I wouldn't worry too much about the wagenmeister," Tjaard confided. "Old Anton's been riding around like he's sitting on piles for a week now." Tjaard laughed loudly then punched Erik in the shoulder with his fist, which was a bit like punching a rock wall. Sharing a Frisian upbringing and dialect, Tjaard and the Teutonics had quickly established a friendly relationship. Tjaard, who had learned his gun master skills while serving aboard a Swedish warship, was highly adept at loading and firing cannons under tight and bumpy conditions. After a chance meeting with Herr Buhl in Brunsbuttel, and being very much sick of the sea, he signed on to this most unusual post with Buhl's Hanseatic Overland Trader Shipping. He was fairly satisfied but also underutilized, as his position was more a matter of posturing than actual fighting. Still, Herr Buhl paid well and the job was uncommonly safe for a gunner; more importantly, it was not at sea, so Tjaard was content with his lot.

At one point, while Marco was working on the wagon, an aristocrat's carriage drew up rapidly from the rear. Showing no signs of slowing down, the driver seemed intent on blowing right past the whole bottleneck, which was undoubtedly the smart and safe thing to do. Unable to resist using the opportunity to hone his skills, Tjaard excitedly grabbed Erik's hand and asked him to assist. With Erik's help, Tjaard spent the entirety of the carriage's approach aiming and re-aiming his falconette until it was almost upon them. Then, at just the right moment, he feigned lighting it off before falling backward and making a very loud KA-PLEWEY sound with his mouth. "Got you, you rich son-of-a-bitch," he shouted out through his laughter. Not quite sure if Tjaard was crazy or simply board, Erik chuckled politely then helped his companion back to his feet.

"Now that's not something you see everyday," Erik muttered with a smile.

"What? Do you have some kind of problem with it?"

"Not at all, Tjaard, we're just having a little fun, eh." Erik punched the gun master back lightly in the arm, almost knocking the smaller Tjaard to the floor of the wagon. The men had come to a meeting of the minds, and Tjaard now understood who was dominant.

While Marco and the Teutonics worked on the stalled wagon, Nickolaus, Michela, and Stefano strolled along the side of the road, munching on snacks, always staying very close to the convoy. Michela was relieved that the drinking issue had finally been brought into the open, and she believed that her husband's acknowledgment of the problem was a huge step forward. No longer a big secret, she felt free to bring it up if he appeared to be slipping. Nickolaus, who had begun feeling progressively more human as the day wore on, was comforted by the compassion and acceptance Michela had shown on the matter. She had always been his most reliable and devoted supporter. Unfortunately, the better he felt, the more he could feel his resolve to remain sober waning. Soon he began to fantasize downing a nice, cool schnapps or two, preferably peach, at the tavern when they reached Itzehoe – not much, not enough to get drunk, just enough to make him feel normal, or maybe slightly better than normal. However, he kept those notions to himself, since he knew such conduct would only serve to betray Michela's kindness.

As they approached the jammed wagon, it was obvious that Marco and the Teutonics were having difficulty. Despite an abundance of clanking, pushing, clunking, groaning, and swearing, nothing was moving. Stefano looked on with curiosity, remembering Chief Grumbach's advice, "If you find yourself forcing something too hard, then you're either doing it wrong, or you're trying to stick it in the wrong place." Stefano was still confused as to why the chief had snickered and elbowed him in the side when he said it, but it seemed to make perfect mechanical sense, so he'd taken it to heart.

Stefano turned to Nickolaus. "Do you think I could take a look?" Nickolaus immediately recalled Stefano's impressive display of technical jargon and apparent mechanical aptitude.

"I don't see why not."

"Just be careful," Michela warned maternally.

Stefano stepped up to Marco. "Do you mind if I slide under there and take a look?"

"What?" Marco snapped, frustrated by his lack of progress.

Nickolaus edged forward. "Stefano wants to take a look. He's small and has a keen eye. Why don't you give him a chance, Marco?"

"No disrespect intended, Nico, but the boy's got the silky soft hands of a nobleman and the mushy mind of an artist. What could he possibly see under there that we haven't?" Watching the discussion from a short distance, Heinz stepped up.

"Give him a chance, Marco, looking at something with a fresh set of eyes never hurt anything."

"Oh, all right, Stefano, go ahead and take a look," Marco conceded skeptically as he and the Teutonics reluctantly moved aside. Nickolaus truly hoped that Stefano would find something, if only to show up his cocky friend.

Stefano ducked under the wagon and looked closely in several locations from different angles. "Marco, come here, I think I see something." Marco slid under the wagon. "Look here, that bracket bolt has slipped part way out of the wagon and imbedded itself in the yoke. That's why it won't move. If you don't clear that bolt, you'll just break the yoke trying to jam it free."

Marco poked around a bit. "God damn, Steffy, you're right. Christ, you are handy after all. Glad I invited you in. Now clear out so I can get the big guys in here to fix this thing up." Marco nodded his approval. "Great find, Paesano."

Stefano smiled. "My pleasure," he replied, sliding out from under the wagon. Relieved to be vindicated, Nickolaus winked at Stefano as the young man stood up and stepped clear. They all moved back and watched as Marco and the Teutonics went to work. After about five minutes of clinking, clunking, cursing, and a loud thump, a yelp of joy emerged from beneath the wagon. Marco and the Teutonics swiftly moved to the front of the wagon where they grabbed the freed yoke and swiveled it back and forth in a gesture of victory.

"Now all we need is a horse," Ludwig proclaimed. The man who owned the wagon rushed forward and shook hands heartily with Marco and the Teutonics, lavishing them with words of praise and thanks, none of which Marco understood.

"Your horse," Ludwig demanded. "Where is your horse?" A moment later the other man with the group wandered up to the wagon leading an ox.

"No horse, just an ox, but she's a good ox," he announced simple-mindedly.

"That'll do nicely," Heinz declared. Marco and Ludwig quickly set to work helping the man hook the ox up to the wagon. Moments later, the sleepy animal pulled the wagon over to the side of the road, safely out of the way.

"Load up," shouted Anton. "We've got to get moving right away." The Teutonics hastily began helping the family reload their belongings.

Heinz shook his head then glanced over at Nickolaus and Michela. "Our wagenmeister has quite the special way with people, wouldn't you say?"

"It's sorrowful, if you ask me," Nickolaus replied disgustedly. "He's about as caring as a prickly pear. And thank you, Heinz."

"For what?"

"For helping these poor people out," Michela explained. "I didn't think we should just leave them here."

"Nor did I, and we didn't. You should go find your places now. Good work, Stefano."

"Thank you, Sir," the young man responded, beaming with pride as he led Nickolaus and Michela back to their wagon. A few minutes later, the convoy was off and moving again, leaving a very grateful family waving their heartfelt thanks as it pulled away.

# Chapter 25 – Party Time

Racing against November's limited daylight, the convoy spent the next three hours traveling as rapidly as possible trying to reach its destination before dark. Itzehoe, an ancient regional capital, finally came into view just before four o'clock. Everyone was exhausted despite the relative ease of the day's journey compared with what it could have been. The convoy planned to spend the night at a carriage inn near the edge of town where both horses and people could safely be accommodated at reasonable prices. The inn seemed a bit rustic to the Silberbachs at first, but it turned out to be pleasantly comfortable just the same. Heinz made sure the wagons were parked in a block formation and closely guarded. Anton claimed the extra precautions weren't necessary, but Heinz was adamant, insisting, "It's my responsibility and reputation on the line, not yours, Sir, I'll do as I see fit." A mysterious animosity seemed to have erupted rather quickly between Heinz and wagenmeister.

After settling in to their small, modestly furnished room, Nickolaus took his leave to check out the neighborhood while Michela rested for a while, at least that was what he told her. Stefano headed off to the inn's dining room to find something to snack on. Despite having been specifically warned by Heinz to stay at the inn, Nickolaus decided to take a stroll along the rugged sidewalks that lined the shipping district of Itzehoe. He had no particular purpose in mind except, perhaps, finding a bit of privacy. After passing several dark, unremarkable shops, he crossed the street and headed back toward the inn. A short way along, he chanced upon a humble tavern where he noticed light from a crackling fire gleaming through a quirky stained glass window that graced the front façade, almost as if it were a tiny church.

Unable to resist its warm, beckoning invitation, he stepped inside, seeking a cup of hot tea, or maybe some other spirit-lifting beverage. However, it was a tavern, not a café, so tea would have been an unlikely item to find on the menu. He took a seat and, after a brief internal debate, ordered some peach schnapps. He simply couldn't resist. Then he ordered a second. Soon he began feeling very good, but also guilty, so he ordered a third, after which he began to feel a sense of righteous indignation that anyone would question his judgment over the matter. After about forty-five minutes, he threw back the last few gulps of a fourth schnapps then, sporting a fool's grin, slipped out the front door and headed back down the sidewalk.

Just as he was about to cross the street back to the carriage inn, he happened to glance down a narrow alley where, through the dimming twilight, he spotted Anton the wagenmeister talking in animated whispers with two other men – a clergyman of unknown denomination, and a rough looking character that reminded him of the thuggish men he used to see meeting with the corrupted Father Raimondo back at Saint Matthias in Genoa. After a few moments, the would-be pastor suddenly pointed toward Nickolaus, which caused Anton and the other man to turn around and stare at him as well. Feeling significantly light-headed, Nickolaus smiled, waved slightly, then quickly turned away and crossed the street. He wasn't sure what any of it meant, but his instincts left him feeling concerned over the affair.

Upon he reaching the carriage inn, he immediately grabbed a mug of hard cider – the everyman's daily beverage of Itzehoe – then climbed the stairs to meet with Michela for dinner. Served fest style in the crowded dining hall, guests would either eat when served or not eat at all. As tired as she was, Michela spruced herself up a bit and then headed down to the dining hall, suspicious the whole time that, despite their earlier conversations to the contrary, Nickolaus had overindulged in the spirits once again. But she was sleepy, and he smelled mainly of cider and fruity wood smoke, so she let it go for the time being, hoping that her perceptions might be flawed.

Within a few minutes, the Silberbachs and the rest of the convoy members were hungrily spooning away at Stamppot (mashed potatoes with sauerkraut), ham, and dumplings in gravy, all washed down with generous mugs of the local brew. With Michela's ready blessing, Stefano joined Marco and Vinny in the opposite corner of the dining hall where the three of them would later play cards with two of the wagon drivers from the convoy.

It was a delicious and comforting meal, though somewhat heavy for Michela's fragile stomach.

After about ten minutes, Anton strolled in - by himself - apparently having concluded whatever business he had been engaged in with his two cronies. Upon seeing the wagenmeister, Nickolaus was immediately reminded of his earlier sighting in the alley, which he then resolved to inform Heinz of as soon as possible. After loading up his plate and filling his mug to the brim, Anton sat down near the serving bar and dug in, stopping only occasionally to tease or, more accurately, harass one of the serving maids with whom he seemed to be particularly interested. It appeared to Nickolaus as though the two had a history, a history that seemed amusing to Anton but not so much so to the overworked bar maid.

Once Michela had downed all she wanted, which wasn't very much, Nickolaus helped her back up to their room and then returned to the dining hall to find Heinz. First, however, he had the serving maid dish him up a nice slab of apple strudel before stepping over to the bar to obtain a mug of peach schnapps, indeed, a double serving. He then invited himself to sit down next to Heinz, who had just finished his meal. "Heinz," Nickolaus whispered loudly, "any luck with the captain's medicine?"

"No, I didn't have a chance to look for it. To be honest, I didn't hold out much hope for finding it here."

"That's unfortunate. Perhaps you'll have better luck in Lubeck." Nickolaus slid a little closer. "Heinz, I don't know if this means anything, but before dinner I saw Anton having what looked like a very serious conversation with a pastor and a rough-looking character over in the alley across the street."

Heinz turned to him, frowning. "What were you doing over there? I asked you to stay here where it's safe. You know how Genoa is down by the wharf at night? Well, that's what kind of neighborhood this is." Nickolaus felt ashamed but also insulted that he was being scolded like a child. He was also growing quite drunk.

"I just wanted to get out and be by myself. I'm sorry," he offered curtly. "Just forget I said anything." Nickolaus started to stand up, but Heinz gently pulled him back down.

"No, I'm sorry, now what was it that you were saying about seeing Anton in the alley?" Nickolaus repeated what he had seen, explaining that the light had been very dim, and that the three men had all noticed him staring at them. "Odd, very odd. Did they say anything to you?"

"No, I just waved briefly before moving on, and that was the end of it."

"That sounds damned peculiar to me. Why would Anton be meeting with men in an alley rather than right here where he's staying? I don't like this at all, Nickolaus. I have to confess that I'm none too fond of Anton, though I can't say for sure why. There's just something about him. Thank you for telling me. By the way, is that schnapps in your mug?"

"What, you too? How much I drink is my own damned business and no one else's."

"Good Lord, Nickolaus, I only asked because it smelled so good. Now I want some for myself. Pardon me for saying so, Maestro, but you seem a bit touchy this evening. Maybe you should call it a night and get up to bed."

"My apologies, Heinz, I thought you were referring to … oh, forget it. I'm going to go over and sit by the fire for a while. I'll see you first thing in the morning. Good evening, Commander."

"Yes, same to you, Maestro." Feeling both troubled and confused as he watched Nickolaus sit down in a chair near the fireplace, Heinz stepped up to the bar and ordered a small mug of peach schnapps before returning to his seat to ponder the worrisome meeting between Anton and the two other men. By the time Heinz decided to head upstairs to his room, Nickolaus, who had spent most of the evening putting on quite the eclectic floorshow, was laid out sloppy drunk next to the fire. Once again, Heinz ordered Eric and Ludwig to help the Maestro up to his room and into bed. Momentarily cross, Michela rolled over almost immediately and fell back to sleep.

The next thing Nickolaus knew, Michela was shaking him silly. "Get up, Nicki, get up now. We're going to be late. They're probably already waiting for us. Damn you," she grumbled, pulling helplessly at her husband's floppy arm. Michela seldom swore, so she had either been influenced by the sailors or she was very angry.

"What? What is it, for God's sake?" Nickolaus groggily rolled over and opened his foggy, bloodshot eyes. "Michela, what do you want? What happened?"

"You tell me. You said you were going hold back on the spirits, and now I wake up and find you like this. I don't know what to say ... or ... or what to do, but I know you have to get up and get ready to leave. Right now!"

"Oh, my Lord," Nickolaus mumbled as he painfully pulled himself up and sat at the side of the bed. He burped then gagged slightly. "Oh, my God, what a headache. I think I'm going to die. Damn me."

"Well, what do you expect? Do you even know how much you drank?" Nickolaus stood up unsteadily then, after nearly overwhelming the chamber pot, clumsily began dressing.

"To be truthful, my dear, I don't even remember how I got up here."

"It was Heinz and a couple of the Teutonics – again. Good lord, I can't even imagine what Stefano thinks of your drunken antics. Truly, Nicki, I don't know how to deal with you when you're like this. Do you have any suggestions?"

"I'll stop. I told you I'd stop and I will. I promise."

"Promises are what you make to your priest when you're trying to get out of the confessional. I don't need promises. I need ... we need you to stop. In all honesty, I don't understand where this came from so suddenly, first on the voyage, and now this, this ... whatever this is. It's not like you, Nicki, and you know it. You've always avoided spirits in the past because you never know what they're going to do to you." When he was finished dressing, Nickolaus splashed some water on his face, rinsed his mouth out, and then headed downstairs with Michela in tow, lugging their overnight belongings in a canvas bag. He felt like he'd spent the night hanging upside down over a still.

Heinz, Marco, and Vinny were seated in a corner engaged in furtive conversation. They looked grim and intense. Nickolaus flopped down on a bench while Michela served up some scrambled eggs, ham, and pastry on a single plate for them to share. Nickolaus wobbled over and acquired a sizable mug of hard cider. He was very thirsty and the modest amount of alcohol in the drink would help quell some of his hangover jitters. Pressed for time, both ate very quickly, which was not the best thing for either of them, but it seemed to be the way of the road, so that was what they did.

A few minutes later, Gertruda, the wife of the family-owned establishment, walked into the dining hall from the kitchen and began gathering up plates and spoons left by the patrons. When she spotted Nickolaus, she quickly made her way over to his table. "That was quite the show you put on last night, Maestro. Your man's got a nice set of pipes," she excitedly told Michela, who shook her head in dismay while staring angrily at her husband.

"Oh, it wasn't much. I just sang a few old tunes, nothing special. I don't even remember it all that well."

"Well, I do," exclaimed Gertruda. "You had the guests clapping and laughing and singing their hearts out. I'd like to have you put on a show every night. That'd really spice things up around here." Feeling like a total fool, Nickolaus blushed as he stuffed his mouth full of eggs, hoping to avoid answering for his forgotten evening of roadhouse showmanship. As Gertruda walked off, Michela turned to her husband and looked him straight in the eyes.

"Now if that doesn't make you want to stop drinking, I don't know what will."

"Christ almighty, Michela, I barely recall it. It's like a big hole in my memory. I can't believe I would do something like that in public. I'm not that kind of singer."

"But you do sing well, and you are a performer at heart, so you shouldn't be surprised at having put yourself out like that, especially considering your condition at the time."

"Well, it won't happen again. I'm through. I feel like hell, and I've made myself into nothing but a source of ridicule, as if I were some cheap street act or an alley burlesque singer. Lord, what an ass I've been."

"Feeling sorry for yourself won't solve anything, Nicki. Forgive your transgressions and move on. Today is another day - make this one right."

"I will. I promise, my love."

Michela softly kissed her husband's reddened cheek. "We'll see," she hedged. A moment later, Anton stepped in and shouted out the departure warning. Nickolaus shoveled the rest of the eggs into his mouth then gulped down as much cider as he could swallow. On the way out, Michela stuffed a few pastries and some bacon into their travel pouch.

Stefano met them at the door. "I thought I was going to have to come in here and pull you two out again. Anton is really in a foul mood this morning. He claims he won't wait for anyone."

"To hell with Anton," Nickolaus growled. "This is our damned parade, not his. Who the hell does he think he is?"

"He thinks he's in charge of moving the convoy, and he's basically right," advised Stefano.

"Well, that doesn't make him right about everything," Michela protested as the three of them crossed the street and climbed onto their wagon. "Lord, I'm not looking forward to another day up here," she complained, puffing up some blankets and pillows to soften her seat.

"Better than heaving up and down on the open seas all day, my love."

"You've certainly got a point there, Nicki."

Up ahead, after receiving Anton's final order to move out, Heinz, Marco, Vinny, and the Teutonics parted ways to find their places, each looking back, nodding knowingly at each other. Heinz halted for a moment.

"Erik, are you certain we can count on the gun master?"

"Tjaard will do what's right if we need him. I'm sure of it."

"Good," Heinz acknowledged as he turned and hustled over to his rig. Oblivious and impatient, Anton shouted the order to move out then waived the convoy forward. It was another cold, foggy morning, but at least it was still dry – quite amazing for November in Holstein. After just a few minutes, they had passed through much of Itzehoe and reached the bridge over the River Stor, a small tributary of the Elbe. This was where Anton had warned that either his personal influence or Nickolaus's passage document might be necessary in order to avoid undue taxes, tolls, penalties, inspections, delays, or some combination thereof. As the convoy pulled up near the gate and stopped, Anton rode ahead to the gatehouse where he dismounted and began conversing in a familiar manner with the crossing guards.

"Here we go," mumbled Heinz to Vinny. "I'm sure they'll find some excuse to search the wagons or impose some cockamamie fee."

"Maybe, but I see Anton smiling," Vinny whispered. "Look, he just handed something to one of the guards. Hey, what's that damned pastor doing there? What the hell? Are they going to try to impose some kind of church toll, too? Vaffancullo, bastardo," Vinny hissed.

"Not so fast, Vinny. They just shook hands. Now Anton's on his way back with a smile on his face."

"Well, maybe there's hope after all."

When Anton was within earshot, Heinz asked him if they needed Nickolaus's passage document. "Not necessary, Gentlemen, I used my pull to get us a pass. We need only pay the bridge transport toll and we're through."

"Do you need some money?"

"Already taken care of, courtesy of Herr Buhl. You can buy me a mug or two this evening. It's going to be a long day. I plan to reach Bad Segeburg by this evening, even if we have to travel after dark. There's a great place to hold over there, and then a short day to Lubeck tomorrow." Anton rode back to the Silberbach's carriage at the middle of the caravan and yelled out the plans for the day so that everyone could hear. As soon as he was finished, he motioned the convoy forward. Marco shot a questioning glance forward to Vinny, who tilted his head while holding his hands out in a gesture of perplexed acceptance.

As soon as the convoy began moving, and he was sure Anton was out of range, Heinz turned to Vinny. "Anton suddenly seems to be in uncommonly good spirits, don't you think?"

"I'll say, too good if you ask me. I don't trust him."

"Nor do I, Vinny. Let's just move forward as though everything is as it seems. We'll assume the best but stay prepared for the worst." Deep in thought, Vinny passively nodded as he resumed closely surveying his surroundings.

# Chapter 26 – Teaming Up

Even though the road ahead was supposedly smoother and straighter than that of the first day, the second day of travel promised to be far more punishing. Anton made it clear from the outset that he was determined to reach Bad Segeburg by that evening no matter what the cost. At a distance of nearly thirty-eight miles, the convoy would have to push at its best possible speed for seven or eight hours, and that assumed everything went as planned.

Suffering from a hellacious hangover, Nickolaus dropped down on the bed in the back of the carriage as soon as it started moving. Michela insisted on sitting upright and looking forward out the window, as it seemed to calm her pregnant morning stomach. Their carriage driver, Hans Wagner, who seldom spoke but often smiled, proved to be a very skilled coachman, constantly initiating small, gentle swerves that somehow managed to maneuver the carriage around many of the worst ruts and bumps.

Throughout the entire morning, Anton kept the convoy moving at four or five miles per hour, which was almost dangerously fast for such heavily laden wagons riding over a provincial country road. Around lunchtime, the convoy rolled into Bad Bramstedt where it stopped to feed and water both people and horses. Having finally sobered up to a tolerable state of cognition, Nickolaus suddenly realized that the tough-looking character he'd seen speaking with Anton and the pastor in the alley the night before had quietly taken the place of one of the four original mounted guards. He told Michela right away then hustled over to inform Heinz. Upon hearing the news, Heinz glanced over at Marco and Vinny and nodded slightly. "Thank you, Maestro, your keen eye is most appreciated. It may be nothing, but I'll ask Anton about it just the same. I think we should know who we're working with." Heinz's calm was only an act, for he was actually quite concerned over the unexplained overnight change in personnel, especially given the circumstances. Accordingly, as soon as he was finished with his meal, he slipped over and sat down next to the wagenmeister. "Anton, I noticed you replaced one of the mounted guards this morning. Was there a problem?"

Anton blushed, cleared his throat, and then found his voice. "Oh, yes, I meant to talk to you about that. Gerd was suddenly called back to Brunsbuttel. His father fell very ill. They sent Erwin Niedstedt with the message and to work in his place. Erwin is a very good man, believe me." Anton looked over at Erwin and waved. Erwin looked away, then back, then waved uncomfortably, and then looked away again. "I've worked with Erwin for many years. There's none better, trust me." Whenever a speaker followed a statement with the words "believe me" or "trust me," Heinz assumed there was a good chance they were being deceptive.

"Ah, so that was the purpose of your rendezvous in the alley last night." Anton grimaced slightly, remembering that Nickolaus had spotted them in the alley the night before during their private parley. He stewed silently for several seconds, seemingly flustered.

"Uh … yes, and we contacted a pastor to comfort Gerd. Yes, yes, Gerd is very close to his father, you know."

"A pastor?"

"Why, yes, Commander, I'm sure Nickolaus saw him with us last night."

"Right, the Maestro did mention that." Heinz crooked his head slightly. "But if Gerd was already rushing back to Brunsbuttel, why was the pastor still hanging out with you and the new man in the alley?"

Anton stared hard at the ground as he spoke. "Oh, uh, we're old friends, Commander, just talking over old times. You know how it is."

"Hmmm, I see. Well, good then, I hope Gerd got back home in time to help out."

"Oh, I'm sure he did. By the way, Commander, we'll be leaving shortly, so you should begin gathering up your people."

After lunch, Nickolaus switched places with Stefano, taking a seat beside Marco. Stefano stepped back and rode in the carriage with Michela who, having grown tired, decided to take advantage of the makeshift bed in the rear of the carriage. Mainly due to Nickolaus's shifting moods and Marco's constant guard duty, the two lifelong friends had barely managed to spend any time together during the sea voyage. For about the first hour and a half, they shared memories of earlier years while also recounting some their experiences and impressions of their time spent aboard *The Paradise*. Marco suddenly turned serious. "Nicolo, I know this is a touchy subject, but I'm going to wade into it anyway. I'm truly beginning to worry about your sudden love of drinking. It's not like you at all. Not long ago, it was you scolding me about drinking too much. You wouldn't even rent me your apartment for fear that I might damage it. Now, my boy, I'm afraid it's you who's acquired an over-fondness for the spirits. Wouldn't you agree?"

"Damn it, Marco, did Michela put you up to this?"

"What? No! What are you talking about? She's been very patient with you - a lot more patient than Vinny is with me."

"You're absolutely right, Marco, she's been very understanding about it, except that I don't really see it as a huge problem, do you?"

Sighing, Marco's eyes bulged out slightly. "Well, maybe not so much now, but you have to admit that it could easily grow into something serious and life-changing pretty damn soon, like maybe yesterday. You've really been in to it over the last several days. Do you even know how drunk you've been at times? Well, I sure do, and I've been there myself, on far too many occasions."

"Tell me, Marco, how did you manage to stop?"

"You mean this time? There've been several."

"Yes, how did you do it?"

"Well, this time around, Vinny told me if he found out I'd been drinking anything other than a sufferable amount of hard cider or beer, he'd beat me down and then fire me."

"Truthfully?"

"My oath on it, Nico, but I'm not sure how seriously I take his threats anymore. I could probably put him away long before he ever hurt me much. Lord knows he's got at least twenty-five years on me. And at this point, he's not exactly in a position to fire me, since the only job he has to offer is parked back at Bishop Caravaggio's villa in the Ligurian Hills. I suppose if and when we return to Genoa, we could carry on with our livery service, but who knows? We might just be arrested the moment we step ashore. None of that matters anyway. I just keep his well-intentioned threats in the front of my mind as a reminder, and he is my friend, so I abide by his rules. Besides, I know he's right. I just don't like it. Either way, thinking that way helps me to stay off the spirits."

"God dammit, Marco, I don't know why I've started drinking so much. I really don't. I know it feels good, and it relieves my nerves for a while - I mean, you know how bad my nerves can get - but then I feel like hell. I know it's wrong, but then I do it anyway. Michela hates it and so do I, and I know I have to stop. I guess I'm just sort of floating right now. It felt safe for a time, but it doesn't anymore. Does this make any sense to you?"

"Hell, yes, Nicolo, you're preaching to the choir." Having shared years as choristers, they looked at each other and smiled at the inside joke. "Well, Nico, at least you're being congenial about it. As I recall, I was pretty much of a horse's ass."

"That you were, my friend, but at least you had good reasons for your excesses. What excuse do I have?"

"I think we both know the answer to that. Between your shifting humours and all you went through in Genoa, it's a wonder you haven't been soused up for months."

"I did start drinking a lot on the ship. There it was, right in front of me, and I had nothing to do, and I felt so bleak and melancholy, so I used it as a salve. You know, Marco, it really doesn't work very well for that."

"I know, Nico, it never does, but that doesn't stop a man from trying. We are who we are. We always think this time around will be different, but it never is. And for those of us who thirst for it most, there's always some damned reason to drink. Hell, you know that as well as anyone."

"You know, Marco, every morning I solemnly promise myself that I'll stop, but as the day wears on, my determination seems to disappear. Then late afternoon and evening roll around, and it just feels right. I swear it's like an evil spell."

"Damn right to that, my boy. Listen, Nicolo, once we get to Lubeck, you'll probably be able to put things back the way they were. Normal times will strengthen you, give you some stability."

"I hope so."

"In the meantime, just do your best and …" Marco suddenly stretched forward and began squinting ahead. "What is that up there? Is that another wagon blocking the road? Do you see that, Nico, just past where that smaller road forks off and runs down into that ravine?"

"Yes, and there's a man standing next to it, just waiting. I wonder what Heinz thinks of this?"

"I'm sure we'll be finding out soon enough. Stay sharp."

A couple of hundred feet or so before reaching the parked wagon, Anton motioned for the convoy to pull to a stop. He turned somewhat awkwardly toward Heinz and Vinny. "Hold up here. I'll find out what's going on." He nodded at Erwin Neidstedt, who accompanied him forward to the man standing next to the stalled wagon. Once there, the three men conferred quietly with dour faces, and then a few chuckles, which seemed a bit out of place. After a few minutes, Anton headed back toward the convoy, leaving Erwin with the stalled wagon and its driver.

"There's been a bridge failure up ahead. We're being diverted down that smaller road for a short piece, then we'll rejoin the main road just past the bridge. It shouldn't cost us much time. I'll go tell the others." Anton rode back to the middle of the convoy and shouted out the new orders.

Still seated in the front wagon, Vinny turned to Heinz. "What the blazes is this? That seems horribly suspicious, don't you think?"

"That's an understatement, Vinny. We aren't going anywhere until I check this out. In the meantime, slip back and tell Marco, Nickolaus, Stefano, and the three Teutonics to be prepared for trouble. Be subtle about it. Tell them to behave like a gang of happy innocents so that none of Anton's men will suspect anything. And most importantly, tell them to follow the lead wagon – our wagon – no matter what. And if we get way laid, tell them to follow Marco's wagon and then the carriage. Also, arm Ludwig and station him in the carriage with Michela and Stefano. I want both of them well protected. And last but not least, speak only Genoan - the chances of any of these provincial Holstein folks understanding Genoan are virtually nil."

"Capisco, Comandante." Vinny slid off the right side of the wagon then quickly made his way back through the convoy alerting the others of possible trouble.

After conferring briefly with two of his mounted guards, Anton drew forward and stopped at the front wagon. "Hey, where's Vinny?"

"He went over to relieve himself. He'll be back in a minute. What can I do for you?"

"We're turning down that side road and he's the driver of the lead wagon. Where is he?"

"Relax, I told you he'd be here. I have to say, Anton, this seems highly unusual. How could a bridge go out in this kind of weather? Are you sure you can trust that man up there?" Anton was obviously taken aback by Heinz's mounting suspicion. He looked forward toward Erwin at the wagon, and then turned back to Heinz.

"Of course I trust him. That's Wolfgang Dorn. I've known him for years. The Duchy pays him to watch over the highways. Believe me, if he says the bridge is impassable, then you know that it is, I can assure you of that. He has full authority to close and reroute highways. Don't worry about it, Commander, I've been through this before. Trust me."

"I think I'll go up and talk to Mr. Dorn myself," Heinz declared as he climbed down from the wagon and began walking toward the highway master.

"No, no, that won't be necessary," challenged Anton sternly, stepping directly into Heinz's path. "We need to get moving right away so that we can beat the darkness." With bodies poised for conflict, the two men stared threateningly into each other's eyes for several seconds. But just as the nascent standoff was about to explode, Nickolaus, who had stepped down from the second wagon to relieve himself, suddenly flew around to the front of the lead wagon to warn Heinz of a new realization.

"Heinz, I must speak with you right away," Nickolaus insisted, nodding his head backward. "It's very important, Commander." Sensing Nickolaus's state of alarm, Heinz immediately withdrew from the standoff, temporarily staving off the fight.

"What is it?" he whispered.

Nickolaus pulled Heinz to the right side of the wagon, out of Anton's sight. "The man up at the stalled wagon is the same man I saw dressed as a pastor in the alley last night."

"What? Are you sure?"

"Absolutely certain, Commander, it's the same man. I don't know for sure what it means, but I think we have no choice but to treat this as some kind of an ambush. I suspect if we turn down that side road, we'll not come out at the other end, if there even is an other end."

"I agree, Nickolaus. I'm glad you were alert." Heinz leaned in and began speaking very quickly and clearly. "Maestro, slip back to other wagons and tell Marco and the Teutonics that a betrayal is in progress – probably an ambush. They'll know what to do. Tell them that something, though I know not what, could happen at any moment. Keep a low profile and speak only Genoan. Vinny is off warning them now to prepare for something unexpected. He's also telling them to keep it light-hearted, so don't be surprised if you find them acting a bit jolly. If you run into to Vinny, tell him to come back up here right away – armed and ready. Make it quick, and when you're finished, join Marco in the second wagon. Can you drive, by any chance?"

"Vinny taught us to drive a team when we were teenagers. It's been a few years, but I'm sure I can handle it if need be."

"I know you can, Nickolaus. Now smile, laugh a little, and then get to it." Nervous though determined, Nickolaus headed off down the right side of the convoy. Heinz climbed onto his wagon to keep an eye on the exchange between Anton, Neidstedt, and the supposed highway master up at the barricade wagon.

"My sister wants to know what the hold-up is," Stefano shouted up at Heinz from the left side of the wagon, having run forward from the carriage. Startled, Heinz instinctively grabbed the truncheon he kept hidden behind the seat and poised it to strike at Stefano.

"Dammit, Stefano, you scared the hell out of me. Don't sneak up on a man like that unless you mean it. I almost bashed your face in." Heinz relaxed slightly then grinned. "I'm glad I didn't. Now climb up here and sit down next to me, then smile when I talk to you, and don't look around."

"What?"

"Just do as I say." Heinz's tone instantly put Stefano on notice, so he jumped up onto the wagon and sat down. "There's not much time, so listen closely." Heinz quickly apprised Stefano of the situation and their plans to deal with it. "Now go back to your carriage and help your sister take cover in the back – it's the most protected spot in the carriage. And it wouldn't hurt if she slid under some covers until whatever this turns out to be is over. You would do best to take cover yourself, but knowing you as I do, I suspect you won't, so stay low and don't try to be a hero. By the time you return to your carriage, Ludwig should already be there, armed and ready to fight. Also, the driver always carries a sword and a club up front with him. I can't say whether he knows how to use them or not, but I'm almost certain he'll support us. Got all of that?"

"Yes, Sir."

"Good, now laugh a little and then head back to the carriage. Buona fortuna, Stefano."

"Si, mio amico."

A few moments later Vinny slid up and laid a loaded, long-barreled handgun known as an arquebus onto the floor of the forward wagon.

"Do you know how to use that thing?" Heinz whispered.

"Tjaard taught us how this morning when he was showing them off."

"Are there any more of them?"

"Three more - each of the Teutonics has one."

"Do they know how to use them?"

"I hope so. We were all together this morning. Also, I sent Ludwig to the middle carriage as you ordered. He has an arquebus and a club, but I'd wager his size and determination are his most potent weapons."

"He is a brute. What about Tjaard?"

"He says he's with us, but he doesn't have a clue as to what's going on. I'm almost certain that Hans, the carriage driver, and Wilhelm, driving the fourth wagon, aren't part of any conspiracy."

"Let's hope not, Vinny. I'm not sure about the two mounted guards back on the left, but I'm assuming they're part of whatever this is going on here. And the falconette?"

"No use in close quarters like this."

"It's kind of a strange thing to carry, don't you think?"

"Tjaard says there are constant turf wars going on in this territory. Herr Buhl likes to be prepared, if only by way of posturing. Tjaard looks to be a skilled and experienced gun master. Add in your strategic abilities, Commander, and I bet the two of you could turn some heads with that dainty little piece of artillery."

"I suppose so, Vinny, but right now it's time to get down to the business at hand."

"Right, Commander, so here's what I saw: Neidstedt is forward with Anton and that character at the barricade wagon. Dolph is over there on the right, standing beside his horse, staring down the detour road. God only knows what's on his mind, but after speaking with him for a while last night, I'm guessing not very much. The other two horsemen are on our left, one near the second to the last wagon, and the other hanging back about fifty feet behind the convoy. I don't know if they're part of any ambush or not, but they both seem damned suspicious to me, and Anton did station them there. We have to assume they're part of whatever this is. At the moment, no one seems to be paying any attention to the right side of the convoy."

"And that is where we'll make our moves if and when they become necessary. How is Marco with his sword?"

"Damned good, and with his dagger, too. He's a trained and experienced soldier. He survived the Corsican campaigns and that's no small accomplishment."

"I'm impressed, Vinny, then he'll do fine without an arquebus."

"He's probably the best fighter here, Commander; besides, you only get one shot with the arquebus, then it's back to swords and knives.

"How about the Teutonics; they're big men with naval skills, but can they shoot?"

"I don't know, Commander, but they certainly look threatening either way. I noticed Anton carries a knife and an ax, and he also has a sword strapped to his mount."

"I certainly wouldn't consider all those weapons to be part of his daily regular. He's set for a fight, no doubt about it. My concern is that we don't have a plan."

"How can we form a plan when we don't know what's coming? Hold on, it looks like Anton and Niedstedt are heading this way. This is could be it."

"Let's keep our wits about us, Vinny."

Marco had already moved his wagon slightly forward and to the left in order to gain a clear view past the front wagon. Heinz leaned out of his wagon and looked back. Marco nodded that he was ready.

After swaggering across the breach, Anton marched up to the forward wagon and barked, "We've confirmed the problem, now let's move these wagons down the detour road. Just follow Dolph; he knows these roads like the back of his hand, believe me." Anton headed toward the rear of the convoy, erroneously assuming that his orders would be followed without question.

"I guess we know Dolph's involved," Heinz whispered to Vinny out of the corner of his mouth. "That makes at least six of them against four of us and Nickolaus."

"And Johann, the Buhlswagen driver, he's with us," Vinny added.

"I'm sure the carriage driver can be trusted. He's Herr Buhl's longtime coachman. And Dirk, driving the fourth wagon, he's also a veteran driver. He's not part of any highway gang."

"You know, Commander, there are probably men down that detour road waiting for us. My gut tells me that these guys are just here to move us down into that gully where we'll meet up with the rest of the gang. That's the God damned plan, I'd swear to it."

"Well, you know what, Vinny, we aren't going down into that gully. And you can be sure that when they hear a ruckus, or get a signal, or hear an arquebus fire off, they'll be up here before we can spit. We'd better be ready for that. If we could just get Tjaard to load up that falconette and lob a cannonball into whoever comes up out of that valley, I'm sure it would set them back a few paces."

"It's already loaded. I told him I wasn't exactly sure what we could do with it, but since he never gets to use it, he chose to take my warning as an excuse to load it up. It's ready to go, Commander, and so is Tjaard, maybe too ready."

"Well, damn, Vinny, that's a bit of serendipity."

"A bit of what?"

"Never mind, it's a word Nickolaus uses. It means I'm glad the cannon's ready and waiting to be used. Damn, it looks like they're planning to go through with this. Now listen, Vinny, when they give the order to move, that's exactly what we'll do, except we'll put on as much speed as we can, and when we get to the detour, we'll keep going straight, pass around the barricade wagon, and then head straight down the highway toward Bad Segeburg. We'll just have to fight back at whatever they come up with to try and stop us."

"I'm with you Commander. I drive – you shoot – I prefer to use the blade. Give the word and I'll take off. I just hope the others follow."

"Anton just climbed on his mount. Get ready. Wait for him to give the order to move – and – there it is – let's move!"

As soon as the front wagon began rolling, Anton rode forward and took a spot at the left side of the convoy between the first and second wagons. Neidstedt abandoned the barricade wagon and took Dolph's position about twenty feet down the detour road, planning to ride closely in front of the lead wagon. Within moments, all five wagons were in motion. The detour road split off to the right about seventy-five feet before the spot where the barricade wagon was positioned. Vinny pushed his horses as hard as he dared, pressing the wagon to gain as much speed as possible. Marco knew to keep pace, as did the carriage driver, who always stayed in tight formation during convoy situations. It instantly became apparent to Dirk, driving the fourth wagon, and Johann, driver of the Buhlswagen that they, too, had better follow closely behind the others. By the time the lead wagon reached the detour cut-off, all five wagons were tightly bunched, moving rapidly in virtual lockstep right past the detour road toward the barricade wagon, which they swerved around before heading straight down the main road toward Bad Segeburg.

Caught completely off guard, Anton was forced off the left side of the road into a stand of tall, tangled grass, which caused his horse to grind to a sudden halt before rearing up and dumping its surprised rider back-first into the tangle. Meanwhile, Dolph was headed down the detour road without bothering to look back to see if the convoy was even following him. The third mounted guard, to the left of wagon number four, then raced forward to assist Anton, but he too was forced off the road into a trough filled with stones and grass where his horse decided that its best move was to light out at full speed across the fallow field next to the road. With the wagons speeding by in close formation, Neidstedt was in no position to spot Anton's predicament until the convoy was already past the detour road and well on its way around the barricade wagon. At the very last second, the highway master tried to push his wagon in front of the oncoming convoy, but it was too heavy to move, so he screeched and howled as loudly as he could, attempting to spoof the horses. That also failed.

Suffering from marked nearsightedness, it took Neidstedt several seconds to realize what had happened to Anton. As soon as he saw Anton climbing slowly to his feet while also calling out for his horse, Niedstedt turned and screamed at Dolph, "Get your dumb ass back up here or I'll cut your damned head off." Dolph, always a bit slow and increasingly annoyed by the near constant stream of insults from his comrades, decided to take his own good time rejoining the rest of the gang up at the main road where the regrouping was already in progress by the time he got there.

Once the rider taking up the rear of the caravan saw what was going on, he decided to prod his horse as swiftly as possible up the right side of the convoy, not realizing that he would be cut off by the barricade wagon. But being shocked and confused, he headed up the right side of the road anyway - straight into an ugly heap of briars and rubble that had been gathered up from the cabbage field next to the road. The horse tripped through several feet of the prickly debris until it ground to a sudden halt, throwing its rider head over heels into the briar patch.

As soon as Anton managed to get to his feet, he ran over to his horse and blew the signal horn that he kept lashed to the back of his saddle. He then tried to remount his horse, but the animal was so badly frightened by all of the commotion, that it refused to stand still long enough to allow him to climb on. By that time, the mounted guard whose horse had sped out across the field was finally returning to rejoin the gang.

Meanwhile, the convoy, still in tight formation, was racing as rapidly as possible down the highway, knowing full well they had almost no chance of outrunning Anton's contingent. In response, Heinz and Vinny decided to focus on finding a defensible position where they could stop the wagons and strategically deploy men and arms against the robbers as they approached from the rear. "What the hell do you suppose was waiting for us down in that gully?" Heinz shouted to Vinny over the din of the speeding wagons.

"I figure a well-armed pack of thieves."

"No doubt," Heinz agreed sourly.

"We really need to find a wall or a hedge to pull up behind, Commander."

"Vinny, up ahead, is that the bridge that's supposedly out?"

"That must be it. Christ, that may not be much of a bridge, but there's not a damned thing wrong with it either. I suppose we shouldn't be surprised."

"No, I would say not. You know, Vinny, if we can get the wagons over that bridge and then park the Buhlswagen directly in the middle right at the entrance, we'll have an excellent fighting position. Those brambles at the edge of the gully are going to force them to use the bridge unless they want to take a big risk of losing their mounts. I doubt if they're that reckless. All right, let's do it, Vinny, it's all yours!"

"I hope the other wagons follow our lead, Commander. This isn't exactly a well-trained regiment, you know." Heinz leaned out of the wagon, stared straight at Marco, and then made a slow, sweeping downward motion with his arm and hand wide open, a signal often used on *The Paradise* to indicate a slow down. It was the only thing he could think of to do. Looking back even farther, he saw several mounted men chasing up the road behind them. The large space between the two groups indicated to Heinz that the robbers had run into difficulty regrouping before they could get back on the move, but that gap was closing rapidly.

"They're coming, and they're moving up behind us damned fast," Heinz exclaimed.

"Is there enough time to make the bridge, Commander?"

"That's up to you, Vinny. You're the lead driver. We're all counting on you."

"Well, then, I better get to it."

# Chapter 27 – Fireworks

The wagons generated an ear-splitting racket as they raced in close formation across the overburdened bridge. Given the extreme weight of the convoy, it was a miracle that the bridge didn't collapse completely, but there were never more than two wagons crossing the span at any one time, and they passed over so quickly that the stone structure was able to hold the weight with nary a creak or a groan. Fortunately the convoy's alert drivers managed to slow down in near perfect concert with the lead wagon, though the horses seemed none to keen about being jammed up and cajoled so aggressively. Vinny managed to stop his rig almost precisely where he wanted it before handing Heinz the reins and then jumping off the wagon. After directing the other wagons into position, he tore back across the small bridge as fast as his aging legs would carry him. The Buhlswagen had stopped right at the edge of the bridge, creating a nearly impassable roadblock. Just as he reached the rear of the Buhlswagen, its reinforced rear hood suddenly flew open, revealing the ominous barrel of the loaded falconette, ably manned by its trigger-happy gun master. It was a moment Tjaard Hegseth had dreamed of for years.

A moment later, Erik jumped out and rammed a set of heavy, custom-cut wheel jams under the front of each of the rear wheels. He then reached in and pulled out two additional jams, which he slammed into place at the back of the rear wheels. It was rightly a job for two men, but Erik handled it like an expert. "Vinny, run forward and steady the horses. We're going to fire the cannon in a few seconds," Erik shouted as he swiftly pulled himself back up into the Buhlswagen. Without pausing, Vinny shot forward and grabbed the reins of Albert and Bauser, the two hefty draft horses that had faithfully led the team pulling the heavy Buhlswagon for several years.

Ka-BOOM! The cannon spewed forth its sizzling, two-pound, iron ball of death directly toward the rapidly approaching horsemen. The Buhlswagen rocked forward violently, looking at first as though it might smash into the horses, but the hefty stabilizers held firm as the wagon rebounded back and forth several times between the wheel jams. The horses whinnied and snorted a bit, but never moved more than a few inches out of place. They had been well trained to maintain their positions. Vinny peered around past the rear of the Buhlswagen, hoping for the best.

Tearing headlong into an oncoming cannonball was absolutely the last thing Anton and his ragtag band of thieves expected to encounter at that moment in time. Nevertheless, there it was, without any warning, finding its mark with astonishing accuracy. In fact, it was nothing less than a bulls-eye hit, striking Erwin Neidstedt directly in the chest, instantly transforming him into a human battering ram as he slammed backward into one of the gully horsemen that had taken the first position behind him. Both men hit the ground directly in the path of Dolph, whose horse tripped over the carnage, dumping its shell-shocked rider into the ditch next to the road. The big man landed on his head and never moved again. The cannonball then ricocheted diagonally across the highway, forcing the second gully man off the road into some brambles where his horse threw him to the ground and then took off running. The broken and bloodied rider immediately pulled himself up, but after thinking about his circumstances for a few moments, quickly turned around and began limping back down the road toward Itzehoe on what was sure to be a long and painful journey.

"There's only four of them left," Vinny shouted. "Only a gang of fools would keep after us now. Let's see if can't convince them to stand down." At just that moment, Heinz showed up at the rear of the Buhlswagen.

"What the blazes, Vinny, who gave the order to fire that cannon?"

"Tjaard took it upon himself, Commander, and from the looks of things, I'd say he made a premier command decision, wouldn't you?"

"Spot on! Well done, Tjaard. Now we've got to convince the rest of these idiots to give it up before any of our people get hurt." Heinz, Vinny, Erik, and Tjaard watched anxiously as the four remaining horsemen suddenly ground to a stop about two hundred paces behind the Buhlswagen. After maneuvering their jittery mounts into a muzzle-centric circle, they embarked upon an angry and disjointed squabble over who was to blame and what they should do now that their plans had been shot to hell. It rapidly became apparent that the third gully man was furious with Anton for having misjudged the readiness and resolve of his convoy targets.

"God dammit, Mogensen, you told me they'd fold like dough. Now does that look like dough standing over there with their guns and swords just waiting to punch holes in us?"

"Listen, Woepert, I'm not a common thief like you and your gang. I told you I'd deliver them wherever you asked, and I did. I warned you this detour plan wouldn't work. If you think these people are as dumb as you are, then you might want to consider finding a new profession."

"Go to hell, Mogensen. This is all your fault. Don't try to lay the blame on me. Look at those men you brought. Dolph is as dumb as a brick, and those other two guards of yours ride like they just saw a horse for the first time yesterday. Where'd you come up with this band of fools, anyway?" Suddenly, Daag Hansen, one of Anton's remaining guards, spurred his horse forward.

"Hey, far be it from me to interrupt your dispute, but I suggest we either attack right now, which looks to me like an act of lunacy, or turn tail and get the hell out of here as fast as we can. Either way, this damned bickering is of no benefit to any of us. Also, if you take a look behind you, you'll notice that your decision had better be a quick one." The four men turned toward the Buhlswagen where they spotted Tjaard standing proudly next to his reloaded cannon, holding its lit firing stick in his hand. Marching down the road and approaching rapidly were Heinz, Vinny, and Marco - each with swords drawn, and the two oversize Frisian guards, Helmut and Ludwig - each pointing a loaded arquebus straight at the pack of thieves.

"Let's try to keep the peace," urged Heinz. "We can handle this like gentlemen. There's no need to get people killed for nothing. Now drop your weapons and surrender. We'll make it easy on you, I swear."

Mounted guard, Daag Hansen, suddenly turned his horse away from the Buhlswagen. "I don't give a damn what the rest of you do, but I'm getting out of here right now. And you'd better not turn me in, or I'll find you and cut your balls off, you stupid sons-a-bi …" His words trailed away as he raced off down the road.

"I guess that pretty much settles it," Anton declared. "This whole God damned thing is over. Let's get the hell out of here." And with that, Anton, his fourth mounted guard, and the third gully man all took off as swiftly as their horses would carry them. Unable to resist a perfectly good opportunity to shoot at something, Tjaard grabbed his arquebus and aimed it as close to the right side of the rapidly retreating contingent as possible. He had no intention of hitting anyone in the back, as he felt to do so would be both cowardly and criminal. Providently, a wayward ricochet nicked the hoof of the gully man's horse, causing the frightened animal to slide off the road briefly, throwing its stunned rider into the rubble-strewn trough at the edge of the road. Apparently uninjured, the rider-less horse tore off down the highway chasing after the others.

"Oh, how the mighty have fallen," taunted Vinny, chuckling as he and Marco marched up and stood imperiously over the fallen bandit. "This oughta give us a chance to find out who the hell's actually running this miserable pack of thieves. What say you, Marco, a nice round of Genoan-style interrogation for this sorry piece of trash?"

"Sure, why not? That's the best way I know to get to the truth." Marco abruptly poked the point of his sword directly against the gully man's lower back. At the same time, Vinny leaned over and twisted the thief's arm upward against his neck, setting off a sadistic back-and-forth of pain and torture that was certain to extract information from anyone. Anyone, that is, so long as they spoke Genoan.

"Hey, you two, hold up on that, right now," Heinz ordered firmly. "I'll not tolerate any of that inquisitional horseshit under my watch." Vinny nudged Marco in the side.

"Well, what do you expect us do? Are we supposed to shove some sauerkraut under his nose, turn our backs, and then break him down with that frigid silent treatment you Saxons are so fond of?" Vinny and Marco both snickered." Heinz grinned and nodded.

"Not bad, Vinny, but I can assure you there are plenty of brutal methods of torture up here, too. Neither the Germans nor the Danish are particularly well known for their patience or hospitality toward their prisoners. That being said, I do not approve of torture as a method of extracting information, so I suggest we first try standing him up like a man, and then asking him directly for the information we seek. Perhaps he'll choose to spare himself a grand ration of pain and suffering and just give us some straight answers instead."

"Hell, Commander, what's the fun in that?" goaded Vinny. "He's ours now, and he's got the information we need. If you ask me, he deserves whatever he gets." Heinz glared sternly at both Vinny and Marco. "Oh, all right, Commander, have it your way." Vinny released his grip on the gully man, winked at Marco and Heinz, and then stepped back a few paces. He'd been posturing all along without appreciating the fact that his target couldn't understand a word he was saying.

"That's better, men. We'll try it my way first, and if that doesn't work, you can whip up a batch of your famous Genoan wedge cake for our wayward friend here." Heinz pulled the gully man up, brushed off his coat a bit, and then grabbed him tightly by the collar. "Make it easy on yourself, mister, or I'll let those two have their way with you after all. Now what's your name?" The man stared at Heinz with silent impudence then sighed a big waft of very foul breath.

"Swenhardt, Hermann Swenhardt, what's it to you?"

"Good, that's good. Now let's just keep this nice and friendly, Herr Swenhardt. So who was in charge of this attack?"

"Why should I tell you? What difference does it make now? You broke it all up. We're finished. Why don't you just let it go, and while you're at it, let me go, too?" Vinny and Marco watched impatiently, understanding very little of the conversation other than Swenhardt's insolent tone.

Vinny edged forward. "Shall we take over now, Commander?"

"Nice try, boys, but not yet. Listen, Swenhardt, how about if I meet you halfway?"

"What does that mean?"

"If you tell me who's in charge and who's involved, I'll let you go. You can climb on one of your horses and ride away so long as you head east toward Bad Segeburg and swear not to rejoin your friends."

"Friends? To hell with them. I plan on heading over to Saxony, as far away from those bastards as I can get."

"All right then, you have nothing to lose and everything to gain if you just tell us what we need to know." Swenhardt looked around at his captors, then the ground, then the sky, then back down the road from whence he'd come.

"You swear to uphold your promise?"

"Listen, Mister, I'm a commander in the Hanseatic Maritime League, I will do as I say."

"Then it's a deal, Commander." Swenhardt put out his hand, which Heinz reluctantly took hold of and shook." Vinny grumbled a few unintelligible epithets under his breath then grudgingly re-sheathed his sword.

"Well, let's hear it, Herr Swenhardt. And you'd better be truthful."

"Dorn, Wolfgang Dorn is ... was the head man, the main force behind the plan."

"The highway master with the wagon?" Heinz asked incredulously.

"Yes, Sir. He's known as The Priest among the lowland commoners of Holstein. He's little more than a common thief nowadays, but at one time, he was a respected priest."

"That's impossible to believe, Swenhardt, you can do better than that," Heinz insisted.

"No, it's the truth, I swear. When Luther's followers forced the Catholics out, he turned rogue - claimed he was trying to recoup some the losses suffered by good Catholics at the hands of thieving Lutherans. I'm sure none of the Catholics who lost anything ever received so much as a penny from Dorn's thievery, but he's grown into a legend just the same." While Swenhardt related his story, Vinny and Marco were busy scanning the horizon.

"I wonder what happened to Dorn, anyway?" Vinny wondered aloud. "I didn't see him around during any of this brouhaha." Heinz overheard the comment.

"Where is Dorn now?" he demanded of Swenhardt.

"Right after the convoy blew around the barricade wagon, he took off, wagon and all, and headed down the detour road. He damned near ran us down when we were coming up from the gully. He's probably standing around at the bottom of the hill waiting for us to show up with your wagons full of gold."

"That seems damned cowardly to me. Where I come from, a captain never abandons a ship before his crew. That's a serious dereliction of duty. A sea captain could go to prison over a gutless act like that."

"Well, this isn't the sea, sailorman."

Heinz shook his head in disgust. "That's not the point, Swenhardt. It's damn low anywhere, even for a common thief. Why do you follow such a spineless bastard?"

"I've been with him for a long time now, and for a man with my skills, he offers the only game around. Besides, if I try to leave, he'll have me hunted down and killed."

"Got yourself in a bit of a stew, eh? Well, Herr Swenhardt, what I want to know is how he came to know about the nature of our cargo."

"You mean its value?"

"Yes, they came after it as if it were the Holy Grail. How did they even know what we were carrying?"

Swenhardt threw his head back mockingly. "Huh, some idiot cook's mate from your ship told us about the gold during a confession with The Priest. Or maybe I should say that The Priest tricked the information out of him. From what I heard, it wasn't much of a challenge."

"Ugh, it was that damned Martinello," Heinz related disgustedly to Marco and Vinny. "How did that young fool even know about the gold? Only the officers and a few of the crew knew about it."

"It had to be Pietro," accused Marco angrily. "He had his hands in everything, and he had a personal and financial relationship with someone at the Bank of St. George in Genoa, but most of all, he was an unrepentant thief. That bastard couldn't do a single good thing to save his soul."

Heinz turned back to Swenhardt. "How, when, and where did Martinello manage to find The Priest to confess to?"

"You've got it backwards, sailorman. The Priest found Martinello, not the other way around. He has a special way of discovering these kinds of things." Swenhardt grinned smugly.

"How's that?"

"I'm not sure, but I know The Priest has a brother from Papenburg who is also a priest. Peter, I think. I heard the brother was living somewhere in the Italian states, probably Genoa from the looks of things." Swenhardt chuckled. "Anyway, once The Priest found out what was in those wagons, he knew it was worth taking whatever risks were necessary to get his hands on it. As for Anton Mogensen, he's been crooked for years - Herr Buhl just never recognized it. Big man Dolph will do just about anything he's told. The other two mounted guards, Daag Hansen and Sjord Falsgraf, simply fell to the temptations of greed. Gerd, the mounted guard they sent home, turned out to be an honest man. When they realized he'd never go along with the plan, they replaced him with Neidstedt, who was planning to join up with us all along but got held up in Brunsbuttel for reasons that I'm not privy to. To be honest, I'm not sure why they didn't know of Gerd's loyalties in the first place. Anyway, they sent him back to Brunsbuttel by telling him a lie about his father dying. Damned clever, eh?"

"Damned cruel, if you ask me," countered Heinz.

"I swear that miserable Pietro is reaching out from the grave to have his revenge on all of us," griped Vinny after hearing the translation. "Well, to hell with him, because it didn't work."

Heinz turned back to Swenhardt. "If you knew what we carrying, how many good men we had, and how well armed we were, whatever led you to believe that you could get away with this? It seems like a damned fool's errand to me."

"Maybe so, but we almost succeeded, so I suppose it wasn't that far-fetched after all. Let me ask you, Commander, just how much do you think that gold you're carrying is worth?"

"I don't know. I'm a mariner not a banker."

"The whole of this duchy couldn't hope to parlay that much gold in a decade. I can promise you that."

"Come on, Swenhardt, the Maestro couldn't possibly be that well set."

"Oh, I'm sure he has plenty, but it was mainly the gold of the Bank of Saint George that attracted our attention. Apparently the cook's mate told The Priest that his sponsor, Father Pietro, had spoken several times about a huge portage of the bank's gold being transported on board your ship. I'm not sure how this Pietro character came to know of it, but we figured he must have had an inside contact at the bank." Heinz shook his head in disgust, spit on the ground, then turned to Marco and Vinny and relayed the information.

"That God damned Pietro," grumbled Vinny. "I don't know how, but he probably set those pirates out after us too."

"I'm sure he did," agreed Heinz. "He's no doubt the brother of The Priest."

Vinny shook his head. "What a bastard! He could have gotten us all killed."

"Thank God his scheme caved in on him," Marco declared.

"I'm still not satisfied," Heinz objected, turning back to Swenhardt. "How did your people find out about us in the first place, and how did they put this plan together so quickly? Listen, if I think you're holding out on me, I'll turn you over to those two. Remember, your freedom and your life are at my prerogative."

Swenhardt scratched his head intensely then adjusted his manhood. "I've told you everything I know. What do you want from me?"

"I want to now how The Priest knew to set this up. For God's sake, man, it's that simple."

Heinz stepped back. "Okay Vinny, bind this idiot's wrists and tie him to the back of the fourth wagon." Vinny and Marco both smiled then stepped forward as Vinny tugged a sturdy leather strap from beneath his cloak.

"All right, all right, give me some time to think, for Christ's sake." Swenhardt rubbed his chin and stared up at the sky. "All right, The Priest found out about it from the crew of that ship you damn near blew out of the water outside the Elbe. He only met with Martinello to confirm the story. He didn't trust the pirates enough to go ahead without checking it out for himself."

Heinz turned to Marco and Vinny and nodded. He felt personally vindicated for having recommended sinking the pirate ship rather than setting it free, as the captain had ultimately insisted upon. "Well, boys, it was that son-of-a-bitch pirate ship we let go. Somehow members of the crew contacted The Priest. I knew we shouldn't have let those bastards get away."

Swenhardt stepped back a pace. "Are we through here? I need to be on my way."

"Not a chance. I want to know how to find Wolfgang Dorn, and how your group intended to escape with so much gold. I need details or I can't tell whether or not you're telling me the truth, so let's hear it, man!"

Swenhardt looked up and down the road a bit then spit on the ground next to where Heinz had just spit. "The Priest moves up and down the Elbe between Brunsbuttel and Hamburg by boat, usually disguised as a common fisherman, but the men at his side don't look particularly handy with any damned nets. That's where you'll find him. Neidstedt, The Priest's right hand man, was on that pirate ship you should have sunk. He made his way straight to Brunsbuttel. I'm afraid you let the wrong people get away, Commander. Not so smart after all, eh?"

"I'll say. And what were you going to do with the wagons? Speak up, man."

"There's a little known wagon trail off the detour that leads to a side road that goes directly to the Elbe. The Priest's boat is tied up there. We were going to deal with your people and then take off with the gold wagons. By the time anyone thought to look for us, we and the gold would be long gone."

"What do you mean when you say you were going to deal with us?"

"To be honest, Commander, I don't really know. I'm not sure whether they planned to tie you up down in that ravine and leave you there, or shut you up permanently. Most of us just wanted to tie you down and leave, but Neidstedt and The Priest are pretty damned brutal. They love hurting people. They get pleasure out of it."

"How lovely of them." Heinz shook his head. "Well, then, Neidstedt definitely got what was coming to him. I have to say, Swenhardt, those friends of yours are quite the dregs of humanity, aren't they? Oh, never mind, now describe Dorn's boat and give me its name." Swenhardt crossed his arms and pursed his lips in defiance. Vinny snapped his leather strap, as if it were a whip. "Well?" repeated Heinz.

"Oh, to hell with them. It's a clean, red fishing boat named Die Rote Henne. They keep it neat as a pulpit and adorned with a hanseatic trade banner. No one would suspect a thing unless they boarded it, and no one would do that if they ever caught sight of its crew."

"Was Anton planning to go with them? He's an outlaw now; he has no future in the company of honest men."

"Oh, he was planning on joining them all right, at least for a while, but they'd probably just assume kill him and take his share of the gold rather than worry about him mucking things up. He might just discover later on that he has a conscience after all, which would make him quite a problem."

"I doubt that. He struck me as a remorseless jack ass."

"Maybe so, but that's none of my concern anymore. Can I go now? I'd like to get a fair head start on you and your men."

Heinz looked questioningly at Marco and Vinny, both of whom shrugged their shoulders. "All right, Swenhardt, as far as I'm concerned, you've complied with my conditions. You're free to go, but I hope you realize just how lucky you are to have been granted this reprieve. Don't squander it. I'm giving you an opportunity to turn your life around. Use it wisely, man. Now get the hell out of here, so I can stop looking at you."

"Gladly, sailorman." Swenhardt limped back down the road a ways then climbed onto Dolph's horse, which was grazing peacefully next to its apparently dead rider. As he rode forward past the convoy, he waved mockingly. "It's been a little bit of pleasure, gentlemen. I hope I never have to see any of you again. Auf Wiedersehen!"

"Bastardo," Vinny hissed. "Well, the light's burning, Commander, I suggest we get these wagons moving so we can get to Bad Segeberg and tell the authorities what happened here."

"What about the corpses?" Marco asked. "We can't just leave them here like this."

"We've neither the time nor the space to deal with them right now," Heinz stated coldly. "Besides, it's probably best to have the constables see them where they fell. Are we sure that big fellow is dead?"

"Oh, he's dead all right," confirmed Ludwig, just then returning from having checked out the various casualties strewn about the highway. "His head was smashed wide open on a sharp rock. His brains are lying on the ground." Everyone grimaced. "The other two are just as dead - blood and guts everywhere."

"Wonderful. Thanks for the fine detail, Ludwig."

"Well, he asked, didn't he?"

Marco shook his head in dismay. "Commander, if we leave them here, won't their bodies be scavenged by morning?"

"Possibly, but I'm afraid that's how things will have to be. Anyway, those bastards deserve whatever they get."

"I say we get the hell out of here right now," implored Vinny, seemingly a bit spooked.

"Aye, Vinny, and the sooner the better."

# Chapter 28 – Bent Expectations

Bad Segeberg may not have been a worldly city, but it was the most cosmopolitan town on the road to Lubeck. After pushing as hard as possible for the next few hours, the convoy rolled into the ancient burg at twilight. Because of his personal relationship with Herr Buhl and his exceptional knowledge of Holstein's roads, carriage driver Hans Wagner quickly fell into place as the new wagenmeister, though Heinz retained overall command of the mission. Having acquired near hero status among the travelers, gun master Tjaard Hansen suddenly found himself swimming in newfound respect and prestige.

Bringing up the front position as the convoy approached Bad Segeberg, Hans Wagner led the group to an upscale carriage house where the wagons and horses could safely be consolidated and the travelers put up in near luxury lodgings, at least compared with those of the previous eve. It took a couple of hours for Nickolaus and Michela to calm down after witnessing another stunningly violent and nerve-shattering encounter. However, by the time they pulled up to the carriage house, their shock and anxiety had given way to a great sense of relief, and then to outright giddiness. Rightly or wrongly, they felt as if they had finally cleared the last hurdle in their long journey from Genoa to Lubeck.

After settling into their overnight lodgings, Nickolaus, Michela, and Stefano headed to the dining hall where they met up with the rest of the victorious entourage. There, in the presence of friendly souls, scrumptious food, and plentiful libation, Nickolaus's well-deserved sense of joy quickly morphed into a massive personal celebration, which, for him, meant drinking ungodly amounts of schnapps – his favorite poison – until he barely remembered where he was or what he was celebrating. Not wishing to badger her husband, Michela had refrained from mentioning the subject beforehand, but as she watched him transform from the man she loved and respected into an

261

annoying, amateur sot, she wished she had been both specific and insistent about her wishes and expectations. Blaming herself was absurd and wrong in so many ways; nevertheless, she felt partially responsible for his downfall, as if upping the game on her presumed wifely duties might somehow have prevented her husband from sinking into another drunken stupor. Deeply troubled, tired, and disgusted, Michela asked Stefano to take her back up to their room shortly after dinner and a bit of conversation.

Considering himself the life of the party, Nickolaus once again decided to perform a few rounds of song, which actually turned out to be a surprisingly inventive and energetic revue that left the dining hall patrons feeling highly entertained and thoroughly impressed. Around ten o'clock, Marco and Vinny came around to collect the drunk and weary Nickolaus and then take him upstairs to his room. Michela, who had already fallen into a deep sleep by the time they arrived, barely awakened when the two men loaded Nickolaus into bed. "He'll be all right, Signora," Vinny tried to assure her. "Marco and I will take care of this. We'll get him turned around once we get to Lubeck. He just needs some normal times so he can get his head straight."

"What, straighten what?" Michela mumbled.

"She's not really with us," whispered Marco. He nodded and smiled at her. "We'll talk about this tomorrow."

"Thank you – both of you," she muttered before laying her head back down and then quickly turning away from her husband, who had already begun wheezing out a classic drunken snore. Marco and Vinny both nodded at Stefano and then left.

"I hope we can bring him around," Marco confided to Vinny. "He's sure fallen hard and fast. I've never seen anything like it. It's almost like the plague."

"Yeah, well that's the way it is with some men, Marco. We'll bring him back one way or another, I can promise you that."

The schedule was less pressing the following morning, as the final leg to Lubeck required only about four to five hours of travel. Nickolaus awoke with start. For a moment he thought he was still down in the dining hall, but it was only the clattering of Michela swinging open the window shutters, allowing the muted but probing early-morning sunlight to penetrate the room and strike him directly in the face. This did not sit well with the disturbingly hung-over composer, who moaned woefully before rolling over and burying himself in his bed covers. Undeterred, his smiling wife seemed to enjoy taking a measure of vengeful delight at being the immediate cause of her husband's suffering. "Time to get up, Nicki," she chirped cheerfully. "Heinz says we leave in an hour."

"Close that shutter. You're blinding me."

"Only if you promise to get up, clean-up, and eat a proper breakfast before we go."

"What in God's name are you talking about?"

"You heard me. If you're going to act irresponsibly, then I'm going to have to treat you like I'm your mother." He rolled over and glared at her.

"Are you joking?"

"Not in the slightest." The two stared at each other for about ten seconds, until Nickolaus finally realized what he'd done – again - so he decided to act both remorseful and apologetic which, for what it was worth, he truly was. He also came to realize just how badly he needed to use the chamber pot.

"You're right. I'll get up, but please close that shutter. It's blinding me." Nickolaus drug himself out of bed and complied with Michela's orders, fulfilling his normal morning rituals without prompt or complaint. When he was ready to dress, he found one of his Maestro's evening suits laid out neatly on the bed.

"What is this, my love?"

"We'll be reaching our future life today. I thought we could arrive in style as gentleman and lady. I see no reason to show up dressed like paupers when we have a trunk full of gold in the wagon."

"No, I suppose not. Good thinking, sweet one."

"Besides, maybe it will help give you back a sense of yourself, remind you of who you were and who you can be again." He stared at her with his head cocked slightly, trying to decide whether she was trying to pick a fight or just help him find his way. It was the latter, of course, and he well knew it.

As they were dressing, he glanced over in her direction. Still barely showing but shy over her pregnancy nonetheless, she kept her back turned to him; however, that only seemed to draw his attention even more. As he stared at her temptingly slim neck, with it's soft, pale skin that he so missed and desired, he was suddenly given to urges that he hadn't experienced for quite some time, indeed, not since early on in the voyage. He placed his breeches back down on the bed then stepped over and gave her a gentle but sustained kiss on the neck. She startled slightly at first, but then turned around and hugged him as she kissed him back. They stared into each other's eyes momentarily then she softly murmured yes. He quickly stepped over and barred the door.

They didn't have much time, but neither did they need much time, for despite his diminished condition and her reticence to engage, they coupled quickly but lovingly. Fearing he might injure his pregnant wife, he restrained himself, keeping things simple and gentle. In truth, she was not nearly so fragile as he imagined. In most respects, there was nothing particularly romantic or enduring about the interlude, more of the proverbial quickie, if you will, but it was pleasant and satisfying for both of them just the same. In a few short minutes they were finished, leaving Nickolaus with a welcome surge of confidence, followed promptly by a strong desire to lie back down in bed and steal a bit of time while he basked in the afterglow. It was to this northern land of his childhood where his mind often flew during these coveted minutes of ecstasy after fruition; however, all he had felt so far was anxiety, drunkenness, and hung-over. Unfortunately, his appointment with euphoria would have to be forfeited on this day, as Michela promptly pushed both of them to finish dressing so that they could get down to the dining hall. For the first time in several days, it was morning and Nickolaus was hungry; in fact, he actually felt famished. Michela, too, felt a sense of relief, as perhaps this was the first step on their return to normalcy.

Marco and Stefano met them the moment they stepped into the dining hall. Marco immediately handed Nickolaus a stein of hard cider that he'd spiked with a strategically measured amount of apple schnapps. He knew from personal experience that his friend's excruciating hangover would be almost unbearable without it. "Drink all of this with your breakfast – no more and no less. It will ease your way into the day, Nico." Marco leaned over and hugged Michela briefly then stood back and stared at the couple for a moment. "You two certainly look refreshed this morning. Did you manage a good night's sleep?"

"Yes, and more," Nickolaus boasted, grinning slyly. Michela blushed then smiled coyly.

"Oh … Ooohh, I see. Why, Nico, you old dog, you, struck by a bit of the frisk, eh? Well good for you, my boy. Maybe you're not as hard up as I figured."

"Let's just get some breakfast, Marco, I'm starved. Where's that bacon?"

After a hearty breakfast of fresh eggs, bacon, and pastry, Heinz marched in and announced a quarter hour departure warning. A moment later, Ludwig trudged through the dining hall carrying the Silberbach's travel trunk over his shoulder. Apparently, he had personally packed it up for them. He looked at them and smiled in an odd sort of way then winked at Nickolaus, which left all of them feeling embarrassed and somewhat violated.

After fifteen minutes, with everyone and everything loaded onto the wagons, Heinz gave the order to move out. At about five hours, the trip to Lubeck wouldn't normally be that much of a challenge; however, Heinz made it clear from the outset that, despite feeling safer, they would still remain as vigilant as ever. At least on this final day of travel, everyone shared the same goal, that is, safely reaching Lubeck. Early the prior evening, Heinz and Hans Wagner had scrupulously informed the sheriff of all the details of their criminal encounters so, hopefully, the constables would already be on the lookout for members of the gang. Heinz and Vinny figured the whole crew was undoubtedly long gone, quietly cruising down the Elbe in *Die Rote Henne* toward somewhere else – anywhere else.

The closer the convoy got to Lubeck, the more heavily traveled the road became, including foot traffic and several slow, two-wheeled ox carts similar to the one Nicolo had traveled up to the Ligurian Hills on every summer as a child. A few people even waved at them, apparently recognizing Herr Buhl's personal carriage, or the Buhlswagen, or perhaps both. The warm reception served to imbue the members of the caravan with a sense of friendly celebration.

As they approached Lubeck, the surroundings began feeling familiar to Nickolaus. With a growing sense of excitement, he began recognizing memorable landmarks, large old trees, unique houses, and even the entrance to the old road that led to the Silberbach Estate a few miles down the lane. At last he was feeling a true sense of arrival – he was finally home.

Before long, the glorious red brick towers of the Holsten Gate, which stands at the western entrance to Lubeck's central city, came into view. Seemingly ablaze in the late afternoon sun, the giant towers gleamed like great beacons, warmly welcoming the Silberbachs to their new life. Beautifully crafted in the 1460's, the gothic style gate consisted of two large, red brick towers - several stories high - with conical roofs separated by a matching central section that included a pediment and gate. This is where they stopped and presented their entry papers. Heinz planned to drive the convoy directly to the Lubeck branch of the Bank of St George where he intended to offload the gold as rapidly as possible in order to have it safely stored away in someone else's protected custody.

As they rode past the towering hanseatic trading houses - all decked out like Christmas gingerbread - the new arrivals quickly came to realize just how different their new world would be. These great houses, built of north German red brick and held together by posts and beams, were sensationally adorned with solid, elaborate, darkly colored trim of the most masterly construction. Even the warehouses were like architectural works of art. It was all very Germanic and most impressive. Although they had originally imagined their initial passage through Lubeck as some sort of grand arrival; instead, they were barely noticed at all as they passed slowly through the brick and cobblestone streets of the central city. This was a place of both vibrancy and reserve, with abundant mercantile activity and plenty of money hiding behind its tall, dark, rather foreboding facades. Showing off here was considered crude and garish, though these denizens certainly had their own ways of letting everyone know who they were and what they had. There was also a sense of collectivism about it, a unity of purpose, perhaps, even if that purpose was to control as many conditions as they could while also making as much money as possible.

It was nearly dark when the convoy pulled up in front of the Lubeck branch of the Bank of St. George, which, irrespective of the bank's Genoan heritage, was virtually indistinguishable from every other hanseatic trading house on the square. Even in the dim light of dusk, it was apparent that everything on and around the square was as neat and orderly as could be; however, with the brisk chill and a damp, billowy fog rolling in, it also seemed depressingly bleak to the exhausted travelers.

Heinz immediately jumped off his wagon, squared away his uniform, then bounded up the stairs and through the heavy, ornately-carved, double front doors. He had arrived just in the nick of time, as the bank was already closing for the day. A few minutes later he returned, accompanied by a stolid-looking gentleman and two brawny, well-dressed guards. "Greetings, Maestro Silberbach, I am Herr Weldon. Would you and your family please come with me? Herr Von Württemberg has been looking forward to your arrival and cannot wait to welcome you personally. Also, he has some very important news for you."

"You know who I am?" Nickolaus asked, pleasantly surprised.

"But of course we do, Maestro. We've been expecting you. Please, follow me." Nickolaus looked at Michela then shrugged his shoulders. She cocked her head in response.

"Well, let's do as the man says," Stefano blurted out. "This is what we came here for, isn't it?"

"I suppose so," agreed Nickolaus. "Hold on a moment." He reached back and pulled a pouch out of their travel trunk. "Please lead the way, Herr Weldon." Nickolaus helped Michela down from the carriage then followed their host into the front lobby of the bank. It was smaller than expected, nothing like the Genoan branch's great ceremonial hall; instead, it was conservatively appointed, dimly lit and, except for one remaining guard, empty of people.

"This way, please." Herr Weldon directed them through another heavy door then down a narrow, nearly dark, wood-paneled hallway where he stopped and knocked on another ornately carved door, this one with gold leaf trim and what appeared to be a gold, metal-cast coat of arms.

"A moment please," called out a muffled voice from within. Twenty seconds later, the door opened, revealing a tall, richly dressed, bearded man, sporting a broad and friendly smile. "Please, come in, I am Wilhelm Von Wurttemberg, director of the Lubeck branch of the Bank of Saint George. I'm so happy to make your acquaintances." He graciously shook his guests' hands then led them over to three lavishly upholstered chairs that surrounded his immense, elegant, dark wood desk. Although she barely understood a word of what was being said, Michela swiftly discerned a common thread among her new Holstein surroundings – dark and woody. This must be the way of the north, she thought to herself.

"I am humbled that you have graced us with such a personalized welcome, Herr Von Wurttemberg," Nickolaus offered. "It's certainly far more than I expected."

"Not at all, Maestro, you are a very important client to the Bank of Saint George, and soon to be one of our first citizens in Lubeck. We welcome you with open arms, to be sure."

"I must say, our trip here has been an exceedingly harsh and harrowing journey. To be truthful, I'm surprised we're even here at all, but here we are, and here we plan to stay and make our lives."

"Excellent, Maestro. That's wonderful for all of us. Do you have the papers that Herr Albioni provided you with?"

"I most certainly do." Nickolaus pulled a sheaf of documents from his leather-bound portfolio and handed them over to Herr Wurttemberg, who then turned up his lamp and immediately began sorting through the several sheets of deluxe quality, parchment paper.

"I ask your indulgence while I take a look at these, Maestro. Shall I have Herr Weldon bring anyone a beverage?"

"No, no, please go ahead and read."

"As you wish." The Silberbachs looked on as Herr Wurttemberg poured through the documents, nodding here and there, and voicing a random uh-huh every now and then. During the process, Nickolaus began nervously tapping his foot to a rhythm that had formed in his head. He suddenly realized he was craving schnapps, rather badly in fact, and that he couldn't get the thought out of his mind. He cursed himself then began looking around for distractions.

"Well, it looks as though everything here is in order. You've done quite well, Maestro, we shall be glad to serve your banking needs if you will have us. We have already vaulted your gold, so you can rest assured that it is safely protected. I would like to extend an invitation for you and your fine family to enjoy dinner at my home this evening. In the meantime, with Herr Weldon's assistance, I have taken the liberty of arranging a suite for you at the Grand Lubeck Inn. If that is satisfactory, I will have one of the guards carry your belongings for you."

"That will be excellent, Herr Wurttemberg," Nickolaus replied.

"Please, Maestro, call me Wilhelm. With your approval, I shall have our solicitor prepare the life estate acceptance documents for presentation to the Baron Von Silberland. You should know that there might be some legal issues involved with the estate, owing mainly to the continuing turmoil between Lubeck and the Danish Sovereign, but we can discuss that tomorrow. In the meantime, with your permission, I would like to arrange a meeting for you tomorrow afternoon with the Most Holy Pastor Klaus Werner across the square at Saint Mary's Cathedral."

"Wait. Hold on a moment. I'm confused."

"I know, and I'm sorry to be springing this on you so soon, but the church has expressed a sincere interest in possibly bringing you on as an assistant Kapellmeister."

"Seriously? Why? How did they even know I would be coming?"

"I'm not sure, Maestro, but they seem to have received word that you would be arriving in Lubeck to stay."

"Well, this is quite the mysterious surprise."

"Indeed so, but I think this probably isn't the best time to discuss the matter. I'm sure you and your family are tired and hungry. Shall we consider it later, perhaps?" Feeling an acute sense of panic, exhilaration, pride, confusion, and craving, Nickolaus looked at Michela, then at Stefano, and then agreed.

"We'll talk, but this is not at all what I had expected."

"I know, Maestro, but sometimes our expectations must bend in order to give way to new opportunities."

"I suppose so," Nickolaus agreed reluctantly.

# Chapter 29 – Just Like Old Times

Wilhelm Von Wurttemberg's home and family conformed perfectly to what the Silberbachs had come to expect in their new Saxon surroundings. Their hosts were outwardly friendly and inviting, but they also seemed careful, reserved, somewhat closed, and clearly under the thumb of the master of the house. Their home, in all it's dark, woody splendor, came replete with meticulously crafted panels, finely carved trim, gothic tapestries, masterpiece furniture – some of it almost alarming in appearance, and a perfectly measured ration of fine Germanic bric-a-brac displayed in a seemingly modest yet certain to be noticed fashion. The servants were impeccably dressed, polite to a fault, and supremely disciplined, all of which led to a machine-like serving up of fine aperitifs, followed by the precision delivery of a perfectly prepared meal of ideal proportions. Despite his best intentions, Nickolaus requested peach schnapps, which Herr Wurttemberg gladly delivered in both quality and abundance. Michela squeezed her husband's hand several times, hoping to communicate a suggestion of restraint, and he did seem to be holding back to some degree, as he had so far managed to remain bright, polite, and witty, if not occasionally a bit silly. Mainly, though, he came across as genuinely happy and relieved, which was a good thing.

As dinner came on, so did the German white wine, a fine period Riesling of enviable vintage, but Nickolaus found it so distasteful that he chose to drink hard cider instead. This was also a favorable turn of events, as it prevented him from getting too drunk. In fact, as the meal wore on, he actually began sobering up a bit – a seeming paradox that demonstrated just how accustomed he'd grown to drinking large quantities of alcohol. Due in part to his well-lubricated condition, eager conversations covering his time in Lubeck as a child, his life as an orphan, his musical training, preferences, and experiences, as well as with his life and times with Michela and Stefano flowed forth with pleasant ease. It soon became clear to Wilhelm that Nickolaus was not destined to farm, manage a rural estate, or even thrive under such circumstances. The Maestro was a musician and composer, and probably a good one. Music was both his greatest strength and his undeniable destiny. There was simply no getting around it. And in the process of relating so much cohesive information under such relaxed and temperate conditions, Nickolaus also came to the same realization, which was, for him, an epiphany.

At the conclusion of the evening, Wilhelm had one of his servants accompany the Silberbachs back to the inn. The evening was cold and still, conditions that invited a deep, penetrating November fog to encompass all of Lubeck. When they finally reached their room, they found welcoming warmth and a crackling fire in the small fireplace. This was fortunate, since the entire party was chilled to the bone. Shortly after their arrival, the inn's night steward showed up with a pot of warm cider, which was received with pleasure, although Nickolaus still couldn't clear his mind of his cravings for more schnapps. In front of a frowning Michela, he asked the steward where he might acquire more potent spirits, but the tavern and libation services were closed, so unless he was willing to leave the inn in search of schnapps or other hard spirits - a truly absurd notion - he would have to make do without. This, too, was a good thing, though at the time he did not see it that way.

Having grown accustomed to imbibing large amounts of alcohol as a sleeping potion, Nickolaus found himself wide-awake and jumpy as a fly. Totally exhausted, Michela and Stefano turned in right away, leaving Nickolaus pacing around the room looking for some way to distract himself. He munched down a couple of cookies from a small plate on the table then poured himself a mug of warm cider. This instantly made him acutely homesick for a nice cup of the warm lemon tea he had virtually survived on in Genoa. There would be none of that here, at least not for now, since tea and, more particularly, lemons were exceedingly rare. He finally stretched out in a cushiony chair and put his feet up on a dark wooden ottoman. He stared off into the dimly lit room and began pondering his circumstances and options, something he had not done for quite some time.

Before he knew it, he dozed off into a fretful, dream-laden sleep from which he soon awoke with a start. He adjusted his position then dozed off again until he was startled awake by a different nightmarish dream involving a pile of snakes and cockroaches fighting in a pit. He drifted off again, but was reawakened a few minutes later when the snakes in his dream started crawling up his legs. He let out a tiny squeal then jumped up from the chair, trying to knock the imaginary snakes off. Michela mumbled something then rolled over, apparently undisturbed. He took a few deep breaths and a sip of cider then sat back down and closed his eyes. He was suffering from alcohol withdrawal, but he didn't know it, so the process continued for several hours until he finally woke up after a three-hour stretch of dreamless sleep. Somehow he had managed to acquire a few hours of sleep, on his own, and without being saturated through and through with alcohol.

"Nicki," Michela whispered, "come to bed. It's almost morning." Nickolaus yawned then stretched.

"If you insist," he whispered back as he quietly hobbled over and slipped into bed, immediately forming a love spoon with his sleepy wife. When he woke up an hour later, he was still in the exact same position but endowed with a solid case of early morning tumescence. Unfortunately, with Stefano sleeping just a few feet away, there was nothing he could do with it. Squirming slightly in response, Michela felt warm at heart that her husband was there, reasonably sober, and definitely still attracted to her.

Before long it was time to arise. As soon as Nickolaus stood up, he realized he was still dead tired, almost to the point of loopiness, and a bit shaky, but he had important things to do, so he moved ahead despite his splitting headache, jumpy nerves, and nauseated stomach. Michela got up at the same time and discreetly helped him out. She knew he was suffering, as he often did in the morning, but especially now that he needed some alcohol to help ease things along. As soon as they were dressed, they went down to the dining hall for breakfast and a hearty size mug of hard cider, hopefully with just enough alcohol to ease his jitters and smooth him over for a while. It seemed to work.

Halfway through breakfast, which was not nearly as tasty as the one in Bad Segeberg, Herr Weldon showed up to deliver Nickolaus a message. "Maestro, Herr Von Wurttemberg has arranged a meeting for you with Pastor Werner and Kapellmeister Hasse at two o'clock this afternoon. Also, if you should be so disposed, Herr Von Wurttemberg would like to meet with you alone in his office at eleven this morning to discuss various contingencies that might affect your future. He apologizes for the rush, but the life estate acceptance deadline with the Baron Von Silberland is rapidly closing in on us.

"Yes, thank you, Herr Weldon. Think nothing of it. Wilhelm's prudence is greatly appreciated. Please inform him that I will gladly accept both appointments."

"Excellent, then we shall see you later, Sir." Nickolaus smiled nervously as Herr Weldon, fastidiously dressed and almost soldier-like in character, quickly retreated and returned to the bank. It was obvious to Michela that her husband was nervous about the meetings, but she also rightly sensed that he was excited.

"You know, Michela, I cannot fathom how they know of my credentials, or why they would want to hire a composer of Roman church music for this great Lutheran cathedral. How do they even know who I am? How can they know what I've done musically, or what my artistic proclivities are? And I still can't imagine how they ever discovered that I was coming to Lubeck. This is truly a great mystery to me."

"Well, you'll be having a meeting with them in a few hours. I guess you'll find out then."

"I think it's very intriguing," remarked Stefano. "You know music is your being. I don't know how they came to know of you either, but this could be a huge opportunity. I'm just not sure how well you would fit into the Lutheran musical culture."

"I'm not so sure myself," Nickolaus confessed, "but I suppose it's worth finding out."

"Agreed," Stefano and Michela declared almost in unison.

Nickolaus's morning meeting with Herr Wurttemberg left him just as confused as ever. During most of the session, he had great difficulty paying attention because of his sudden and unexpectedly passionate concern over making a good showing at Saint Mary's. This certainly spoke volumes about his changing priorities. Herr Wurttemberg informed him that, after a series of decades-long conflicts between the Independent City-State of Lubeck and the Kingdom of Holstein - at that time controlled largely by King Christian III of Denmark - involving land security for debts owed to Lubeck, opposing territorial claims, ambiguous treaty agreements, religious turmoil, and various military threats, the Baron Von Silberland had ultimately managed to secure at least a life estate in his barony that was guaranteed by both Christian III and the City-State of Lubeck – but no more. That mouthful alone was enough to give Nickolaus a severe case of brain paralysis. And there was more. No one had specifically declared that the Silberland Barony would cease when the Baron died, but no one had guaranteed that it would continue either, leaving its future beyond the present Baron's life in a state of complete limbo. Moreover, even if the barony did survive his death, the Baron had but one living son, who was both physically estranged and hopelessly incommunicado. And since Nickolaus's Silberbach Estate had been carved out of the highly contingent and woefully fragile Silberland Barony, its future beyond the life of the current Baron generated an extraordinary degree of uncertainty. The present Baron was in his mid-forties, which left only a limited number of years for the Silberbach Estate to continue with even a reasonable level of assurance. Worse yet, the reality was that the Baron could die or be killed on any given day; hence, installing any substantial improvements, or counting on the estate land for a long-term family home would be highly risky to say the least – something akin to building a house on a melting iceberg. Nickolaus was virtually dumbstruck. Finally, after squirming through a dizzying hour of incomprehensible explanations and juxtapositions of options, he finally threw his hands in the air and exclaimed, "Oh, my God, if I don't get out of here, I'm going to lose my mind!" Startled by his client's sudden outburst, Herr Wurttemberg wisely relented, quickly closing up his folder of papers and then taking Nickolaus out for a much needed lunch break.

After a delicious and refreshing mid-day meal that included a pleasantly ample and immensely appreciated stein of lager beer, Nickolaus thanked Herr Wurttemberg then headed off to find the pastor's office at the strikingly gorgeous Saint Mary's Church. He felt nervous, but also slightly subdued by a mild buzz from the noon hour beer, just about the perfect level of sobriety for the task at hand.

One of Saint Mary's church deacons met Nickolaus in the church's outer vestibule and accompanied him to his appointment. As he passed through the cathedral on the way to the pastor's office, he was struck by the awesome size and magnificent beauty of its great gothic splendor, which dwarfed in every physical way his humble church home at Saint Matthias in Genoa. It still lay beyond his imagination how structures of such size, weight, and complexity could actually be designed and built; nevertheless, there it was, bigger than life itself. He stopped momentarily and scanned the breadth of its colossal nave. The whole thing seemed virtually impossible, even miraculous. Sadly, he couldn't help but wonder what had become of all the elaborate decorations and iconic adornments that he knew must have once graced the now drab, empty walls he was seeing. What a waste of so much fine art and beauty; worse yet, he knew in his heart that none of the proceeds from those riches had ever reached the common citizenry of Lubeck. Still, taken as a whole, Saint Mary's was as impressive as it was imposing.

Pastor Klaus Werner was a thoughtful and respected man in his early sixties. He'd been an esteemed member of Lubeck's leading echelon for decades. In many respects, he reminded Nickolaus of Bishop Caravaggio in the way he instantly exuded an obvious sense of power, experience, and distinction, but he was also different, more restrained, less gregarious than the outwardly friendly and oft-jovial Bishop. Admittedly, Nickolaus had known the Bishop as both friend and leader for many years, so an instant comparison might not necessarily have been fair or reliable.

After several gentle knocks on the door and an agonizingly long wait - actually about fifteen seconds - the pastor graciously invited Nickolaus into his office then immediately introduced him to Saint Mary's revered Kapellmeister, Georg Philip Hasse. Plumpish and finely attired, the Kapellmeister shook Nickolaus's hand guardedly, smiled wryly, and then took a seat off to the side and slightly behind Nickolaus. The Kapellmeister seemed markedly reserved and most likely uncomfortable, which Nickolaus could not help but interpret as a sign of personal disapproval. After sitting down on the wooden, pew-like chair offered by the pastor, Nickolaus took a quick inventory of his surroundings. Unlike the rest of the church, Pastor Werner's office had not yet been stripped of its prior Catholic glory. Beautifully inlaid wall panels decorated with gold leaf, a rich, beam-latticed ceiling, and painstakingly polished hardwood floors that gleamed like fine marble all served as a stage for several magnificently framed works of museum-grade art, including at least two pieces that Nickolaus believed to be of Italian origin. Just as before, he couldn't help but wonder how many of these fine paintings had once graced the walls outside of this office for the entire congregation to enjoy and admire.

After Nickolaus had spent several minutes unabashedly extolling the many fine virtues of Saint Mary's and reminiscing affectionately over his fond memories of growing up in Lubeck, the trio finally turned to the business at hand. "You know, Maestro, I knew your father before the horrible tragedy that befell your family." Nickolaus found this revelation quite surprising, since he knew his father had barely been religious enough to get by in society, let alone circulate with the likes of Pastor Werner. "I regret to say that he did not strike me as an enthusiastically religious man; however, I felt strongly that he was a faithful Christian follower to his very core. And I know for certain that he was a firm supporter of Martin Luther's highest ideals." Nickolaus also knew this to be false, but he smiled just the same. Although his father had favored many of Luther's more pragmatic reforms, he had never expressed any particular affinity for Luther's brand of faith and practice, or anyone else's for that matter. Essentially, his father had played along, neither zealously nor apathetically, so as to draw as little attention as possible to himself or to his secretly Jewish wife. The strategy had worked well for both him and his family, and Nickolaus had skillfully applied his own version of the same approach in Genoa.

"You know, Nickolaus, may I call you Nickolaus?"

"Most certainly."

"You come very highly recommended." The pastor shuffled several papers around until he was holding three high quality parchment sheets, two stamped with official Catholic seals. "Let's see what we have here. Ah, yes, first, we have this stirring recommendation from a retired Bishop of Genoa, one Giovanni Di Caravaggio, stating that you are the finest conductor and composer of church music that he knows of in the world. He also states that you were instrumental in exposing a rogue priest involved in a forbidden indulgence scheme, and that despite your intense faith, you have never been able to break free from your Lutheran roots. Do you agree with his assessment?"

Nickolaus blushed, then hemmed and hawed a bit. "I loved and served the Bishop and Saint Matthias to the very best of my abilities as their assistant music director and then as Maestro Di Cappella. I must confess that I did have some difficulty attending to certain aspects of the Catholic liturgies, but I always did my best to serve their needs faithfully. And while both the Bishop and our congregations expressed much favor toward my compositions, they were not of the musical mainstream. Instead, my goal was to compose music that soared to the loftiest expressions of faith, love of God, and appreciation of his universe."

"Excellent, Maestro, excellent indeed, and we're very glad to see that you succeeded in rooting out another evil scheme of indulgences. This shows that you, too, are an ardent and loyal follower of Luther's highest ideals. Furthermore, the fact that you apply your prodigious musical talents in the service of our Lord proves that you are most certainly a true and faithful Christian of proper mind and spirit." Although he was disgusted by his own grotesque expedience, Nickolaus humbly nodded in agreement just the same. This was not the first time he had allowed people of religious conviction to presume his faith in order to achieve his greater goals. The pastor continued. "I also have a recommendation here from a Father Paolo Di Flagello of Palermo, formerly Maestro Di Cappella at Saint Matthias in Genoa. He reports that you are a superb teacher, an excellent musician, a peerless choir director, and that you were loved and respected by everyone at Saint Matthias." The pastor looked up and noticed that Nickolaus was again blushing and shifting nervously in his seat. "And last but not least, I have here a very warm recommendation from the esteemed composer, Orlande de Lassus, who states that he knows you to be a talented, skillful, and faithful musician and composer." The Pastor glanced over the de Lassus paper, nodded his head, and then looked straight at Nickolaus. "Quite impressive indeed, Maestro, you must know that these are not trivial recommendations."

Shocked to the very heart of his being, Nickolaus barely knew how to react, let alone what to say. He was so stunned by the kindness of his old friends that he wanted to cry. When and how had they done this? And concerning his old acquaintance, Orlande de Lassus, how and why had they ever contacted him? And how did he even remember Nickolaus? They had only spent time together twice. Utterly speechless, Nickolaus turned around and smiled at Kapellmeister Hasse, swallowed the lump in his throat, took a deep breath, and then turned back around toward Pastor Werner. "Well, I have to admit that I am truly at a loss for words. These fine gentlemen were my friends and peers, but I had no idea that they had sent these remarkable letters of recommendation. I am astounded and grateful in the extreme."

"Yes, I would say that you should be. These are absolutely glowing, but I have to ask, are they truthful?" Nickolaus stared at the floor for several seconds.

"You know, I suppose that on the whole they are. Music appreciation is an aesthetic variable, of course, but I must humbly admit that the congregations at Saint Matthias did love my music, and I did manage to create a superb choir out of very meager resources." Pastor Werner glanced over at the Kapellmeister and nodded.

"Perhaps you would be willing to demonstrate some of your talents," challenged Kapellmeister Hasse.

"You mean right now?"

"Certainly, why not? There is an excellent harpsichord in one of the side chapels adjacent to the cathedral. Perhaps you could give us a taste of some of your finest musical offerings."

Nickolaus cringed slightly. "Sure, I suppose I could do that," he agreed reluctantly. "Although I have to warn you in advance that I haven't so much as touched a keyboard for several weeks. However, if you'll forgive a few clinkers here and there, I will gladly give it a try."

Kapellmeister Hasse stood up. "Outstanding, then with Pastor Werner's consent, please follow me." The three men headed off to a chapel situated off to the left side of the main cathedral near the front. The pastor pointed up toward the bank of towering organ pipes that lined the front of the nave.

"As you can see, Maestro, we have one of the most magnificent pipe organs in all of Christendom. Do you play?"

"I'm afraid not. We never had the budget for a pipe organ at Saint Matthias. I've played around on a few, but never seriously."

"Don't apologize. This is often the way of things. Besides, our organist, Herr Ridderbusch, is without a doubt the best organist in all of Christendom. Wouldn't you agree, Kapellmeister?"

"Oh, absolutely, Pastor Werner. Ah, here we are." Kapellmeister Hasse stepped over to a six foot, gaudily ornate, two-manual harpsichord that was obviously of the highest musical quality. "It was just tuned and regulated last week," boasted the Kapellmeister before leaning over to fire off a showy, full keyboard musical sequence. "Lovely, isn't it?"

"In the extreme," agreed Nickolaus. "This instrument has to be the most splendid harpsichord in all of Christendom." Pastor Werner smiled proudly while the Kapellmeister, who was standing behind the pastor, subtly but knowingly rolled his eyes. Nickolaus sat down then let loose with his own version of the same musical sequence played in a contrasting minor key with several harmoniously curious ornamentations. When he was finished, he looked up and grinned.

Pleased rather than offended, the Kapellmeister nodded approvingly. "Very nice, Maestro, let's hear some more, if you dare."

Needing some time to warm up, Nickolaus settled in with a few scales and chords before starting slowly with a simple but tuneful little fugue he had composed as a minor student work, which he then artfully transfigured into a very popular hymn by Martin Luther, Christ Lay in the Bonds of Death. Several of Luther's hymns had made the rounds among church musicians in Italy, though they were mainly a source of musical curiosity rather than something that could actually be used in any Catholic setting. At that point, Nickolaus could feel his audience warming up to him. He then executed a perfect transitional Phrygian cadence, one of his favorite tacks, before launching into a gorgeous keyboard version of the most beautiful and expressive aria from Michela's Stabat Mater, his magnum opus that had brought him such musical fame and success in Genoa. Then, just as the last lilting chords of that heartbreaking piece were fading away, he launched into a forceful but otherwise straightforward version of another Luther favorite, A Mighty Fortress is our God, ultimately finishing off with just the right brand of rousing musical punch that he had heard many Lutherans were fond of.

When he was finished, the pastor and Kapellmeister instantly broke into a hearty round of applause - until they remembered where they were, but when they stopped, the applause continued, carried on by several nearby congregants who had happened by during the performance. Nickolaus stood up and bowed graciously. Highly impressed, the pastor and Kapellmeister each shook the Maestro's hand before directing him back to the pastor's office to speak further about Saint Mary's and its venerable musical heritage.

Nickolaus conducted himself with courtesy and modesty throughout the ensuing discussions, even though, on the inside, he was about to burst from pleasure and self-adulation. He had succeeded far beyond his highest expectations. When he arrived back at the inn shortly after four o'clock, he seemed confused and preoccupied, perhaps even a bit dazed. At first Michela was concerned that he might have gone out drinking again, but when she drew near and kissed him, he smelled only of cider and the raspberry jam he'd enjoyed on his afternoon pastry in the pastor's office. He pulled her close and hugged her for almost thirty seconds then they kissed again and parted. She looked at him quizzically. "Did you find what you expected?"

"Very much so, but not completely. They want to bring me on as an Assistant Kapellmeister."

"Nicki, that's amazing! We just arrived, and here you are with an important musical position already. I'm so impressed."

"Hold on, but not to work at Saint Mary's. They want me to prepare and direct the choirs at one of their smaller churches here in Lubeck."

"Oh, I see. And composition?"

"Yes, yes, they seem very much interested in that. And you know, even though I haven't touched a keyboard for weeks, my audition went very well – compelling, in fact. I'm certain they were very favorably impressed. I must say, though, that preparing and directing choirs at a lesser church reminds me so much of Genoa that I'm not sure how I feel about it."

"Yes, but look at it this way, you would essentially be serving as Kapellmeister in your very first position here. You could end up creating the most sublime music in all of Lubeck."

"You mean all of Christendom," Nickolaus mumbled, smiling to himself.

"What?"

"Never mind, I'll explain later."

"I'll look forward to that. Anyway, that is more than you could ever have hoped for, especially since you didn't even seem to be thinking in that direction at all. I don't think you realized how much you needed your music and a fair share of artistic recognition until they were gone.

"I think you are right, my love. And I must say, they really seem to want me. Can you believe they had personal letters of recommendation from Bishop Caravaggio, Father Paolo, and even Orlande de Lassus?"

"Yes, isn't that amazing?"

Nickolaus cocked his head slightly. "How do you know about that?"

"Oh, I don't really, but I've heard a few rumors here and there."

"What? How?" Nickolaus was totally confused. "I still have no clue as to how they knew I was coming, let alone the source of those letters of recommendation.

"I imagine we'll find out soon enough, my love. In the meantime, Herr Weldon stopped by earlier to inform you that they would be filing papers to accept the Silberbach Estate on your behalf tomorrow morning with the local recorder. Also, with your approval, Herr Wurttemberg has arranged for a carriage tomorrow morning to take us out to visit the Baron Von Silberland in order to present him with your papers of acceptance. Would that be satisfactory?" Nickolaus took a deep breath and then sighed.

"Oh, Michela, this is all going so fast. My mind can't digest all of this information so quickly. I've been lazing around half drunk for weeks, and now this. It's all so unexpected."

"Then we won't make any decisions right away. We'll just proceed as if everything is clear and uncomplicated. We'll go along with all of the appropriate procedures as if we know what we're doing, but for the time being, we won't actually commit to anything. That way everything will remain an option. Nothing will be lost to us, and no one will be hurt or offended. That will give you some time and space to think about your … about our future."

"Yes, yes, that's just what we'll do. My heavens, Michela, what would I do without you?"

"That's hard to say for sure, Nicki, but I imagine you'd figure it out on your own in time. I'm just picking up some of the burden for you. Now let's take a walk before dark and then head over to dinner. We'll make everything as normal as possible." He pulled her in and hugged her tightly again. He needed her badly and she knew it. But she also loved being needed, and even more so, she adored being loved and appreciated.

He kissed her on the neck then whispered into her ear, "I've got an idea for something far more satisfying than a walk."

"You do?" she answered alluringly.

"If you feel up to it, that is."

"Oh, I suppose there'd be no harm in being a few minutes late to dinner, my love. Go bar the door while I turn down the bed." Nickolaus nodded then dashed toward the door.

# Chapter 30 – Watershed

Dinner turned out to be the first of several watershed moments for Nickolaus. He was thrilled that his surprise audition had gone so well, so he really wanted to celebrate. On the other hand, the details of the assistant directorship he'd unexpectedly been offered were somewhat confusing and not necessarily acceptable, so he also felt discouraged. There was also the matter of the highly unsettled nature of the Silberbach Estate, which left him feeling like a man without a home. He wanted relief from his thoughts, but he also didn't want to drown himself in schnapps. He knew he felt better and far more productive when he was sober, but he also wished he could stop feeling and worrying, if only for a while.

Shortly after sitting down in the dining hall, Marco slipped up behind him, slapped him on the back, and then clunked down a hearty tankard full of beer. "Make it last, my boy, it's all you need and it's all you'll get." Nickolaus looked up at him resentfully, feeling both insulted and bullied. Marco patted him on the shoulder. "It's enough, Nico, if you want to keep your wits about you."

Michela grasped her husband's hand. "Let's celebrate for real this evening, my love, truly enjoy ourselves." Nickolaus stared straight ahead for a few seconds then agreed with a nod. He knew they were right. It would be a battle, but he had to try. There was too much at stake this time. Every time he fell under the spell of the schnapps, he lost a little bit more of himself and another sprig of Michela's respect. Fortunately, as soon as he started eating, he sensed his mood brightening. Before long, feeling strong and energized, he joined in the conversation just as he would have done in Genoa. Michela spoke very little German, so she conversed mainly with Nickolaus, Marco, and Vinny. Near the end of dinner, Michela turned to Marco and smiled. "So, what are you and Vinny planning to do with yourselves?"

"Well, as much as we'd like to stay here and help out, I'm afraid Vinny and I must return to Genoa. Our lives and livelihoods are there, and we are of that place. And to be entirely truthful, I don't think I've ever felt so damned cold in all my life." Marco and Vinny looked at each other, both nodding in commiseration. "But we'll be around for a while. Neither one of us is too keen on crossing those miserable seas again, especially through the winter storms. Besides, the voyage getting here is still too fresh in our minds."

"Yeah, and I'm too old to learn German," Vinny added. "That's more than this old boy can handle. I don't even like the sound of it. Too much shush-schvussshing for my taste."

"I know what you mean," agreed Michela. Nickolaus thought about it a few seconds then chuckled.

"I guess that's just one more sacrifice we'll have to make," he proclaimed lightheartedly.

For the second night in a row, Nickolaus succeeded in remaining essentially sober. He initially climbed into bed with Michela, but after an hour or so of fretful tossing and turning, he climbed out of bed, paced a bit, and then took a seat in the chair next to the bed. He really wanted to quench his special thirst with schnapps – or anything spirituous – but somehow he managed to talk himself out of it. Half way through the night he climbed back into bed and fell asleep, perched as close to Michela as he could manage. When he awoke, he was once again sickeningly tired, but he was sober, and at least he felt a little better than he had the day before – not quite so hollow and shaky. At breakfast, Marco rationed up another mug of hard cider, this one containing only two-thirds as much as the day before. Disappointed though he was, Nickolaus raised no objections.

When Herr Wurttemberg's hired carriage rolled up to the front of the inn at ten o'clock, Nickolaus, Michela, Stefano, and Marco were ready and waiting. Herr Wurttemberg seemed at first a bit hesitant about Marco, but when Nickolaus introduced him as his personal guard and special consigliere, Herr Wurttemberg felt obliged to invite him along. For the first time in weeks, Nickolaus was actually excited about doing something. Despite the tragic circumstances of his departure fifteen years earlier, he held many warm childhood memories of the Silberbach Estate. He wondered what Gustav would look like, and how surprised he might be, or if Gustav would even recognize him as an adult. He was both curious and concerned about what condition the estate might be in after so many years. He already knew that the manor house was little more than a foundation and some rock walls. Mainly, though, he wondered if the estate, taken as whole, would be worthy of rebuilding and living on.

"These lands have barely changed at all," Nickolaus marveled. "It's almost as if I never left. I would have expected more progress."

"Times have been hard," explained Wilhelm defensively. "Disputes, wars, plagues, and lean times have cost us a lot. We're proud of what we've managed to accomplish, despite so many setbacks."

Nickolaus shook his head. "No, that's not what I meant. When I said that it hadn't changed much, I didn't mean it in a critical way. I'm just surprised and charmed that so much is still the same. I find it pleasing and quite comforting."

"That's good to hear. We'd certainly like to see you keep your legacy in the family. Your father and his father before him were excellent stewards of the property. I'm truly glad you've returned, Maestro." Nickolaus felt good that he might soon deserve the title of Maestro again.

The Silberbach Estate was located on a narrow but well-used lane off the main road to Baron Von Silberland's mansion. Nickolaus was glad they would be able to see what they were getting into before actually submitting their claim to the Baron – just in case. Several hundred feet up a slight grade, past fallow fields, several small orchards, and a couple of stone-fenced pastures, they pulled to a stop in front of the remains of the old manor house. It was just as Nickolaus remembered. Nothing had been done to it, although it was evident that Gustav had been keeping the tall grasses cut back and the trees pruned away from what was left of the house. About a hundred feet away from the house, the old barn was still standing, in decent condition, and apparently still in use, as the ground around it was worn down and littered with fresh straw. A hundred feet in the other direction up a slight hill, the old gravestones marking the burial sites of several of Nickolaus's ancestors, including his parents, were still standing properly upright among a neatly trimmed patch of grass surrounded by a low-laid but well-tended rock wall. Nickolaus gazed back toward the main road. It was obvious why this site had been chosen for the manor house. Other than the small graveyard, the home stood at the highest point on the parcel, with a commanding view in three directions, at least as commanding as was possible in this mildly rolling terrain.

After a few minutes of discussion, they moved on, this time downhill toward the wooded glen where Gustav lived with his family. Gustav's first wife, Elisabeth, who had so lovingly cradled and tended to Nickolaus after the fire, passed away from consumption several years after the orphaned boy was sent to Genoa. After a respectable period of grieving, Gustav married a younger woman, who then gave birth to two children in close succession. Traveling down the lane, it was clear that Gustav still loved his roses. Dozens of them still clung tightly to the manor fences, though they had mainly lost their blooms and leaves so late in the season. "You know, in the summer when the grasses are green and lush, and all the roses are in full bloom, this lane looks just like an artist's masterpiece."

"I can believe that," remarked Michela. "Nicki, I think I could easily grow to love this place, that is, if there were a home to live in."

"Indeed, that does pose quite the problem, doesn't it?"

"It's certainly not something that couldn't be remedied," Wilhelm chimed in. "You could live in town and spend your time acclimating to your new position while the old manor house is rebuilt, or you could build an all new home if you wished. The choice would be yours." Nickolaus and Michela gazed at each other for several seconds.

"Tell me, Wilhelm, are my resources sufficient to build a suitable home of reasonable modesty while still maintaining a substantial and secure financial reserve?" The banker was impressed by Nickolaus's apparent business acumen.

"Very much so, Maestro, unless you chose to build a castle or something else excessive which, for professional reasons, wouldn't be a wise choice in any event. It would be best not to appear ostentatious in front of the Baron or the Church Council."

"I see your point, Wilhelm. What say you, Stefano?"

"I like it. I could be happy here, although I have to admit that I still feel a nagging itch to return to the sea."

"What?" snapped Michela. "You can't be serious. That would be totally unacceptable. I could see that you were enjoying yourself out on that ship, but why would you choose a life like that? I don't understand at all. You're joking, aren't you?"

"I didn't say that I was actually planning to go to sea. I just mentioned that I was curious. Commander Buxtaholda told me that he would take me under his tutelage as a junior officer if I put in some time at the maritime academy near Lubeck before *The Paradise* was repaired and ready to return to service. It was just an innocent conversation. I'm not being impressed into service."

"Damn him," cursed Michela. "What is he thinking, anyway? Stefano, what about your music and your education? You would just throw all of that away?"

"I said I was just thinking about it; besides, it's my choice, not yours. You have your own life with Nickolaus."

"You're too young. I won't hear of it. Perhaps when you're older and more experienced, I will let you choose, but not now."

Nickolaus shook his head. "Michela, I love you, but if he truly wants to go, I do not believe it is in your power to stop him." Stefano nodded assuredly then eased back into his seat. "Let's talk about this later, my love, under calmer circumstances?" Sober and relaxed, Nickolaus was quite capable of being a voice for reason and reflection.

"You can be most certain that we will," Michela asserted forcefully. "You can count on that, Master Stefano." She turned away and then, other than the occasional sigh, stared silently out the carriage window as an awkward tension filled the coach. Fortunately, a few moments later they pulled up in front of the old caretaker's cottage and ground to a halt, except that it was no longer a mere cottage. For the benefit of his new wife and growing family, Gustav had made considerable improvements to the old place, including a couple of decent-sized, lean-to additions to the main house, a second fireplace – probably for a better kitchen, and what appeared to be a recently re-thatched roof. He had also added a small barn and stable farther down the hill near the bottom of the gully, close to the stream. The stream marked the eastern property line, except for the canyon portion upstream, which belonged in its entirety to the Silberbach Estate. Since it was nearly impossible to access from anywhere other than the Silberbach Estate, the landowners on the east, namely,

The Independent City-State of Lubeck, had ceded it to the Baron Von Silberland, and he, correspondingly, to the Silberbach Estate. Enchanted by its unique beauty and singular isolation, Nickolaus had spent many a day up there playing and exploring as a child. There were dangers, of course, and if he had ever been hurt, it might have been quite some time before anyone ever thought to look for him up there. Nevertheless, it had all been worth it, for his memories of that place were fond and plentiful.

Eager to see his old friend, Nickolaus jumped out of the carriage before it even came to a complete stop. Stefano followed closely on his heels. Michela seemed stuck in place, still brooding over her brother's unexpected rebelliousness. A few moments later, a late middle-aged man with two children behind him came out of the stable down near the stream and headed up the hill. The man had no idea who had come to visit, and since the carriage was so grand, he feared that it might be the Baron, or perhaps some other grand Poobah coming to evict him and his family from their home and livelihood. Earlier that morning, Herr Weldon had sent a messenger to the Baron's estate informing him when they would be visiting; however, he had not bothered to notify mere Gustav, whom he viewed as a lowly caretaker. The Baron, on the other hand, did not share Herr Weldon's diminutive view of Gustav, nor did Nickolaus or Wilhelm, both of whom knew better. For nearly a quarter century, Gustav had maintained the Silberbach Estate through thick and thin with great effort and efficiency, resulting in healthy profits and royalties for both Nickolaus and the financially struggling Baron. Indeed, the Silberland Barony would probably have collapsed in the absence Gustav's relentless endeavors.

Half way up the hill, Gustav stopped, squinted, shielded his vision from the sun, and then suddenly shouted out, "I can't believe my eyes. Is that you, Nickolaus?" The Maestro started down the hill. "It is you. Stay there, I'll be up shortly. My God, man, I can't believe it's you. You made it at last!" As Gustav neared, Nickolaus ran down to meet him. They embraced enthusiastically, slapping each other on the back several times. "Have you come to Lubeck for good? Are you going to claim your rightful estate? Nickolaus, please tell that me you are. I can't stand being unsettled like this. I've been stewing over this for months, for years."

"It's good to see you, Gustav. I was so sorry to hear about Elisabeth." Gustav pushed Nickolaus away slightly then held him by the shoulders and looked him straight in the eyes.

"It was truly sad, Nickolaus, and I loved her dearly, but now I have my mein liebster Elsa, and my two beautiful children." He stood back and pointed to each. "Meet Gunter and Hilda Lenzmann." They smiled then looked down shyly toward the ground. "Children, run in and tell your mother that we'll be having four guests for our midday meal." He looked pleadingly at Nickolaus. "You can stay for lunch, can't you?"

Nickolaus glanced at Wilhelm, who smiled and nodded favorably. "I believe we have the time, Nickolaus. I suspected you might want to visit with Gustav for a while, so I took the liberty of scheduling your appointment with the Baron at two o'clock." A moment later, Michela floated up and placed her arm around Nickolaus.

"Ah, Gustav Lenzmann, this is my lovely wife, Michela." She curtsied. Gustav smiled and bowed slightly. "She hails from Genoa, as does her younger brother, Stefano."

"It's very nice to meet you, Michela. Nickolaus is a lucky man to have found and married such a remarkable woman." Nickolaus translated Gustav's greetings to his wife.

"Yes, I believe he is, and so am I." She smiled warmly as Nickolaus translated back. Gustav turned and shook Stefano's hand, which he immediately recognized as being soft-skinned but sturdy, a condition not uncommon among dedicated keyboardists.

"It's nice to meet you, Herr Lenzmann," greeted Stefano in an admirably clear, north German dialect while continuing to shake Gustav's hand in a manly fashion.

Gustav grinned. "Ah, you already know our language. That will be of great help to you."

"And this is Marco Di Caniglia, my personal friend and consigliere." Marco stepped forward and extended his hand, but when he did, his outer wrap fell open, revealing both his sword and a sizable dagger. Gustav glared at him suspiciously for a moment then realized the true nature of Marco's roll. Gustav saluted informally then shook Marco's hand.

"Nice to meet you, Marco." The two men smiled at each other, but Marco spoke not a word in return, as the language was little more than a jumble to him. "Yes, well, please follow me. Elsa will be thrilled to meet all of you." They headed down the flagstone walkway and entered the Lenzmann household, which was as neat and tidy as a queen's bedchamber. Elsa greeted them warmly then immediately set back to work preparing the meal. Despite being an attentive and hard-working wife and mother, Elsa was still young and fresh. She could have passed for her husband's daughter. Gustav offered everyone a chair at the table before sitting down with a slight groan. The children set the table then delivered a generous mug of the new season's hard cider to everyone. Nickolaus took a gulp or two. It was pleasantly and perhaps dangerously harder than expected. With a playful glint in his eyes, he glanced first at Marco and then at Michela, as if he were a child preparing to snatch a forbidden piece of candy. He took one more sizable gulp, and then another for good measure before setting down the mug, planning to sip only stingily while he ate. He turned to his host.

"I have to ask, Gustav, how do you manage all of this? All of these fields and orchards, and the animals – so much work for one man?" Gustav was humored at how little Nickolaus understood about maintaining a farm.

"I have help, Nickolaus. During planting and harvesting, I bring on help." Nickolaus felt stupid for a moment, remembering how Captain Zannaro had been amused by a similar question and answer about ship's operations at the beginning of their voyage north.

"From where?" Nickolaus asked curiously.

Gustav stared blankly for a moment then glanced at Elsa. "They are either traveling workers ... or whoever I can find in the neighborhood."

"Are they reliable?"

"My workers are as reliable and hardworking as you could find anywhere. We're almost like family." Nickolaus was puzzled.

"Where do they live?"

"Oh, down the way a bit, in a village." Nickolaus was still at a loss.

"How about some food?" Elsa interrupted clumsily, rapidly passing around the serving dishes. "Our meals are simple but delicious." Nickolaus recognized the Stamppot right away.

"And on such short notice," added Wilhelm. "Everything looks delightful."

The meal passed quickly with little bits and pieces of conversation flying in every direction, though occasionally complicated by the language barrier. The discussion turned congratulatory and very much animated when Nickolaus unexpectedly announced the news of his wife's pregnancy. Michela had not planned on revealing her condition so soon, but the news was out and everyone seemed truly excited. Elsa momentarily stared wistfully out the window – she wanted another of her own. Around one o'clock, Herr Weldon stood up and declared that they needed to take their leave in order to make their appointment with the Baron. Gustav jumped up and grabbed Nickolaus's hand and shook it earnestly. "I do hope that you and the Baron can reach a fair agreement … I mean, I hope your meeting goes well. You know that no matter what you decide, I will continue to manage your lands as best I can for as long as you will have me." Gustav's words and demeanor struck Nickolaus as being intensely sincere as well as sadly desperate. Nickolaus put his hand on Gustav's shoulder.

"I know, Gustav, but I can't make any promises. I am very impressed with what I've seen here, but there are some odd and complicated legal issues involved. You know I love this place." Nickolaus let go of Gustav's shoulder and addressed Elsa and the children. "Thank you all for your wonderful hospitality. I'm sure we'll be sharing more great times." The travelers all smiled and shook hands before climbing into the carriage. It had been a very pleasant encounter, but now it was time to do business with the Baron.

As they were passing by the old manor house, Nickolaus ordered the carriage to a halt. He climbed down with Michela and Stefano then headed past the old ruins and ascended the hill to the small graveyard. Once there, they turned toward the waning afternoon sun and stared out admiringly over the picturesque landscape that would be theirs if only they chose to stay. "How curious, that looks like smoke rising up from the Silberbach Hollow. I'll have to ask Gustav about it the next time I see him." Nickolaus turned back around and glanced downward, one at a time, at each of the carved stones that marked his ancestors' graves. And in that moment, he came to realize that he had finally found his way home. Michela took hold of his hand and squeezed tightly but said nothing. Despite her huge stake in the matter, she was determined that Nickolaus should ultimately make his own decision. Unsettling and perhaps even unfair, he was totally in control of their destiny. She just wanted him to know that she was with him no matter what he decided. He stroked her hand lovingly then let go and put his arm around her shoulder.

"You know, my love, I must take you and Stefano up the canyon to visit the Silberbach Hollow near the crest of the ridge. It truly is a special place."

"I would very much like that, Nicki." She bumped his hip playfully.

"Michela, with your concurrence, I think we shall make this our home." He hesitated. "Well, not exactly right here. Down there, where the old house stands." She felt a surge of exhilaration as she reached up and grasped the hand he had placed on her shoulder.

"If that is your decision, Nicolo, then I am most pleased." They turned to each other and kissed firmly and deeply, just as they had done during their first passionate kiss in Genoa. Stefano turned away and pretended to stare out over the horizon. They parted then gazed intensely into each other's eyes for several seconds while Stefano meandered down the hill, embarking upon his own life's journey. Nickolaus wiped a few tears from Michela's cheeks then kissed her on the forehead.

"It's time to go meet the Baron, my love"

"You lead the way, Nicki, I'm all yours." He took hold of her arm as they headed down the hill.

"Shall we do this together, my dear?"

"By all means, I wouldn't miss it for the world."

**Coming in the future:** *Songs of The Hollows,* Part Three *of The Lives of Nickolaus*

## A Message to Seafarers Everywhere

Please forgive the many instances of literary license taken by the author with respect to maritime affairs. While some of these infelicities result from a lack of available information concerning ships, designs, and protocols of the era, their presence is mainly a product of abundant and liberal artistic license indulged in by the author with the hope of telling a grand tale of the sea.

## Acknowledgements

First and foremost, I must thank Cindy Roof, my lovely wife of forty-five years, for her love, companionship, support and, last but not least, for being a fantastic and loving mother to our three wonderful children, Abe, Ashley, and Melanie. I must also thank all of the people who expressed their sincere wishes to see more stories about the lives of Nickolaus. Lastly, I would be remiss if I failed to mention Paul and Sheryl Shard of the Canadian television program, Distant Shores, for providing me with a fair measure of information and inspiration to send Nicolo across the Land of Seas on his voyage home.